A FLAME TREE
BOOK OF HORROR

BEYOND THE VEIL

An Anthology of New Short Stories

Edited by Mark Morris

This is a **FLAME TREE PRESS** book

FLAME TREE PRESS
6 Melbray Mews, London, SW6 3NS, UK
flametreepress.com

US sales, distribution and warehouse:
Simon & Schuster
simonandschuster.biz

UK distribution and warehouse:
Marston Book Services Ltd
marston.co.uk

Thanks to the Flame Tree Press team, including:
Taylor Bentley, Frances Bodiam, Federica Ciaravella, Don D'Auria,
Chris Herbert, Josie Karani, Molly Rosevear, Mike Spender,
Cat Taylor, Maria Tissot, Nick Wells, Gillian Whitaker.

The cover is created by Flame Tree Studio with
thanks to Nik Keevil and Shutterstock.com.
The font families used are Avenir and Bembo.

Flame Tree Press is an imprint of Flame Tree Publishing Ltd
flametreepublishing.com

A copy of the CIP data for this book is available from the British Library
and the Library of Congress.

HB ISBN: 978-1-78758-463-1
US PB ISBN: 978-1-78758-461-7
UK PB ISBN: 978-1-78758-462-4
ebook ISBN: 978-1-78758-465-5

Printed and bound in Great Britain by Clays Ltd, Elcograf S.p.A.

A FLAME TREE BOOK OF HORROR

BEYOND THE VEIL

An Anthology of New Short Stories

Edited by Mark Morris

FLAME TREE PRESS
London & New York

CONTENTS

INTRODUCTION

I was delighted with the response to *After Sundown*, the first of Flame Tree's annual non-themed horror anthologies, which came out in October 2020. When I delivered the book in January of that year, Covid-19 was being mentioned only peripherally, as a strange new illness that was affecting people in Wuhan, China. Certainly very few of us at the time thought that the situation would escalate into a global pandemic that would have such a devastating impact on all of our lives.

One story in *After Sundown*, Michael Bailey's *Gave*, was about the entire world's population slowly but surely succumbing to a mysterious blood disorder, and one man's desperate, life-long attempt to reverse the trend by donating his healthy blood to those in need. It's a measured story – no jump-shocks, no cheap scares, no violence, no monsters – and yet its implications are devastating, dealing as it does with one of our most fundamental fears: human extinction.

Despite its reticence, an outraged few might argue that Michael's story is in bad taste, appearing, as it does, to profit from the pandemic, if not to reduce a horrifying global event to a piece of entertainment. However, aside from the fact that *Gave* was written at least a year before publication, when the pandemic was still an unanticipated future event, these outraged few will also have missed the most important factor of all, which is that *After Sundown* is an anthology of *horror* stories, which, by their very nature, are intended to shine a light on our darkest fears and taboos.

If you're coming to this anthology with the hope of experiencing nothing more than a few cosy and familiar chills, therefore, then I'm afraid you're in for a rude awakening. As editor, I found the timing of Michael's very relevant story to be serendipitous rather than unfortunate. I'm not interested in reassuring tales of monsters vanquished and the status quo restored. Horror stories to me should be confrontational. They should be about things that truly disturb us; things that prey on our minds. Things like loneliness and isolation; loss and grief; illness and death; the fear we feel for our own personal safety when faced with intimidation, violence and abuse.

A friend recently said to me that he thought most horror stories stemmed from a loss of control, and that's certainly true of many of the characters and situations you will encounter in these pages. As human beings we kid ourselves that we have a semblance of control over our lives, our circumstances, our environment, our health... but if the year of the pandemic has taught us anything, it is that it doesn't take much for that control to be wrested from us, and for the rug to be wrenched violently out from under our feet.

And *that* is the essence of true horror.

Mark Morris

THE GOD BAG
Christopher Golden

I never knew where she got the idea for the God Bag. In the waning days, when my mother's memory turned into a source of constant pain and confusion, I asked my brother and sister about it, but neither of them knew the origins of the threadbare velvet thing, or even when she started stuffing prayers into it. The earliest any of us could recall Mom mentioning it was shortly after she and Dad divorced. I guess I'd have been around seven years old, which means my brother, Simon, would have been nine and Corinne, our sister, about fifteen.

"I'll put it in my God Bag," she'd say.

I remember the look in her eyes when she talked about it, as if she assumed we all knew exactly what she meant. I honestly don't recall if she ever explained it to me or if I figured it out through context clues, but the gist was clear – when Mom was troubled, wrestling with something in her heart, or when she'd lost something and needed to find it, she'd scribble a prayer on a scrap of white paper, fold it up and stick it into the God Bag.

Reading that, you might assume we were a religious family, but I wouldn't go that far. Corinne, Simon, and I attended Catholic schools from first grade up through high school graduation, but we were never regular church-goers, not even when our parents were still married. Dad's religion was self-indulgence; bars were his church, women and alcohol his communion. Mom had a more eccentric sort of faith. She burned St. Joseph candles, had psychics read her tea leaves, was devoted to the predictions of her tarot cards... and she had her God Bag.

Years passed the way they do, and occasionally I'd remember the existence of the thing, but only as a funny anecdote from childhood. College came and went, I built myself a sustainable career as a graphic designer, I married Alan Kozik and we found a surrogate to carry our baby, which made us dads. Being gay complicated my relationship with my mother, but I'd heard worse stories and we all survived the turmoil. She loved Alan, and she loved our daughter Rosie even more. Her first granddaughter – it meant everything to her. Yes, my siblings were older, yes they'd had their own weddings, yes they'd had children of their own, and Mom loved each and every one of them. But Alan and I had the only girl, the only granddaughter. Any resistance my mother had to the idea of me being married to a burly, bearded guy who liked to hold my hand just about every minute of the day... that went out the window when Rosie came along. From then on, Mom acted as if she'd never had an issue with me being in love with a man. I still nurtured some resentment, but I let it go the best I could. Why fight the tide of joy?

Joy.

It never lasts.

We began to notice Mom's memory failing a year or two before the dementia really dug its claws into her. For a long time, her lapses seemed mundane enough, but when it began to really fail, there could be no denying it. One week it manifested in simple things like misplacing her phone or forgetting plans we'd made, but soon after she would finish a phone call with Corinne and then call her back half an hour later with no recollection of the earlier conversation.

Mom despised going to the doctor. She hated for her children to know her personal business, including her health. She held on to this weird intimacy as long as she was able, but eventually Corinne insisted she be allowed to accompany her to the doctor, and the news was grim. Smoking had done more damage than we imagined, and in ways we had never anticipated. Yes, Mom did have a tumour in her lungs, but it was small and slow-growing and far from her biggest concern. She also had COPD and end-stage emphysema, as well as vascular dementia. Decades of smoking had narrowed the blood vessels in her brain and in her extremities, and the blood that did flow wasn't carrying nearly enough oxygen.

Every day, it would get a little worse. Eventually, either the constricted blood vessels in her brain would cause a stroke or her blood oxygen level would fall so low that a heart attack would kill her. She would stop being able to draw in enough breath to keep herself alive.

Meanwhile, the dementia ravaged her in other ways. She had never been a healthy eater, but now she tended to forget or lose interest in anything but draining cans of Diet Coke and crushing butts out in the same stainless steel elephant ashtray she'd been using for forty years. Loose, dry skin hung from her arms and legs and her hair remained in constant disarray. Her moods had always been mercurial, and now they ranged from near-catatonia to pure joy, from loneliness to rage, sometimes in the space of minutes. She had delusions, mostly harmless, a way for her unconscious mind to fill in the vast, empty spaces in her memory.

"Oh, it's up on my bed," she'd say of the memoir she claimed to be writing, or a book she thought she had given you, or records of some improvised bit of personal history. Photographs of a trip to Ireland that I'd taken – a trip she insisted she'd been on with Alan and me. She had photographs to prove she'd been there "up on my bed".

She'd never been to Ireland in her life.

On a Tuesday morning in late August, I took the day off work to bring her for an MRI. We knew what the results were likely to be, but in order to get Medicare and the local elder services to give her the coverage she needed, we had to jump through the hoops. I hated doing it, but not as much as Mom hated having to go. Even at her most confused, even when her memory turned to smoke around her, she still understood that visiting doctors at this point was futile. Nothing we did could keep the train she was on from crashing, but we had to keep Mom going to her appointments and try to remind her to take her medications, because that was the only way to be sure Medicare would cover the costs of what was to come.

My mother wanted to stay in her home, to live out her last days there, and we were doing everything in our power to grant that wish. Soon that would change. Something would happen, some household accident, some injury or emergency that sent her to the hospital, and then the whole paradigm would shift.

But that Tuesday had been quiet. Just me and Mom. I brought her a couple of glazed doughnuts – one of the few things she would eat – and then drove her to the MRI appointment. She didn't complain, even seemed in good spirits, but then she had always loved the summer and the sun. Eighty degrees, windows down, I drove her to the doctor's office and checked her in. As I sat in the waiting room reading the historical novel I'd brought along, I kept losing my place on the page, worried by how long it was taking and whether the staff might be having difficulty keeping her on task. But when it was over, the nurse walked my mother out to me and the two of them seemed to have become fast friends. As horrible as she could be, Mom also knew how to charm strangers when she felt like it.

We drove home with the music up loud and the sun shining. Shortly after two o'clock, I pulled into her driveway and killed the engine. She'd gone quiet, slipping into that numb, hollow mood that came over her so often now. No matter how bad her memory might be, how confused, she knew that arriving home meant I would be leaving soon and the shadow of that knowledge darkened her features.

I helped her up to her room, cracked her a fresh can of Diet Coke, and chided her when she tried to light up a cigarette. I had always hated the damn things, and now more than ever. For twenty years she had remembered not to smoke in front of any of her children, but now even that was slipping. She crinkled her eyes and gave me a pouty look, but she put her cigarettes aside.

"I wish you didn't have to go," she rasped in her gravelly voice, pausing every few words to catch her breath. "I get so lonely."

The words were familiar now, but no matter how often I heard them, they carved my heart out.

"I know. But I'll see you again in a few days. Corinne's visiting you tomorrow, and tonight you'll see the nurse. Who's on Tuesdays? Sylvia?"

"Yep, Sylvia. Yes." She nodded, brows knitted gravely in an attempt to communicate confidence. I knew the expression well – it meant she had no idea which nurse would be working tonight, helping her bathe, keeping her company, keeping her out of trouble.

The bedroom wasn't hoarder-level disaster, but it was close. Stacks of books and documents everywhere, pill bottles, a hundred antique knickknacks that would have to be sold eventually but none of which my mother would part with, even now. Especially now. Her queen bed looked more like a nest, with too many pillows, blankets, and two different comforters, both of them with stains I didn't want to think about, no matter how many times they had been washed.

Mom slept alone on the left side of the bed, the right side piled up with bags of Cheetos and mini-Reese's cups, cigarette cartons, her chequebook and bills that Corinne would take the next day to make sure everything was being handled properly. Left to her own devices, Mom would either not pay the bills or overpay someone she didn't actually owe. There were notebooks she had scribbled in, some DVDs Simon had brought for her to watch, and sticking out from beneath a dirty pink sweatshirt, a familiar faded blue velvet with gold tassels.

"Mom, is that the God Bag?"

The question confused her. She frowned as if remembering what the God Bag was to begin with, then she glanced at it and nodded. "Of course. I have a lot of prayers these days. If I'm going to die, I want to make sure I get a good reception on the other side."

I laughed, but it wasn't funny. Once I would have reassured her, told her she wasn't going to die anytime soon, but even she knew her time was limited.

"I didn't realise you still had this," I said, studying the bag.

It was a royal blue, faux-velvet, drawstring thing with obscure origins, but I assumed it had originally held a bottle of fancy scotch or brandy. Mom's generation had given bottles of alcohol as holiday or housewarming gifts when they couldn't think of anything more personal. The drawstring was a golden, corded tassel. The God Bag had seen better days, but it still served its purpose. The latest couple of notes jutted from the overfilled bag.

"Are your prayers ever answered, Mom?"

I don't know why I asked. Truly, I don't. The words skipped over the thinking part of my brain, went right from the impulse to my lips, and the moment I spoke I wished I had kept silent. If the prayers she put in her God Bag had been answered, she wouldn't be lying in her bed waiting to die.

But her eyes widened a bit, glinting with a clarity I hadn't seen in them for months. "Always," she said, laser-focused on me. "They're always answered. You're happy, aren't you? You and Alan and Rosie?"

Her voice didn't rasp or falter. Her gaze felt sharp, her focus weighted. She almost never remembered Alan's name now, didn't mention him until I mentioned him first. I didn't think it was her old Puritanism returning, just the rockslide of her memory carrying Alan over the cliff into obscurity. Right then, though, I could see she remembered everyone, everything, with utter clarity.

"You prayed for me and Alan?"

"Of course I did. I wanted you two to have a family. I wrote it down and put it in my God Bag, and I got my only granddaughter."

She smiled when she mentioned Rosie. As she always did. Her life had been a series of resentments and vendettas, a terrible example for me and my siblings and for our children, but in her imagination she and Rosie shared a bond, and I never had the heart to shatter the illusion.

"Well," I said. "I'm grateful."

I started to open the drawstring. "Maybe I should put my own prayers in here."

Mom ripped it from my hands. "Get your own God."

I held my breath, worried she would topple over into one of her rage moods, but once she had the God Bag tucked against her chest, she seemed comforted, and in moments her eyes glazed over again. Whatever had prompted her outburst, it had passed.

"I'm going to get you something to eat. Some of that chicken salad from yesterday." I had been perched on the edge of her bed. Now I stood and left the room, her words echoing in my head. Of course she had meant to say "Get your own God Bag", not "Get your own God." She missed words all the time, or mixed them up, and that was obviously what had happened here. Even so, I felt a cool prickle at the back of my neck as I went down to the kitchen.

Get your own God.

The joke was on her. I didn't believe in anyone's god, and I certainly didn't have one of my own.

I went down to the kitchen, which held its own nightmares. It felt like a relic from another age, maybe the galley in a ship found adrift at sea with all hands lost. When had she last been down here to get some food on her own? Some of the plates were set out on the counters. Several knives crusted with dried peanut butter were in the sink. There was a home health aide that helped with such things, but it wasn't fair to always leave it to her, so I reminded myself to run the dishwasher before I left.

I fixed Mom a chicken salad sandwich – on a hot dog roll, because it was easy for her to handle and she wouldn't have eaten an entire sandwich anyway – and carried it upstairs on a small plate with a handful of grapes. I hadn't been gone much more than ten minutes, but I could smell cigarette smoke and she had turned up the TV nearly to max volume.

"Your lunch, madame!" I announced as I entered the room.

The cigarette had already been stubbed out in the ashtray. She'd taken maybe three puffs. She lay in bed, her head slightly tilted, mouth open, eyes closed. If not for the wheezing labour of her breathing, I would have thought she had died.

She dozed off fairly often in those days. Fifteen, twenty minutes, sometimes as much as an hour. I glanced at CNN on her TV to check the time and decided I would wait for her to wake. I hated the idea of disturbing her almost as much as I did the idea of her blinking back to consciousness and finding herself alone. Would she even remember that I'd been there? I wasn't sure, but I didn't want to leave without being able to say goodbye. Just in case.

I set the plate with her chicken salad roll amidst the debris on her nightstand and turned the volume down. My phone lay dormant in my pocket and I knew I could kill time on Twitter or playing Wordscapes, but I figured I would just sit in the chair at the end of her bed and watch the news for a while, let my mind rest.

Then I saw the God Bag again. Such a strange artefact from our family history, as if someone had dredged up a long-forgotten photo album. I knew it was private, and yes, it felt like an intrusion even when I was reaching for it, but my mother was dying and soon enough we would all be rooting through the detritus of her life. Her mind, the person she had been, was already being erased, and given how tenuous our relationship had often been over the years I could not help myself from wondering.

I dug in, sifted around at random, and pulled out a folded piece of white paper. When I unfolded it, I found her familiar scrawl and realised this one had to be at least a couple of years old – written long enough ago that her handwriting remained crisp, with the

confident loops and flourishes I associated with the younger version
of my mother.

A better job for Simon, she'd written. Just those five words, and the
date – 10/11/17. I smiled as I studied the words, barely a prayer, more
of a wish. I tried to remember how long ago my brother had quit
working for the German company whose CEO treated his employees
like they were competitors in some kind of reality show, where they
were judged on loyalty, forced-enthusiasm, and the ability to come to
work and feign good health even when they were sick as dogs. The
job had been withering Simon's soul, but he'd been afraid to talk to
headhunters for fear someone would tell the boss and he'd be fired.
Now he worked at a Boston tech firm whose office culture was the
polar opposite and I could see the difference it had made in him, both
physically and mentally. I wondered when he had gotten that job.
Early 2018, I thought, and it made me smile again as I realised Mom
would have taken the credit. She'd put the wish in her God Bag and
it had come true. That would have made her incredibly happy, to
believe she'd had a hand in changing Simon's life for the better.

Mom's breathing grew worse as I sat there. I glanced around in
search of the inhaler she was supposed to use twice a day, but it was
nowhere in sight. The nurse would find it later, but as I watched my
mother I was reminded of the first weeks after we'd brought newborn
Rosie home from the hospital. Alan and I had put her cradle in our
bedroom and I remembered lying awake at night, listening to her
breathe, terrified that she would stop.

It's strange the way life echoes. Strange and terrible.

When I felt confident Mom wouldn't die in the next five minutes,
I dug back into the bag and pulled out more of the folded prayers.
Family trip to Florida was in there. So were three versions of *I want
Corinne to move home,* from back in the days when my sister lived in
Arizona. *Someone to paint the house* was among the more mundane
wishes, along with *A better car* and *I pray for my back to feel better.*

Some of them were a bit more vindictive. Mom had a history of
suing people for just about anything, particularly if she herself had
done something wrong and decided that pretending to be the injured
party would get her out of it. There were negligent injury lawsuits
and real estate lawsuits. When my grandmother had died, she'd ended

up in a legal fight with her siblings over the will. As I dug through the God Bag, I found half a dozen notes wishing for victory over her enemies. Some of them were court cases but there were other, more petty disputes.

Kill the raccoons. That one made me catch my breath with its cruel brevity. There had been raccoons on her property for ages. Sometimes they became brave and rooted through the trash or found a way into the garage and clawed at mouldy old boxes of things Mom should have discarded decades ago. For that, she had prayed for God to kill them.

"Jesus Christ," I whispered, staring at that single creased sheet of paper.

I folded the raccoon-murder-wish again and tucked it into the God Bag. There were so many of them. The dates ranged over the course of many years. Nearly all the prayers had been written on white paper, but I was intrigued to find that some of them were red. No other colours that I could see, only white and red. I began to unfold the red ones.

A kidney, said the first one. It had been written in black marker, the lettering somehow shakier than the others. Thick and blocky, though. Determined.

My diamond.

Annabeth.

The cottage.

Cosmo.

I confess that at first none of them made sense to me, not because I didn't understand the references but because they broke the pattern. Mom had fought uterine cancer years ago and during surgery the doctors had discovered that one of her kidneys had been badly damaged. I couldn't remember the details, but I knew they'd had to remove it. Had there been damage to her remaining kidney? Had she feared she might need a kidney transplant, which would explain her wishing for one?

About a dozen years before, she had lost her wedding ring on the beach in Florida, so that one made sense.

Annabeth had been her closest friend for nearly forty years before they'd had a falling out and Annabeth had moved to New Mexico to be with her son and his family. Warm and funny, with a wicked sense of humour, I'd always loved Annabeth and had been sad to see their friendship destroyed. Shortly after she had moved to New Mexico, she'd had a bad stroke. Annabeth survived – as far as I know she was still in New Mexico – but the stroke damaged the language centre of her brain, making it virtually impossible for her to have an ordinary conversation. She could still write, though not with the eloquence she'd once had, and had sent letters to Mom several times. Whatever had happened between them, it must have been awful, because my mother never even opened those letters. She put them in the garbage.

The cottage had to refer to the one up in Maine. My father had inherited it from his parents, but Mom had gotten it in the divorce – she said because we kids loved it so much, but we all knew it was just one way for her to hurt him. He had it coming, of course, but from that point on I could never feel completely comfortable there. When she'd reached her early seventies, Mom had started to falter financially. She made bad decisions, took risks, got into a few real estate deals with men she should not have trusted. Without telling us, she mortgaged the cottage until it was underwater, ended up in a court battle to try to save it. That would have been around 2009.

Cosmo had been her dog. An adorable little terrier who mostly liked to sit on the sofa next to her with his head on her lap. She loved the little fellow, scratched behind his ears, fed him, even took him out for a stroll up and down the sidewalk in the days when she could still manage that without having to stop every twenty feet to catch her breath. A UPS truck had struck him. The injuries had been enough to kill him, but not quickly. When Mom had been told he might linger for days, she'd had to make the tough decision to put him down.

I stared at the red prayers, trying to figure out what I found so odd about them. Yes, they were even more succinct than the wishes written on white paper. Instead of *Save Cosmo*, she had just written his name. Instead of *Let me find my diamond* and *Help Annabeth get well*, she'd written only *My diamond* and simply *Annabeth*.

I started opening white prayers again and when I came to one that said *A happy and healthy baby girl for Tom and Alan*, I swore softly to myself. Obviously her wish hadn't been the reason we had Rosie – Alan and I had wanted a baby, a family – but I had thought it was entirely a delusion when she had given herself credit. Yet some part of her dementia-stricken mind had remembered writing this prayer down, and she certainly had asked God for a granddaughter. No wonder she put so much faith in the ridiculous bag.

I stared at that prayer again, touched by the kindness of Mom's wish but also deeply frustrated by the way it had fed her constant need to be in control. I loved her, but her narcissism and passive-aggression had been poisoning that love since the day I was born. As I folded the paper and began returning the various wishes to the bag, the answer struck me – the reason the red prayers made me uneasy.

How had she known?

The red prayers had not been granted. If God really was out there listening to Mom's prayers, able to read or intuit the wishes she placed into her God Bag, then he had ignored the ones on red paper. Actually, much worse than ignoring them, he had done the opposite of what she'd prayed for. You want your diamond back? No. You want to make peace with your best friend? She'll move thousands of miles away and nearly die. You want your dog to live? How about I make him die in agony instead?

Shuffling again through white prayers, I couldn't have said if most of them had been granted, but there were certainly some that God or fate had granted her – that family trip to Florida, a better car, and a granddaughter. A happy life for me and my husband and our daughter. I wasn't ready to credit Mom's God Bag – or the existence of any deity – for our happiness, but the difference between the prayers written on white versus red paper seemed clear.

I stuffed the others back into the bag, but I held on to a red one. Unfolding it again, I stared at the single word there – *Cosmo*. Beneath it, Mom had scrawled the date, as she had on all of the rest. The 12th of July, seven years before.

I couldn't breathe for a moment, staring at the date.

Alan often teased me about how poor I'd always been at judging chronology. A vacation we'd taken ten years earlier would seem only a few years ago. I knew the year we'd married only because I had memorised it. Some dates stuck in my mind but that 12th of July wasn't one of them – I might've been doing just about anything that day. The next day, though…

The 13th of July was Alan's birthday, and that particular year had been his best ever because that day we'd gotten the phone call that the agency had found us both an egg donor and a surrogate willing to carry our child. That was the day we learned we were going to have a baby, be a family.

Our joy had been slightly diminished by the phone call I received from my mother that night telling me Cosmo had been hit by a truck, that he'd lingered for hours before she'd had the vet put him down.

I stared at the red paper in my hand and the date on it. The day before Cosmo had been hit by the car. Why had Mom been so worried about him – worried enough to put a prayer into her God Bag – the day before he'd been hit?

"She wrote it down wrong," I whispered to myself. That had to be it. She'd simply gotten the date wrong.

Her bedclothes rustled. Her legs jerked beneath the spread.

"Put that back," she rasped – more of a growl.

I snapped my head up and met her eyes. She didn't look at me, only stared at the red paper in my hand, the bag on my lap. Then she jerked forward, tangled in the sheets, spindle-legs bare as she crawled toward me.

"That's not yours!" she cried. "Not yours!"

The mad look in her eyes made me think she didn't recognise me, not in that moment. But maybe she did, and the fact I was her son didn't matter at all. She thrust out a hand but out of reflex I jerked away from her.

"Give it to me! It's *my* God. Mine! Give me the fucking bag!"

"Jesus, Mom," I said, tucking the red prayer back into the bag and cinching the drawstring.

She snatched it from me with more strength than I'd seen in her for months, then held it against her chest and collapsed at the end of her bed, chest heaving as she tried to catch her ragged breath. When she started to cough, I saw red-flecked spittle on her lips, hideously brown mucus that only hinted at the rot in her lungs.

"I'm... I'm sorry..." she managed to wheeze.

Exhaling, I began to reply, hoping to offer her some comfort, but then I saw her apology hadn't been meant for me. She'd been speaking to the bag, holding it against her chest as if it were her only love. She'd gasped out her regret, but it had been offered to a faded faux-velvet sack instead of to the son she'd just shrieked at. She'd been talking to God.

Her God, anyway. She'd made clear she didn't think he belonged to me.

I'd had enough for one day. Pointing out the sandwich I'd made for her, I waited for her to settle back under her covers, confirmed that she had the TV remote control, and made my departure. I needed out of there, away from the smell of cigarettes and my unbathed mother. I wanted fresh air to clear my head, but even when I had gotten into the car and driven away, windows open to let the breeze blow in, my mother's screeching voice lingered, as did some of the things she had said.

Get your own God.

★　　★　　★

Weeks passed. I visited every few days as her mind and body continued to deteriorate. The God Bag had vanished, though I knew it must be under the bed or in her closet. I thought about it often, usually in times when my own mind ought to have been quiet, out for a run or in the shower, but I didn't search for it. Mom had been deeply upset when she saw me holding it, and I decided there was no point in agitating her further.

But her words still lingered, as did the savage, desperate gleam in her eyes when she screamed at me to hand it over. And the prayers themselves, the folded scraps of red and white paper, and the dates. I never brought it up to Alan – he had lived with me through a lot of the pain my mother caused us both over the years, and now he watched as I had to process the war between empathy and resentment that was going on in my head. The last thing I wanted was to have him think I was losing my mind. What else would he think, after all, if I told him the dark thoughts I'd been having about the correlation between the white prayers and the red ones?

But the dates on those paper scraps – the one about Cosmo and the one wishing Alan and I would give Mom a granddaughter – they made the back of my head itch, and late at night when I couldn't sleep, sometimes they gave me a chill. I wondered about the other paper scraps, about what would happen if I matched the dates on the red prayers with the dates when she lost her diamond, or when Annabeth got sick, or when she'd lost her court battle up in Maine and the family cottage along with it. I wondered if I looked back far enough, if I could find earlier batches of notes from the God Bag, if I would find red paper scraps where she'd written down *My marriage* or *My ex-husband*. Had she chosen these things to sacrifice?

The concept of a God who loves you unconditionally and doesn't ask for anything in return except your faith and love – that's a product of the modern world. Old gods – even the early Christian god – demanded offerings and sacrifices, blood rituals, slaughtered lambs. In the Old Testament, God told Abraham to murder his son in the name of the Lord. Abraham was about to do it, too, before God said, *Hang on, Abe. I was just fucking with you. Did you really believe I wanted you to cut your child open and let him bleed out just for my entertainment, just to make me feel good about myself? To prove you love me? Yeah, okay, maybe I did want that, but now that we're here and I see how sharp that knife is, I guess it's enough that you, his father, were willing to murder him for me. And that Isaac will live the rest of his life knowing that. I guess that's sacrifice enough… for today.*

And the Old Testament God was far from the only cruel, bloodthirsty, needy fucker. Most of those old gods – and demons, let's not forget them – were happy to bring a little magic to your life, answer your white-paper prayers, if you had the right red-paper sacrifice to offer up in return.

The more I thought about it, the more absurd the whole thing seemed. There were no gods, not in those ancient, violent days, and not today. My stress and anxiety had combined with a dying old woman's dementia and obsession to turn simple coincidence into heinous divine intervention.

On a Sunday afternoon, nearly a month after the incident with the God Bag, I went to spend a few hours with Mom. She found it difficult to concentrate on much of anything by then, but she always liked watching New England Patriots games, so I thought I'd keep her company. I figured she would ask me the same dozen questions she asked every time we spoke and I would give her patient answers, and then she'd ask them again and I'd be a little less patient, but I'd still indulge her. That was the way it had been going lately, and at least that day we would have the football game as a distraction.

That was the plan, anyway.

Just after one o'clock, I walked into her room. As usual, the volume on her TV had been turned up much too loud, but when I saw she was sleeping, I left it that way. Even over the blaring voice of the announcer and the roar of the stadium crowd, I could make out the guttural rattle of her breathing, shallower than ever.

She lay with one skinny leg uncovered save for a thick purple woollen sock that bunched around her tiny ankle. The God Bag lay beside her, but its contents had been spilled onto the floor next to the bed, a small mound of white paper, sprinkled through with the occasional slice of red. I'd had my phone in hand, scanning Twitter for the day's insanities, but now I set it on the nightstand, knelt by the pile of prayers, and began to sift through them.

From the corner of my eye, I noticed a little pile of scrap paper to my left, as if it had fallen off her bed and slipped down beside the nightstand. I pushed my fingers into that space and pulled out a little stack, mostly white but a handful of red pieces, too. On her nightstand I spotted a stubby little pair of scissors and a few thin strips of the red paper, as if someone – the home health aide, perhaps – had indulged her by cutting it up for her, then scissoring off the uneven edges.

A tightness formed in my chest.

Shuffling through the mound on the floor again, I spotted only her old handwriting, back when she could still write in cursive and remember the dates. There was nothing new in that stack, at least not at first glance.

I rose to my feet and stared down at her. The God Bag lay in a pile with a cigarette carton, a bag of fun-sized Milky Ways, and a faded pink sweatshirt stained with chocolate and Diet Coke and things she spit up when she couldn't find a napkin close at hand. I stared at the bag. The drawstring was loose, the bag deflated so that it looked empty, but when I noticed the black Sharpie lying on top of the sweatshirt, I thought she might have written a final prayer.

On television, the action halted. The referees huddled for a conference to see what penalties they felt like calling. In my mother's bedroom, I reached for the God Bag and snatched it off the bed. As if sensing its absence, Mom groaned and began to cough in her sleep, breath hitching. Her lips, I noticed, had turned a deep blue.

I reached into the bag and pulled out a scrap of paper.

White paper.

I unfolded it. Mom had used the Sharpie to write a sentence, and though the letters were poorly formed and some forgotten, I could make out her prayer. *Want my mind back.*

The words, stark and jagged against the white paper, cut me open. My left hand rose to cover my mouth. Tears welled in my eyes and I lowered my head, the prayer dangling in my right hand before I let it flutter to join the rest of the old prayers on the floor.

"I'm so sorry," I whispered. "You didn't deserve this."

She began to cough again, worse than before. I watched her strain to breathe. Simon and Corinne and I had agreed to co-operate with Mom's wishes on this. Machines might keep her alive a bit longer, but by then she would have wanted to die. Thinking of my siblings, I realised I should probably call them. Mom might have months to live yet, but in that moment it certainly did not seem likely. She looked paler than ever, and though her cheeks reddened from coughing, her lips darkened and the bags beneath her eyes seemed to be turning blue as well.

Gasping, Mom opened her eyes. I could see in them the profound shock of a woman who understood, truly, at last, that she was going to die. She had prayed to get her memory back, when what she ought to have prayed for was the ability to breathe freely. But it was too late for any of that. The years of oxygen deprivation had already done too much damage to her brain and lungs and circulatory system. How many mini-strokes or mini-heart attacks had she already had?

"Mom," I said. "It's okay."

What else could I say?

In spite of her panic and the blue tint to her skin, she spotted the God Bag dangling in my right hand and her desperation seemed to grow. Her fingers scrabbled at the bedsheet and she tried to reach out for me, or for the bag.

"It's okay. We're all going to be all right," I told her. "You shouldn't have to be afraid to go. It's okay."

I moved toward her, and my shoe pushed over the mound of prayers. I remembered today's wish, that final scribble. She'd finally admitted to herself what had been happening to her, and she had turned to her old faith. I looked down at the pile now spread across the floor and saw the red prayers again, and the pattern returned to me. The method to her madness. The white prayers, and the red ones.

Her coughing continued, but grew thinner. She managed to speak my name, and I decided the hell with it. I could not stand there and watch her die, no matter what Simon, Corinne, and I had agreed. That conversation had taken place in a time when none of us imagined we would be standing by her bedside when it happened. I couldn't just stand there and keep telling her it was okay.

"I'm sorry, Mom. I'm going to call an ambulance. You shouldn't... I can't just..."

Words failed me. I felt the tears on my face. I reached for my phone.

As I did, she made another weak grab for the God Bag. I wanted to scream at her, to tell her to forget it. No gods were listening to her. She was dying, and no amount of bizarre faith would save her. Her lunacy could not give her the oxygen she needed or fix her brain.

She stared hungrily at the bag. A dreadful idea occurred to me, a sickness in my gut. I opened the bag and reached down inside. Yes, there was another prayer in there, a folded slip of paper. Even before I drew it out, I knew what colour that paper would be.

Red, of course.

I dropped the bag to the floor. When I unfolded the prayer, my heart filled with hatred. In her childlike scrawl, in thick black Sharpie, my mother had written my daughter's name – the name of the granddaughter she had always wanted, the child whose birth had given her such joy. In exchange for getting her memory back, she had offered up Rosie.

On the nightstand, my phone began to buzz.

It was Alan calling me.

On her bed, my mother's eyes cleared. I saw her blink in surprise as her fear abated. She tried to get control of her breathing.

"Mom?" I said.

When she focused on me, I saw the recognition there. The calculation and intelligence.

"Tom," she said. "Help me up. Get the nebuliser and... look around... for my inhaler..."

It seemed impossible, but I couldn't deny what I saw in her eyes, the clarity and knowledge there. My phone had stopped buzzing, but only seconds later it began again, vibrating on the nightstand next to my mother's overflowing ashtray. Alan was calling me again.

I picked up my phone. Tapped to accept the call.

"Hey, honey, I'm with my mom. Can I—"

Alan cut me off, but I couldn't understand a word he said. He wailed into my ear, catching his breath, *trying to tell me*. The only word I was sure I'd heard was "Rosie".

I looked down at the red prayer in my hand.

My mother saw my face, looked at the letter, and the new clarity of her mind filled in the rest. I saw her understand what she had done, saw the moment of realisation, of horror.

She tried to scream. Gasping, wheezing, face and lips darkening further, she reached for me and slid out of her bed, sprawling in the pile of red and white prayers.

I ended the call with Alan. It wasn't fair to him. He should have been able to share his pain with me. But I couldn't give him that just yet.

Numb, I slipped the phone into my pocket, turned, and walked out into the hallway. Once I'd left the bedroom, I couldn't hear my mother's struggles anymore. Not over the volume of the television set.

Downstairs, I sat in the chair where she'd spent decades smoking herself to death.

My mother had wanted to die at home, and I decided to grant that wish.

All of her other prayers had already been answered.

CAKER'S MAN
Matthew Holness

They keep asking me but I can only tell you that it wasn't that kind of cake at all. It had no icing, and no candles. It really wasn't a birthday cake in any way, no matter how much he insisted it was. But my mum took it from him nevertheless, and promised him we'd eat it that night, and agreed again that he'd been right in thinking it was my birthday. Then, when he'd finally gone, she tore it up and fed it to the birds in our back garden, and told the three of us we'd had far more to eat than was wise for small stomachs. I can remember Jamie and Connie being upset about that, but I wasn't. They tell me that's because I was the eldest and had to set the example, but the truth was I was glad about it. So glad that I even got up early the next morning to watch Mum, through my bedroom curtains, examining the lawn out back. Most of it was still there on the ground.

We didn't know his name. He'd lived across the road from us for the best part of a year, Mum said, before she'd ever even spoken to him. For us children, that was an eternity, and for the longest time he was just the back of a large, grey head in the window of the house opposite ours. Jamie would sit beside me, staring at the man's strange, wild hair through our lounge window as we counted cars and burnt our arms by accident on the radiator, delighted in the secret knowledge that he could see nothing of us. Then I'd tell Jamie stories about the head, pretending it wasn't him at all sitting there, but an ogre instead, or monster. Then my little brother would start to cry and Connie would rush in, upset by the noise, and I'd try my best to turn the head into something else.

But still we'd watch it, knelt together on the sugar-stained couch our mum got to keep, studying the head and wondering why it never moved from that position, until one day the back of it opened up like a mouth with teeth and we ran into the kitchen, crying with fright. Then, because I was the eldest, I crept back to the window and saw it was a furred hat he'd been wearing, pulled forward to cover his face. And now it was up, and he was smiling at us, and waving, and I realised he'd been watching us all the time.

It was Mum who suggested we visit him one day, having learned that his wife had died unexpectedly the month before. We'd never once seen her over there, however, not even in the days following that first signal to us, when he'd begun beckoning us over whenever we made eye contact. From that point on, I'd started to observe his house more closely from the safety of my mum's bedroom, which was situated directly above our previous position in the lounge. I watched him on my own now, whenever Jamie and Connie played together on the far side of the house.

I'd sit in my mum's chair, peering at him through the hinged gaps in her three-way dressing mirror. At times he'd venture outside to water his front path or clip the hedgerows, and whenever he'd stop to glance up at my mum's window, which he did frequently, I'd flinch back instinctively from her mirror, then slowly summon up the courage to move back. Whereupon, he would smile up again in my direction, wave his hand, then carry on calmly with his work. Meanwhile I would sit stunned, catching my breath and berating myself for not having kept still, yet relieved that the ordeal was over, and with little in the way of consequence.

Mum felt guilty, I think, because we'd missed the funeral car entirely, and he'd apparently attended the service alone, putting a brave face on it, he said, their friends being too old to travel down and "pack her off". So our mum took us out that afternoon to the florist in town to find him a nice bouquet, and when we pulled up outside our house that evening, she insisted we go over there to hand it to him in person. I begged her to let me stay in the car, knowing I wasn't yet allowed to be alone at home by myself, but Jamie and Connie were still rowdy from the sweets they'd eaten, and insisted on going in with her. Besides, Mum explained, appealing perhaps to a burgeoning maturity she sensed in me, it would cheer the old man up to see some children.

Before Connie had a chance to ring the bell, he'd opened the door from inside.

"Are you hungry?" he asked, beaming at my sister with a wide grin.

Connie, startled, looked up at Mum.

"Well," Mum replied, herself a little thrown, "we're having tea in a while."

"We are indeed," said the old man, making room for us to enter. "Come in, come in."

He stepped back into the darkness of his hall.

I didn't like his hair. It resembled a judge's wig up close, made up of small, white frizzy curls with two strange corkscrew ringlets dangling down, past his ears. I hoped Mum would say no, but instead she ushered us in. I held back for as long as possible, until eventually she went in before me, her hands on Connie's shoulders.

"We can only stay a short while," she said, and I wondered whether she was feeling as unsure about things as I was.

"Come in, young man," he said to me, almost sternly. As I stepped inside, he began humming an old-fashioned tune I didn't recognise.

There were no lights on in the house, but our eyes were young and sharp and I studied him closely as he beckoned me forward. His head was large and rectangular, with an unusually high forehead. His wide-set eyes were marked with broken vessels, and his flushed complexion seemed rather pronounced, as if the redness in his cheeks had been deliberately painted on. In certain places, too, his face looked like it had been dusted with a fine layer of powder.

He reminded me of an illustration I'd once seen in a history book at school. It was an early newspaper caricature, from the days when men wore wigs, tailcoats and funny tight trousers. One of the figures depicted in this particular picture had frightened me. It was a gentleman of some kind, because he'd been dressed in a frock coat and smart buckled shoes, but his head was far too large for his body and was drawn like an ogre from a fairy tale.

Although my teacher had done her best to explain that this was because the illustration was exaggerated and not a picture of a real person, I nevertheless dreamt about it for months afterwards, and in this particular context, being unable to distinguish between what was real and what wasn't, the hideous figure from the book became as lifelike to me as anyone I'd ever met.

My subconscious mind was dwelling on this when the old man's eyes darted suddenly from Connie to me, and I had the uneasy impression he'd apprehended my thoughts. The motion of his head followed after, as though it were a separate entity, while his mouth remained fixed in that unnerving smile throughout our whole visit, entirely divorced from the expression above. His teeth were large and very white. Possibly false, I thought, although the neat, sizeable gaps between them looked very different from those I'd seen in other old people. In fact, they drew my attention so much that I almost failed to see his tongue was completely black.

"Liquorice," he said, sticking it out at Connie.

"It's a sweet," I said, sensing she was frightened. "Like Black Jacks."

He smiled at me oddly, like his eyes didn't mean it.

"Shoes off, children," Mum said. Dutifully we obliged, expecting the old man, like every other adult we'd ever met, to insist otherwise. But instead he merely nodded rather solemnly, waiting for us to remove them.

"We came round to give you these," Mum said, handing him the flowers.

He took them without comment, and at first I thought he was struck with a sudden sadness, until I saw it wasn't the flowers that were distracting him but Connie again, who was clinging to my mum's dress in an attempt to balance herself.

"We're very sorry for your loss," Mum added.

"You are?" he replied, sounding surprised.

I'd removed my shoes at last, and could feel the unpleasant touch of his cold, tiled floor beneath my socks.

"We really can't stay long," Mum said.

"In," he replied, rather shortly, pointing to an open door beside us. "Through there."

Mum held Jamie's hand, instructing me to take Connie's.

"You have beautiful children," the man said, following us into what I knew to be the lounge immediately facing ours. "I watch them every day."

"Thank you," Mum replied, taking the seat he was pointing her toward.

"This one especially," he continued, stepping between myself and my sister. "Such beautiful skin. Like porcelain."

He dumped the flowers on a small coffee table in the middle of the room, then placed both hands gently on my sister's shoulders. He turned her around slowly to face him, as if she were a museum exhibit.

"Do you know what porcelain is?"

"No…"

"They make dolls from it. Pretty dolls."

Connie smiled.

"Would you like a pretty doll to play with, Connie?"

"Yes, please," she said, in a tone usually reserved for the family doctor.

"Then I'll send you one. A pretty doll for a pretty girl."

Mum looked like she was going to object, but remained silent.

"I'm starving," I said instead. "Can we go home?"

The old man turned to me.

"I imagine you'll be wanting a pretty doll yourself, soon enough?"

I don't think I quite knew what he meant, but I didn't like it.

"How do you know my sister's name?" I asked him coldly.

"I know all your names. You're very loud children. Shouting all day and night, upsetting my wife on her deathbed."

Mum glared at me from across the room, but I ignored her, my attention focused on the fact that there weren't enough seats for us all, and Connie and I had been left standing, close by him. I had a suspicion he was about to pick my sister up and sit her on his lap, so I positioned her near me, beside the door, and sat down between them.

"I'm sorry if they've been any trouble," said Mum.

"No trouble. She was a *horrid* snorer. Like a big pig."

He grinned at Jamie.

"Actually, we ought to be going," Mum said, suddenly checking her watch. Relieved, I stood up.

"It's past their tea time. I had absolutely no idea."

"So soon?" he said, signalling me to sit down.

"Perhaps another day."

"I will hold you to that, Mrs. Ellis."

It was my father's name.

"Miss Radford, I mean. Slip of the tongue."

He poked his black tongue out again, this time at Jamie.

"Come on, children," said Mum, rising from her seat.

"Before you go," he said, waving her down again, "I have something for you."

He walked over to the bay window, winking at Jamie, and took three small paper bags out of an old tea chest. There was something inside each of them.

"These weren't touched."

He turned to face us, holding up the bags.

"A slice of cake for every child. A gift, from my wife's deathday party."

He emphasised the word, but unlike Connie, I didn't find it funny.

"You like birthday parties, don't you?" he asked my sister, giving her another big smile from across the room.

"Oh, yes!" she exclaimed.

"Well, a funeral is the same thing. Only it's a deathday party, instead. See?"

He walked back, close to Connie, and held out one of the bags, too high for her to reach. Finally he let her have it, then looked at Jamie. My little brother stood, excited, and ran to him.

"Wait your turn," the old man said, pulling the bag away rather sharply. Then offered it to me.

"No, thanks," I said.

His smile dipped a little.

"More for Connie."

He handed my sister a second bag, then gave her the third as well. He glanced down at Jamie, who looked like he was about to cry.

"*Share.*"

Jamie nodded, then looked tearfully at Mum, who sat there in her chair, watching us and saying nothing. She looked shocked, like she did whenever she'd rowed with my dad.

"Let's go home," I said.

"Home," the old man repeated, rolling up both shirt sleeves. "My, it's hot in here, with all these excitable children."

His arms were covered with tattoos. The one nearest me resembled a mermaid, but turned into something else when he flexed his muscles. He did this subtly, I noticed, so only I could see. It became something like those pictures scrawled in the concrete tubes we used to play in at the park. When my parents were off having one of their fights.

"Shall we arrange another visit soon?" he asked as my mum stood up again. I think she'd been sitting in something wet, because she kept feeling the back of her dress.

"Just the two of us."

She straightened it downward, over her legs, and addressed me.

"Toby, take them out and help them put their shoes on."

I nodded and moved Connie back toward the door, away from him.

"Jamie. Come on."

My brother walked past the man without looking at him, and followed my sister into the hall.

With both of them gone, the old man looked at me.

"The new man of the house."

"Excuse me," said my mother, edging around the coffee table in the direction of the door. He stepped in front of her, blocking her way.

"I'm a widower, after all," he said, his voice becoming noticeably louder. "And you've lost your husband. We might have a good deal of fun together."

"Let me through."

"You heard her!" I shouted, from behind. "Let her through!"

"How about tomorrow?" asked the old man, stepping aside.

"Stay by me, Toby," said Mum, walking past him into the hall.

"Tomorrow would be perfect," he continued, following us out. "I have so many of my wife's clothes to sort through, and I need a woman's touch."

I rattled the handle of the door.

"Would you like to try on some of my wife's clothes?" he asked, behind us. "Before I burn them all?"

"It's locked," I said, fighting panic.

"That's because," he replied softly, "I have the key, here in my pocket."

Mum held out her hand.

"Give it to me."

With an air of faint amusement, he reached into his trouser pocket, rummaged for a moment, then pulled out a small silver Yale key. He held it close to his chest.

"Here it is."

Steeling herself, Mum reached out and grabbed it from him. Then inserted it into the lock.

"I think you'd look attractive, wrapped up in my wife's dresses."

It was the wrong key.

"Or your porcelain daughter. A good many slices of cake and she'll fill out rather nicely."

Mum whirled around, pulling Connie and Jamie close to her. I stepped forward, putting myself between her and the old man.

He gave a comic sigh. "Wrong pocket."

He moved his hand over his flies and thrust it inside his other pocket. He rooted around again for a few moments, then drew out a second key, attached to a piece of grubby string. He dangled it before us, looking at my mum.

I snatched it.

As I handed the key to Mum, he reached out and pressed her stomach lightly with his hand.

"Any more?" he said.

Mum turned, unlocked the door quickly and pushed it open. As we stepped into the cold night, he adopted a friendly tone.

"Thank you for the flowers. I'll return the favour. Very soon."

Mum herded us over the road, into our drive. Behind us the man was muttering something to himself. Then he raised his voice and spoke to us, clearly.

"I'll send you a pretty doll. A slice of cake and a pretty doll."

He began to sing. The same strange, old-fashioned melody I'd heard earlier.

> *"A slice of cake and a pretty doll,*
> *The Cake Man gave to me,*
> *A slice of cake and a pretty doll,*
> *Is all the life I'll see."*

Moments later we were back inside our house. I removed my shoes on our entrance mat, felt the familiar softness of our hall carpet under my socks and swung the front door shut behind me. As I did so, I glimpsed him, still watching us from his front doorstep.

I locked him out.

Jamie was irritable all evening and didn't want his tea. I didn't feel hungry either, so I gave him and Connie their baths and read them both happy stories to get them to sleep. Eventually they nodded off, and when I came downstairs again, Mum was busy examining the slices of cake he'd given Connie. They were stale and hard as rock, so she threw them in the bin.

I left her watching television in the lounge and went up to bed with my stomach hurting like it used to whenever Dad came home. On the way to my own room I slipped into hers, which was unlit, and peeked through her dressing-room mirror to spy again on the old man's house through the curtains. There were still no lights on inside, but as my eyes slowly adjusted to the surrounding darkness, I could just make out his grey head opposite, crouched down like a monster in his horrible lounge.

★   ★   ★

The next time he came to us. It occurred three nights later, not long after my mum had gone to bed. The front doorbell woke me from a dream, but I only rose and crept downstairs when I heard voices. My mum's was the loudest – he didn't shout at all, in fact – and she'd evidently been under the impression that it was a policeman at the door, because she sounded angry and was telling him to go home or she'd call them for real. He spoke to her politely and calmly, explaining he would do that very thing, only he wanted to give us the cake first, with her blessing, and she need only open the door for a moment so that he could hand it over. He insisted he was sorry about the other day and had been up all night baking it for us because nights were now unbearable for him. He grew sad at night, he said, and it was all he could do to keep from despairing over there in that lonely house, all by himself.

Mum's manner grew politer then, despite her obvious exhaustion, and she told him she'd accept it from him the following morning but not before. At once he became friendly again, almost jolly, and said he'd be over first thing. But he never came.

We didn't hear anything further from him for several weeks, and I saw almost nothing of him through the gaps in my mum's mirror. Yet occasional deliveries were now left for him on his front doorstep. Supermarket carrier bags, stuffed full of shopping, which invariably disappeared whenever I'd leave the room to eat or relieve myself.

We didn't really talk about him. Mum grew distant whenever I brought the matter up and just said he was old and grieving and needed time to himself. But Jamie and Connie weren't sleeping well. The garden was too noisy at night, Jamie insisted, and Connie began talking about a man who came into her room and sat at the bottom of her bed when it was dark. I was also experiencing bad dreams, along with the return of my stomach aches, and wondered if Connie was mistaking the old man for me, as the first thing I did upon waking and realising where I was, was to go through to their rooms and listen for the sound of them breathing.

When my birthday came around, I received presents and a visit from my aunt, but nothing from Dad. Mum said his gift would no doubt arrive later that day, but I could tell she was upset. That afternoon, the doorbell rang for a second time and I rushed through to the hall, hoping his present had arrived after all. But when I opened the door, before me stood the old man.

In his hands he held something vaguely resembling a brown loaf, wrapped in a fresh, striped towel.

"Happy birthday, Toby," he said, holding it out for me to take.

I didn't say anything to him, and I didn't reach for his gift.

"A birthday cake, Madam," he said, looking at my mother, who, I was relieved to discover, had followed me from the kitchen. "For the master of the house."

"Thanks," she said, taking it from his hands.

Before she could shut the door, he began talking about the cake in some detail. How long it had taken him to bake and how thoroughly he'd perfected the recipe, working night after night, ensuring it was exactly right before bringing it over.

The cake didn't look perfect to me. Like I say, there was no icing on it, and no candles either. Mum pulled back the towel politely to take a look, and I knew from her expression that she too thought there was nothing remotely nice about it.

"That's kind," she said, attempting again to close the door.

"And I got the right day?"

She hesitated, briefly.

"Yes."

"How much of it will you eat, Toby? The whole cake?"

He laughed loudly. I didn't say a thing until Mum nudged my arm.

"Yes, thank you."

He continued to grin at me, staring into my eyes, then finally turned back to her.

"And I got the right day?" he said again.

"You did," Mother replied, swinging the door further shut.

"And you'll eat it today?"

"Of course."

"Remember to share, young man. With your greedy brother and sister."

Mum closed the door on him and ushered me away, back toward the kitchen. Then she knelt down quietly on the carpet and carefully raised the flap of our bronze letterbox. She watched the old man walk back across the road and re-enter the house opposite. Then she stood up again and sniffed the man's cake. I followed her as she took it through to the kitchen.

"Are you going to cut it now?" I asked.

"No, Toby."

She placed the cake on our kitchen top and unwrapped it from the striped towel. Then she dug her fingers inside it and tore it apart, dragging the sponge and sifting through the crumbling fragments.

She gathered the remains inside the towel, took it outside into the garden and scattered the lot over our lawn. When she came back in, she dropped the towel in the bin and washed her hands with soap.

When she looked over at me, I was crying.

"Toby, darling," she said, coming toward me. I wept into her jumper as she hugged me close. Jamie and Connie came down from upstairs, hearing me crying, and cuddled me as well, and then Mum made tea for us all. When nothing further came for me that afternoon, I went up to bed, trying hard not to be sad about my dad, and fell asleep above the muffled sounds of her crying on the lounge sofa downstairs.

★   ★   ★

The next morning I pulled back the curtains and watched her examining what was left of the cake on the lawn below. It was nearly all still there, the birds having hardly touched it, but when Jamie got up he said he'd heard someone in the garden during the night, and when I went out with Mum to look around we discovered a pair of muddy footprints on the compost sacks Dad had left under our side-window, which someone had evidently climbed up on to look in.

"I hope you aren't feeding my cake to the birds," the old man said later that day, bending down to address us through our letterbox. We were sat around the kitchen table, picking at our food, and Mum was holding one finger over her lips to keep Connie and Jamie quiet.

"No good for birds," he said, rattling the bronze flap up and down with his fingers. I stood up then, Mum whispering at me to stop, but I ignored her and walked over rather more boldly than I felt, toward the kitchen door. At the far end of the front hall I saw his eyes staring in at me through the letterbox. Aware that I was watching, he raised his head so that I could see only his mouth.

"I've baked another cake, Toby," he said. "Let me in and I'll give it to you."

"No," I said.

"Open the door, Toby. Let me in."

I heard my mother moving up behind me.

"Go home," I shouted, suddenly angry. "We don't want your stupid cake."

The flap snapped shut loudly and the mouth disappeared. There followed a long silence, the gloomy atmosphere of the hall lit only by the sun's final rays passing through the frosted glass panes either side of the door. I heard the muffled voices of Connie and Jamie close by and realised Mum had her hands clamped over their mouths.

Then the letterbox snapped open again and something came flying through it onto the hall carpet. Mum hugged me close and told me to look after my siblings. Then silently she moved forward, by herself, into the hall.

The object was an envelope, addressed to me. She recognised the handwriting and opened it. Then threw it back down almost immediately. She wouldn't let me read it, not even later, when the police asked to see it. It was a birthday card from my father, apparently, sent in good time, but when I managed to glimpse some of the writing while they were checking the envelope for fingerprints, I saw something horribly familiar scrawled in the margin. It was the picture from the old man's arm, and there were lots of other messages in funny handwriting too, which my mum told them wasn't my father's hand, and that's all I ever knew about it.

The police didn't do much in the end, although the old man's visits stopped soon afterwards. About eight months later we found out he'd died, alone in his house.

I watched the van arrive to collect his body. It was a white transit, which surprised me, having expected, for some reason, a black hearse like the ones we'd occasionally drive past in town. They brought him out of the house in a bag and dropped him accidentally while lifting him into the vehicle. Mum said he had no relatives at all, and as nobody we asked knew what his name was, Mum searched through the local obituaries the following week, hoping to identify him. There were no accompanying photographs, but one entry referred to a former merchant seaman who'd later worked as a Punch and Judy man, while another described a retired council officer who'd once run a bakery business in the north of England.

I grew quickly bored of Mum's searching and was drawn instead to a picture on the opposite page which upset me; a photograph of what I took to be a local pantomime dame, despite it being summer, taken close-up through a funny lens. The face looked a little like the figure in my old schoolbook and I threw the newspaper out as soon as my mother was finished with it.

Jamie, whom we'd hoped might forget our old neighbour completely, instead began to point every so often to the house over the road while singing an odd little song. He claimed he'd dreamt the melody up himself, but I recognised it as the one the old man had sung to us. Jamie called it 'Caker's Man', a title Connie also adopted. Regrettably it stuck, and the old man slowly, despite my mother's best efforts, became something of a permanent family memory.

A few months later Jamie joined Connie at school for the autumn term, and the change in routine helped them both. I, on the other hand, was losing a great deal of weight and continuing to experience severe bouts of stomach cramps. I kept this largely to myself, but by December Mum had arranged for someone to come to our house, explaining initially that the lady was a babysitter. It soon became apparent to me, however, that she was also my carer.

The arrangement made sense as we could no longer rely on my father's payments, and instead Mum had to find a job with extra hours. In turn, this meant she was unable to collect us from school each day. Although I explained I was old enough to walk my brother and sister home, she wouldn't let me do it, and soon we were being driven home instead by Lucy, a ginger-haired woman in her late twenties, who had pink, rosy cheeks and wore very bright clothes.

She was funny and pretty, almost like one of Connie's new ballerina toys. Lucy made our meals, supervised our homework hours and occasionally stayed the night when my mother was working out of town.

She also used to make us shriek with laughter by driving so fast over bumps in country lanes that we'd get flung in a heap onto the floor of her Mini.

Mum never told me why Lucy was really there, but one night when she was at work, Lucy took me aside and set down, on our lounge floor, a heavy and serious-looking grey binder. From it she removed several sheets of paper containing long lists of food types, which she asked me to tick in a particular order. She wanted to know which foods made me feel most ill. She also wished me to identify which of them made me physically sick, which was always cake. She said I had to draw that particular food over and over, so that eventually it wouldn't make me feel ill at all. It didn't matter if I couldn't do it now, she said, reassuring me. She promised I would soon be able to, and that I'd be so happy with the pictures I eventually drew that afterwards I wouldn't feel remotely sick at the thought of eating them.

The night after, she stayed over again and did the same thing, talking to me alone while Connie and Jamie were both asleep, asking me to draw pictures of birthday cakes, insisting I would soon be adding nice things to them, like striped candles I liked. She said I could pick whatever crayons I wanted and colour them in like I had done when I was small. I remember wondering if she realised how old I was, and when I told her how silly that would make me feel, she laughed out loud, agreeing with me, but insisting I must do as she said.

Not long after Lucy had begun staying over, I began to suffer a recurring nightmare not dissimilar to the one I had experienced when younger, only this one was more intense, taking place in an exact replica of our house. So convincing was it that whenever I woke up, I was never quite able to tell which house I was in.

It always featured me and Connie, although my sister was much older in the dream. We were both in the house, but never together at the start. The ordeal would begin in my mother's bedroom. The light outside was soft and dull in the dream, like a cold afternoon, making everything inside feel dark and heavy. There was a faint pinkish tinge to the sky, like a summer storm was approaching. I sat behind my Mum's dressing mirror, watching the house opposite through the gaps between its reflective panes.

After some time, and in complete silence, a car would draw up in the street outside. It was a strange looking car, made entirely of glass, so that I could see right through it. Some nights it looked different, more like an old-fashioned carriage from a fairy tale, but I was never able to make out its driver. Having pulled up outside the old man's house, the car, or carriage, would wait there in silence for some time, completely motionless, until gradually I began to feel frightened. Then the front wheels would turn and the car would move across the road toward our home, pulling in somewhere directly below me. It was hard to know when it had completely vanished from sight, because the car became almost entirely invisible when it moved, save for reflections, usually of the house opposite, which rippled through it like a passing current.

I would hear the front doorbell ring downstairs, and sense, soon afterwards, Connie running through from somewhere behind me. I would get up from my mother's chair and leave her room, entering the upstairs hall just in time to see the back of my sister's head descending the staircase ahead of me, but no matter how fast I ran I could never catch her.

As I followed her into the front hall, I would glimpse something move from the frosted glass window beside the door, to hide, unseen, behind it. Connie and I would then stand in silence, watching the bronze letterbox intently. After a while the doorbell would ring again, followed by three loud knocks. We were both too terrified to answer, yet I was somehow aware that whoever was standing outside had a gift for me, and wanted me to let them in. I would start to dread the bronze letter flap opening, until suddenly I would hear three more knocks, this time from the rear of the house, and Connie would run through the kitchen behind me towards the door leading to our garden.

I would follow her, not daring to call out, then catch again the sight of someone in the act of hiding themselves behind our house, only this time its shape appeared to float downward from the roof, passing the horizontal window above the doorframe, to land somewhere immediately behind. The little I could make out as it vanished from sight vaguely resembled a human face, only one that was unnaturally large and brightly coloured, like a party mask.

As Connie and I stood before the garden door, dreading the knocks we knew would come, behind us we would suddenly hear the unmistakeable sound of our front door swinging open. Then I would turn and see, set in the exact centre of our hallway carpet, a perfectly round birthday cake.

Realising I'd forgotten about Jamie, and that it must be he who'd opened our door, I would suddenly be gripped with a swift and terrible anxiety, and the dream would reach its inevitable conclusion as I crept reluctantly over to the cake, which was coated with sugared icing and decorated with pink and yellow candles, and plunge my fingers inside, tearing the whole thing open. And there I would find the mouth buried within, and the two rows of small white teeth set together in a smile. And as they fell away beneath my fingers, I'd recognise them as Connie and Jamie's baby teeth, and know that the cake had been made from my brother and sister.

★　　★　　★

"Try this one," Lucy said one afternoon, leaning down beside me and holding the plate of brightly coloured fairy cakes beneath my chin. Most of them had gone already, with Connie and Jamie now looking rather ill, having gorged themselves the second Lucy had prised the plastic lid from her pink Tupperware container. She had enjoyed bringing them out, declaring the dinner she'd accidentally ruined had been saved after all.

I think that was the first time I noticed she looked different to how she'd appeared when I'd first met her. It was hard to tell exactly, and it was only when I pictured Connie's precious ballerina dolls that I realised she no longer quite resembled them in the way she once had, but she seemed a little fuller than before. Her make-up was also different, with her face even pinker now, both cheeks noticeably redder, as if she'd been painting the colour on. Her lips looked much thicker too, and were no longer pleasant to look at, forever smeared from constantly kissing me.

"No, thank you," I said.

"Go on. Just one."

"No, thank you."

"Try the smallest one."

"I'm not hungry."

She put her arm around me and leaned closer.

"You'll eat them, Toby. I promise."

"I know I will," I said, looking round at her to let her know I meant it. "Just not today."

"No, you'll eat them now."

I noticed Connie and Jamie looking at me. Like they'd also sensed the change in Lucy.

"I can't," I said.

"I made them for you, Toby," she said, close to my ear. "Especially."

I could smell her breath. It was sweet, like warm caramel. I picked up the one nearest to me; a small fairy cake with pale orange icing. It was too soft and I felt the sponge giving way between my fingers as I placed it back on the plate.

"No, thank you," I said again.

Lucy rose abruptly and took the plate away, setting it down between Jamie and Connie. Her smile had gone.

"You two can fight over it," she said, stuffing one of the remaining cakes in her mouth. Then she walked over to the pedal bin and tipped the rest in. She was right, of course. My brother and sister did indeed fight over it. So loudly that when Mum finally came home, I got the blame.

★   ★   ★

On my thirteenth birthday I received several books. One was a collection of fairy tales from my dad, which were all too young for me, even though Lucy insisted they weren't, and one a large history book which turned out to be the same one I'd read at school, only with a newer cover. Mum assumed it had to be the other half of Dad's present, because the book had been left on our doorstep later that day, with a note from a neighbour saying it had been opened in error.

I glanced over the road as I picked it up, thinking I could see the old man's grey head again, in the lounge opposite ours. But when I stood up I saw it wasn't there at all, and the house was still as empty and uninhabited as it had been since the day he'd died.

When I had a moment to myself that afternoon, I took the history book up to my room and looked up the picture of the strange gentleman which used to frighten me. It was even worse than I remembered, and immediately I hid the book in the lounge cupboard downstairs.

The rest of the day was miserable. Connie and Jamie were upset I hadn't been given any toys they could play with, while the shaving kit Mum bought me ultimately sat in my bedside drawer, unused, for a whole year.

The big event came later that evening, after Lucy had dropped off some shopping for us, with Mum telling me to look upon it as a "strange" sort of present. She was sorry, she insisted, but she had to work late again at very short notice, meaning Lucy was unable to look after us like she usually would. My mother had no alternative, therefore, but to leave me in charge of Connie and Jamie until she returned later that night. It was a big responsibility, she told me, but perhaps I was old enough at last.

"After all," she said, forcing a smile, "you're the man of the house now."

I asked her if she could call in sick, but she refused, and when I began to play up she told me off, telling me I was being childish, then apologised and insisted there was nothing she could do.

It would be good for me, she said.

★   ★   ★

Before leaving for work, my mother left me detailed instructions about where the keys were, what to cook Jamie and Connie for tea, what time they had to be in bed, and finally she gave me Lucy's number in case of an emergency, which I already had as Lucy herself had once handed it to me, saying I could call her if I ever needed to. Finally, the door was shut, locked firmly from outside, and then all I could do was watch Mum's car disappearing down the road between the gaps in her dressing mirror.

It was the middle of winter and already getting dark outside, so I immediately went around the downstairs floor, closing all our curtains and making sure there weren't any gaps.

Then I switched the radio on and made Connie and Jamie toasted cheese. I couldn't handle the grater properly and grazed my fingers, so I made a game of it with Connie, letting her put plasters on me while Jamie played on the couch with his action figures.

I'd finished their baths and we were all watching a music programme on television when it happened. I was about to send them up to bed when my brother and sister became suddenly secretive and ran into the kitchen. I continued watching the screen, distracted by the female singer who looked a bit like Lucy, when I suddenly heard a shout of "Surprise!" and looked round to find Jamie and Connie standing there with a plate balanced in their hands. On it sat a perfectly round birthday cake, covered with sugared icing, and thirteen pink and yellow candles arranged around its rim.

"Happy Birthday, Toby!" they said together.

"Where did you get it from?" I demanded, feeling a familiar stab of pain in my stomach.

"We made it, silly," said Connie.

"Mummy helped," added Jamie. "After lunch. When you were in your room. It's a surprise."

I took it from their hands and went through to the kitchen. I put it on the table and covered it with a cloth, then realised I hadn't thanked them.

"Aren't you going to have some?" asked Connie.

"No," I said.

"Can we?" said Jamie.

"Not now."

"Mummy said we could have some."

"You're about to go to bed."

"Why can't we have some?"

"Because it's bedtime."

"But Mummy *said*."

Connie was welling up. I was tired and didn't want a fuss, so I took two plates from the cupboard and a knife from the drawer.

"Aren't you going to light the candles?" said Jamie, leaning over the cake, his nose practically touching the icing.

I opened another cupboard, took out the matchbox and lit one. Connie puffed with excitement as I set one of the candles alight. Then, reluctantly, I went round each candle in turn, lighting them all.

"There," I said, watching the soft glow light up their faces.

I knew I was being horrid and felt terrible. To make things worse, Jamie and Connie began to sing to me.

"Happy Birthday to you, Happy Birthday to you…"

I forced myself to join in, putting my arms around them and kissing them on their foreheads.

"Why are you crying?" asked Connie.

"I'm happy," I said, drying my eyes. I let them blow out the candles for me. As the smoke wafted between them, slowly dissipating, I picked up the knife and cut into the cake.

I examined each slice as I laid it on the plate. There was a pale layer of cream in the centre, but nothing else. It smelled very sweet.

"Are you having some?" said Jamie.

I felt another pain in my stomach, but took a third plate from the cupboard. I cut myself a small piece, held it to my nose for a moment, then sat down between them.

"You won't sleep," I warned them.

"Mummy *promised*," Connie replied.

And with that we all ate our cake. They appeared to enjoy theirs, but I could barely get mine down. Eventually, I pinched my nose between my fingers, shut both eyes and imagined it was something else. When I finally allowed myself to smell again, I had to cover my mouth, fighting to keep it down.

"Yum," said Jamie.

"Can we have more?"

"No," I told Connie, taking their plates away. "Up to bed now."

They didn't sleep, like I'd said. Instead, they were up for hours, white as a sheet, heads craned together over the toilet bowl, clutching at their stomachs. When one of them was finally sick, the other joined in almost immediately, and I spent another hour battling my own pangs while attempting to feed them the water they craved. But every time they took some down, they brought it up again almost immediately. They begged me to call for Lucy but I told them she was away and I was in charge. They cried even harder at that and when I finally had them in their beds with buckets by their sides and towels spread across the floor, they drifted into a feverish, troubled sleep.

They both had high temperatures, as had I when I checked. After I'd done my best to clean up the bathroom floor, I made my way unsteadily downstairs, put the rest of the cake in the bin and checked all the locks again. Then I fought back a fresh urge to bring everything up and staggered up to bed.

I'd just pulled my bedroom curtains across when I heard the front doorbell ring downstairs. I sat up suddenly to check the time on my bedside clock. It was past eleven o'clock and the act of sitting up almost made me sick over my covers. I climbed out of bed and crept over to my door, hoping I'd imagined it.

The doorbell rang again. It was most likely Lucy, I reasoned, checking in on us after a late evening call from Mum. But instead of going down to see her, I moved quietly into my mother's bedroom and crawled over to her dresser.

Crouched in her seat, I leant my head against the mirrored glass and peered through the gaps between.

As I looked through, I realised I'd forgotten to draw the upstairs curtains. The room, including its reflection around me, was bathed in stark moonlight, throwing the frames and edges of my mother's furniture into sharp, unworldly focus.

I sat for some time, looking out between the gaps at the house opposite, which was dark and empty still, hoping I'd hear whoever was downstairs, waiting outside our front door, give up at last and walk away. But instead the doorbell rang a third time.

I'd somehow forgotten how ill I'd been feeling. Only that the pain which had surged through my stomach was now focused instead in my head. Yet it was not quite pain – more an uneasiness of mind and a distorted sense of things, as if the room before me was shimmering in a thick haze, and I was perceiving everything through the clammy fog of swelling fever.

I stood up with difficulty and lurched over to the landing, glancing into Jamie and Connie's rooms to check they were still asleep and breathing, then sat on the top stair and edged myself downward, step by step, toward the silence and darkness of the hall below.

I saw it almost immediately, staring in at me through the pane of frosted glass beside the door, as it had done in my dream. No longer attempting to conceal itself, the dark contours of the giant head filled the pane, pressing itself against the glass as I reached the floor. Though greatly distorted, I could make out the bold colours of a vast painted face, with huge cheeks daubed red above its wide mouth.

I knelt on the carpet, unsure whether it could see me or not, feeling suddenly as small and vulnerable as Jamie or Connie. Then, in a smooth arc, like something slowly waving at me, the face moved back behind the door.

My gaze dropped to the bronze letterbox and a dreadful moment passed. With intense trepidation, I crouched on the floor, dragging my fingers anxiously through the carpet. Then the flap sprung upward.

Beyond, all was black. I could see nothing, yet smelled a sweet, saccharine odour wafting through the hole in the door. It was the unmistakeable aroma of ovens, and a cake slowly rising. I felt the nausea I'd suppressed swell up again, and thought I glimpsed something move in the darkness of the gap. But what I thought was a hand, holding up the bronze flap, instead writhed and darted through the hole to lick me. As I lurched backward, desperate to avoid its touch, I saw what was slowly growing each side of the door. Blurred horribly through the frosted panes, lined with teeth, was the vast, widening smile of a colossal mouth.

I cried out for my mum and fled back upstairs toward my bedroom. As I passed along the landing I heard something like feet pattering over the roof above, and when I entered my room and threw myself under the covers, I called out for Jamie and Connie, realising I'd left them alone. But they didn't come, and as I tore back the sheets again, knowing I had to get out and save them, I saw the brightness of the full moon beyond my window, vast and white, illuminated through the nylon fibres of my bedroom curtains.

Then I heard the sound of plaster splitting as shards of paint and brickwork crumbled like powder from one corner of the wall. I stared, dumbfounded, as long, spider-thin cracks worked their way downward from the ceiling, casting fragments of the wall outward, onto my carpet. Then the moon outside began to move across the sky. Convinced the house was collapsing, I flung back the curtains and saw it looking in at me, the vast whiteness of its giant eye moving slowly from side to side like a mechanical head luring children to a terrifying funhouse. The pair of immense lips below it were stretched wide apart, the interior of its mouth darker than anything I had ever known.

Its teeth, white and monstrous, yet unbroken like the rows of brickwork they were fixed upon, shone bright in the glare of the real moon above. With a terrifying crack, the immense jaws clamped downward, biting on the wall between us, and I knew it was making its way in.

As the room fell in around me, I heard my brother and sister scream for me in the dark. Aware I could do nothing to help them, I cried out for my mother to save us all, knowing the thing was above me, its pink, painted cheeks and blood-red lips stretched into an infinite grin as it leaned down over my bed, preparing to eat me up.

Then I smelled the scent of my mum's perfume and felt her arms around me, and knew at last where I was as I cried myself to sleep.

★   ★   ★

Later, amid tears, Jamie admitted it was Lucy who'd baked the cake, having handed it to him and Connie earlier that day when Mum was in the garden. Connie never spoke about her, but Jamie said Lucy had frightened them into it, although he would never tell us how. The police believed there was nothing in it, perhaps recalling how things had been with us, or perhaps my mother, when she'd previously reported the old man. We only saw Lucy once after that, when she turned up, accompanied by her estate agent, to view the house opposite ours.

Mum handled that by herself, and we watched our old babysitter for the last time through the gaps in our mum's dressing mirror, arguing and shouting loudly about us from the old man's drive.

We were eating our tea later that evening when Connie told us that Lucy had been wearing his wife's clothes. When Mum pressed her, my sister insisted they'd belonged to the old man who'd once lived opposite, and were the same clothes he'd asked her to put on.

"You're too young to remember that," said Mum, a little nervously. "Besides, you never saw them."

"I did," Connie said, playing with her fork. "He used to come into my room at night and sit at the bottom of my bed. Then he'd wake me up and show me pictures of her."

That's all I can tell you, except that I ate the cake, like he wanted, and somewhere it's still inside me.

THE BEECHFIELD MIRACLES
Priya Sharma

Brexit Britain. Blackout Britain. Britain on the brink. Our United Kingdom is divided. Democracy broken by coalitions and divisions. This small island has made waves. There's no backstop for the ripples.

Bad times breed despair and prophets. Soap-box messiahs and evangelists are springing up all over. They're the drug of choice in some quarters. Not everywhere though. A street preacher was stoned to death in Crewe. Another nearly drowned when locals baptised him in the Tyne.

Journalism's a grubby trade nowadays. The money's in celebrities, not news. When Alan called me to cover a story for his scandal mag, I was low enough to bite. He liked to have a few true-life stories, the weirder the better.

What have you got to lose? At worst, you'll have a piece on social enterprise that you can flog to the Guardian *website, if you're lucky. At best you'll have covered the second coming.*

Alan's the only person who'll touch me. Funny. There was a time when I had ideals and wouldn't have wiped my backside on what he was printing.

I got off the train at Beechfield Station. Beechfield was built on cotton mills and steam power. Terraces clustered around the river. On one side, high up the hill, there was an estate of pebble-dashed council houses. Beyond that were rolling moors of rough wind-flattened grass. Who the hell had dubbed it Beechfield?

A young man waited for me on the platform. He held up a piece of cardboard with my name on it. We were the only two people there.

"Where's the limo?"

"Pardon?"

"Just joking. I'm Rob Miller."

"Pleased to meet you, Mr. Miller." His politeness was careful, as if newly learnt and in need of practice. "I'm Peter Watkins."

I was already filing him away for later. The odd formality, his earnest handshake, the sovereign rings, and his black nylon trousers. The darkness of his tattoos showed through his thin white shirt.

"Jasmin sent me to fetch you."

We walked through old Beechfield. The sunlight was thin, as if light was a commodity the North couldn't afford. The red lines of terraces could've been any industrial town but Beechfield was different. Most of the houses had window boxes. They contained Little Gem lettuces or radishes, even though it was April.

"Come on."

We turned a corner.

"Christ."

There was an open patch where the houses had been torn down. The end terrace bore faded, tattered wallpaper. Peter had wanted me to see this.

The ground had been cleared of rubble and turned to reveal rich, dark earth. On one side were potato plants, the other carrots. My granddad was a gardener right up until he died at seventy-eight. Carrots pulled straight from the ground smell sweeter than anything shop-bought.

"This used to be condemned houses. The council didn't like us planting here but they daren't move us on. They haven't the manpower anyway. Better food than weeds. Go on, take some pictures."

"May I?" I motioned to him, wanting to include him in the photo.

Peter nodded. I knelt down, making him a giant at that angle, dwarfing the rows of green. The end of the terrace, with its exposed wall, looked like something from the Blitz.

Perfect.

"How have you grown this stuff out of season?"

"Love and care."

I've seen hoaxers of every stripe. I imagined a crowd of them, planting everything up the night before. I still look at the photo sometimes and wonder what kind of men we both are.

"We should go. This way."

We turned down an alley that ran between the backs of the houses.

He stopped halfway along, leaning on a wheelie bin. I hadn't given Peter a reason to kick the shit out of me. Not yet anyway.

"What are your intentions, Mr. Miller?"

Peter was a big lad. He could've shoved me in that bin, head-first, and not broken a sweat.

"I'm a journalist. I'm here to write a story."

Nothing's more disarming than the truth.

"Newspapers lie."

"I'm only here on invitation."

"Jasmin wants you here. She says you're important. You're a witness."

Gold, I thought. *This is going to write itself.*

"Tell me, Peter. Help me understand." I had a repertoire of faces. I pulled out man-in-search-of-the-truth.

"I don't need to. You'll see for yourself."

*   *   *

Peter was a lamb for the rest of the way. He even offered to carry my rucksack.

"How did you meet Jasmin?"

"Outside a pub. I was about to stick a knife between my dad's ribs."

"Fucking hell."

"Jasmin took the knife out of my hand. She said, 'Kill him and you'll go back inside. Your dad's wrong about you. You're not a worthless piece of shit', which was what he always called me. 'You're special. There's something that only you can do. Follow me and you'll see.' She cried as she said it. And she stayed with me when the police came. 'You'll sit by my side, I promise. I'll look after you.' And she did."

Peter turned another corner. He was deliberately taking a tortuous route.

"I'd be dead now if it wasn't for her. I worked for a bad man. Done ugly stuff."

"Like?"

"Guns, drugs, sex trafficking, pharmacy robberies."

Pharmacies got raided for methadone, then antibiotics when the shortages set in. The bottom dropped out of that market because most of them stopped working. God help you if you get super-gonorrhoea.

"Didn't a few people get shot during pharmacy raids up here? Wasn't there some local lord who masterminded them but got let off?" Lords, as they'd been dubbed, ran the towns that couldn't escape themselves. "What was his name?"

"Bill Wheatley." Peter's jaw clenched, like he was scared he'd invoke the man then and there. "This is it. We're here."

He banged on a back gate. When he rapped a second time it opened. The flagged yard was crowded. People sat on upturned crates and plastic garden chairs. A few turned to look at us.

"Is this him?" A woman squared up to us. "Give me your bag, sunshine."

"Nice to meet you too." I handed her my rucksack. "Are you chief of security?"

She rifled through my gear, pulling out clothes. Deep furrows marked her forehead.

"I'd have packed my best undercrackers if I'd known they'd be on show." She ignored me, laying out the contents of my washbag on a picnic table and inspecting each item. Then she repacked everything with more care than I'd taken. She hadn't finished yet though. "Jacket off. Hands against the wall."

"Seriously? Are you ex-army?"

"Sorry." Peter held my jacket. "You won't get past Fiona without a pat down."

Fiona kicked my feet apart. Suddenly Peter seemed like a kitten.

"Has Jasmin been threatened?"

"Pimps. Dealers." Fiona's hands slid up my legs, onto my trunk and then around my arms. "Religious nuts."

I was glad I was facing the wall. I couldn't suppress a smirk.

"You can go in now. She's waiting."

I paused at the kitchen door. The threshold is the best part of any story, when there's a million possibilities and before reality disappoints me.

The kitchen was lit by a fluorescent strip. Two women were seated at the kitchen table. The older one wore a dark blue nurse's uniform and the other one was eating a bowl of cereal.

"Jasmin?"

The young woman stood. Her cheap acrylic jumper was heavily bobbled around the armpits. I put her in her early twenties. Younger than I'd imagined. Round cheeked, with faded acne marks.

"Welcome, Mr. Miller." She held out a hand.

I realised I was staring.

"Call me Rob."

"Tea or coffee?" The nurse got up.

"I'll do it, Saira. You should go." Then to me by way of explanation, "She's a midwife. Got a shift."

Saira kissed her cheek and gave me a wan smile as she left. Jasmin spooned out coffee from a jar as the kettle boiled. The domesticity of it brought me back to the moment. She wasn't John the Baptist. She was just a girl.

"Thanks for seeing me." I normally started with a brash question. "There's a lot of people looking out for you. Who are you hiding from? The police?"

"I've not broken any laws, have I?"

Jasmin directed the question to the corner behind me. I hadn't noticed the man, perched on a kitchen stool.

"No, you haven't."

"Good." Jasmin smiled. "I'll make you a sandwich, Rob. Ham okay?"

"Great."

I extended a hand to the man. He looked incongruent in a dark grey suit. "I didn't catch your name."

"That's because I didn't say it. I'm Jonathan Knox."

"How do you know Jasmin?"

The back door opened. It was Peter.

"Just in time. Mr. Miller was asking how I know Jasmin."

"I introduced them." Peter's teeth were irregular and stained. "Jonathan represented me when my dad pressed charges."

"Here." Jasmin put a plate and a mug down in front of me. I took a bite of the sandwich. It was a proper doorstopper, made from homemade bread.

"I wondered if you'd like to stop with us for a few days." Jasmin wiped down the worktop.

"Is that a good idea?" The solicitor stood up.

"Are you planning to brainwash me?" I grinned at her.

"It's not a cult."

"I think you should have the right to veto anything he writes." Jonathan was frowning.

"Are you Jasmin's solicitor too?"

"I wish I were."

"Jonathan, Rob must do as he sees fit." She laid a hand on his forearm. "It's okay."

I nearly choked on my sandwich. Jonathan looked doubtful but didn't press the point. She commanded all these hardened, worldly people.

"Maybe I could talk to some of your disciples."

"They're not disciples. I'm not a guru."

"Well, there's plenty of people interested in what you have to say."

★   ★   ★

My alarm woke me at 7:30 a.m. I lay there, basking in the fact I'd actually slept through the night. A deep and dreamless sleep that left me rested. The first time since Kim Roth. I'd been given the converted attic room. I realised what a luxury this was when I went downstairs.

I pushed open one of the bedroom doors that had been left ajar. It contained bunk beds, an arm's length apart, each neatly made with a washbag and pile of folded clothes lying at the foot of the bed. The other bedroom was the same. The small back bedroom was different. It contained a single bed, the mattress bare.

I followed the sounds down to the kitchen. Peter was handing round plates of toast.

"What's the plan?"

"Busy day ahead," was all he would say.

I pulled up a chair at the table. The man beside me held out his hand. "I'm Hrithrik."

Hrithrik made introductions. It was a relief that nobody knew who I was or didn't care. My normal mode was defensive. Kim Roth's sister spat in my face after the inquest and called me a pariah. She had a point.

Jasmin came in through the back door. She looked flushed. Her hair was pulled back in a stretchy headband.

"We should head off."

A group of younger men gathered up plates and started to wash up. Everyone had a role.

There were half a dozen white trucks parked along the street.

Fiona climbed into the driver's seat of the lead one. Jasmin got in beside her. Peter went to follow.

"Pete, Rob comes with us. Will you drive the next one?"

The old truck roared into life as I buckled up.

"Be careful. You'll make Peter jealous."

Fiona gave me a narrow look which deepened the lines on her forehead, then checked her wing mirror before pulling out.

"Be gentle with him," Jasmin said. "He's the most emotional person I've ever met. He's been through so much."

Her tone stung. It felt like when my grandfather said *I'm disappointed in you.*

I resented my sudden softness. I had work to do. I pulled out my Dictaphone.

"May I?"

"Of course."

"What are we doing today?"

"Food distribution."

"In Beechfield?"

"No, Norton."

"Where's the food from?"

"We've grown the fresh stuff. The rest are donations."

We headed over the river and up through the newer housing, then took the road out that skirted the reservoir. Its grey expanse was wind-rippled. One side was banked by stone containing the dam's outflow gates to the river.

The ground fell away on either side of the tarmac to become moorland. Where the road rose ahead of us it looked like we were headed into white sky.

"Have you ever worked, Jasmin?"

Fiona gave me another skewering look but Jasmin wasn't bothered.

"Hospital cleaner. Supermarket work."

"What about your family?"

"I've broken with that life."

"Why?"

"There's only room for this now."

"What's your surname?"

"You'll find out."

"Are you Christian?"

"No. Religion doesn't matter to me. I welcome all faiths. And the faithless."

"So you don't believe in God?"

"I didn't say that."

"So you do?"

"I didn't say that either."

I gave her time to expand on that, but she didn't.

"If you're not on a religious mission, what's your plan?"

"To help. We waited for the government to help us. For the council and local charities. We're not deemed worthy or we're too easy to ignore. We need something different. To change things ourselves. If we show people it's possible, what we do here will spread."

"Are you a revolutionary?"

Revolutions are for young men and philosophers, not checkout girls, but I wanted her to say, *Yes, I'm going to burn it all to the ground.*

"Poverty's ancient. The rich need the poor. For someone to have more others must have less. Children huddle together in bed for warmth. It's Victorian. Except now we can see how the rich live on TV. It's shoved in our faces. Britain's become Poundland. The best we can hope for is to go shopping for tat and buy lattes, and we can't even do that anymore. There's only one way to live and if you can't afford it, you're screwed."

"That's quite a speech. You've been practising. Who's to blame? Politicians? Bankers?"

"I feel as much contempt for them as they do for us. They don't want to listen. They don't want to change a system that works for them. Their lies and theft are institutionally sanctioned. The whole system is rotten."

I wondered if Jonathan Knox was feeding her lines.

"Are you a Communist?"

"No. I want something more basic."

"What's that?"

"Compassion."

The road dropped and we coasted into Norton. Beechfield looked affluent by comparison. Condemned houses were boarded up. Shop windows were shuttered. The school was a flat roofed

1980s monstrosity that needed bulldozing. There were portacabins in the playground.

We were expected. A man waved us into a public car park that had been blocked off with orange cones. We pulled in, the other trucks lining up alongside. People were already waiting. The back of the trucks went up and Jasmin and the others started to unload, boxes being handed down to waiting hands.

I got out and walked down the queue, talking to people. There were young women with toddlers in prams. Scrawny teenagers. Old women leaning on shopping trolleys. A group of them had left home at dawn to ensure a place in the line. A man in his sixties showed me his arm.

"Who's Jack?" The name was driven deep into his skin in ink. He'd done it himself.

"My boy. They told him he couldn't have a support worker anymore. He wasn't high risk for self-harm. Not ill enough. He cut his wrists. Only twenty. He was a stubborn bugger. Always liked to prove people wrong."

Some allowed me to take their photo, but I stopped when one man hung his head. "Leave us a scrap of dignity, eh mate?"

"I'm here to show the world what it's really like." Hollow man, reaping their pain.

"Everyone thinks we're cockroaches. Seeing this won't change that."

It was my turn to hang my head.

Muttering came down the line. *They're running out of food.* There were at least another seventy people waiting. I'd covered the Sheffield riots of 2024. The first of many. I knew how a crowd can turn on a pin.

It started as a hush, then quiet mutterings and the shuffling of feet. The voices got louder. I tried to stroll rather than run back to the one remaining truck. The others had driven off after they finished unloading.

Jasmin and Hrithrik were inside, handing down boxes to Peter and Fiona.

"Jasmin, how much is left?"

I climbed in to join them beside the last crate. Jasmin and I looked in. Only one box was inside.

"We need to leave. Now."

"Not while people are still here." She pulled the box out, cradling it to her body.

The orderly queue dissolved. People crowded around the truck, jostling one another. Peter and Hrithrik were backed against the tailgate.

"Jasmin, there's going to be an almighty kick off when they realise there's nothing left."

Fiona joined us.

"Why didn't you tell us we'd run out?"

Jasmin was firm. "Form a chain. We need to work quickly. Rob, next to me. Pass this along. Go on, Fiona."

Jasmin gave me the box which I handed along. It contained toothpaste, toilet roll, cans of beans, pasta, fruit and vegetables.

"Pass it down, Rob."

"For fuck's sake." *They're going to dismember us and eat us.*

Jasmin gave me another one. Nappies, soap, formula milk, canned meat, vegetables and a loaf.

Then another. And another.

I know for a fact there was only one box left. I saw it myself. I counted out another seventy-six boxes, one for every pair of hands that waited.

There it was. The first miracle of Jasmin of Beechfield.

★   ★   ★

I didn't know how to look at Jasmin after that. She sat between Fiona and me in the truck's cab. Fiona and I looked straight ahead, as if the thing would be undone if we acknowledged it.

I lay awake all night, hands behind my head, staring at the ceiling. I couldn't rationalise it. I'd checked the last crate myself. There wasn't a false bottom or side. Nowhere those boxes could've been hidden.

I wanted to stay beside Jasmin. Forever. What seemed like naivety yesterday was now divinity.

Peter stood beside me as I washed up after supper. I felt a sharp dig in my ribs as he elbowed me. When I looked up he was smiling at me as though to say, *You see now, don't you?*

I went up to my room and wept. It was the strangest thing. Not from sadness. It was poison being drawn. I was a child again, safe in the arms of my parents. I wanted to believe in something other than money or the dark things that we do. I wanted to believe, because if miracles could happen there was a possibility I could be saved.

I got up at 4:00 a.m. and opened my laptop. I wrote it all up and emailed it off.

Alan, the editor, called me the next day.

"Jesus, Robbie, what's this shit?"

"The truth."

"Are you smacked up to the tits?"

"It happened."

"You've been had, son." He said *son* like he'd forgotten we once shared a desk. "I can't publish this pseudo-religious claptrap. Look," he tried to soften it, "you're not yourself after Kim—"

"It's got nothing to do with that."

"Bollocks."

I hung up. Fuck Alan. I'd tell the world myself. What else was social media for?

★   ★   ★

We went out for a drive, just Jasmin, Fiona and me in an old Fiesta. Peter stood on the kerb and Jasmin put her head out of the open window.

"Peter, there's clean bedding in the airing cupboard. Will you get the back bedroom ready?" She meant the unoccupied one. "The lamp in there needs a bulb."

The domestic chore chafed. She put a hand on Peter's neck, pulling his forehead to hers. I couldn't catch what she said except for "... you do me a great service..."

When I looked back Peter stood in the road, hands in his pockets.

Fiona drove us up to the new estate. The pebble-dashed grey houses leached the colour from the world. A pack of mutts crossed the road in front of us. One stopped to push an inquisitive nose into an overturned wheelie bin.

"There."

We pulled up outside the house Jasmin pointed at. It was at the end of a road, looking out onto coarse grass. There would've been a time when it was coveted for its view.

Fiona unbuckled her seatbelt.

"Just Rob and me."

"Jas."

"Wait."

The wind poured down the hill towards us. The clouds were dark streaks.

Jasmin rang the bell. A shadow grew behind the patterned glass. A wraith opened the door. She wore purple velour shorts with dirty white trimming and a strappy vest, despite the chill. Her bare feet were as dirty as the carpet.

"It's double for both of you."

"I just want to talk."

"Same cost."

She couldn't have been more than twenty-five. Dead-eyed. Self-regard long gone. She went back inside, not caring if we followed.

Damp clothes hung on the hall radiator. Moisture gathered on the windows, framed by black mould on the window seals. We followed her into the lounge. She lay back on the stained sofa cushions. A chipped plate balanced on the sofa's arm, piled with cigarette butts and smears of dried tomato sauce. Condoms were kept handy. There was an ashtray full of them.

The woman's flesh was sallow in the harsh light of the unshaded bulb. It revealed her scars, skin damaged and thickened beyond use to the needle. There were pits and pockmarks from old abscesses. Her thighs and forearms bore the parallel lines of the razor blade, some silvery and faded, other fresh studies in self-disdain.

"What's your name?" Jasmin asked.

"I always have to have the money first."

The hollows of her face were filled with grey shadows.

"What's your name?" Jasmin asked again.

"Lola." She stretched and yawned. Her top rode up.

"Your real name."

"Magda."

"Where are you from?"

"Romania."

Jasmin grasped her wrist lightly. Magda tried to pull away.

"They're filling you with crap to control you. It's killing you. It has to come out."

Magda's chin slumped onto her chest. The needle marks in her arms opened up. These stigmata wept. Not blood, but straw-coloured liquid. It ran down her arms and dripped from her fingers. I thought she'd wet herself, then realised she'd injected her groin too because it was trickling down her thighs.

"Jesus, she's dying." I put my face close to her mouth and the flat of my hand against her bony chest. Then I felt her slow inhalations.

"Magda." I shook her, little bag of bones.

"I'm tired," she muttered.

Jasmin knelt beside us.

"She's very precious, Rob, but you can't tell anyone yet."

★   ★   ★

It was getting dark. I bundled Magda up in a blanket and lay her on the back seat, her head on my knee. Her eyes fluttered and I wondered what she was dreaming about.

We drove back to town by the road that circumnavigated the estate. Coarse grass and heather stretched away into the falling night. There was a thundering sound that grew louder. The sky was falling in.

Then they came into view. Pale shadows ran alongside us. I'd read reports of the diminished horse population up on the moors. They were being caught and eaten.

There were three at first, then half a dozen, then more. They raced as close to the car as they could, for half a mile nearly. Unbridled wild things, with mud up their legs. I opened the window a fraction so that I could hear their pounding hooves, their snorts and whinnies.

They had grace and strength, a supernatural sensitivity in their liquid eyes and quivering nostrils. They were utterly divine.

★   ★   ★

"Rob, wake up." A hand gently shook my shoulder. "Fiona's in the car. We'll wait for you. Don't be long."

It was Jasmin. She put a finger to her lips to shush me. I picked up my phone. It was one in the morning.

The floorboards creaked as I tiptoed past the dormitory. The sound made me pause, wincing, but nobody stirred. The door to the private bedroom, now Magda's, was closed. She'd been with us for a week. This privilege wasn't questioned.

I sat on the bottom step of the stairs to lace up my boots. I'd become used to communal living, to chatter and industry. The silent darkness seemed strange. Odd too, how I'd hungered for company without realising it.

Fiona was in the driver's seat and Jasmin beside her. The engine was running. I got in the back.

"I think we should bring Peter." Fiona's fingers drummed on the steering wheel.

"Not for this." Jasmin was resolute.

Fiona's gaze caught mine in the rearview mirror. She stopped drumming.

"Where are we going?" I asked.

"To meet someone. Fiona, we need to go *now*."

I don't know what scared me more. Seeing Fiona wound tight or Jasmin's urgency.

"Who?"

Neither of them answered. It had rained all day. The roads were soaked in sheets of water, the drains overflowed. Beechfield was sodden.

"Pull over there."

We'd reached the bottom of the old town. Jasmin pointed to the layby just before the bridge.

"Jasmin." My mouth was dry.

She wasn't listening. She was already out of the car, standing in the drizzle that blurred the light from the streetlamps. The road beyond the bridge climbed up the hill into the new estate. Rows of darkened houses were shrouded in cloud.

"I need you to both promise me something."

"What?" Fiona was guarded.

"Both of you stay here, by the car. It doesn't matter what you see."

"Why? What's going to happen?"

Fiona was as clueless as I was.

"Promise me you'll stay put. Please. Help me."

I'd never heard Jasmin plead like that. It cut through me.

"Yes, we will," I said, but I was sorely afraid.

"Fiona?"

"Okay."

Jasmin went from us and stood on the middle of the bridge. All I could hear was the churning river and the wind. We waited.

"There." Fiona nudged me.

Her eyes were sharper than mine. Twin specks of light moved on the hill opposite. They grew brighter and larger each minute, then multiplied. A line of headlights.

The transit van was at the head of the convoy. It stopped on the bridge, pinning Jasmin in its glare. The van's engine rattled and died. Cars pulled up behind it, men piling out. They carried baseball bats, knives, one even had a Samurai sword. They were fired up, keen for blood and angry at being taken by surprise, even if it was a poor reception.

They'd planned to tip us from our beds and beat the crap out of us.

A man waved them back. He was in his sixties. His fleece was zipped up to the neck. His short hair was silver.

"Wheatley. He's come himself." Fiona spoke under her breath as though they could hear us.

Peter's old boss. Trafficker of girls, drugs, guns. Extortionist and robber. He wasn't made criminal by circumstance. It was his calling.

"So you're the one causing all this fuss."

Jasmin, a young woman in drenched plimsolls and anorak. I put a foot forward, but Fiona pulled me back.

"You've got something of mine. I want it back."

"You mean *her*. Her name's Magda."

"Her name's whatever I say it is."

"She's under my care now."

"*Under your care?* You're fucking hilarious. I've turned a blind eye to you so far but you've overstepped the mark. This is my manor. I'm going to slice up every single one of your happy fucking clan and then I'm taking Lola back."

"It won't go well for you if you try. I can only give you one warning."

Wheatley laughed, long and hard. "That might work on your weak-minded misfits, but not me. Some people call you the little witch. I think I'll burn you."

"If it's a man, it's a miracle. When it's a woman, it's witchcraft."

"What the fuck are you talking about?"

"I don't consider you my enemy. I don't consider you at all. You've put yourself in my way."

He rubbed his hands together. "I'm going to enjoy this."

"Come on then." Jasmin held out her arms.

More men had joined Wheatley from the cars backed up onto the road. Wheatley walked towards her. She raised her hands above her head.

"Jasmin!" I shouted. Fiona's arms were around me.

The air changed, the ground rumbling. There was a roaring. A wall of water came out of the night, two, maybe three times the height of the bridge. Jasmin had summoned a destroying angel.

The news reported later that the dam had broken, sending a massive swell downstream.

The streetlamps on the bridge died. Cables were torn, sending out showers of sparks. In our car headlights I saw glimpses of heavy branches and rocks in the churning, frothy wave. When it hit the bridge everything within it came crashing down. The cars were picked up like toys, overturned and smashed against the bridge wall or went over the side. There wasn't time for screams. The world was being swept clean.

I fell to my knees. Fiona was howling. I pulled her close. I saw it all over her shoulder. The debris deposited by the water, wrecked vehicles and broken bodies. And Jasmin stood there, dripping, her arms still raised.

★   ★   ★

I'd taken to walking. Being outside made me feel better. I went through the town, down to the park. The central playground and football pitch remained but the rest was given over to raised beds.

I sat on a bench. Jasmin came over. She wrapped her coat tight around her and joined me. We were both quiet until I couldn't stand it any longer. "Peter's talking to you again?"

"Just about."

Peter was turning the earth, ready for planting. The carnage on the bridge had been a month ago. Peter was furious that we'd gone without him that night, but he'd stayed close to Jasmin ever since, fearing retribution for Wheatley and his men.

"You've been avoiding me, Rob." Jasmin sounded sad.

"Did you know what would happen to them?"

"Power's a knife. Sometimes we use it to prepare a meal for our enemies. Sometimes we have to cut their throats with it."

"Are you going to hell?" My voice cracked. I was afraid for her. As afraid for her as I was when she was on the bridge.

"Sometimes you have to do bad to do good. It was Wheatley's choice. It doesn't matter what happens to me now." She put her hand on mine. "We've all done bad things that we carry with us. What about *you*?"

"You already know."

"Say it aloud."

"Kim Roth." Television darling.

"She was well loved."

"Even more so when she was widowed."

"Then?"

I looked at the sky. Clouds moved overhead. I'd drifted for so long.

"I broke the story about her husband's affairs after he died. All the squalid little details. It was all pretty tawdry and mundane, so I didn't even get that much for it. Kim Roth hadn't known. It broke her heart. She opened her arteries in the bath."

The clouds changed shape. How fleeting their existence. I shrugged, as if I were telling Jasmin how I'd lost my car keys. "Well?"

Jasmin swivelled in the seat and took my head in her hands. She planted a slow, deliberate kiss on my forehead.

I don't know what I expected. Forgiveness? Absolution? Instead there was only sweetness and I remember thinking it wasn't enough.

I'll never be kissed like that ever again.

"These are for you to plant."

She pulled a packet from her coat pocket. I turned the packet over and started to laugh.

"You don't know much about gardening. You need to germinate these first. And they'll never survive out here. It's too cold. You need a heated greenhouse."

"How do you know this stuff?"

"My grandfather had a smallholding. Old swine."

"You didn't like him much."

"He took me in after my parents died in a car crash. He was staunch Catholic. Never forgave Mum for lapsing and getting knocked-up out of wedlock. He despised Dad, who was born Church of England. Religion for softies, Grandad called it. Religion for cherry pickers and special-needs."

"Nice."

"Yeah, I was the *little bastard* for the first year with him. God was a rod for that man, not a staff."

I turned the packet over in my hands, the seeds rattling around inside.

"Do me a favour? Plant them anyway."

She returned to Peter, picking up her spade again.

On my way out of the park I stopped beside an empty bed and pushed the seeds into the ground. The earth was rich.

When I walked past the following day the bed was full. Each plant was a full thirty centimetres tall, in need of staking, as they were so heavy with meaty, pendulous aubergines.

*   *   *

I'd gone back to my flat for the weekend, to check my mail and pick up some clothes. I looked at my things. Stacks of DVDs, books. There was nothing to keep me here. This life was empty.

Nobody spoke to me on the street where I'd once lived. People barely looked at one another. The man outside my flat was odd. *He* was looking at me. I ducked into a café. He followed.

"Cup of tea, please."

I took a seat near the door where I could see the whole room. That seemed to decide him. He ordered and then pulled out the chair opposite me.

"I need to talk to you. You've been writing about my daughter."

Once I would've begged him to talk to me but now I felt queasy at the prospect.

"How do I know you're who you say you are?"

I was stalling. Their genes were on his face. Jasmin had his eyes. He pulled a photo from his wallet. He was younger. Darker hair and more of it. The girl at his side was unmistakeable. Jasmin's cheek was pressed against his, her arms tight around his neck. He got out another photograph. Jasmin was one of a brood. I'd presumed she was an only child. Her mother hugged a tot to her chest while the rest of the children, Jasmin included, crowded around her. They were all laughing at something.

"Jas was always different from the others."

I stared at the picture, as if the difference was visible. He took it back, carefully tucking it away.

"She never cried, even as a baby. And she didn't play like the others did. She always wanted to help. Her mum joked that she wanted so many because she was hoping for a second like Jasmin." There was so much love on his face. "I lost my job when she was ten. Some parents tell their kids everything but that's bollocks. They should be kids for as long as possible. Mel was asleep so I thought I'd go downstairs for a bit of a cry. I left the lights off. I felt a hand on my shoulder. It was Jasmin. She told me that everything was going to be all right. Three kids and Mel pregnant again and my ten-year-old tells me everything will be fine. And I believed her. It felt like an immense weight lifted from me. I trusted her. And she was right."

"I believe you. I've seen things. She's special."

"I don't want you to believe me. You've got no idea what I'm trying to say. She has a way of making you trust her. It's a talent but she's not the messiah. Not like you've said."

"Was she right though?"

"Things worked out because I *had* to make them work. What else was I going to do? I got another job, eventually."

I frowned.

"She's surrounded by freaks and misfits. They've made her into a figurehead. You've been tricked into stoking the fire."

"I know what I've seen."

"You believe what you *think* you've seen. When Jasmin was fifteen she started seeing lights. She was diagnosed with migraine. Then she started to say they were messengers."

"Visions?"

"Migraine aura that she'd incorporated into her delusions about God. I wouldn't mind but we're not a religious family. She was sectioned. Psychosis."

I opened my mouth to speak but I couldn't think of anything to say.

"She didn't want anything to do with us after she was released from hospital. Her psychiatrist saw her last year. She let me go to the appointment with her, to prove a point, she said. He said that she showed no signs of mental illness anymore. The people around her are using her. Coaching her to hide it. They're making her illness worse."

I got up but he clutched at my arm.

"Why are you telling me this?" I tried to shake him off. People stared at us.

"You're adding to the hysteria. I know about you. I've read all your work. When you write about Jasmin you sound like a fanatic. You've already killed one woman. Is that what you're trying to do to Jasmin? Tell the truth and once people know, that bunch of misfits will have no use for her. We can bring her home and get her the help she needs."

★   ★   ★

The train pulled into Beechfield. The town was in darkness. It was our turn for a power cut, shut off for four-hour blackouts around the country, to preserve national resources.

I walked along the main street. A row of torches shone in the distance, getting closer. It was Hrithrik and Magda.

Magda couldn't hide her bump any longer. She must've been about three months gone when we took her out of that house.

"How are you?"

"Well. We went for a scan yesterday. The baby's well, which is good. Healthy."

"That's terrific." More than terrific. Remarkable, considering.

"Yes, it is." Hrithrik put an arm around her, even though he needn't have been defensive of her, not around me.

More people passed us. Some carried bags and flasks, others lanterns. The aim was to keep the streets safe, the shops from being looted. The elderly and vulnerable were visited to ensure they were warm and fed, that they weren't scared.

"I'd forgotten it was powerdown tonight. Do you want me to do anything?"

"No, Rob. Go and get some rest. We've got tonight covered."

"Are you okay? You don't look yourself." Magda tilted her head.

"I'm fine. Just done in. Going back home felt weird."

"Are you sure?"

"Sure." I squeezed her hand. Jasmin's father had opened a pit of worms inside my belly.

I let myself into the house. I was about to call out, but I stopped. To this day I don't know why. I went along the hall in the darkness, towards the glimmering light at the end.

The corridor doglegged into the kitchen. I could see part of the room reflected in the hall mirror from where I stood. Jasmin sat at the kitchen table, pressing the heels of her hands to her eye sockets. The lamps in the kitchen cast giant shadows up the wall.

Jonathan Knox poured a drink from a flask into the mug before her.

"I'm tired."

"You should get some sleep."

"There's so much to do and not enough time."

"Would it help if you stayed at mine for a night? I have a spare bed. You could get some peace, without us all bothering you every minute."

I never knew where she slept. She didn't have a room.

Jasmin twisted around in her seat and then stood to face him.

"Will you hold me?"

"Of course. Come here."

Jonathan put his arms around her. She laid her head on his shoulder and he patted her back awkwardly. Then she tipped her head towards him and pressed her mouth to his. He gasped and broke away.

"What are you doing?"

"Please. I want to know what it means. What it's like. Just once."

"God, please, don't." He pushed her away, staring at her like he didn't recognise her.

"Jonathan…"

He ran from her, into the hall, and into me. He jerked back, startled, then staggered away, weeping, for the door.

Why Jonathan rather than Hrithrik, who had a profile to make angels stare?

Nothing's more dangerous than the righteous when they feel betrayed. I'd wanted Jasmin to be pure in this world of dirt. I didn't want to sleep with her. I didn't want to father her. I wanted to worship her.

Her dad was right. She was just a young woman after all.

★　　★　　★

I had cast myself out. I sat in my flat, night after night, walked the streets by day. I'd lost the purpose I'd found in Beechfield. Food went off in the fridge. I drank for days. Nothing sated me.

It was four months before the phone rang. Fiona flashed up on the screen.

"Jasmin wants you to come." There was no preamble. "I've no idea why."

"She can't summon me as she pleases." I was sour, but something leapt within me.

"You betrayed her. Did it feel good to make the front page again?"

I'd written about everything. Her father. Jonathan. The red-top that took it loved it, and a spate of religious cult exposés followed.

"I denounced her. It's different." I tried to sound indignant. "I told the truth."

"Your truths are cheap. And you're lying to yourself."

"Jasmin's mentally ill."

"Is she?" Fiona laughed. "She told me everything right at the start. She told me that people refused to believe her."

"*I* believed in her."

"You still don't get it, do you? She doesn't want you to believe in her. She wants you to believe in yourself. Come or not, it's your call."

Then she hung up.

★   ★   ★

The trains to Beechfield were booked up for weeks ahead, so I hired a car. My damning article hadn't stopped the pilgrims. Campsites had sprung up at the edge of town. As I sat in the traffic queue people passed me on foot, carrying rucksacks and pushing kids in buggies.

The railings, walls and fences around Beechfield were hung with rosaries, Ganesha posters, Buddhas, and prayer mats. Pentacles were chalked on pavements. I didn't know if they symbolised faith cast off or affirmed. Cardboard signs in the terrace windows said *Free room here*. Beechfield was embracing all-comers.

I knocked at the house. When I got no answer I peered through the window into a bare living room. They'd moved on. It was the start of September, a clear, sunny day with a cool edge. A day to draw people outside.

Hesketh Park had become a paradise. Cape gooseberries grew up the gate, the orange globes hanging in papery lanterns. Rows of raspberry canes bent under the weight of their own fruit. The bed I'd planted with aubergines was now crowded with fat marrows.

None of the faces in the crowd were familiar. Then I saw Magda. Pregnancy had fleshed her out. She wore a blue sundress and was barefoot on the grass, a hand rested on her swollen belly. She drank thirstily from the glass that Hrithrik handed her. Afterwards she lifted his fingers to kiss them. He didn't look at her but turned his face slightly to hide the involuntary brightness of his smile.

Magda spotted me first, squinting against the sun in disbelief. "Rob?" She came to me. "It's good to see you. We've missed you."

"I wasn't sure what kind of welcome to expect. Fiona certainly doesn't want to see me again."

"She's angry at you." Hrithrik clapped my shoulder. "That doesn't mean she doesn't miss you. Or Peter. She can barely say his name."

"Peter's gone?"

"What you wrote caused a real shitstorm. Jonathan's gone too."

"I know what I saw. What Jasmin did."

"Does it make any difference?" Magda asked gently.

"It clearly mattered to Peter." I was clutching at anything that justified what I'd done.

"Peter is a nutter." Hrithrik shook his head. "I'm glad we're shut of him."

"I meant what I said, Rob." Magda, more diplomatic, more gracious. "I'm glad you're here."

"So am I." It was true, but underneath I felt that she was being kind to the man who had been tested and failed. "You can't have long now."

"A month," Magda replied. "Saira will help me when it's time."

"Your own personal midwife."

We both laughed. People looked at us with open curiosity.

A hush fell over the crowd. There was birdsong from the trees, a plaintive rising and falling. A jet stream bisected the sky above us. The clarity of the moment made it unreal.

Then Jasmin was among us, walking through the throng. She reached out to touch someone in blessing. A man lifted the hem of her cardigan and kissed it. She leant towards a woman and said something in her ear and the woman looked upwards, her shining face wet with tears. Fiona walked beside her, anxiously scanning the crowd.

When Jasmin saw me across the clearing a smile curled up the corners of her mouth and her eyes softened. My sick soul was glad to see her. The world rearranged itself around us as I surrendered to something bigger than myself.

How could I have doubted her?

Someone pushed by me, clipping my shoulder. He didn't look back but kept on walking. It was Peter. Fiona opened her arms to him, a mother welcoming a son. I'd not understood until then how she loved him. They embraced, but then he said something to her and put her aside for Jasmin. Fiona was smiling.

Jasmin reached out a hand to cup his cheek and he bowed his head. She nodded as if to say, "Yes, yes."

Peter pulled the gun from the back of his waistband, which was hidden by his jacket. Fiona was on Jasmin's far side, so she didn't see it at first.

The birds in the trees took flight when they heard the shot. Jasmin plummeted to the floor. Then the screams started. People started to run, pushing each other out of the way. Hrithrik pulled Magda to him, shielding her as they ran from the crush towards the far park exit.

Peter had already dropped the gun, but Fiona still wrestled with him. Blood and brain had sprayed her face. He didn't offer much resistance.

"What have you done?" Fiona shouted over and over again. He lay on the floor, weeping as she punched him.

I pulled Jasmin onto my knee. Pieta. Pity, Lord. Her head was a mess of bullet-scorched skin and bone, laid open to the world and leaking onto my lap. I put my hand over the hole, as if this could help.

I could hear keening but couldn't have said whether it was from someone far away or next to us. There was only me and Jasmin now. Nothing else.

"Rob," she gasped. "Magda's baby."

"Jasmin, I'm so sorry for what I did. I'm sorry."

"The baby."

I leant closer, struggling to catch her words.

"I'm just the herald. She's the storm."

The sound of sirens brought me back to the world.

"Jasmin, stay with me, please." I clutched her hand. "Just hang on."

"She'll show no mercy. She'll wash her feet in their blood…"

"Who? I don't understand."

Her lips carried on moving soundlessly for a few moments before falling still. There were no answers in her eyes, just the reflected sky.

CLOCKWORK

Dan Coxon

I found the first piece on the day we buried my father. I'd shrugged out of my black dress, into jeans and a fleece, then headed out back to find a spade and dig up his rhododendrons. I was teasing the root ball out when I saw it: something small and metallic in the soil, about the size of a bottle cap. Before I lost it again I dropped the spade and dug it out with my nails, holding it in my palm to get a better look in the fading light. The mud was claggy and wet, sticking to the metal like plaster, but once I'd managed to clear some of it away with my thumb I could see it was a cog. Eight teeth spaced evenly around the outside, a single round hole in the middle. It gleamed dully, like tarnished treasure.

I uncovered a total of eleven pieces on that first day – nine cogs of varying sizes, a metal spindle about six inches long, and a strange four-pronged fork that I later discovered was called a buffer spring. Two of the cogs still had their spindles attached, one of them with a second row of teeth on another, inner cogwheel. The entire find fitted onto a small side plate, once I'd rinsed them off and poked out the holes with a cotton bud.

There was no indication of how they came to be there, buried in my father's garden, or how long they might have lain hidden in the earth. My father had never been a watchmaker, or an enthusiast of model trains. I had never seen him enthusiastic about anything much, except perhaps the football on a Sunday, or the anger that would rise in him at some perceived slight or injustice towards him. He barely knew how to hammer two planks of wood together; in his later years, I doubt he'd even have had the strength to lift the hammer. Maybe he'd had no idea of what lay silently beneath his rhododendrons, slowly leaching metal deposits into the soil, feeding their roots. Maybe someone else had put them there.

The next morning, once the sun had lifted above the horizon, I went outside and finished the job. When all three bushes were piled on the concrete patio to burn, I took my garden fork and started to turn the soil, looking to see if there were any parts I had missed. Within minutes a small pile of metal was growing on the lawn. The deeper I dug, the more frequent the discoveries became. Each forkful would turn up three or four pieces – mostly cogs, sometimes spindles or springs, occasionally a thing whose function I couldn't identify – and I was three feet down before they started to dwindle again. Midmorning I fetched a bucket to store them in; when that was full, I used two shopping bags.

By lunchtime all three were full to the brim, and I struggled to bring them into the house to clean. They clattered as I tipped them into the bathtub, the dirt swirling brown down the plughole as the spray from the showerhead hit them. It was easier work than spraying Father down during those last few years, enduring his abuse, the slaps from his bony hand when the water splashed into his eyes. The cogs did not brim over with anger and try to dig their nails into my arm. They did not spit at me as I dried them off with a stained, threadbare towel.

I counted them that night. Two hundred and fifty-six pieces of metal, all curiously well preserved. The largest cog was as big as my palm; the smallest, barely bigger than the nail on my little finger. I knew there were more, though, and I went to bed early, conserving my strength for the day ahead. I wanted to find them all.

*　*　*

The funeral was a small affair. My father was never a popular man, even in his youth. He didn't make friends easily, and those he did make rarely stuck around for more than a year or two. If you didn't have to endure his presence, you wouldn't choose to.

His sister Bea was there, wheeled in by my cousin Frank. She sat and drooled through the short ceremony, only shifting slightly in her chair when the celebrant – Mr. Dawkins? Deakins? – started listing my father's achievements. She was probably just resettling herself on her cushion, but it looked as if she was lifting herself up to break wind. I don't remember her much from my youth, but I do know that she wasn't particularly fond of him – most Christmases we would receive a card from her and that was all. I have no idea what he did to sour their relationship, although I can imagine. I always felt it showed great charity and magnanimity on her part that she stayed in touch with him at all.

When we filed up to view his body I could still make out the seam down the side of his head, from the top of his skull to behind his ear, where they'd inexpertly filled and painted over the gash. Someone had tried to comb his hair across it, and now it stuck out sideways like he was standing in a wind tunnel. I resisted the urge to spit in his face.

There was no wake, and once the ceremony was over I was supposed to stand at the door, shaking hands and accepting condolences. When the time came I couldn't face the lies we'd all tell, so I snuck out the back door, walking so fast down the corridor that I was almost running. I stopped when I came to a junction, and peered through an open doorway. The room was stark and uninviting, all cracked linoleum and stainless steel, fluorescent lights buzzing like a beehive overhead. A man stood there, at the door to the incinerator, his hand poised beside my father's cardboard coffin. He looked up, peering at me through thick-lensed spectacles.

"Did you want to say something?" he asked, his voice high and reedy. "Before he goes?"

I nodded.

"Tell him he can fuck off."

I didn't linger to see his shocked expression, or to watch his finger come down on the big red button that would set the conveyor belt moving, but as I walked out into the sunlight I imagined I could hear the crackle of the flames as my father began to burn.

★   ★   ★

It was on the third day of digging that I dug up the mask.

I'd spent the morning burning the rhododendrons, the smoke puffing skywards in thick black clouds as the greenery smouldered and died. It smelled like engine grease and rot, the stench lingering on my fleece, perfuming my hair. Eventually, when the branches and leaves had been rendered to grey dust, I abandoned the ashes and returned to my spade.

The finds had begun to thin, and I was close to taking a break when the blade hit something solid in the dirt. I'd uncovered a few of the larger cogs this way already, but this sounded different: a hollow ring, like I'd struck a bowl, or the bottom of a buried plant pot. Dropping to my knees,

I used my hands to shovel the dirt away from whatever it was, a ceramic object of some kind that was only a little smaller than a dinner plate. My fingers found the edge, scraping the soil off in increments, revealing the cracked white glaze beneath. An ovoid curve to the edge, then a slit, a raised protuberance. Two divots painted like eyes.

I stood staring at the face that looked up at me from the bottom of the pit. It may have once been considered lifelike, but years beneath the ground had rendered it dead, the surface spiderwebbed with tiny cracks, the painted eyes dirty and dull. There was a single thick line bisecting it from the top of the head to the middle of one side, where my spade had struck it. As I lifted it from the soil it broke into two pieces, one slightly smaller than the other. I remember being relieved that it had broken so cleanly. It wouldn't be so hard to glue it back together.

The first hand emerged from the dirt later that afternoon, the tip of one finger chipped off and missing, but otherwise intact; the other appeared the following morning, its thumb lying severed next to it, although not due to my spadework this time. I was being more careful now, using a hand trowel to scrape away the surface, patiently revealing my treasures. Two indistinct blocks of clay that I imagined must be feet, intended to be hidden in a pair of shoes; four long metal rods to form the legs; four shorter poles for the arms. There were a number of smaller, more fragile rods too, slightly curved, and it took me a while to realise they formed the ribcage, protecting the delicate machinery that once lay within. In places there were scraps of leather still holding them together, but much of it had rotted away. I laid it all out on the grass and sprayed it down with the hose, washing it as clean as I could. Then I took them inside and my work began in earnest.

I have no technical training, no engineering degree – I barely have any qualifications at all, my father took that from me – but it's amazing what you can find on the internet these days. I joined the AmateurAutomata forum, posting photos of my finds, and within hours the thread was buzzing with eager enthusiasts, in awe of my good fortune. It was an original automaton, they told me, hand-crafted and bespoke, probably made for a private collection, or a fairground. They bickered for a while over whether it was late nineteenth century or early twentieth, British or French, but these details bored me. I wanted to use their expertise for one purpose only.

I wanted it to move again.

★   ★   ★

My parents were already old when they had me. My mother was in her forties, my father almost fifteen years older, eyeing his retirement. I don't think they wanted a child, although they never spoke those words aloud. Certainly, my father never showed me any warmth, and my mother lived in perpetual fear of his moods and his bursts of anger, which came without warning or provocation. I only saw him hit her two or three times, but one of my earliest memories is of a crude trail of bruises up her arm. She always wore long sleeves when we were out of the house, even in the middle of summer.

Her death felt long and drawn out, but in reality it took a little less than a year, from diagnosis to funeral. I was only eleven years old at the time, so living with it felt like an eternity. As her cough worsened, the fits spasming her body for minutes at a time, I imagined I could see the life being expelled from her mouth, each cloud of tiny particles whittling her away a little more. I was the one who found her when it finally happened. Father was out somewhere, I don't know where, and I returned from school to discover her body stick-thin and lifeless under a pile of blankets. The skin had drawn back so much on her face that I remember thinking she looked like a skeleton already, as if someone had dug her up, several years from now, and travelled back in time to place her in the bed as a prank.

It took only a year or two for my father to find a new punching bag. He was careful to restrain himself to body blows only, at least while I was still in school. If the teachers had any idea, they never mentioned it. You had to allow a widower his grief. Back then, things stayed behind closed doors.

When I dropped out of school at sixteen to care for him, I told myself it would only be for a year or two. He was showing signs of early onset dementia, and his body was wasting away, as if he was determined to outdo my mother in his race to the grave. If I'd known it would take another ten years for him to die, I'd have abandoned him there and then. Let him fester, and moulder, and rot.

But I didn't, and I lost those ten years to a man who never loved me. It's remarkable how much damage a soul can endure.

* * *

It took me a few days to identify those who could help me, and those who were nothing more than eager enthusiasts. I pruned my contacts in the AmateurAutomata forum until only three remained, and then I set them to work. I snapped a total of twenty-six photos of the cogs and other machinery I had uncovered in the garden, then I shared them with the group, asking them to piece my jigsaw back together, to reassemble my automaton.

The key cogs and springs were in place after five days, cleaned and greased, dirtying what used to be the kitchen counter. I would wind them up and let them whirr; and there it sat, the living, beating heart of this new man. I felt I should chant incantations over it, paint it with sacrificial blood, but I had nothing of the sort. In the end, after a bottle of wine one evening, I staggered in with the plastic tub of my father's ashes and sprinkled them over it, anointing it with a cloud of grit that had once contained a life. Then I licked my fingers clean and went to bed.

I was a better machinist than expected, and mostly I took to the work with enthusiasm and determination. I had never anticipated that I might be good at something, and the dexterity and confidence with which I slotted tooth into groove caught me by surprise. All those years cutting my father's toenails and trimming his thinning hair held me in good stead. Even the group seemed surprised by my success when I shared the work in progress with them. TheRealSpalanzani sent a short message of congratulations:

I don't know if you're attempting what I think you are, but if you are, ALL THE LUCK IN THE WORLD. Hopla! Hopla!

While not exactly a standing ovation, it was the first time I could remember being praised for something I had done. Beneath the streaks of grease and dirt, I blushed.

Ten days after I began, the work was finished. I lifted the automaton down from the counter, his feet clunking on the tiles. He was lighter than I expected, this man of steel and clay. We stood there for a moment, two dancing partners, his pale, cracked head only reaching up to my chin, so it looked as if he was staring at my chest. I steadied us for a minute, letting him find his centre of gravity. Then I let go.

He teetered, rocking on the balls of his artificial feet. I imagined him crashing to the floor, the mask splitting into hundreds of tiny shards this time, an injury beyond repair. But he didn't. He stood there facing me, this thing I had made, and I smiled. I reached out a tentative hand and flipped the switch.

With a flutter and a whirr the machinery came alive. He lifted his left hand, gradually, holding it up in front of his unseeing face. Then the right, and he looked from one to the other, as if surveying them for the first time. Apparently satisfied, he lowered them to his sides and took a slow, graceless step forward, his foot never leaving the floor but sliding along it, the clay block tracing a pale scar on the tiles. Then the other foot, so he stood nearer to me now, close enough that I could smell the grease warming in his chest.

There was a heavy *clunk* that made me startle as he raised his left hand again; then, his right. Hand down; left foot, right foot.

Clunk.

Hand.

Hand.

Feet.

Clunk.

It didn't take long for his faltering rhythm to bore me. I'd seen what he could do, and it amounted to little more than a toddler's first steps. But still the fact remained: I had made a man.

★   ★   ★

Father's clothes fit the automaton remarkably well. In his final years he had been little more than a bundle of skin and bones. The shirt was easy to get on, buttoning up the front of the mechanism, hiding the magic away. With my teeth I tore a small hole in the back, so that the switch might poke through. His trousers were more difficult, its legs stiff and unwieldy, the clay feet snagging on the fabric and tearing it in a couple of places. Once they were on, I fastened them with Father's belt. I was pleased to see that it tightened to the same notch he had used, the hole slightly wider than the rest.

His shoes were too big, so I tugged four pairs of socks onto the clay feet. They still smelled of my father, a rancid milky odour that made me wrinkle my nose. Once the shoes were laced up it stood a little steadier.

I stood back to admire my handiwork. A dark stain ran down the shoulder of the shirt, the cotton crusty and stiff. There were four marks on the leg of the trousers, too; evenly spaced, like fingerprints. Had he touched his head as he bled out? I couldn't remember. Maybe the fingerprints were mine.

It took some effort to manoeuvre it to the top of the stairs. Eventually, I dragged him by his armpits, his clay feet thumping against each step as we ascended. I almost lost him halfway up, my grip slipping so that he slid down several steps. When I managed to get him under control again I heaved him up the rest of the stairs, scared of letting go and watching him thump down to the ground floor, nothing but a heap of cogs bundled inside some old rags. I had plans for him.

Once we were at the top, I balanced him back on his feet and caught my breath. I should have been used to the exercise, after all the times I'd had to haul Father in and out of the bath, from the bedroom to the toilet in the middle of the night, but I was several weeks without him and my body had already become flabby and tired. Too many takeaway pizzas, too much cheap wine.

We stood at the top of the stairs, the automaton and I. He swayed slightly on his feet, and I placed my hands upon his shoulders, settled him where I wanted him; just so. My hand reached around to his back, and with my fingertips I found the nub of the switch poking through his clothes. As I flicked it on I could hear the cogs stutter and whirr next to my ear, a first, ragged breath. The brush of his hand as he raised it to his face.

Stepping back, I surveyed him from further along the landing. I had been in the bathroom at the time, mopping up where Father had pissed all over the floor. I came out onto the landing, like this. My hands raised, so.

I screamed at the same time as I pushed him in the chest, his body toppling backwards in slow motion, wobbling on the brink before gravity took him and he fell, down, down, his back striking the wall halfway, his feet lifting into the air, his head cracking against the newel post. I stood, panting, at the top of the stairs, surveying my work.

The whirr of cogs as he tried to raise a hand. A click as something broke inside. The spasms of a program stuck on repeat, his hand lifting, then lowering, lifting, then lowering, over and over again.

I didn't have to walk downstairs to see that he wasn't right. The mask was still intact, the collision had barely damaged his limbs at all. The satisfaction I craved was missing.

He was not my father.

I would have to build him again.

★   ★   ★

The next time was better. It had taken me two days to correct the damage, to reset the cogs, realign the springs. When I'd finished, he was like new – no, he was better than before. I detected a vigour in his movements that was lacking on the first attempt, a violence that spoke of my father. The hand moved sharply when he raised it, and I almost flinched. He was ready.

I found it easier to drag him up the stairs this time. There was an excitement within me, a hurricane in my blood. I knew what I wanted more clearly. Setting him on his feet, I smoothed his clothes down, brushed back non-existent hair from his painted eyes.

I let him take two faltering steps forward before I ran at him, my arms outstretched again, palms thudding into his hollow chest. It felt better, but still not right. He tumbled sideways halfway down the steps, the back of his head bumping off each stair as he fell, his feet hitting the ground first and his legs crumpling beneath him. One of his feet twitched as I approached. I watched him for a while before switching him off and carrying him back to the kitchen.

Third time's the charm – isn't that what they say? I'd been drinking for most of the evening, but that hadn't kept me from my work. The damage to his internal workings was only slight, and it was easy enough to realign the slipped cogs, sliding tooth back into groove. There was a slight tear to the sleeve of his shirt, which I mended inexpertly with needle and thread.

Standing at the top of the stairs, I felt unsteady on my feet. The second bottle of wine had risen to my head. I found myself leaning on him as much as he leant on me, his body reassuringly solid beneath my arms. I don't recall taking extra care setting him on his feet, but when I stepped back to survey my handiwork he looked perfect, exactly the way I remembered Father looking that night. My breath caught in my throat as his hand raised sharply up, as if he was about to slap me across the face, dig his cracked nails into the flesh of my arm. He looked inhuman in a way that only my father could.

As he took that first step I jumped forward like a released spring. And in that moment, as he tottered towards me with outstretched hands, I saw not a man-made thing of steel and clay, but my father, the heartless shit who had raised me like a dog and then left me, parentless and adrift, in a world that cared for me no more than he did. My hands collided so hard with his chest that it jarred my arms, and in that instant I was taken back to the night of the accident, the night I finally killed the man who had stolen the first thirty years of my life.

I watched, stunned, as he tumbled backwards, his head cracking against the wall with a sickening wetness, his skeleton limbs pinwheeling as he crashed down to the ground floor and lay still. I stood as I had that night, watching the blood pooling about his head, letting the life bleed from him until I was sure that he was dead.

★   ★   ★

Before collapsing into bed, I took a few minutes to clean the automaton. There was a new crack now, where its face had hit the wall; a second dark seam across its porcelain features. I considered repairing the fracture, but decided against it. It still held together despite the crack, and it gave it some character, some context. We all gather damage over time.

I'm not sure what made me take it into the bedroom with me. It felt like the right thing to do, after everything I'd put it through. Its shirt was still crusted with Father's blood, but I didn't care as I bundled it into my bed, too drunk and tired to mind the brown flakes moulting onto my sheets. I hauled its legs one by one onto the bed, then tugged the duvet up to cover its chest. There was still room for me, so I crawled in next to it, fully clothed, my head already beginning to pound with tomorrow morning's hangover. Despite the brain fog that was blowing in, I remained aware of the automaton lying beside me in the dark, creating its own gravity well in the mattress.

I was almost asleep when I heard it stir. Just a flutter of cogs, a faint smell of machine grease. Then a hand, cold and hard, resting gently on my shoulder, pulling me close to the machine that was not, and would never be, my father.

SOAPSTONE

Aliya Whiteley

She couldn't make the choice.

Jen played the future over and over in her mind, imagining the packed church, the bowed heads and black shoes, the timing of the slow steps of the pallbearers down the aisle. What song would be best for the entrance of Sam's coffin? She made a list. The closer she got to whittling down the options to one, the more she found it hard to envisage herself there, taking part in the ritual. And even though she never thought she'd use one of the many excuses she'd concocted in her head, she found herself phoning Sam's mother's answering machine while she sat in the café on Gloucester Street, two miles from the church, at the time when the service was meant to begin.

Then she watched the clock on the wall, and drank her coffee slowly.

The café was warm and quiet, the radio on low in the background. She told herself that her pain was not like everyone else's pain. She could not name it, nor find the edges of it. It had no musical accompaniment. It was better to stay away, to leave their mourning uncontaminated by her own. She should never have been given the responsibility of choosing a song for such a moment. She couldn't decide. She would never decide. Somebody attending, somebody older and wiser, would choose instead.

Tyler phoned her later, in the early evening. She answered quickly, determined to get it over with, but he took her by surprise, using his gentle voice, as if feeling his way into the argument. "How's the toothache now?" he said. "Are you okay? How did the emergency appointment go?"

"Fine."

"So there was an appointment, then?"

She didn't answer. She'd never expected anyone to buy it, least of all Tyler.

"Thought not," he said. "I'm coming over."

Jen put the phone down beside her, on the sofa. She'd gone from the café to the supermarket, and bought vodka, the kind he liked. It was already in the freezer, getting cold.

★   ★   ★

"They were looking for you. Afterwards, outside the church. His gran asked me where you were."

"I left a message on his mum's phone."

"So you phoned when you knew she wouldn't pick up, I'm guessing," Tyler said. He crossed his legs at the ankle, stretching them out under the kitchen table. "When she was actually in the church?"

"Listen, I'm doing my best."

"Well your best is—" He stopped himself; she saw the effort of will it cost him.

"My best isn't good enough, is that it?" She reached behind him, to the freezer, took out the bottle and refilled his shot glass.

"I just think it's not *your* best. To not attend your friend's funeral because you're upset and you can't pick a song. We're all upset. I miss him too. I was close to him too. Or are you filtering me out of all your memories? I'm – I can't even feel anything properly right now, and I need you to be up to this. Can you understand? It's unfair that he's gone, when it could have been – it should have been—"

"It should have been me?"

He closed his eyes and held out his hand, across the table. She couldn't take it. He was still in his funeral suit, black and sharp; how serious he looked. Like an adult, when she had only seen the remnants of the teenager in him before. "Don't even say that."

"You said it, not me."

"I didn't say it! Why would you even think I would say that?"

Jen couldn't think of a reply. She reached back into the freezer, retrieved the bottle once more, and drank straight out of it, taking long noisy swallows. The liquid was icy, the bottle numbing her fingers. When she looked back at Tyler he was smiling at her. He said, "You idiot." Then, "At some point we'll feel better."

"He dropped dead," Jen said. It was the first time she'd spoken the words aloud, although they'd been circling in her head, nonstop, since it had happened. "A problem with his heart that nobody knew about, and he just dropped dead. We don't get to feel better about that." She couldn't bear the thought of being stuck like this, in this pain, for an age. Surely pain passed. She needed to find a place to put it.

"You're right," he said. "We don't get to feel better."

"I'm right?"

"Well, you had to be right about some part of this mess eventually." He reached out his hand again, with determination, and this time she took it. "So we feel terrible. That I can agree with. But we do have to move on from today. Let's help each other move on."

★   ★   ★

They ended up in bed together, not as lovers but as comforting bodies, there only for warmth and presence. He curled around her, both of them in their underwear, and she pressed her back against his chest. She cried, a little; then she listened as his breathing subsided into sleep.

Her thoughts were on the last time they'd slept that way, during university, when they had shared a hall of residence and gone through a phase of crawling into bed together after drinking too much, occupying the bed without intention. The phase had lasted a month or so, before she became an item with Sam.

Sam she had wanted physically, with an urgency that she'd never felt before or since. He had a passion for life that she had craved, wanted for herself. She had been his girlfriend, for a few months, before realising she could not become part of him in the way she wanted. She had decided being friends, all together, was better. Sam: Tyler's room-mate, and her ex-lover. He had been the connection between them, the one in the middle that bound them. And now Sam was dead.

★   ★   ★

She woke and felt a moment of relaxation, deeper than anything she'd experienced in weeks. He was facing away from her, and he was so still. Too still.

Panic shot through her, but then he breathed in, and she became acutely aware of his smell: the remains of yesterday's aftershave, mixed with his sweat. How would she smell to him? Her bad breath, her body. The duvet cover, and the sheet; she hadn't changed them in weeks. She found herself willing him to wake up just so she could strip the bed back and throw everything into the washing machine. Boil wash. No, that wouldn't do. She'd have to take them out back, to the communal garden for the flats, and burn them.

But Tyler showed no sign of noticing the duvet cover, or her body, when he woke. He simply got up and started to dress, not even bothering to throw her a look. His eyes were unfocused, his movements languid. She remembered, then, how he had always been that way in the morning, sharpening during the day to a cutting edge, but soft, unformed, at first: it took him time to become who he was. Or, at least, who she thought he was. For the first time she wondered how much of it was an act. It made her want to cross-examine him, to find the boy she thought she knew again.

"You and Sam were so cute at uni," she said, as she made him toast and tea. "Always together. Both studying chemistry."

"Organic chemistry."

"Yeah, organic chemistry."

"But he was actually good at it," Tyler said. "And you liked history."

"Yeah," she said, although that wasn't exactly true. She had been good at it; interpreting the past from the clues left behind came easily to her.

"You remember how he could crack on with stuff when we were saying *come out, we're off to The Black Horse, you can work tomorrow*? I wish I'd told him I thought that was amazing. I used to have a go at him about it; he probably never knew that I admired it."

"He knew," Jen said.

"You talked about that, did you? His feelings?" Tyler gave a short laugh. There it was: the sharp edge of him, hardening. "We spent far too much time in The Black Horse, didn't we? He'd always meet us later. He was forever coming along later, just before closing time. Too busy for time-wasting. He'd drink three pints quick, before the bell went."

"It was cheap, remember?"

"And it had a great jukebox. A big old thing."

"It had that song Sam really liked on it." She named it, fresh in her mind from her deliberations.

He frowned. "He liked that? I don't remember that. I thought you liked that one."

"He loved that one! Maybe I should have chosen it. What did they go with, in the end?" The toast popped. She put the two slices on a plate, one on top of the other, and passed them over.

He said, "They never played any music in the end."

Jen stared at him. The funeral was nothing like it had been in her head, after all. She should have been there. She realised it with sudden, astonishing pain. She should have chosen a song and stood there while they played it. "So what did they do instead?"

"Forget it. You can't be bothered to be there, you don't get to know." He buttered the toast methodically, ate fast, and left without touching her.

There was plenty of time to get ready for work, but Jen found herself phoning the office with another one of her ready-prepared excuses, and an hour later – without much thought, with nothing but the desire to see the place once more in her mind – she was on a train, heading for the coast.

★   ★   ★

She hadn't chosen Brighton; it had been the only university that offered her a place, and she'd accepted without seeing the town. Perhaps that was why she'd never really warmed to it in the way many of the other students had. Some, like Sam, had been evangelical in their love for it, having chosen it, and felt chosen by it. Still, she had enjoyed her time there, and when a job in administration had come up in London after graduation, she'd left it behind without much thought. It had been coincidence that both Tyler and Sam had ended up in London too. Or had Sam got a job in the City first? Yes, Sam first: of course. It had made it easier to move there. Tyler had come along afterwards.

Five years had passed since she'd last been in the town. Many things were different. If she'd thought she didn't belong before, it was beyond obvious to her now. The students were their own group, walking the promenade, blithe in their ownership of the strip between the buildings and the sea. She sat on one of the benches for a while, her hands deep in the pockets of her coat, and watched them cross before her, loud in their conversations. She heard some planning a Halloween party; it was only days away. Maybe they were first years, only there for a month so far, caught up in the possibilities of adulthood, not the realities.

She had no idea where the time had gone.

She watched the sunset, unspectacular, a simple failing of the light, and got up. The plan was to return to the train station, but somehow she found herself at the familiar double doors of The Black Horse, the sign the same, the frosted glass tinted orange by the light within.

Inside was the Brighton she knew.

The bar was already busy for early evening, warm and welcoming in its noises, and the jukebox was the same, flashing away on the back wall, next to the toilets and that old heavy green curtain that closed off the passageway behind. Jen approached the bar, and caught the eye of the older man serving; it wasn't a familiar face, but how much attention had she ever paid to such faces, anyway? It was enough to order the usual pint, and find it was still available, and not much more in price than the last time she'd been there.

The man served it with a smile. "Nice to see you back," he said. A trick of the trade, no doubt.

"Thanks."

She walked over to the jukebox, pint in hand. The song – the one she'd told Tyler about that morning – was still there. It was so easy to feed the machine, press the button, and imagine Sam and Tyler sitting in one of the booths behind her, waiting for her to turn around and come back to them.

She took a seat. Not in one of the booths, but at the bar. One pint, one song, and she'd be gone, back to the train, back to her life.

Her phone rang.

Tyler said, "Listen, I've been thinking about last night. I should come over."

"I'm not home," she said.

"Where are you?"

"The Black Horse."

A silence. "Seriously?"

She held out the phone to the jukebox. The song was approaching the second chorus, with its catchy melody that Sam had loved to sing along to. She put the phone back to her ear, and said, "See?" even though he couldn't see at all. It was a ridiculous thing to say; how stupid he always, always made her.

"I'm coming down," he said. "I'll be there in an hour."

She put the phone back in her pocket. The song played on, then came to an end. Now she was stuck at The Black Horse for at least an hour, waiting for him to catch the train down – and for what? To boss her into doing what he wanted? She pictured him walking in, standing in the centre of the room, head raised, eyes hard. Then he would see her, and come over, and tell her why she was an idiot for being there. She drank down her pint and ordered another.

"Been stood up?" asked the man behind the bar.

"I wish."

The man laughed suddenly, silently, his shoulders moving. The bar was getting busier, a student crowd arriving. Jen got up and returned to the jukebox before they commandeered it, selecting the song again, and as it started up a voice on the other side of the green curtain said, "Once more, with feeling! That's a winner." Not with sarcasm, or annoyance, but with pleasure. The voice came again: "Yes, perfect, doesn't get any better," and the curtain moved, just enough to pull away at the side. A face appeared in the gap; the eyes were dark brown, amused, under hooded lids, set in deep folds over a long, fleshy nose and a near-white beard that had been trimmed to give shape to the old face. Something about it seemed familiar to Jen, although unplaceable.

"You're a lucky one," said the man. "Are you playing?"

"Sorry?"

"You're not in the game, then. You a student?"

"Not anymore."

"What, you don't learn anything anymore from anyone? That's a sad state of affairs." The man smiled at her, not exactly mocking her – including her in the joke, although Jen wasn't sure what the joke was. "Great job, anyway. You're about to make me a happy man. The odds came up smiling."

"What odds?"

The face retreated, and in the gap that was left Jen glimpsed a cavernous space, dimly lit, figures inside, their backs to the curtain – a shock, to find such a room where she had pictured a dusty, claustrophobic passageway, beer crates and barrels stacked against brick. How strange, that the room had always been there without her knowledge. It was grandiose, like a long-forgotten ballroom, all the walls lined with the same heavy green curtains. "Come on," said the man, "come in, come in," and she pushed through to emerge in that world, nobody turning to greet her, nobody seemingly surprised at her admittance at all.

In her jeans and coat she was underdressed for this occasion, whatever it was. Everyone else, fifty or so people, were in suits or long dresses, and all their high heels and polished toecaps were pointing towards the same spot – the centre of the room, where there stood a large, sleek table of some dark wood, mahogany or walnut. Their attention was absolutely fixed upon it, and she recognised that stillness, that contained energy, from a place she had once visited with Tyler and Sam: a last-minute, end-of-finals, trip up to one of the big London casinos, back when such things had been impressive to them. *Let's go win big*, Sam had said, and somehow they'd got in, wearing their charity shop ties and her only smart summer dress, with the bouncers exchanging a bored look. Sam had been the only one to place bets on the roulette wheel, the whole lot at once, and he had lost everything, of course. Then the sense that their short time was up had swept over them all, and they had run out, laughing. They hadn't belonged there.

She should feel the same here, surely? That sense of being an interloper at some event not designed for her. She moved forwards, and the people parted for her, allowed her access to the table. She looked down on carved objects, white soapstone and black jet playing pieces, each one big enough to fill her hand. They were arranged in rows on either side of one central, empty strip that ran the length of the board. At the top of the table was a rectangular box, made of a lighter wood – a plainer piece compared to the white and black.

She made a show of studying the set up. It wasn't chess, or like any game she knew. But undoubtedly everyone else in the crowded room felt something important was happening; she stole glances at their faces, as they concentrated on the board. Nobody moved. They were older than her, in the main, she thought; the dim light was gentle but it cast long shadows under eyes and chins. From the main bar, Sam's song was still playing, clearly audible, and they stood there in silence as it hit the final chorus and faded away.

Only then did the atmosphere break. The people turned away, or to each other, and began quiet chatting, exchanging smiles or frowns. Jen felt sudden pressure on the centre of her back, and then the old man appeared at her elbow. "What did I say? Lucky."

"You won?"

"And here comes the next round. You want the honours?"

"I don't... I haven't—"

"Here." The man leaned over the table and retrieved the wooden box. He placed it at the foot of the board, then arranged the soapstone and jet pieces, his hands working at speed, to regular spacing, in their rows. The attention of the crowd was turning back to the board, tension in their expressions, the way they leaned forward.

Something was expected from her.

'I don't know—"

A song began on the jukebox. It wasn't one she liked, particularly, but she did recognise it. Fast-paced, a brash quality to the voice: she assumed the students had put it on to get themselves in the mood for a big night out, on to a club perhaps. Something about the thought of it exhausted her. Music, and life, really had moved on.

"Now," said the man.

"What?"

"Now!" The urgency shifted Jen to action; she reached out and picked a piece at random: a jet one, short, with a wide oval base. Her fingers found slight notches and grooves in the surface. Was it her imagination or did the crowd, collectively, hold their breath? She moved the piece to the right, keeping it in the same row, and put it down again. A few people nodded, or shifted their weight, but the feeling of expectation did not pass. There was more to do.

All right, then, she thought. *All right*. She picked another piece: a white one, slim, tall with a square base and a curve, like a downturned mouth, across its body. She moved it from the back of the board to the middle. A few faces frowned, a few smiled. The song finished its first verse, and circled back around to the chorus. She shifted a few more pieces, at random, and found a rhythm, moving them in time to the beat, becoming more adventurous. Some she gathered together and some she placed in the empty central section. The wooden box, she avoided. She wasn't sure why.

The song built up, and up, and stopped suddenly. No fade out, just a crash down into silence, and Jen took her hand from the board, and looked at the pattern she'd made. It meant nothing, of course. At least not to her. But the crowd broke into applause, a solid clapping that felt genuine, warm and affirming.

"Amazing," said the older man, as the sound died down and the people turned away. "And you say you've never played before?"

"No, never, but I like games," Jen said. If they were going to praise her then she felt it would be churlish to deny any ability at all. And it was true, she did like games. She'd played chess with Sam sometimes, using an old set in the common room, and had always won – mainly because Sam had always been in such a rush to get through it. She didn't have illusions about her skill at such games, but still, it counted for something that she wanted to play at all, surely? And why shouldn't she be good at this game? It felt like a small payback from the universe, for all she'd been through in the last month.

"It shows, it shows," said the man. He sorted out the pieces once more, back to their regular starting positions. "Up for another round?"

"Okay," said Jen. "Since I'm lucky for you."

"For us all. For us all."

When the next song started, she was ready. It was a ballad, one from the Eighties, full of swelling chords and throbbing emotions, and she used wide, sweeping gestures to move the pieces, this time choosing to create a heart-shaped pattern into which, at the last chorus, she placed the box. The wood was unvarnished, grainy. And it was surprisingly weighty; something heavy was inside it.

The song faded away, and this time there was no applause. There was a sound of soft crying, somewhere near the back of the room, and for a moment Jen felt her sudden confidence drain away. She was terrible at this – how could it have been otherwise? But then the older man leaned over and whispered in her ear, "Beautiful," and she realised everyone's eyes were shining with amazement at what she'd done.

"Set them up again," she said.

★   ★   ★

She had no idea how much time had passed when her phone rang. She didn't let it interrupt her concentration, finishing the song, completing her pattern. The beeps of her ringtone even seemed to fit well to the music, dovetailing with the beat of the dance-floor banger as the crowd swayed along. Only when the round was over did she retrieve the phone from her pocket and listen to the message.

"I'm here," said Tyler. "Where are you?"

"I have to go," she told the man, but he grabbed her arm, and said, "You're on a roll! Come straight back, all right?" She nodded, pulled away, and stepped through the green curtain to an audible groan from the crowd. There, at the busy bar, he stood, looking around the place, scowling at the students. It was just as she had imagined. When he saw her, his frown deepened.

"You look weird," he said, as she approached.

"Thanks very much."

"Tired. Older. I don't know. I've been here for ages. Where were you?"

"I only just got your message," she said. "And you didn't have to come down here. I'm perfectly fine."

"Listen, it just – I don't like how we left things. I didn't realise you were struggling so much, I should have seen it, but I'm struggling too—"

"I'm not struggling."

"Then what are you doing here? You just…" He flung out his arms wide. She hadn't realised how angry he was. "…decided to have a pint in The Black Horse. Just like that."

She didn't want him there: his anger, his demand that she respond to him. What was it he had said to her last night? *We do have to move on.* But she didn't want to move on, to find out what happened next. "So what if I did come down here?" she said. "That's my business, not yours."

He flinched, as if she had hurt him. He said, "We're friends, right? We'll still be friends, even without him. If you'd come to the funeral you would know that, because I stood up and said that."

"What?"

"To make up for the lack of music everyone stood up and said what they were grateful for, and I said I was grateful that he'd made me part of a group of three friends. Real friends. The kind who can get pissed off with each other because sometimes that's the best thing you can do for a friend."

She tried to picture that – him, in the church, dressed in his black suit, telling them that. She couldn't see it. Where had he been sitting? How had the others looked at him?

"And maybe the worst thing about all this – the thing you don't want to face – is that you never asked him how he felt after you broke up. And you never once acknowledged that he was waiting around for you to want him again. And you know how he hated waiting. He spent all his time, hanging around for you, and it turns out that there was no time at all. All this is terrible, right? It's terrible to think about. But it will be okay. As long as you come with me, and we talk about it, we'll be okay."

It was too much to take in. She pushed it away, concentrated instead on Tyler. "So what do you get out of this, then, if I'm such a terrible person? If I ruined his short life? Why are you here?"

"Because I don't want to give up," he said. He was so tall and solid, planted before her. "Not on you, not on Sam. Not on life."

Jen hadn't seen it before. But his anger at her – it was a mask for his fear. He was afraid. As scared as she had ever seen him. There he was again: the teenager she had curled up in bed with, to help each other through those first lonely nights away from home, in a strange town where they were suddenly meant to be adults. They had helped each other so much, back then. Warm bodies, together. She reached out on impulse, pulled him into a hug. His heart was a solid thud against her chest.

It opened up her own terror, the one she had been trying so hard not to feel; she was equally as afraid for him. It was the reason she couldn't go to the funeral, the reason she couldn't bear to hold him for long. She bore it for as long as he could, memorising him, his heartbeat, the way he cared for her.

"Come back with me," he said.

She stepped away. "I'll meet you outside in a minute," she said. "I'll just..." She made a vague gesture, in the direction of the toilets, the jukebox.

"The next train goes in twenty minutes," he said. "We'll get back, I'll make you supper." She managed a smile: painful, fleeting. He walked away.

Jen returned to the jukebox, pushing through the students to stand before it. She selected Sam's song. *One more time*, she told herself. Then she pushed through the green curtain, and the crowd in the room parted easily so she could stand before the board once more.

A cheer went up. The older man, so familiar, put his arm around her and said, "We've been waiting for you. Ready when you are." A song started up. Not Sam's, but one of those standard tunes that always got so much play on the radio, and people often picked as their favourite. The singer sang of a broken heart as Jen let her hand hover, wondering what to touch first.

There was a thick soapstone piece, solid, with a domed head and a tapering body. She picked it up and found it cold, perfect in her palm. Her fingers picked up curves and indents in the stone: perhaps two eyes, a nose. She put it in the centre of the board, leaving it standing, and slowly knocked all the other pieces over, to lie on their sides. It took time to get everything positioned just as she wanted. When she finished it was a pretty picture, one she wanted to fix in her mind forever.

No. Not quite.

Something wasn't right.

The box – the box needed to be moved, but she didn't know where.

"It's all right," said the old man. He reached over her and swiped the box from the board. Something about his eagerness, his speed regardless of his advancing age, reminded her of Sam's energy. That desire to be busy, but concentrated on this one task alone. This game. And, yes, he looked a little like Sam, too, she realised. "You can open it. You can do anything you like here."

She took the box in her hands. How heavy it was, and warm. Was it her imagination, or could she feel the rhythm of the music moving inside it, beating in time? She felt around the edges – yes, there it was. A small catch, that she pried open. She swung back the lid. Inside was… nothing. Wait. The bottom of the box was not made of wood at all. She brought it up to her face, and realised it was a mirror, reflecting the dim lights above. She tilted it towards her face and saw her own eye, in close detail. But it was not a young eye anymore. Time had rushed past, abandoned her here, and the eye that looked back at her was almost lost in a nest of deep lines and wrinkles. It looked tired, and worn, and done. Surely it was only the lighting that made her look so old, just as old as the others who surrounded her, waiting for her to finish her move.

She closed the lid and put the box back on the table, next to the soapstone piece that remained standing. That was better. It felt like a good move. What an easy game this was for her. And the others were so happy; as the song ended they clapped her, and someone even gave out a cheer.

"One more game," she said, and the old man started to reset the pieces. Soon, Sam's song would come up again, and she would set the board up perfectly. Yes, she would stay until she'd made all the right choices. It wouldn't take long.

"Isn't it amazing how you always win in here?" said the man, as he took the soapstone piece and shifted it back to its starting position. "Isn't it just so great how you always, always win?"

THE DARK BIT

Toby Litt

I usually start by apologising; because we are upper middle and white and weren't badly off, and already that must mean, before you even know what we're like, that you're not disposed towards us – as people, as people you might care about.

But even though we aren't particularly sympathetic, or even interesting, what happened to us is – I assure you. Though 'interesting' isn't the first word that would come to mind; not according to the internet.

'We' is myself, Pyotr, and my wife, Anaïs – mid-thirties, corporate (I admit it), South London, trying for a baby since Anaïs hit twenty-nine.

And, yes, our house had white shutters on the inside of the front windows. And, yes, we ordered takeaways every other night. And, no, I'm not going to tell you what we earned.

By now you hate us, and would be glad if very bad stuff was going to happen to us. Well, good – because very bad stuff did happen to us, and it started like this:

Anaïs woke up in the middle of the night, because she'd had a nightmare. She got them quite often, particularly during this period, and they mostly related to children drowning.

We talked about this nightmare quite a lot afterwards, because we were trying to work out whether it had anything to do with what followed. Not that it instigated the whole horror, but maybe it was significant in some way – prophetic, even, if that's not putting it too strongly.

(I am including it here although some people have advised me never to mention it again. Even counsellors.)

In her nightmare, Anaïs was herself but a lot older – and she knew she didn't have children. "I don't know how – I just knew," she said. "Like you do in dreams."

"It was a nightmare," I said.

"It became a nightmare," she said. "It started out as a dream. I was in a beautiful swimming pool. Somewhere sunny. But there was a lid on the pool. A strong glass lid that suddenly slid across the top of it. Right on top of the water. I banged against it with my head, but I couldn't get my mouth up into the air. And then, when I looked around, I saw that it was only me and this one black boy in the pool. His friends, I knew, were safely out, already above the glass. Walking on it. I saw their pinky feet above me. I looked around, but I couldn't see an edge. I felt like I couldn't breathe, and that scared me, but it didn't seem like I was drowning. I think, by this point, I knew I was sleeping and it was a nightmare. So I swam over to the black boy, to see if he was dead. And when I got there, I was afraid, because I knew I would have to touch him to see if he was dead – and I didn't want to touch him, because I knew if I touched him I'd turn black, too. It seemed to go on for a very long time, with me waiting to see if he was still alive. The longer it went on, the more I knew he was going to open his eyes and shock me, and I didn't want him to open his eyes and shock me, so I woke up."

This is how Anaïs told me her nightmare, the first time. But that was the next evening. When she woke up that night, around 3:00 a.m., she went downstairs to the kitchen. She did not wake me.

Ours is a normal Victorian house layout – attic conversion, kitchen with a side return, two parlours knocked through on the ground floor, cellar for storage.

To get into the kitchen, Anaïs had walked in a big Z-shape – out of our front bedroom, along the landing towards the rear of the house, then turned and gone diagonally down the stairs to the front hall, then she doubled back on herself and went through the dark bit and into the kitchen.

Anaïs told me she didn't switch the lights on, because she didn't want to wake me. So the dark bit just before the kitchen was really completely black when she passed through it and felt something across the bridge of her nose.

I should probably have said that Anaïs has long blonde hair. But she knew straightaway it wasn't a hair, even though it felt like one, because when she tried to brush it off, it wouldn't brush. However, she was mostly thinking about her nightmare at this moment, and wasn't one hundred per cent concentrated on her face.

"It wasn't like I stopped and screamed," she said weeks later, the last time I saw her, when they'd stopped us, and we were in institutions – but they got us together for a session. "Although, if I'd known what was coming, I suppose I would have done."

"You don't regret it, do you?" I asked.

"No," she said, and touched the bandages covering her face.

Then the psychiatrist intervened.

★ ★ ★

At first the landing of the thread didn't bother her. Anaïs was groggy, not fully awake. We kept our house clean – we had a cleaner who came in on Fridays and Mondays – but still you get spiders and spiders' webs, don't you? Even if you're not living in the country. Anaïs thought what she felt might be a strand from one of those, across the bridge of her nose.

As she drank her milk, she tried to pull the thread away, but it wouldn't come. She couldn't get hold of it.

"I thought then it might be some weird nerve-damage thing," she said at one point. "I was worried I might be having a stroke, but I didn't have any other symptoms."

When I asked her, on another occasion, if she ever thought of waking me up, she said no, it didn't seem worth it.

Anyway, the milk did the job. She felt a bit better, and came back to bed. I woke up enough to say, "Okey cokey?"

"Fine as wine," she said, and did go to sleep.

★ ★ ★

The next morning, she didn't even mention it to me – the line on her face – although she could still feel it just as vividly present. She just got up, had breakfast, got dressed, went to work – with it there all the time.

It's not hard to describe or to imagine; it's just like a very thin thread laid across the surface of the skin, touching it. Not burning or agonising or anything – just *there*.

I got my first one that evening, in the same place in the house, the dark bit at the back of the hall. It wasn't across my nose, though. Mine was at a slight angle down and across my chin.

Unlike Anaïs, I mentioned it straightaway. Because I put my hands to my face, and brushed and then scratched, but I could still feel this thin line of *presence* left to right.

"Can you see anything on my face?" I asked when I got into the kitchen. "It feels like I scratched it."

"Oh, you've got it, too," she said.

I asked what, and she told me about the night before – after telling me about her nightmare. The black boy in the pool.

"And you've been able to feel it all day?" I asked.

"Every time I thought about it, it was there."

I kept rubbing at my chin.

"Why didn't you tell me first thing?" I asked. "I'd have told you."

"I thought it was nothing. I just thought it would go away."

We were eating toast and Marmite. Neither of us had felt like a takeaway. Anaïs was drinking camomile tea. I had put on a comfortable cashmere jumper, and my favourite old pair of white corduroys. We had been happier the day before, without knowing it; but this quiet time in the kitchen was as content as we were going to be, together, again.

(At this point, I would like to interrupt myself to make a point: You will have noticed that there was no infection between us. Anaïs told me nothing about her so-called symptom before I got mine. This is not a case of *folie à deux*, which is what we're constantly being nudged towards. Whatever caused the threads, it was outside us – and has nothing whatsoever to do with abnormal psychology of any sort. It could happen to anyone in any house.)

I finished my toast; I was that calm.

"Where's yours?" I asked, and Anaïs showed me.

"Yours?" she asked, and I drew a line across my chin with my fingernail. This gave a strange effect, because for a moment I couldn't tell which was which, the line or the tracing of the line, but then the real thing was the one which lingered.

Anaïs asked, "You don't think it's some rare kind of spider, with an acidic web, or something like that?"

I picked up my phone and searched. Nothing I could find seemed likely – not even the horrible creatures that sneak here from Australia, in containers, with fruit.

We went to the dark bit, to have a look. It wasn't actually dark then

– I'd turned on the little-used light by the cellar door. Anaïs waved her hands through the air at the point where her face had been, when the first thread was laid upon her.

"No," she said. "Nothing."

"Are you scared?" I asked.

"No," she said. "Annoyed."

I told her she looked beautiful, which she did. Her eyes are very big, and seem to be a combination of chestnut and violet. The skin on her face was smooth, pale, only slightly wrinkled at the corners of the eyes. Yes, that's how the skin on her face used to be, when she had skin on her face. Her face-type is ovoid, and – though I am unaware of any genetic link – there is something Inuit about her bone structure.

"I am very lucky to be married to you," I said.

"Even though we both might be going mad," she said.

Amazing as it is, we went back into the kitchen and had another round of toast. So English! We just accepted it, the inexplicable; just put it to one side, and spread a bit more butter on than we'd normally do. What did it matter?

That was the Friday, and the weekend went past without us getting any more threads. That's what we had started calling them, although I can't remember if it was Anaïs or I. To begin with they were 'mine' and 'yours', then they became 'my thread' and 'your thread'. Soon enough, they became plural. Then they went back to being 'mine' and 'yours', as in 'How are yours today? Mine aren't too bad'; but I'm jumping too far ahead.

We didn't go away that weekend. We had a lazy time with the newspapers and a trip to the Farmers' Market on Sunday. But we were both a bit irritable, and spent quite a while in front of the bathroom mirrors. We had three – a tall oval one above the sink, a magnifying one you could flip round for real close-ups and a full-length one.

Anaïs got her second thread early on Monday morning. It wasn't the first time she went through the dark bit that day. She'd gone in to put the kettle on, and come out to ask me if I wanted toast or cereal, and gone back in to get the cereal from the cupboard. And I'd come past, too, in my dressing gown, ready for breakfast.

It was only when she was on the way towards the stairs, after we'd tidied up, that Anaïs stopped dead and said, "Another one."

"Really?" I said.

"Yes," she said.

"Where?"

She turned round. She was wearing her soft cotton pyjamas, the ones with blue and white stripes – the ones they have let her keep, because the waist is elasticated.

"Here," she said, and drew a line across her clavicle bones. So delicate. That used to be my favourite place to kiss.

"All the way across?" I asked.

She stood for a moment, feeling her skin. "Yes," she said, "all the way across."

"Interesting," I said.

"Why?" she said.

"Well, it is interesting," I said. "They're not natural. They're not in the air, waiting for us – they are different. They appear when it's time."

"I understand."

"Do you want to go to work?" I asked.

"Of course," she said. "This isn't any reason to stay off." She indicated her body.

For some reason, I could feel my thread particularly intensely at that moment. Partly, I suppose, because I was trying to imagine what it felt like to have two. I hadn't got used to the first one, not exactly. But having one was, during that time, the normal state of affairs; having two would be different, and perhaps more upsetting.

I didn't have long to wait to find out.

Dressed and ready for work, just popping into the kitchen to fill a bottle of water for the commute, I felt my second laid upon me. It ran directly across my chest, cutting each of my nipples in half.

"Bugger," I said. "It got me."

But Anaïs had already left.

★   ★   ★

Looking back, you start to wonder if it was all meant to mean something. Were the threads like the first white hairs? Or the first heart murmur? Something to do with age, the drag of age. And death, of course.

But you also face the greater possibility that they were – in fact –

meaningless. On this account, the threads were merely to be ranked among those inexplicable things that happen to random people, and that they spend the rest of their lives trying and failing to understand.

Two threads – we both had two threads at the start of the second week. In retrospect, it seems so few.

And over the course of the second week I received only one more – this time across my forehead but not, because we checked, in the exact same place as Anaïs. She, by contrast, ended that week with five threads – the two original ones plus one across her very flat tummy, one down by her slender ankles (on both legs) and one at the very crown of her lovely skull.

So, to all appearances, the threads seemed to be randomly distributed both in time and space; randomly, except we only accumulated them when passing through the dark bit.

Of course, we began to wince slightly as we approached it – anticipating, fearing, that *this* time, we'd be blessed with another thread.

★   ★   ★

"Mine are strongly there," said Anaïs, on the Wednesday, as she was getting off the exercise bike. "Don't yours feel more and more present?"

"I try not to think about them," I said. "I think we should really try not to mention them, or think of them – not any more than we have to."

And so we said nothing for the whole of Thursday and Friday.

We managed without speaking at all.

★   ★   ★

Imagine it was happening to you – what would you do? Go to the doctor? There's no point going to the doctor when you know exactly what the doctor is going to say, and that it's going to be rubbish and banal and no use whatsoever to anybody.

I suppose there was a slight chance it might have been nerve damage, rather than something genuinely inexplicable. But that we'd both suffered the same kind of nerve damage on the same day of the week…

★   ★   ★

It was mischievous of us, and perhaps immoral, but months earlier we had invited some friends to dinner that Saturday – Charlie and Shirley – and we didn't cancel.

I cooked something Palestinian, and drank a bottle of wine doing so.

Anaïs came down looking gorgeous in Gucci – the last time she would ever be this straightforwardly beautiful; although, of course, I love her as she is now, with her different, more exacting looks.

Our guests arrived. We ate nibbles in the front room, then they followed us through into the kitchen.

We talked about upper middle annoyances, nothings.

"They're going to promote me into a position I really just don't want," said Shirley.

"I can't get a decent gin and tonic in Balham," said Charlie.

"I'm sure our babysitter makes more in a day than I do," said Shirley.

"Every day at the lido, without fail," said Charlie. "Twenty-eight lengths even when it's six degrees."

Shirley went through the dark bit eight times during the course of the evening, and Charlie six. Neither of them mentioned any strange sensations or seemed to touch their face more than usual.

Anaïs did. I watched her hands. She disguised her touchings as strokings of her eyebrows or tuckings back of the hair behind her ears. But I could tell she was checking.

In bed, after the guests had gone, she told me she kept feeling that the lines were becoming visible – that they were starting to glow red, and that soon other people would be able to see them.

"That would be better," she said, "in a way. Then they'd be a subject, and I wouldn't feel I was hiding something important from the world."

I offered sex and she refused.

"You were touching yours," she said. "You're a little red here," she said, and touched my forehead.

★   ★   ★

On Sunday, Anaïs made a shopping list:

Cleanser
Toner

Moisturiser
White vinegar
Chisel
Wire wool
Razor blades
Small delicate hooks?
Needles
Surgical tape (lots)
Plasters
Milk
Bread
Passata
Some kind of acid

I understood immediately, and asked her to promise me she would never harm herself in any way.

"Not harm," she said. "Experiment. I'm sure there's something we can do."

These words clarified my understanding.

★   ★   ★

That afternoon we went to the chemist's and then to the supermarket and then to the ironmongers. It seemed necessary, I can't say why. At a certain point, you start to feel not in control of your own actions. You must know that state? You've already eaten the biscuit before you've been able to tell yourself not to pick it up.

It was a very large ironmongers – a chain store. We walked along the aisles, Anaïs pushing a shopping trolley. There were so many tools of which I couldn't fathom the use. Nothing was as delicate as we wanted it to be.

"Really we need a proper medical supplier," I said.

She agreed.

We had stopped not talking about the threads. Now, it seemed, we didn't really talk of much else.

★   ★   ★

"I'm glad we're taking action," said Anaïs, as she was parallel parking the car outside our house. The bags clanked in the boot. "We'll know more soon."

"Yes," I said, although I was afraid in a way that was entirely new to me. I knew Anaïs, and her determination, but I didn't know her physical fearlessness.

She would have been a wonderful mother.

I feel appalling writing this. It shouldn't be written, but I have to get rid of it somehow. I am disloyal, to myself in the past as much as to Anaïs in what counts for her present.

Both of us are held in stasis, until we can somehow get away.

Children aren't an impossibility.

★   ★   ★

We began gently, in areas that could easily be covered over. The problem with this was, it was the earlier lines that were the more intense – those ones on our faces. They hadn't exactly started to burn, but they were more irksomely *there*.

Anaïs had never liked her stomach, although it was perfectly toned. We hadn't managed to get any delicate hooks. That's what we really wanted – something that could neatly get in under the surface of the skin, then grab whatever was running through it. Instead, we had razor blades – packs of ten – and that's what we started with.

Although she could easily have done it herself, Anaïs said she thought I could get in at a better angle. First, though, she drew the belly line across her skin with eyeliner. Once she'd started, there was something freeing about it. She did the thread across her nose, and the other three. I took the eyeliner from her and did both of mine.

Then I began to cut.

The first incision was quite delicate, vertical. Looking back, from where we got to, our beginnings were extremely conservative.

"Can you see anything?" Anaïs asked.

"No," I said. "I think I may need to go a bit deeper."

"Fine," she said.

I made a cut about an inch in length but only a quarter of an inch deep and pulled the flesh apart.

"Let me see," said Anaïs.

"I'm afraid there's nothing to see."

Anaïs reached in with her left index finger – she is left-handed. Her nails, which were real, were quite long. She tried to use her nail as a hook, to get the thread out.

"No," she said. "No use."

A trickle of blood was running down her upper thigh.

"I think we might need to follow the lines," she said. "Not cut across them."

It was what I'd been thinking, too.

"Let's try the one up here," I said – and tapped her clavicle with my finger.

"Hey," she said. "Gentle."

"Sorry," I said.

"Start here," said Anaïs, touching near her right shoulder. "I still want to be able to wear that yellow summer dress."

I knew the one. She always looked delicious in it – like a model from an advert for yoghurt.

The razor blade was already a bit sticky, so I washed it clean. Seeing the blood in the basin, spiralling down – I think that was the last thing that might have stopped me.

"Hurry up," said Anaïs.

I resumed work. We found nothing. Anaïs rooted around inside herself, up to half an inch deep, with tweezers – no thread came out.

"Now you," said Anaïs.

"I've been feeling rather left out," I said.

Anaïs was more confident than I had been. She drew the razor blade neatly sideways across my chest.

"Not the nipple," I said. "Not yet."

"Why not?"

"I don't know," I said. "It might cause complications."

We didn't want complications.

Anaïs looked closely into the red ditch she had created below my right arm.

"I can't see it yet," she said.

"Perhaps that's enough for now," I suggested. It did sting a bit.

I could tell Anaïs was disappointed.

We closed up the wounds with surgical tape, and put on dressing gowns, then got our laptops.

★ ★ ★

After this, we fell into something of a routine. Every evening, after dinner, we would continue our investigation.

On Tuesday, I got my fourth and fifth lines. The fourth was almost at the soles of my feet. The fifth one ran across my thighs and the tip of my penis. By this time Anaïs had eight.

We did not just use the razor blades. We tried the wire wool, but it was clear pretty soon that was useless. The acid wasn't strong enough to do anything much. Anaïs put some in the first cut I'd made – the one across her belly – which she'd done some work on widening. Afterwards, for a moment, she said, "You know, that feels a bit better."

"Really?" I said.

"Maybe it's dissolving it."

The effect soon went away. Everything seemed to be happening both very fast and extremely slowly.

Anaïs had already booked the next week off work, as annual leave. Neither of us were sleeping very well. The hidden thread across my chin vexed me more than the cuts across my thighs.

We thought about avoiding the dark bit – not getting any more gifts bestowed upon us. But it hardly seemed worth it. The fridge was in the kitchen. Where would we keep food, if not there?

Even so, we upped our consumption of takeaways. Sometimes I was bleeding quite badly, beneath my clothes, as I answered the door. But you don't have to fiddle with cash these days, do you?

Still, we only ever did a weekend online shop. So sometimes, midweek, we needed milk and bread and alcohol and other basics. I was only out for ten minutes at most, on the Wednesday afternoon, but when I came back Anaïs had opened up her face.

"Naughty," I said. "Couldn't you wait?"

"It felt so good," she said. "I felt I was really making progress."

I kissed her. I knew I had to. And I knew I had to start on my face, too. My chin was so annoying.

That weekend was the most intense. Almost every time we passed the dark bit, we got new lines. And we became sort of high on the pain, and also – I suppose – on the vodka and painkillers.

Why did no one find out and stop us? We didn't have much to do with our neighbours.

Anaïs had a video call with her mother, but she said she hadn't done her hair, and left the camera off.

By Monday morning, we knew neither of us was likely to be able to go back to work; not for quite some time. I called in sick.

On Wednesday I resigned.

You probably think we were mad to keep going. But there were moments, like with the acid, when we really had hope. We gained ourselves whole half hours of relief. There must be something there – something just a millimetre further in. If only we were brave enough, we'd hook it out.

Looking online, we'd eventually managed to source some really good hooks. These were a game-changer, when they arrived on Friday. We were able to dig in at any point along the line where it felt closest to the surface. But still no joy.

I did an online shop, and asked them to leave it outside the door, in bags. But when the man came, he knocked anyway. I put a towel around my face and he pretended to ignore it. Afterwards, I saw there was blood on the towel. Most of our towels were pinkish, by this point.

We were sleeping less and less. Of course, there were no cuts across our backs, so lying down wasn't painful. But those across our faces and stomachs burned.

This continued until the following Wednesday. Anaïs, always the strongest of us, had pushed on in her explorations across the clavicle area. Finally, she went too deep with the hook. There was a major artery in there, and considerable leakage ensued. The wallpaper and carpets suffered. I was left with no choice but to call the emergency services.

An ambulance arrived. They were experienced medics but even so the two of them did a lot of swearing and gagging when they entered our house.

"What the fuck?" one of them kept saying, the man, which I thought was very unprofessional.

Very soon after the first responders came the police.

At that time, Anaïs had seventeen lines and I – still not having caught up – was blessed with a mere fourteen. But I had just removed the tip of my penis, so I suppose we were even.

Anaïs needed to be operated on immediately. In the front room, the medics began to load her onto a trolley. I held her hand.

"Sir, if you could explain," said the police officer, who was black.

Anaïs looked at him in horror, and said, "Swimming pool. Swimming pool." They carried her out. They would not let me go with her in the ambulance.

"Sir."

Politely, I showed the police officer the dark bit.

I could not explain. I asked him to walk back and forth until something happened. He did, but nothing happened.

They took me to hospital. Someone else must have locked up the house – we were not burgled, not that I've been told.

There were more questions, more doctors, more police.

I could not explain and I still cannot explain. Not to therapists, not to bloggers.

Everything we did was logical, and necessary, given the fact of the threads. I do not think either we or the house were evil.

Just because we are who we are, and earned what we earned, and did what we did, we do not deserve what is happening to us – despite what the internet says.

We should be released immediately.

PROVENANCE POND

Josh Malerman

To look at it, you'd say it's just a pond, which I suppose it always was, but at an important time in my life, it was not.

Look: tufts of brown grass, overwatered, outlining a quarter of its circumference, evergreens mountain-high; green earth curtains, creating, always, the sense of a stage. Listen: frogs in conversation, ducks wading, snapping turtles lunging only when they are absolutely certain of their catch. This *was* a stage, you see, for me and the few friends I shared it with. There was more to see then, more to hear. Though I suppose even words sounded larger, louder, when you were small.

Mother didn't love the pond, though she tried. For her it was a constant struggle: overrun with algae in the summer, dead ducks at the beaks of those snappers, the surface not quite ice-strong enough to hold me, skating, in January. You could always tell when Mother was placating, kind-hearted as she was, when she ruffled my hair, when she said, *You do love it out there, don't you, Rose?* Father was different. He never employed tact, and he outright told me, myself aged ten, that what I'd mistaken for theatre was only nature, bland at that, as we didn't live too far from the city. I tried to tell them otherwise, Father especially, to explain how anything, literally anything, could be a stage, and anything curtains, so long as the players performed.

To look at it now, it's small, though, mercifully, not man-made. And even as I study it through the eyes of a woman, no longer a ten-year-old child, I see it as it was.

Father was unimpressed. Why do I think of this still? Why do I care? His cynical nature was never in doubt; not even the school disciplinarians saw things with less magic. And each time I thought I'd perhaps made ground, he'd scoff, he'd frown, he'd plant a hand on his hip and point with the other, point to the pond, and say:

Look, Rose, it's water and flowers. Listen, Rose, it's ordinary.

The unspoken, of course, was that there was nothing special about *our* pond, seeming to suggest nothing interesting about *his* pond, and more, it seemed, nothing unique about *mine*.

But it was special. It was interesting.

It was frightening, too.

There was Kathy, for one. And while I couldn't see her, she rode the tree-swing with me every time I swung. She laughed when I eyed the thick rope, following it all the way up to the thick oak branch, the one that would crush me if it ever broke free of the tree. Kathy assured me this would never happen. And I believed her.

Marcus was unique, too. And, while I couldn't see him either, I knew he was always smiling, as he stood on the other side of the pond, just before those evergreens, waving good day each time I approached and goodbye whenever I ascended the grassy hill back to the house.

Was ten too old for imaginary friends? Father certainly thought so. He and Mother argued about it one night when they believed I was out of earshot. Looking back, I wonder if they thought I was at the pond that day. Mother attempted to quell Father's indignation. I heard her use words like *natural* and *healthy* while he combated with fierce terms like *frivolous* and *mad*. There was never a question of my mental stability, to this day I've held jobs, relationships, and nobody has ever intervened on my behalf. So, even at ten, I wondered as to Father's overreaction. What did he so detest about my imagination? There were times I worried he didn't like the pond itself, as if it somehow represented a poor purchase on my parents' part; perhaps, to Father, a pond, of any sort, was nothing more than a hole in more potential land.

I wish I would've told him it was a door.

A third friend arrived, unannounced, one afternoon, the sun on high for all the world, it seemed, to see.

Because I *could* see Theo, understand. Watched him rise from the dark water, first only the mud on his scalp and a pair of eyes larger than my own. Then, fingertips, as if Theo were climbing up, the disrupted surface of the pond as stable as the rock of a cliff's edge. From our first encounter to our last, he only ever appeared as he actually was; bulging eyes and wiry frame, tall as Father though thin as the runners on the high school team, the older boys Father cheered for at the track meets so many of us attended. Theo made himself known in dramatic fashion, I thought then, employing all elements of the stage, rising at last to his full height, as I turned to ask Kathy if she too saw the man in the pond. But Kathy was no longer beside me on the swing.

"Good day," Theo said, his first two words so uncharacteristic, though I couldn't have known it at the time.

"Good day," I said in return, eyeing the seaweed that clung to his white legs, thin as the branches of the lesser trees between where I sat and the house.

I looked for Marcus then, wondering what his take on this might be. But, unseen or not, I knew Marcus had receded farther into the evergreens.

"The reason you can see me," Theo said, "is because I am your real friend."

I freeze a little inside now just as I did then. I say to myself: it's just a pond.

He stood in water where snappers lived, and the dark wounds along his body were proof.

"I am Theo," he said. "You are Rose?"

"Yes," I said.

And I freeze again now as I did then.

"May I join you on the swing?"

I didn't like this notion. Kathy was my friend to swing with, Marcus my friend in the trees. Theo would have to find his own place with me.

"Shore, then," he said, not waiting for a response, taking exaggerated strides toward the grassy lip before crouching and reaching it with his fingers first. Theo crawled on all fours toward me and I slipped quietly off the swing and stood behind the wide wood board.

"Shore," I said, indicating that he should remain there. But, unlike my other friends, Theo tested the rules from the start. "Shore," I said again.

He came only a little closer, until I could see the pupils in his eyes, the layers of muck on his forehead and face.

There he remained, seemingly mid-reach, as if I'd frozen him in a game of Simon Says. I thought to turn then, to run to the house, to tell Father he was wrong, so wrong, the pond was anything but ordinary, the pond was not bland.

Instead, I spoke to him.

"Where did you come from?"

To think of his expression now, I can name it. *Despair.* But at ten I hadn't a clue.

"Right here," he said, indicating the water that had gone still again behind him.

"Do you live in there?"

He moved then and, in my mind, I was already halfway to the house. But he was only lounging on the shore, leaning on one impossibly bony elbow.

"Do you dream?" he asked.

I told him I did. I told him only a fool didn't dream.

"Do you plan?" he asked.

"What a silly thing to say," I said. And it was.

"Do you wish?"

"Why would I wish? I have everything I want here."

Again: despair. But I couldn't have known.

He laid out then, fully on his back, his body curving slightly with the contour of the pond.

I stepped out from behind the swing.

"What is your name?" I asked.

"Theo," he said. Even at ten I understood that he wasn't looking at the sky just because his eyes were pointed that way.

"You're silly, Theo," I said.

I seemed to blink, and he was looking at me. Then, without speaking any more, Theo slid back into the water, his eyes set on mine, even as the algae rose to their bottoms, even as the algae touched the pupils I watched sink.

That night, I told Mother and Father about my third friend of the pond. Father didn't like it.

"Another one?" he said. He moved the centrepiece vase of flowers so he could get a clean view of Mother. I recognised the look he gave her. And the one he gave me. "Rose... you're supposed to *lose* imaginary friends the older you get, not gain them. Got it?"

"What's his name?" Mother asked.

"Elaine," Father said. "*Please.*"

"Theo," I said.

Dad huffed. The subject exasperated him as it always did.

"No more," he said.

"Roger," Mother said. "There's no harm."

But they'd gone around this subject so many times. There was less force behind her protestation than his.

"Kathy is my swing friend," I said, not letting Father win. Not with this subject. If they weren't going to love it, the pond was mine.

"We know," Father said. "And Mark is your tree friend. Christ, Rose."

"*Marcus* is my tree friend. And, now…" I paused to consider. Did I really number the thing I'd seen lounging at the lip of the pond a friend? Under the false light of the kitchen, every little detail of the food between us, the full oddity of Theo struck me. But I decided yes. "And Theo is my shore friend."

"Shore friend," Father said. "I don't even want to know what that means."

"Does that mean he comes on shore?" Mother asked.

I shook my head. No. But I smiled.

"That means he has to *stay* at the edge of the pond."

"Oh," Mother said.

"Rose," Father said. "Let's talk about school. Math. Please. It's time to put your toys away."

I recalled Theo sliding back under the water.

"Okay," I said. I liked math. But I wasn't quite ready to move on. "He asked me if I dream," I said.

Father set his fork down. He shook his head slowly as he stared at his plate. Then, to Mother, he said, "Elaine? A little help here?"

"Rose," Mother said. Placating. Humouring. Mother was kind. "Your father just wants you to know what's important."

"I want her to be prepared, for Christ's sake," Father said. "Ten isn't so young, Rose. Ten is old enough to start really thinking about where your life is heading."

"Roger…" Mother said.

"No. Listen to me. Ten will become fourteen real fast. Then you're in high school, getting the grades you need to get into college. And once you're in college, forget it, Rose. You think college students have imaginary friends?"

"Maybe," I said.

"They do *not*," Father said. "And I don't wanna hear another word of this garbage."

"Roger..." Mother said.

"No," I said. "It's okay. We can talk about math. I like math, Father. Two plus one equals three. We can talk about math."

The next afternoon, Mother and Father up at the house, I sat on the tree-swing with Kathy until Theo crawled out of the water again.

He paused like he had the day before. Mid-reach. One arm forward, fingertips on the grass, bony back arched, eyes on me. He smelled of the bottom of the pond.

"Shore," I said. But I didn't mean it. And, Kathy gone, I slid over on the swing, making room.

Theo joined me there. He smelled of the bottom.

"None of your dreams will come true," he said. "None of your plans will happen. And none of your wishes will be answered."

"That's silly," I said.

His profile bothered me. The nose. I had to look away.

"All your love affairs will end in heartache. You will be abandoned, gaslit, treated terribly by those you mistake as kind."

"I'll certainly never have any of *those*."

I laughed.

Now, looking across the pond again, I do not.

Theo went on:

"You will come to resent and to blame and to loathe. You will not be strong enough to endure the hardships of your life. You will find you are too weak. The joy you feel now will wilt. You will not notice this as it happens. It will go slow."

"Silly, Theo," I said.

"The innocence you possess now will be taken from you, in the form of meannesses from others, embarrassing mistakes you make, by way of both the body and the mind. You will battle yourself, distrust yourself, hate yourself. The life you have ahead is war and you will not survive it."

"Well, I think I'd make a good soldier."

I looked to him, only to find him doing the same.

He was sitting too close.

I got off the swing. I walked. The grass was vivid green beneath my shoes. I wondered if Kathy and Marcus might return.

"You will gossip, you will lash out, you will burn bridges, you will lie, you will deceive. You will blame everyone but yourself. You will cheer for strife and for poverty. You will want others to fail as you fail."

"And *you* are mad," I said, turning to face him, only to find I'd taken fewer steps than I thought. "And you look funny, too."

I smiled. I felt funny myself.

Then, the oddest thing: Theo seemed to *slide* from the swing, as though he were made of putty. Boneless and without form. Dirty snow melting onto the grass. I stepped toward him and saw his eyes were still on mine. Eyes in the impossible form of the grass.

"Silly, Theo," I said.

Then he slid toward the pond, feet stretching for it first, before entering the dark water, and vanishing once again.

That night, I told Mother and Father I'd seen Theo again.

Father took me by my wrist and led me to the couch. He ordered me to sit. Mother and Father remained standing.

I did not describe for them what Theo looked like.

"Your mother and I have decided," Father said. "It's time you talked to someone."

"I talk to you two," I said.

"Dear," Mother said. She knelt by the couch. "You are an optimist, Rose. And it's my favourite thing about you. But what your father is trying to say is—"

"I'm not *trying* to say anything. I'm saying it. It's not right for a ten-year-old girl to hang on to her childhood this long. It's desperate and it's dumb."

I looked to Mother and laughed. I saw she was upset.

What a silly thing for Father to say.

"Your father wants you to speak to a counsellor at school," Mother said. "It's not unusual for kids to do that. You can tell your counsellor all about Kathy and Marcus and—"

"Theo," I said.

"Yes. Him, too."

"But you can't keep talking about them to us," Father said. "No more."

I nodded. I loved them both dearly. I understood they were only trying to be parents.

But when I saw Theo again the next day, no counselor was on my mind. In fact, explanations and descriptions were the last thing I was thinking about.

He didn't sit on the swing. He stood in the grass while I sat and plucked yellow clovers and made pictures on the lawn.

"You will come to despise this life," Theo said.

I laughed.

"You will detest friends. You will not achieve any of your goals. You will be average at whatever it is you attempt to do. You will discover you are not special. Nobody will see anything special in you. Lovers will use you for your body and employers will use you for your time. You will waste your years on matters that mean nothing to you. You will age before you know it. Time will have passed you by. You will die alone, without joy, heartbroken, angry, envious, and mean."

"Look," I said, pointing to the clover petals. "This looks like you!"

I had made a likeness in the grass. When I smiled up at him, I saw Theo was not interested in what I had done. Rather, he studied me, incredulous, it seemed, though I did not know that word then.

"Happiness is an illusion," he said, stepping toward me, then stepping onto the petals so that I saw his muddy toes up close. "You will become greedy. There will be no satisfaction. You will suffer anxiety and angst, jealousy and doubt. You will doubt everything you do. You will lose all belief in yourself. You will mistake chance for success, then realise your mistake, and live with your mistake, too."

"You ruined my picture," I said. "But don't worry. I can make another. Maybe this time... Father."

Theo sat close to me, his legs crossed like mine. I looked away from his legs. The way they bent. It hurt to see.

I look away from the grass now, too. It still hurts to see.

"Rose," he said. But I couldn't look Theo in the eye for long. He reached across the smashed petals and took my wrist. "You will not succeed, you will not be loved, you will not be happy."

"You're getting excited," I said. He was. His voice had more urgency. He quite nearly hissed.

Sometimes, now, I hear similar sounds in the folds of daily life. In the woods, as I hike.

"Are you listening, Rose?"

"This could be Mother's ear," I said.

"Are you listening, Rose?"

"Yes. I am listening, Theo."

We held eyes then, the longest we ever did that. I smiled and tried to channel all the warmth of the sun and the day. I wanted to make Theo smile.

He did not smile. Rather, he looked like he'd swallowed sadness and it was lodged in his bony throat.

"Do you have hair?" I asked him, my eyes back on the petals, arranging them into a face. "I can't tell for all the mud. But if you do, I could use some of these stems for that. Then we could get some muck from the pond and—"

But Theo was gone. And when I looked to the surface of the water, I saw the faintest echo of a ripple and I knew he'd gone back under again.

That night, I did not speak of Theo to Mother and Father. Still, Father went on about the world, complaining about the people on television and the people at work. He spoke about money and Mother smiled sadly and reminded him that we always seemed to *make it work*. I liked that phrase then and I like it now. But Father, he couldn't be stopped, it seemed, ranting about the neighbours next and then his own brother, my Uncle Jerry. He said Jerry was wasting his time on the *investment* and that he, Father, ought to talk him out of doing it. Mother agreed but reminded Father Jerry was his own man.

"He sounds excited," I said.

Father looked across the table to Mother as if I'd brought up Theo and Kathy and Marcus again. But I hadn't.

"He is," Father said. "And that's exactly the problem."

I look back to the house now, can see it so easily from the height I've grown to. It felt so far in those days, as if the pond were another country, another planet only I knew the pleasure of.

That night, from bed, I heard Mother gasp down the hall, but she was laughing by the time I'd reached their bedroom door.

"Never mind," Father said to me. "Your mother just got scared by a piece of fuzz."

Mother looked to me and laughed some more and then I laughed, too. She didn't like bugs. Didn't want them in her bedroom anyway.

"It's okay," she told me. "Go to sleep, honey. We love you."

Father rolled his eyes at Mother's being afraid and I turned and took the dark hall back to my bedroom. On the way, I saw Theo in the dark at the bottom of the stairs.

"Theo," I whispered.

His eyes darted around the first floor and I thought, *He's never been in a house before.*

He looked up at me, started climbing the steps.

He said:

"There is only failure and doubt in your future, Rose. There is no pleasure, no resolve, no closure. You will find nothing when you seek meaning. You will be jealous of the relationships your friends have with one another and with their lovers. They will not be real friends to you. They will not care about you. You will come to hate them as they hate you."

"Theo," I whispered again. "You shouldn't be in here, silly!"

"Rose," he said, with what I now know to be desperation in his eyes. He left mucky footprints on the steps. "There is no happy ending. No real friendship. No joy. You will not discover some secret meaning, there is no meaning. You will die sick, diseased, unsettled, alone."

I looked to Mother and Father's door. They were still in there. I thought of Mother frightened of a piece of fuzz. I looked to the bony, muddy man climbing the stairs. He was almost at the top.

"Shore," I told him. I can still hear my own voice saying it. Sometimes, I can even imitate it exactly as it was done. With strength.

Theo paused at the top of the stairs. His eyes close to mine. Only the banister between us.

"You will resent."

"No, Theo."

"You will loathe."

"No, Theo."

"You will hate."

"*No,* Theo."

"Rose?" Father called from up the hall. Theo's eyes glistened in the dark house.

"Yes, Father?"

"Are you in your bedroom?"

"Almost!"

"Why only almost?"

Theo tilted his head then, as though interested in something he'd just learned.

He said:

"You will blame your father for your worldview. You will resent his worldview even after he dies."

I shook my head and smiled, but it felt like Mother's style of smile. Not quite full.

Theo began to back up then, to vanish into the darkness of the stairs.

"Yes," he said. "You will resent…"

"Wait!" I said. Because I didn't like how our conversation ended. I didn't like how I felt.

Theo's eyes shone once more, halfway down the steps, just as Father stepped out of the bedroom.

"Rose," he said. Anger in his voice. "Tell me you are *not* talking to your imaginary friends right now."

He had a hand on his hip. Another balled in a fist at his side.

"I was," I said, smiling. And I felt, for a second, like myself again.

Father grabbed me by the wrist and dragged me hard to my bedroom.

"Roger?" Mother called. "What's the matter out there?"

At my room, Father used as much force as he ever had, shoving me forward toward my bed. In the lamplight, I saw exasperation on his face, even as he stood upon the dozens of drawings I'd made.

I can still hear the crinkling of all that paper. I can still feel the worry of his bare feet ruining what I'd done.

"Rose," Father said. "That's *it*. *No more!*"

He was shouting. Mother called from down the hall.

"Father—" I said.

"No, Rose!" he said. "I will not let my daughter grow up with her head in the clouds, believing everything is a *Goddamn* daydream."

"Father—"

"*No.*"

With finality. An ending.

I kept quiet, watching him as he decided he'd made his point. I saw, too, as his eyes travelled to the floor, to the dozens of drawings he'd asked me to pick up all the time.

I can still see his expression, now, as if he too was standing out here between the house and the pond.

Father's expression changed.

"Rose," he said, his voice vulnerable now, softer. "Is this... Theo?"

He crouched and came up with a drawing I'd done the night before.

"Yes," I said.

We stared at one another for the longest time ever.

I hadn't told Mother or Father what he looked like.

"Theo..." he said.

I hadn't told Mother or Father what he looked like.

"Yes."

He studied the drawing, held it carefully.

"I'm sorry," he said then. "I'm... sorry I shoved you."

"It's okay," I said. "You were just angry."

I expected him to get frustrated with that. But this time he didn't.

He only looked once more at the drawing.

I hadn't told Mother and Father what he looked like.

And I hadn't lived long enough yet to know that what he was doing was remembering.

He let the paper fall to the floor.

And I, looking out at the pond, can see the wrinkles in that paper as I see the ripples the ducks make in the water. The family that lives here now was kind enough to allow me to take a look, as I'd been in the neighbourhood and struck with the desire to see it again.

Father, I think.

To look at it, it's just a pond. And I suppose that's all it really ever was. But there was an important moment in my life when it was more than that. When it was the stage upon which enormous characters performed.

I turn away from it, having had my fill. But I glance back once, just long enough for Marcus to say, *Goodbye.*

FOR ALL THE DEAD

Angeline B. Adams and Remco van Straten

Those were different times, you have to understand, before the sluice was built and the brick road was laid, and before the steamships came to the Soltcamp, though Geertruida had already seen them in her visions. She'd seen that other thing too, but few had believed her then; not until it was too late. Not until the sea had taken most of the men.

★　　★　　★

There were not many of us there on All Saints' Day that year, and I was the youngest. I thought I was already a woman like the rest of them, though I was still as flat at the front as at the back. We huddled around the grave, with our dark shawls drawn tight against the rain and the cutting wind. Just the one grave, one slab of stone, with a single date and over three-score names below it.

We all thought back to when it happened, twelve winters earlier, to the day. I was little, and hid behind my mother's skirts when she opened the door to the rain-soaked men. They had their hats in their hands. One of them smiled at me, though his eyes looked away. Father was lost at sea, he said, and Mother gripped my hand so tightly that it hurt. She'd been up all night as the storm howled around the house, she told me much later. I'd slept through it; the sleep of the innocent, she said. A dozen of the Soltcamp's boats, most of the village's fleet, hadn't come back to the harbour that morning. At first I thought that if my father was lost, he could be found. When I asked my mother about him, her mouth would pull into a thin line, and she'd shake her head. When I asked again, later, she snapped at me, told me not to be stupid, so I learned not to ask. It was a long time, though, before I stopped looking out of the window when the wind had blown landwards overnight, still hoping he'd come walking up the street.

★   ★   ★

The way my mother told it, at first, after the storm, there had been
sympathy aplenty. Our plight had been reported in newspapers far and
wide, and parcels with food and clothes streamed in; more than we knew
what to do with. The government started a relief fund and thousands of
folk contributed, even half cents and wooden bits from poor people with
little to spare, and the newspaper men were there to note down our tears
of gratitude. Then the order of the day resumed for the rest of the country,
and the women of the Soltcamp moved from the front pages to the small
print in the back of the papers, and slowly we were forgotten. All too soon,
the fishing boats had to pull out again; old boats that had been patched up
by old men, sailed by young boys. Nobody cheered for them when they
pulled out, and there were tears on the decks and on the shore, but what else
could they have done? Fishing is the life of the Soltcamp; saltwater courses
through our veins, and our men know how to do nothing else.

  All the widows and daughters, mothers and sisters came to the cemetery
on the first anniversary of that night. I don't remember much of that first
time; just that I wanted to play with the autumn leaves between the grey
stones, but Mother held me close. I'm not sure who first thought of it. Old
Martje, probably, who'd lost most of all – with a husband and her six sons
gone, she forged a new family from the women of the Soltcamp. She'd
bent down and said something to me. I can't remember what; just that it
felt right. Old Martje went only a few years later. She'd never complained,
but died of a broken heart just the same. Or so my mother said.

★   ★   ★

I looked round at the weathered faces as the pastor made his way through
the sermon. Don't ask me what he preached; it's not important. My
mother listened with her expression drawn in, thinking her own thoughts
as usual. But she was there, at least, unlike so many others. Some had died,
or become too frail to come out to the cemetery. Some of the younger
women had moved inland, and we never heard from them again. Then
there were those who just stayed away.

  "It's in the past," they said, and who can argue with that? Bertha was
there, though, and Sijke. Aafien was there too. She'd married again, only

to lose another husband to the sea. That's bad luck of the cruel sort. But it didn't happen to most of us, I told myself. I was engaged to a fisherman, after all. Well, nearly engaged. I was so sure that he'd ask me soon, though he was only sixteen himself, and not long out on the boat.

So many of the women who had come even one year earlier were not there now. I'm sure that Bertha had gone round to see them all, God bless her. A large woman, with wet brown eyes like a seal's, she stood next to the pastor and nodded encouragement at his words. She'd been the first to welcome him when the new road had brought him to the village this past summer, and she'd asked him to speak, as our old pastor had done. Maybe that's what had kept the others away; they were wary of the young man, as they were of the road that now linked us with the other villages. With his spectacles, shaven chin and straight trousers he was, as they said, "not of the sea". Our old pastor had been a fisherman's son and now lay nearby, under the elm tree. Would it have made any difference if he'd been alive? Would more of us have turned up that late afternoon in November? Well, the new pastor was here now, and the few of us who'd come listened dutifully as he wrestled through the words on his sodden bit of paper.

"And although the grave of these husbands, fathers, brothers and sons is the sea, their immortal souls are in Heaven. Oh Lord, may we give praise to Thee, who gathered them in Thy arms, to keep them until the day of Resurrection." He used language like that when he preached, peppered with *thines* and *thous*, and *shalts* and *speaketh*. I suppose they taught them that at the seminary.

"Well, he's still young. He'll silt over," Bertha muttered. A final "Amen" rippled around the group, then we slowly stood back from the stone slab.

"But we mustn't forget about the sea!"

We turned at the sound of the voice. Geertruida emerged from under the large elm tree that watched over the old pastor's grave. I'd not noticed her, but she had a knack for not being seen if she didn't want to be. Some, though, swore they'd seen her kneeling at the old pastor's grave at night, gesturing as if she was talking with him. She was so old that nobody could remember when she hadn't been old, and she stood propped up by her layers of black skirts and the kind of starched bodice that no one else wore anymore, even then. A few wisps of fine, white hair had escaped from Geertruida's cap and stuck to her wet forehead.

"Yes, the sea," she said. "I hear talk of God and of mercy, but who spared a word for what really rules our lives?"

The pastor looked her up and down, his eyes bulging and his mouth opening and closing like a landed herring. "But know ye not, woman, that God is the master of all, including the sea?"

"Aye. God may be the sea's master, but the sea doesn't always listen to Him." She snorted and spat on the ground. She raised her voice and adopted his tone. "The sea is like Himself: she gives, and she takes away."

Aafien and Sijke nodded. They'd heard it before, as had we all. It was part of the ritual: the acknowledgement that though we lived off the sea, we paid a steep price for it. But Geertruida's tone had never been scornful before. She lowered her voice again.

"And from all of us, the sea has taken away so much, so very much. How many brothers have you lost, Sijke? And how old would your son have been now, Bertha?" Neither of them answered. Her pale eyes met mine and she looked straight into my soul. "What do you remember of your father, Hanne? Just his face and hands? Or do you still remember his voice, the way he walked, and how he smiled when your mother was nearby? No, I didn't think so."

Geertruida never made examples of us individually like this, and it hurt that she paraded the fleeting nature of my memories to tell the new pastor what he should have known: that God had no answer or balm for our grief.

I glanced at my mother, wounded, but her face was closed off again. Others murmured and shifted uneasily. We waited for Geertruida to continue, but she dismissed us with a curt nod and hobbled off. We stood there for a time, remembering the truths she had told us each year since the men were lost, after Pastor Arend had spoken: that the sea's voice carried the promise of a bountiful catch, but sometimes that promise was a lie, and the sea's true gift was a wet grave. Then she'd remind us of how the sea gets hold of you, drawing you to herself. "Wade in just a few feet, and you'll feel her pull."

"The men of the Soltcamp lie with their Mistress Sea at night," she'd say. "But she's fickle. She loves them, but she also hates them; hates how they plough her with the keels of their boats at night, and then go home to their wives to be fed and to sleep." I'd giggled at that just the once, when I was old enough to understand her words, but Mother had cuffed me, and I'd nodded along sagely since. It felt wrong not to hear those words this year. We all glanced at each other, and then quickly away again, self-conscious and lacking the closeness Geertruida's words always gave us to the men we had lost. When it became clear that nobody was going to speak up in her place, Sijke said, "Well, that's another year gone," and that brought a guilty relief. The group dispersed.

My mother still stood there as their broad shapes swayed towards the churchyard gate, her face as empty as the grave in front of her. Then she nodded at the pastor, and hooked her arm through mine. It was all I could do not to shake her off.

★ ★ ★

Silence hung between me and my mother from the moment we left the cemetery gate behind us. We rounded the bend of the old chalk oven and walked in the shadow of the dike that kept the sea from the low houses of the Soltcamp. "I've never seen Geertruida angry," I said finally.

My mother shrugged. "I've seen her angry, Hanne. But there's anger and anger. There's the violent tempest, and then there's the cold, frosted-over anger that endures."

I didn't see then what I now know: that my mother meant her own anger and resentment, kept away from me, kneaded up like a heavy ball deep inside her. That was why she grew so silent every year, fearing she'd say something that couldn't be unsaid, that shouldn't be spoken out loud. Because just as you can't curse God without being cursed, you can't throw insults at the sea without them being answered. Maybe people from further inland can, but not the people of the Soltcamp. No, not us.

"But why did Geertruida leave?" I asked. "Would she not speak because there were so few of us? Was she angry that the others didn't come?"

"Maybe. Or maybe it's because Pastor Arend is below the soil now instead of on it. Yes, you laugh: him a man of the cloth and her... well, looking to the other side of the dike. But Geertruida and the pastor respected each other, and today... maybe she just doesn't know how to go on without him. You don't know how much you need a person until you miss them. You feel so much that you'd rather not feel at all."

She looked at the dike – or was it away from me? – and I understood that she was no longer talking about the pastor and Geertruida.

"Well, I know what I feel, and how much I love Fedde," I said. "I don't need to lose him to know that!"

Then I did what I did, though I knew that no good could come of it. Why? As I said, I was just a girl, and the stone steps up the dike were there. I ran up them, ignoring my mother who called after me, and looked down the other side. Gulls bobbed on the water, glided on the wind or climbed against it, and the wind brought me their shrieks. The sea and the sky almost blended into each other, and only the slightly darker grey lines, which were the islands, separated them. Beyond, the boats would have cast out their nets, and Fedde would be on one of them. I breathed in deeply.

"You bring him back, you hear?" I shouted, and shook my fist at the sea. "You bring them all back!" As if in answer, a sudden gust of icy wind came from the sea and pulled at my skirts. I turned and skipped down the steps to where my mother waited. I'll never forget the look on her face – it was as if she'd recognised someone she'd hoped never to see again. She grabbed my shoulders.

"You shouldn't have done that," she said, and shook me violently. "You shouldn't have done that."

We walked home in silence, while around us it quickly grew dark.

*   *   *

I took no pleasure in my supper. I don't think Mother enjoyed hers either. Not a word passed between us as we put away the dishes and started our evening chores. The small oil lamp on the table gave too little light to sew by, but we could knit with our eyes closed, and for the next hour the only sound in our small house was the clicking of our needles. Then the banging of unfastened shutters somewhere in the alley disturbed the rhythm. It started with that niggle of irritation at some neighbour's neglect, but soon we both laid down our work to listen to the sounds outside. The windows creaked in their frames and rain clattered against the panes and the clay tiles of the roof above us. My mother reached out and laid a hand on mine.

"There's been worse storms than this," she said. She took in the way my eye went from my father's photograph, in its finely carved wooden frame, to the young man's face in the cheap card frame next to it. That picture was new; it had only been taken that summer.

"He's a good boy. Not the type I'd have pictured you with" – she squeezed my hand and I held back the protest I'd been about to make – "but steady, and he can stand up to you."

"I hope he can stand up to the storm." The knot in my chest loosened when I said it aloud. "I don't know how you did it, waiting for Father."

My mother sighed. "That's what you get when you go with a fisherman, Hanne. You marry a fisherman and you'll fret when the storms come. I don't know a woman that doesn't, not if she's honest. But we put a brave face on it, and we never make a fuss in front of them. They've a hard enough life without thinking of us worried at home. Or you can find yourself a farmer, and know where he is all the time, and that he's breathing air and not water."

"But the farmer – he can be gored by a bull. Or work on the field from daybreak to sundown year after year and then die where he stands." I looked at the knitting in my lap. "Besides, I don't want to choose – I want Fedde."

*   *   *

Fedde. So much time has passed, it's hard to remember what he really looked like. He wasn't very tall, and he had red hair and the pale skin to go with it. You'd not think much of him when you saw him, and it was easy to mistake his quietness for mildness. He knew his own mind, though, and when he spoke it was always worth listening to. I'm sure he could've gone to the city to study if he hadn't had to go to the sea. But he did go, so he left school and childhood behind at the same time as I did, and to mark the passage we went to the May Fair in Ollerom.

We'd saved up what money we could and I had dressed in my Sunday finery, lace cap and embroidered bodice. The women who sat in front of their houses at the edge of the village cooed at us, then shook their heads, laughing, and went back to mending their husbands' nets. From the shadow of the linden trees that lined the dirt road to Ollerom, I waved at the farmhands at work in the fields and wondered if they would be given time off for the fair. When I looked back at the Soltcamp it looked so small to me, dwarfed as it was by the green wall of the sea-dike.

Nowadays you just step in your motorcar and it will take you to Ollerom in less than ten minutes, but back then going to Ollerom was like travelling to a whole different world. None of the weather-beaten, salt-eaten brickwork and parched wood of the Soltcamp met us there. No; where the road turned from mud to cobbles, the houses had white gables and big windows. They had lawns with big trees, and little moats with ducks in them.

We headed straight towards the village green and made a few rounds of the fair to decide how best to spend our money. Fedde smirked when I chose the fortune-teller.

"You might as well throw your money on the cobbles," he said, but he too was intrigued by the old woman with the colourful skirts, who sucked her pipe as she stared into the black mirror.

"So, he's going to be blond and handsome, then, your man," Fedde said afterwards. "She might at least have had the tact to describe someone a bit closer to myself."

"It looked enough like you to me, Fedde," I said to him, but now I'm not so sure. The face I'd seen so dimly could also have been my own warped reflection, a suggestion conjured up by the old woman or an image of the man I'd eventually marry.

I nudged Fedde. I'd seen him frown. "What would you like to do?"

"There." He pointed at a wooden hut, smaller than an outhouse even, picture frames hung on the outside. "Professor Knowler's Daguerreotypes. You saw a fleeting image in that mirror. This promises a more permanent portrait; someone's image fixed with light, without the need of paints or charcoal."

I couldn't help but laugh as the professor fitted Fedde on the chair, and pinned his head in place with a metal contraption. Then he disappeared under a black blanket and looked at Fedde through his wooden box on legs. These moments stand out clearly in my memory, even though Fedde's face doesn't. But our minds are strange, and can be tugged at by small currents even when weighted by heavy cargo. How quickly a mood can turn.

"He'd better towel that seat down when he's done with the fish head." Those words reached me through the crowd; spoken low, yet clear enough for me to hear. I glanced over. Three young men in the brushed black cloth and knee breeches of well-off farmers. One of them raised his eyebrows at me. "What's that, fish head? You want to try a real man?" He stepped towards me, and before I could react he held my arm.

"Breathe through your mouth, though," laughed one of his friends. "And take a bath afterwards," added the other. Then Fedde stood between me and the young farmer.

"Sure, the smell of the sea will wash off," he said. "But the stench of manure will never leave you. It comes from the inside."

And that was all it took, really. They glared at Fedde, and threw some more words at him that we from the Soltcamp were used to hearing. Fedde, though, was not afraid of them, and they were not prepared to get hurt over a slight, even if Fedde would come out of a fight much worse. So they left. The Daguerreotype man was in the outhouse, so his assistant told us, so we waited. Fedde hugged me close and my head rested on his shoulder. I felt guilty when I caught myself sniffing for the smell of fish. Then the professor appeared and held a small, cardboard folder out to us.

"It's done, but I shan't put my name to it," he said, and opened the folder. Inside, as through a sea mist, Fedde's face peered at me.

"It's all I could make of it in my laboratorium," he explained. "You shouldn't have leapt off like a jackrabbit. Still, with the work involved, and the chemicals…"

Fedde silenced him with his hand and paid him his fee. It was a full night's wages, and when Fedde gave the photograph to me I first refused it. What did I care for a blurred portrait if I was going to share my life with him?

* * *

My mother stamped out a spark that had somehow escaped the fireguard and leapt onto the rug. The battering of the rain on the roof had redoubled in force.

"There's another way," she said, and sat down again. She glanced at the dark window with its stripes of rain, and swallowed. She seemed to weigh whether she should go on.

"This other way… is to know for sure."

"What do you mean, know for sure?" It came out more harshly than I'd meant it to, as a lot of things had done lately. Mother gave me that glare that said, *You're no longer a child to smack around the ears. You're a grown-up now, and I don't know that I like the woman you've become.*

"Know for sure whether he'll come back."

"But you can't know that. You didn't know when Father was going to die."

Mother stood up again and began to pull undergarments off the clothes horse. She folded them angrily, keeping her face turned away from me.

"I did know," she said at last, in a tight voice. "I knew because I was told. And it didn't bring me any peace, and it didn't stop me from waiting." She slapped the last of the laundry on the table and sat back again. She took up her knitting, but her hands soon fell down in her lap.

"Oh, Geertruida told me a lot of things, everything I asked, though reluctantly. She warned me, but I wouldn't listen, as you aren't going to listen, because youth is impatient and wants to run ahead of nature's course. I was never one for superstitions or fancies back then, and I wouldn't have gone to her, if it weren't for you. I was so worried. Finally I tucked you in and set off to Geertruida's. And we drank tea, and she read the leaves."

Mother looked exhausted. Though not a young woman, suddenly she looked old.

"On my way over I'd resolved to not ask about your father directly; to find a way of asking, of knowing but *not* knowing. Well, I'd drunk my tea, gave her the cup to read the leaves, and there it escaped from my lips: 'My husband, is he alive?' And she shook her head, and that was that."

"She could have guessed," I said. I couldn't help myself. "It was such a bad storm, and then if he'd come home, after all, you'd have been so relieved you wouldn't have cared that she was wrong."

"No. I knew she was right. I could feel that he'd died. And that meant that all the other things she said then would also come true. And they did! Small things; things you'd laugh about if I told you. All came true but that one thing."

"What was it?" I asked. She didn't answer. A shadow seemed to cross her face. It was as if she'd caught herself in a lie.

"I thought about leaving here and finding a position somewhere as a maid, anything. Then I thought, who'd have me with a little girl in tow? So I stayed, and waited for the tide to bring his body in. The sea, though... she never gave him back to me."

Silence fell between us.

"If it were Fedde," I said at last, "I'd have to see him to believe he'd drowned."

A pit opened up inside me, and within that pit there was a vortex like the ones the men told stories about: a vortex that sucked me into its depths. I rose, my knitting falling to the floor.

"We'll go to Geertruida."

My mother closed her eyes and sighed. "Yes, we will."

★   ★   ★

I still wonder how we got ourselves safely to Geertruida's. It was a violent rage that blew between the houses, and we moved against it slowly and hunched over, propping each other up like crones. From the moment we'd opened the door, the wind and rain had fought us like a living, evil thing. We'd wrapped up in heavy shawls and pulled knit caps over our hoods, but still we were quickly chilled to the bone. We stayed as close to the houses as we could, the dike a black wall across the street. Our storm lantern hardly lifted the darkness around us, and but a few slivers of light escaped from the shuttered homes. When we came to the gap between the houses, where our road met the one to the harbour on the other side of the dike, a roof tile sheared past our heads. We nodded at each other and then, foot by foot, made it across the road, while the storm roared and tore at us.

Brick paving gave way to cobbles, then stone chips and mud, as the storm lashed our faces above the scarves that covered nose and mouth. Geertruida's small house, now gone, was set back from the others at the edge of the village. We fought through the shrubs that had grown over the path, and only felt the scratches much, much later, so cold and miserable were we. Then Geertruida's door opened in front of us before we'd even knocked, and we practically fell into her house.

★   ★   ★

She helped us out of our outer layers, and hung them to drip out on the tiled floor. She gestured us to her fireside, and as we sat down she stirred up the fire and added more wood to it. The room was small and crammed with the remnants of a long life: mismatched furniture, badly drawn portraits of men and women who might resemble her if you squinted, and shelves full of tins, bottles and clay jars; all dented, scuffed or cracked. A paraffin lamp hung low over the dark red tablecloth, where a skinny, old cat slowly blinked at me with its single eye. Geertruida moved about the room, gathering all she needed, I realised, to brew her tea. She hadn't said a word to us yet, and I felt silly for imposing upon an old woman so late at night. Mother stopped me with a hand on my arm when I wanted to offer help. She opened her basket and took out a small loaf and a jar of jam, which the old woman accepted with a curt nod. A transaction had begun, and we had to see it through to the end.

Geertruida assembled the herbs in the pot, boiled the water and steeped the tea.

"Not for me, thank you," my mother said when Geertruida put a chipped cup on a glued saucer in front of her. The old woman smiled.

"The first cup's for warming the insides; the second's for reading. I've told you enough to last a lifetime, and I know why you're here tonight." A look passed between them, and my mother let her pour. "Now, as for you, young lady," Geertruida nodded at me, "drink up while it's hot, and in time you'll tell me what you want to know."

She grabbed a blanket and settled herself in a wicker chair.

"I put a drop of something in, for the cold," said Geertruida, now a bundle of fabric topped with a wrinkled face. The old cat crouched at the edge of the table, judged the distance and leapt into her lap. It curled up in a little ball and its purring joined the ticking of the wooden clock on the mantelpiece. It was just past midnight, I saw, and it was All Souls' Day. I finished my tea. It had a strange, but not unpleasant, aftertaste.

"Gretha dear, put the kettle on for another cup," Geertruida said. Mother nodded and went to fill the kettle. I nursed the empty teacup in my lap and looked at the specks of tea leaf in the bottom, and I had a thought.

"Geertruida, would you read the leaves now? It would soothe my mind as the tea has my body."

She peered at me. A hand came from underneath the blanket and waved me over. I rose and stumbled, turning to the table for support. I held still there, bent over the table, with my own cup still in my hand and my mother's near to it.

"Are you alright, dear?" Geertruida asked from behind me.

"Yes, just got up too quickly. The warmth," I said. As I slowly straightened, I swapped the teacup in my hand for my mother's. Still turned away from Geertruida, I smiled. She would read my mother's tea leaves, and if she predicted a dead sailor, then that'd be my father and not Fedde. If she saw a sailor coming home, then that would only show that she didn't have the sight.

"The future of all is writ," she said and looked me in the eyes, "and while few can know it, none can escape it. Turn the cup upside down on the saucer. Good. Now hand me the saucer, dear."

I nodded and did what she asked. She held the saucer up just below her eye level, then lowered it, turning it now with both hands and looking at the pattern of leaves. Just as I was about to ask what I had come to ask, she shushed me.

"No need," she said. "You're your mother's daughter, more than you know. There's only one thing you'd want to know. I'd urge you not to, but you'd persist. Let's skip all that."

She moved her head close to the saucer and muttered while she moved it ever so slightly. Then she lowered the saucer. "He'll be back at daybreak. That's all I will tell you."

"Thank God!" I whispered.

"No, not God. He's got nothing to do with it." She looked at me, with those dark eyes, and I, I laughed. Was there indeed nothing more to it than some tea with herbs to calm the worried, and a bit of meddling dressed up as fortune-telling to make us feel that we'd got something out of it? If she'd wanted to fool us based on a few tea slops, at least she could have done a better job of it.

"I've waited and worried for hours, and then we both got soaked and frozen to the bone coming here, and that's all you have for me?"

"Hanne, behave!" my mother cut through me. "We came unbidden, yet we were welcomed."

Geertruida drew back into the mountain of her blanket for a moment, and sighed. When she spoke, it was as if her voice came from far away.

"There was a time when I'd have told you all that I could see; when I'd have told you what lies beyond the day to come: the pleasure, but also the pain. You know this, Margretha," she said to my mother. "Tell Hanne what I told you when you came to ask me about Libertus."

I glanced over, but my mother shook her head.

"Hanne, listen to me," Geertruida drew my attention back to her. "Your life's story is not written in leaves on porcelain. The road you'll take is not laid out in the lines on your hands. It's not in the stars and not in a soot-covered mirror either. I know more than other people do, that's true; most of it the gatherings of a long life. If there is a secret, Hanne, it is this: I listen to the sea, and hear her speak in a language that's older than people, older than plants and animals. The men of this village know of this language, know that they're being called, though they don't understand her words. I do, and she tells me things. Sometimes, she listens to me when I talk to her in turn. That's her indulging me, Hanne, not obeying. No: the sea, she may hear you, but never does she obey. Never."

Her voice had grown soft and I'd had to come closer to hear her. The urge to ridicule her had drained out of me, leaving little in its place. Geertruida grabbed my hand and gave it a squeeze. It was a small hand, much like a bird's claw, yet it was firm.

"You'll be fine, girl. Your life won't always be easy, but you're strong, like your mother."

I felt my mother's hand on my shoulder. "Well, Hanne, you've got what you wanted. We ought to grant Geertruida the night's peace and leave."

"You'll do no such thing. Not in this weather," the old woman piped. "You drink your tea, and then take your rest in the bed cabinet."

She forestalled our protests with a quick hand. "It's made up for you. I knew you were coming. I'll sit up here, by the fire. It's better for my aches and pains than the bed."

★　　★　　★

I woke in the grey before dawn to the sound of my mother stirring up the remains of the fire. I rubbed my eyes and straightened the clothes I had slept in. Geertruida still snored gently under her blanket. Her mouth hung open, exposing the brown pegs of her few remaining teeth. The cat still lay tightly curled in her lap and glared at Mother with its one eye.

"You'll wake her," I whispered. Mother shook her head and wiped her hands on her skirts.

"She'll sleep on. It'll save her waking up in a cold house."

Though my outer garments were still damp when I put them on, the sound of birds outside lifted my spirits, and a look out of the small window showed a glow on the horizon, a promise of daylight. My mother scribbled a short note for the old lady before we drew our shawls around us and carefully closed the door behind us.

★ ★ ★

The village had taken a beating overnight. The streets were littered with branches and roof tiles, and we had to scramble around a fallen tree. Shutters had been wrenched off their hinges, and at one house a chimney had been torn out and crashed through the roof.

A fisherman came towards us from the crossing where we'd had such difficulties the night before, where the road went over the dike. He passed us on the other side of the street, completely sodden, his head bent, one foot barely dragging ahead of the other. I didn't know him and thought he must've been one of the men who came from one of the other villages to crew our boats.

"Any news from the *Morgenster*? The Husenga men? Fedde?"

I called out to him when he was close enough. He didn't turn his head, seeming not to have heard me at all.

"Leave him be," my mother said. "After a night like that he deserves his rest. Look, you go straight up to the harbour if you like and meet your boy there. I'll see whether the house still has a roof. I'll have coffee ready for you both."

I thanked her and trotted up the road to the dike. It had begun to rain again, but what was a little rain, I thought, after that night? I was out of breath when I reached the top of the dike, and the strong gusts of wind that came from the expanse of the sea took me aback.

That's why at first I didn't see him. Fedde. The way he stood and his shape, even in the thick clothing of a fisherman; I'd know him at any distance, at the end of the world. He waited at the water's edge and stared towards the dike, to the left of me, his head at an angle as if he was listening to something. Then he started walking. I called to him and waved, and ran down the dike towards him. Then I froze.

There were no masts. No boats had pulled into the harbour that morning.

Behind Fedde, a lad I'd gone to school with hauled himself onto the wooden jetty, water gushing off him. Then came another man, who I didn't recognise. And another, and another. They all walked in my direction, towards the road that went over the dike, as they stared beyond me. They trudged as though they had walked the length of the sea bed itself to return home. I walked slowly backwards out of their way, and just watched as they filed past me, including my Fedde himself. It was all I could do. I thought of leaping in front of him, of stopping him, but then I looked at his unseeing eyes, the strands of seaweed draping his head and his shoulders, and his open mouth in which I thought I saw something moving. I reached out my hand as he passed, then withdrew it because I knew the truth already: I couldn't touch him.

Then I saw the man who I knew only from the little carved picture frame in our front room, and from the glances my mother gave it when she thought I wasn't watching. For a moment I thought he looked at me, then realised his gaze went through me, in the direction of home. A memory perhaps, of who he once was. Then, I could only watch as he too walked past me. My head rang with the words the old woman had said when she looked at my mother's tea leaves: "He'll be back at daybreak."

I turned and saw a blanket of fog where the sea should have been. On the horizon the sun was a pink, flattened disc, trying to escape the pull of the sea, but failing. I no longer heard the wind; didn't hear birds; didn't hear anything. My father crested the dike and bent off to the left, away from the stagnant sun, along with all the other dead men. I followed them into the village, in the silence of that stretched-out moment in which the world held its breath, through the deserted streets up to the cemetery. At the gate, Pastor Arend stood to welcome them, his clothing dusted with the earth he had clambered through to meet them, his faithful Bible in his hand. I waited as Fedde went inside, and then my father and all the other men who'd been gone for so long.

The old pastor closed the gate behind them. At last, they had found their way home.

THE GIRL IN THE POOL
Bracken MacLeod

The day was bright, and closing the door behind him felt for a moment to Rory like having a black bag slipped over his head. He waited by the front door, letting his eyes adjust to the gloom. Before long, shapes began to coalesce. In the room to the left of the hallway, he could see a sofa and an end table. At the far end was a standing chess board with oversized marble pieces and, next to that, a big floor lamp that resembled one of those outdoor sculptures you'd find in front of a bank or a hotel instead of inside someone's house. If it weren't for the small light fixtures jutting from the sides of it, he wouldn't have thought it had any function other than to cost money and take up space. So much of the stuff he found in these kinds of places was like that. A globe on a mahogany stand in a study or a life-sized porcelain wolfhound in a foyer had no purpose other than to justify the size of some interior decorator's fee. The chess board seemed like that. There weren't any chairs nearby where players could sit, just the sofa too far away to be of any use. He had friends who liked chess – they'd learned how to play in the Navy or in prison and their boards were cheap and fit in a box you could store on a shelf. The way this room looked, he doubted anyone spent more time in it than it took to tie their shoelaces on the way out the door. It was a drawing room, not a *living* room. Only the housecleaners who dusted it once a month spent any real time in there.

He followed Tod down the hallway past the dining room on the right toward the stairs. This was a second storey job. While he imagined there were plenty of expensive things on the first floor they could take if they wanted – Bluetooth speakers and nice silverware – the money in a place like this was always upstairs in the bedroom and the office. Places where people kept jewellery and watches and money. If he could find a chequebook, his girl, Gloria, could make it rain before anyone even thought to go looking for it. That sort of thing would be locked in a desk.

As if a desk drawer lock could keep him out when the front door deadbolt had opened up for him like a panhandler's palm.

He followed Tod up. The stairs creaked under his weight and he held his breath, waiting for the sounds of barking and claws clacking on hardwood. He knew the dog was in the beach house on the Cape with its owners, but the smell was there and the scar on his forearm itched. Even if there was no dog, there was a *sense* of hound in the house and that got Rory's hackles up. Fuck man's best friend; he was a cat person. A cat scratch might get infected if you were lazy about taking care of it, but you weren't going to have to get twenty-seven stitches and have permanent tingling in your fingers because someone's housecat tried to bite your fuckin' arm off.

At the top of the stairs, Tod pointed to the left. "Marta says the office is that way. I'll check out the bedroom." He stalked off to the right. Tod was an okay partner; he didn't fuck around, and he didn't have any weird kinks that'd make the police worry the job was done by anyone other than run-of-the-mill burglars. Rory had worked with a guy a couple of times who insisted on taking a pair of women's underwear as a souvenir from each house they broke into. *That* sort of thing gave detectives incentive, imagining it might 'escalate'. Even if the dipshit never graduated from panty-raids to something worse, Rory didn't want the kind of heat that came with getting pinched coming out of a place with a woman's underwear in his pockets along with her jewellery. Prosecutors didn't like burglars, but they *hated* perverts.

Still, better not to get caught either way.

He walked down the hall and opened the door to what was supposed to be the office. He saw a treadmill and a rowing machine inside and thought Marta had gotten it wrong. Workout equipment was the sort of shit people set up in the basement. You saw that stuff, it usually meant there was nothing of value in the room. Nobody paid their bills while doing cardio. He let out a relieved breath when he saw the big partner's desk to his right. Okay, the guy liked to work out in his office. Marta hadn't let him down after all. He sidled over to the desk and went to work.

The thing was an antique, which meant the lock was sturdy, but simple. He had the drawer open and the contents dumped on the blotter in less than a minute. He started sorting through, trying to find anything of value. Credit cards, chequebook, even a notebook full of internet passwords.

Behind him, outside, he heard a shout and a splash. He jumped up and put his back to the wall beside the window. No one was supposed to be home. Marta assured them that the owners went to the Cape every weekend in the summer. He'd confirmed that, casing the place with Tod for the last three weeks. The splashing continued for a minute and then settled down. Maybe it was a neighbour's pool. Sound carried. But it sounded like whoever was out for a swim was right there, like he was sitting on the back porch with a beer watching the kids play Marco Polo in the inflatable. He leaned out from the wall and pulled the sheers open enough to peek outside. Rory blinked, trying to make sense of what he saw.

The girl floated face down in the water. Sunlight sparkled on the ripples surrounding her body like stars. A halo of redness wavered around her head.

Marta said it was just the couple and their dog. No kids. But the person in the pool was a child. Skinny. Twelve or thirteen, maybe. Hard to say from a distance. Peering out of a gap in the curtains, he couldn't tell if it was blood in the water around her head or if she was a ginger. Not that it mattered either way; she was face down and still.

He ran out of the office, nearly colliding with Tod on the landing. "What the hell was that?" his partner hissed. "What's going on?"

"It's a kid!" Rory turned to run downstairs. Tod grabbed a hold of his elbow.

"What d'ya mean, a kid? You said everybody was out of town."

"There's a kid in the pool. She's drowning." He shoved Tod's hand away and ran downstairs, taking the stairs three at a time. Halfway down, he missed a step that rocked his spine, turned his ankle and almost sent him sprawling the rest of the way, but he kept his feet under him and a grip on the banister. He skidded on the hardwood floor in the hallway at the bottom of the stairs. Tod thundered down the stairs close behind him.

In the kitchen, he ran for the double sliding glass door that led out onto the back deck and beyond that, the pool. Half the pool was out of view and he couldn't see the girl, but she wasn't making any more noise. He grabbed the sliding glass door and yanked. Locked, of course. The owners were away.

Tod's hand closed around his arm again, tighter this time. "The fuck you doing?" he said through clenched teeth. "Get your shit together. This ain't our problem."

Rory pointed to the pool. "What's wrong with you? She's drowning!"

"You don't know that."

"Get offa me." He shoved at Tod.

His partner's face turned a dark red. Tod grabbed the back of Rory's head and shoved his face against the glass door. "You see those houses back there? You see the second floor windows all lookin' out into this fuckin' yard? You go splashing around out there for Christ and everybody to see and you're going to get us caught. Chill the fuck out, man."

"She's drowning." Rory's breath steamed up the glass.

"You hear her calling for help? You hear any splashing? She's gone or she's gone home. Either way, it's not our problem."

Rory kicked back with a heel into Tod's knee. It flexed back further than it should have and the bigger man grunted and staggered away. Rory turned and ducked low, jabbing three times fast into Tod's ribs. The big man fell backward on his ass, crimson-faced and breathing heavy. Rory stood over him, fists balled up and ready to knock him back down the second he stood up.

"You put your hands on me again and I'll fuckin' burn you down. Understand? I'm not Marta. You don't fuckin' scare me."

Tod's expression darkened, but he didn't argue. Rory grew up in the gym and was fast and hit hard. He was pretty sure he'd broken a couple of Tod's ribs, not that it bothered him. The guy deserved it. No one put their hands on him. No one. When it was clear Tod wasn't getting up to fight, he turned back to the sliding door. He flicked the lock and pulled again.

The door resisted and his hand slipped off the handle a second time. "Fuck!" He kicked at the doorframe in frustration. He looked down and saw an inch-thick wooden dowel in the track, bracing the door closed. He yanked it out of the groove, threw it across the kitchen and slammed the door open.

Tod said, "You go out there, I'm taking the fuckin' car and leaving."

Rory looked over his shoulder. "I give a shit what you do."

"When you get caught, if you tell anyone that I was with you on this job, you will. *Gloria* will give a shit."

Rory felt the urge to lay into Tod a second time at the sound of his wife's name – give him a second helping of what he'd already dished out. A lot more. Rory wasn't a rat and he didn't like being called one, but he liked Tod threatening his wife even less. He wanted to show him exactly what threats bought. Except, there wasn't time to impart the lesson. Every second he spent punishing Tod was another that the girl in the pool spent dying… if she wasn't dead already. He resolved to pay his partner a visit at home if he was still a free man after this was all over. He ran through the doorway into the sunlight.

★   ★   ★

Outside, he felt blinded again; the sudden light made his head hurt. But Rory rushed forward anyway, a hand shielding his face, trying to block the sun glaring off the water. He looked around for the girl but couldn't see her. He'd heard her fall in – *seen* her from the window upstairs. Tod had *heard* her too. It wasn't his imagination.

He squinted and cupped his hands around his eyes, forcing himself not to turn away from the pool and go back inside where it was comfortably dim. And out of sight of the neighbours; Tod was right about those second storey windows.

Then he saw her. A shape in the water, light, but not bright. Pale. And still.

The girl was too far from the edge and Rory couldn't reach her by kneeling and reaching out. He kicked off his Timberlands, took a deep breath, and dove in. Water-soaked clothes made him feel heavy and slow. He fought against his thick work pants and the mechanic's jacket he should've shrugged out of along with his boots and headed in the direction he remembered seeing her body. It felt like he'd swum the length of the pool, but couldn't have. He'd jumped in from the side, not the end. She'd been *right* in front of him. It would have taken only a single stroke or two to reach her. Not this much. He thought he must've come up on the other side of her, swimming away toward the other wall. And then his hand hit something soft and yielding. And cold.

He grabbed the girl's arm and pulled her toward him. He turned her over, slipped an arm under hers and began paddling backward toward the wall, pulling her along. Rory wasn't a strong swimmer, but she wasn't fighting him. While it had felt like an eternity finding her, he reached the edge of the pool in seconds. He scrambled out of the water and pulled the girl onto the patio after him, wincing as her back scraped along the edge of the pool. The tiles caught her swimsuit bottoms and pulled them down to mid-thigh. Embarrassment stung him, but he focused on what he needed to do most. Still, from one of those windows it had to look bad. He turned her head to the side to clear the water out of her mouth. She was blonde, but the back of her head was crimson. He didn't bother pulling her hair away to try to find the gash. Getting her to breathe was his first concern. The cut would have to wait.

He turned her face back toward him, careful about her neck, jutted her jaw forward to open her mouth. Her eyes were open and staring blankly into the blue sky overhead. He leaned down and forced a breath into her mouth. He waited two seconds and blew again. He drew back and looked at her chest to see if it was rising and falling on its own. She was as still as the statue in the foyer. He blew again and again and still nothing. He checked her wrist for a pulse. Cold skin and tendons underneath; bone and flesh and no throb that signalled life.

"Please. Come on," he said. He leaned down to try again.

Water answered. It flooded out of her mouth into his throat and he lurched away. The water slipped into his lungs and he coughed and sputtered, spraying droplets in the air that sparkled and vanished like sparks in daylight. He felt her hand on the back of his neck and her lips and another rush of water flooding his mouth. He tried to resist as it filled him. In his throat and mouth and nose. He was drowning. He shoved at the girl. She was strong and held on. Stronger than he was.

Rory's mind raced. *No! Stop! I tried to save you. I tried to rescue you and I did my best and I'm sorry I was too late it was Tod not me I swear it was Tod who tried to stop me I would have been here faster if it wasn't for him oh I'msorryI'msorryI'msosorry!*

A cool burst of air rushed into his mouth and lungs and he gasped and scrambled backward across the patio, away from the pool and the girl. His back hit the edge of the deck and sharp pain arced from between his shoulder blades down into his spine.

In front of him, the girl lay on her back, pale and glistening like she was made of diamonds. She hadn't moved. Her eyes, wide open and white with cataract, stared at him as a red blanket spread out from under the wet splay of her straw-coloured hair.

Rory coughed and took another deep breath.

"I'm sorry."

She didn't say anything.

He stood up, unsure where to go or what to do. His clothes hung on him like woven gravity. He took a step toward the girl. He waited for her hand to reach out for him, for the solid grip of her fingers – so strong – around his ankle and then the feeling of the bracing, cold water in the pool as she dragged him to the bottom and held him there while he died with her.

Not *with* her.

She was dead already.

Open eyes.

Cataract white eyes.

She didn't reach out for him. She didn't blink. Her chest didn't rise with a shallow breath and then fall. She was dead.

Rory took another step toward the girl. And another. He knelt beside her and pulled her swimsuit bottoms up from her thighs, covering her, restoring the dignity he'd taken, pulling her clumsily out of the water. He put a hand on her cheek and thought about the times as a boy her age that he'd dreamed of being a hero, of running toward danger instead of away, and of the faces of the people he rescued, thankful he'd been there when they needed him and he hadn't shied away, but had done the right thing. Except he wasn't a hero.

He was the villain.

He was the man who broke into your home and looked into your most private places and took your treasures. The one who stole the ring your grandmother gave to your mother, that she passed down to you in turn on your wedding day. He took special things because fuck 'em, they were rich and it was all probably insured and he needed to buy food and a new coat for the kid each winter. But not everyone he robbed was rich. He wasn't Robin Hood. Just a hood. He was the one who took that feeling of safety and left in its place fear and vulnerability.

He'd never wanted to be this person. He'd wanted to be a boxer, a life guard, a good father and husband. But lives didn't work out the way you wanted. And he had a better talent for locks than anything else.

Rory picked up his boots and turned to go inside and dial 9-1-1. He figured he'd set the phone on the counter and leave. They'd trace the call and come eventually and find her. The child from the neighbourhood who'd snuck into the yard with the biggest pool while the owners were away because it was hot and she wanted to have some fun and cool off. They'd find the gash in the back of her head that came from slipping and bashing her skull against the side of the pool, and the blood. They'd find so much blood. But not his footprints. Those would dry in the sun and disappear. He'd leave no trace, except… her lying on the patio instead of floating in the water, and a phone off the hook.

He glanced over his shoulder at the girl, wanting to tell her one more time how sorry he was that he wasn't a hero. He half expected to see that her head had turned to follow him with those dead eyes.

Instead, she was gone.

I left her right there…

He sprinted back to the edge of the pool and searched for her under the surface.

She couldn't have fallen back in. She was dead. The water below was as clear as the day above. On the bottom of the pool, he could see a stone and one of his lock picks that had fallen out of his pocket, but nothing else under the water. No girl.

He stood there looking around the yard, wanting more than anything to catch a glimpse of her slipping over the high stucco wall, returning home.

She was gone.

It wasn't a dream. He'd gone in. His wet clothes were proof of it. He had touched her. Dragged her out. Covered her up. His aching lungs and painful breath were witness that she'd almost drowned him while he tried to give her his breath. She hadn't been a hallucination. Why else would he risk diving in?

The raking tool at the bottom wavered and distorted in the water reminding him, he wasn't done diving.

He dug in his back pocket and pulled out the dripping leather folder that held the rest of his burglary tools. He didn't want to be the kind of man who needed them. That was an easier idea than a reality, though. He didn't have much to fall back on. He simply didn't have much at all, except for these tools and what they got him. He stood, walked into the house.

He made his way through the darkened place to the front door and slipped into his boots before stepping outside onto the front walk. He pulled the door closed behind him until he heard the latch click. The front path led between blooming rhododendron bushes and a large, well-manicured green lawn. At the end of the walk, he reached the tall hedges bordering the property, separating it from the street beyond. He heard a siren wind up in the distance. There were *always* sirens in Boston.

He walked through the lattice archway onto the sidewalk and turned toward where they'd parked the car. He knew both it and Tod would be gone, but that way led also to the Green Line train and home. He would've called Gloria to come pick him up, but his cell phone was still in his pants pocket. He doubted a bowl of rice would fix it. It was dead as...

Around the corner, he spotted the car, parked where they'd left it. Tod hadn't ditched him. Maybe he was having a cigarette, waiting for the sound of sirens to get closer before driving away. Rory started to run, ready to apologise for the work he'd done on Tod's ribs. People did things they regretted under stress. He slowed. He wasn't sorry he'd tuned Tod's ribs – the guy had it coming – but nevertheless, he was glad his partner had waited for him. It was something.

Water dripped out of the tailpipe.

It dripped from the trunk and the tail lights and out the cracks of the doors. It stained the asphalt dark underneath the car.

Everything in Rory said, turn and walk away. He stepped closer and leaned over to look in the passenger window.

Inside, Tod's hair flowed in an invisible current, his arms floating up at his sides. He was pale and his face was bloated. Water lapped at the tops of the windows.

Behind him, he heard the quick slap of bare, wet feet. Like a child running toward the edge of a pool, ready to dive in.

NURSE VARDEN

Jeremy Dyson

Brosnan told himself it started with his knee. It didn't, of course. It went back much further than that, but he was reluctant to own up to that fact. Fear was, for Brosnan, as it is for most of us, a matter of shame.

★   ★   ★

The knee business had begun simply enough. He'd jumped off a wall, trying to impress his nephew. He felt, and disconcertingly heard, a loud pop, as when one punctures a piece of inflated plastic packaging material. Immediately, this was followed by sharp jagged pain. He couldn't stand. His right foot wouldn't bear any weight and he had to sit down, trying not to cry in front of his nephew, who was only eight and didn't want to see his uncle revealed as a suffering human being, not yet. Instead Brosnan tried to channel the expression of his pain into a series of grunts, growls and vocalisations more obviously redolent of manhood – complaints rather than expressions of emotion.

★   ★   ★

After his sister-in-law had picked them both up, she was kind enough to take Brosnan straight to A&E. (It was a St. James' day rather than a Leeds General Infirmary day. The two hospitals alternated their admissions and Brosnan was grateful for that – he never liked going to the LGI, too many bad memories.) Becca offered to wait with him, but he could see she was merely being polite. Freddie, his nephew, was already getting bored and irritable. Brosnan could hardly inflict three hours in a plastic chair on both of them.

"It's fine, I'll be fine. I'll get it X-rayed, strapped up. They'll give me crutches."

"How will you get home?"

"Taxi. It's fine."

"But when you get home…?"

"Becca, it's a ground floor flat. It's fine." Brosnan didn't want to talk. He knew the pain was all too evident in his voice.

★   ★   ★

Once the requisite amount of back and forth that etiquette demanded had been exhausted ('I'll be fine,' 'Are you sure?' 'I'll be fine,'), Becca and Freddie left and Brosnan was left alone. And the fear started to flood in.

★   ★   ★

"Will I need it replacing?"

"What?"

"My knee?"

"Mr. Brosnan, you're fifty-two. I think we can squeeze a little more life from it. We'll strap you up, rest it for a few days and see. It might need some ACL reconstruction."

"What?" Once again, Brosnan struggled to conceal his fear.

"It's a simple procedure. Couple of small incisions. Typically, there's a damaged ligament we need to remove. We can replace it with a segment of tendon."

"Am I awake?"

"I'm sorry?"

"When… for this operation?"

Mr. Manning, the surgeon, who was used to patients' fears in these circumstances, sought immediately to apply his customary balm. He was not to know that in this situation, the balm, rather than soothing, was actually going to inflame. Drastically so.

"No… no no no. It's a minor procedure. We'll knock you out…" Mr. Manning always found the vernacular helped so he applied it without thinking. "You'll be home in the afternoon. A few Nurofen. You'll be right as rain." Well into automatic pilot by now (it *was*, after all, a minor procedure), Mr. Manning failed to notice the ashen pallor that Brosnan had acquired, the fearful mien. For Brosnan, this was the worst thing he could have heard. If he could have this operation under a local anaesthetic he would have been relieved. For his greatest fear was embodied in the thought of an anaesthetic: having to submit himself voluntarily to deliberately-caused unconsciousness. This was a secret he had harboured all his adult life, and one he had hoped desperately to avoid confronting. But now, thanks to something as trivial as a jump from a wall, he was going to have to face his fear, whether he liked it or not.

★   ★   ★

At first Brosnan was bullish. He was an adult. He had courage. He ran his own business, a retail company that sold and fitted wood burning stoves. That may sound like a trivial enterprise but he had had to face all the challenges of the small businessman. Sleepless nights when cash-flow was sticky. Difficult conversations with bank managers, or recalcitrant clients. He knew he was capable of walking into situations he did not want to walk into. He believed that he was able to screw his courage to the sticking place, no matter what. Surely this was just another opportunity to do that. And perhaps, if he'd had someone to talk it through with, an intimate companion, a close friend who he trusted, that would have been enough to carry him over to the other side of the experience. But he didn't. Indeed, his marriage to Suzie had failed for reasons not unconnected with the thing that was causing him so much trouble now. There were parts of himself that he was entirely conscious of, and yet he could not bring them out into the public arena, could not bear to put them into words, to share them. He knew he had a problem, but he could not, for a single second, imagine forming the words that would describe that problem to another human being.

★   ★   ★

And so, because the whole thing remained unspoken, Brosnan found himself sitting in the foyer of the Yorkshire Clinic, his heart pumping so hard he could feel his pulse in one of his fingers, trying to read the form the slightly stern woman on the reception desk had given him to fill in. He could not get beyond the first line. He'd elected to have the surgery done privately (he had a modest insurance policy), rather than wait for the

National Health Service, in the hope that this extra level of control, and presumably comfort, would lubricate his experience enough to allow him to see it through. But now he was there, it seemed like it might not be quite so simple. He watched the clock on the wall with the big face and thin silver hands. He had arrived early in the hope that this would mean less stress. But the precaution had merely created more time for his anxiety to build. All he had to do was sit there, he told himself, be a cork in the water, just be carried along: 'You don't have to do anything, just be calm, be neutral and you will pass through the other side...'

★　　★　　★

For a minute that worked. But only for a minute. And as panic rose within he found himself standing up, throwing the clipboard down as if he was angry with the request for information itself. He heard himself mutter, "I've had enough of this!" and he limped out of the door towards the car. He turned his phone off. And he started the engine.

★　　★　　★

'I'm a man,' he thought as he drove. 'I'm a man. Why should I have to do anything I don't want to do? Why?' But as he pulled into the car park at the back of his apartment block (funny that he lived in a block where it would be impossible to install a wood burning stove. You can't practise what you preach, Jonathan) his knee was already throbbing and he was fearful of the prospect of not being able to walk on it. He felt tears stinging his eyes and he let out a short cry like a child who's fallen over in the playground while everybody else carries on playing around them, oblivious to their suffering.

★　　★　　★

"And when did you first remember having these feelings?"

Whether to have a woman therapist or a man therapist? The advice he received was 'whatever your instinct is, go the other way'. And so Brosnan found himself sitting opposite Dr. Briar Andrews, who seemed sober, attentive, authoritative, if not wise.

"Always. I've always felt like this."

Dr. Andrews looked at him, careful not to let even a flicker of irritation show on his smoothly shaven face. He had the skin of a pre-pubescent boy.

"So, there's no point in your childhood when you can remember being free of these fears? Free of concerns about... consciousness ceasing? Which we could refer to as... 'dying'?"

Brosnan tried to consider this question honestly. He had not objected to Dr. Andrews' conflation of his fear of a loss of consciousness and his fear of death. In fact, Brosnan was comforted that the psychiatrist was right on the money. So what of that question? Had there ever been a time when stories of heaven had helped, for example? 'It's just like going to sleep?' was a phrase he could remember. It brought no comfort. How could it, if there was no prospect of a relieving morning beyond? Brosnan really wanted to co-operate. Wanted to be able to pluck something from his past that might expiate Dr. Andrews' strategy, but there was no such moment.

They sat there in silence for a while.

"I'd like to try another tack, if that's all right?"

Brosnan nodded, miserably. Was there to be no end to this? No solution after all? Dr. Andrews didn't sound hopeful. Patient, but not hopeful.

"What's the *earliest* thing you can remember?"

"The earliest frightening thing?"

"No no no no. Just the earliest thing? The earliest anything? Your earliest memory?"

Brosnan must have looked doubtful for Dr. Andrews immediately clarified: "Here's the point, Jonathan. This is the thought I'd like you to explore. You have already been..." Dr. Andrews searched for the word "...intimate, with non-existence – if that's not an oxymoron." It was, kind of, but Brosnan didn't feel inclined to say it. "Another way of putting that might be to say, non-existence has already featured in your life story and – here's the thing – I'll hazard that it's not a source of fear." Brosnan looked at him, trying not to be afraid of whatever this thought experiment was going to be. "There was a time before you were born." Dr. Andrews paused slightly, for effect. "And I'd like to lead you back there."

Brosnan had encountered this line of reasoning before: 'When you think of the time before you were born, that's not a frightening thing, is it?' It wasn't something that had ever helped him before. But it was also true that it wasn't a thought that automatically brought him fear.

"What I'd like to do," said Dr. Andrews, "is to use your memories as a stepping stone. I'd like to gently lead you back as far as we can, and find a place to rest, just for a few minutes. Would you be comfortable with me dimming the lights?"

Immediately, Brosnan felt himself tense. But he did want to show willing. And even more than that, he wanted to find relief. He eased himself into the angled arm chair, his feet slightly lifting from the ground making him feel like a child. "So, what's an early memory? I'm not asking for the earli*est*, just *an* early memory. One that springs easily to mind."

Brosnan closed his eyes in a slightly theatrical show of co-operation. One did 'spring easily to mind' – a memory of walking into a church hall to take part in a nativity play, clutching a girl's plastic hair band with two grey pieces of card taped to it to form donkey's ears. He knew this was pre-school because his school nativities had taken place in an assembly hall. Brosnan allowed the feeling of it to form and when he felt it had coalesced he told Dr. Andrews about it, in a haltingly self-conscious way.

"Good," said the doctor, "that's good. And what were you... four? Five?"

"Four... maybe even three?"

Dr. Andrews nodded, as if this conformed exactly to his expectations. Emotionally, Brosnan was feeling himself back in that church hall car park. Seeing some grown-ups waiting to go in. 'Fools in old style hats and coats' came into his mind, from the Larkin poem. This would have been the early 1970s. He felt confident, relaxed. Big. A big boy. No different to how he felt now – except he was more confident then perhaps.

"Can you remember anything before this?" said Dr. Andrews, pushing on.

Without straining for it, another memory pressed itself into Brosnan's mind. A red tartan blanket with a rough feel to it. A meadow with lots of wild flowers. It was warm. Mum was there, with Grandma Kay. There were bees but he wasn't frightened of them. A picnic was spread out. Flasks. It was peaceful. Mum and Grandma were smiling. Again, once it had formed he communicated this to Dr. Andrews and he caught himself thinking: 'I hope this is what he wants.'

"Good. Very good. Excellent, Jonathan, excellent. Let's keep going..."

Brosnan wished he could have stayed there, in that Elysian field. The simple perfection. The purity of the happiness. Its matter-of-fact character.

"Is there anything before that? Earlier still?"

How could there be? People can't remember being less than three. Even as he had that thought he was sat smiling opposite Mum – eating a bowl of Batchelor's powdered vegetable soup. How could he remember that? But the memory had presented itself. "We're watching one of the moon landings on TV." He added, "Maybe it was the third one, or the fourth."

"Very good, Jonathan. Let's keep going. Tell me anything else. Anything that comes to mind."

Brosnan didn't think there would be anything else, but almost as he had that thought, there came an image. A flash of pale blue. A big expanse of it. Seen through a frame of some kind. And at his side – hard metal. Shiny. And a feeling – big – hard to understand – something overwhelming.

Dr. Andrews looked on expectantly. Something was clearly playing out on Brosnan's face. But now he wasn't sharing.

"Jonathan?" Dr. Andrews said, prompting him. Brosnan looked up at the psychiatrist. His eyes had been cast down – trying to make sense of the memory. "Jonathan? What is it you were remembering? Was there a memory?"

Brosnan began to try to form words, to speak of the images and feelings but immediately an opposing feeling rose up, a dread coldness, as if someone had piped river water into his belly. His heart rate had doubled. His breathing was short and shallow.

"Jonathan?"

"Nothing," said Brosnan. "There's nothing."

★　　★　　★

Another session was booked in, and Brosnan was encouraged, without strain, in the intervening time, to see if anything else 'bubbled up'. Dr. Andrews really wanted to get to that very first memory if he could. Even as he made the suggestion, Brosnan knew he wouldn't be able to talk about it. It felt too frightening.

★　　★　　★

But avoiding it didn't solve anything. And Brosnan was left with a new problem. He could hardly unremember the image and the feeling it had brought to mind. In fact, he kept being drawn back to it, as a tongue is drawn to a newly broken tooth, obsessively exploring the novel cavity. As he did that, as he recalled the pale blue expanse and the frame and the hard metal – and the feeling – he thought there was a flash of recognition. Could it be a pram? Yes, possibly. The point of view from inside a pram.

★   ★   ★

How could he remember being in a pram? He looked it up online. People's memories didn't go back earlier than the age of three, generally speaking. And he wouldn't have been wheeled around in a pram when he was three. Unless he was. Prams were voluminous back then – like vehicles – big heavy things built from steel and enamel and canvas. Maybe he'd liked getting in it for fun. Or for comfort. Within the mythology of his family he'd always been the nervous one. If Mum had still been alive, he would have called her there and then. Family anecdotes were among the easier things they could talk about. It's possible Dad might know something. But that wouldn't be as easy a conversation.

★   ★   ★

The blue. The big expanse of pale blue. There was a darker patch around the middle. A darker blue. Like a uniform. A nurse's uniform.

★   ★   ★

He woke up the next morning with a tune in his head. Duh duh der, duh duh der, duh duh duh duh duh der der... He kept der-ing it to himself all the way through breakfast. He looked out through the front window across onto Shadwell Lane, lined with wet leaves. Directly opposite was the old primary school with the high wall and the wooden door. It was the wooden door that prompted him to remember what the tune was: the theme to *The Herbs*, a scratchy old stop-motion animation series from his early childhood. The theme tune had been scratchy too – played on a distorted harp that sounded like it was recorded underwater. But this rendition of the melody he had in his head was accompanied by words – and *The Herbs'* theme tune had been wordless. These were the words:

> Here she is, Here she comes, standing out in the Garden
> Waiting there, patiently. "Come and play with Nurse…"

It was referring to the nurse. The nurse standing over the pram. There were two syllables there and he knew, he just knew, that there was a name to go with them. It was there, somewhere in his unconscious, he just couldn't persuade it out into the light. He spent the rest of the day trying to force the syllables into his mind, experimenting with different possibilities – but there was nothing that felt like a true fit.

★   ★   ★

He found out when *The Herbs* was broadcast. It started in 1968, so it certainly would have been on when he was little. On *Watch with Mother* at lunchtimes.

★   ★   ★

"Just let it go," he thought. The whole matter was making him more and more tense. What did it matter? Yes, he wanted to please Dr. Andrews. But he only had to say he couldn't remember anything else – that he had mined the extent of his earliest memories. And they could go on from there.

★   ★   ★

His knee was still painful – and it slowed him down when he walked. He didn't as yet need a crutch, but he had adopted a cane. He hated it. It was a reminder that old age was a real prospect and it would be upon him soon enough. Consequently, he had taken to sitting in the bay window of his flat, instead of going out, avoiding any unnecessary walking. And he was no closer to rearranging his knee surgery. If he was being honest he would rather walk in front of moving traffic. The sessions with Dr. Andrews were designed to help him manage his fear ("We can learn to manage it, which is different from expecting it to go away"). But the fear sat there, as immoveable as ever.

★　　★　　★

The first time he saw her – saw her in the here and now – was when he was sitting in the bay window. It was raining outside, which made the sighting all the stranger. Because she was standing there in the playground of the primary school opposite, the same one that had reminded him of *The Herbs* and its theme tune. She had her back to him – and she wore a pale blue nurse's dress. He knew it was a nurse's dress rather than, say, it being just a teacher in a blue dress, because of the darker blue belt around her middle. It was distinctive enough to be beyond doubt. 'So what?' he thought. 'Nurses go into schools. Maybe she's looking for nits.' But she was just standing there, in the rain. Her back to him. Until she started to inch around, very slowly. It was at that point that Brosnan stood up, despite his tender knee. For some reason, he didn't want to see what she looked like.

★　　★　　★

Of course, this was just ridiculous superstition, like the fear of seeing a single magpie, and if one did, desperately searching around until another one had been located to make a pair ('One for sorrow, two for joy'). It seemed now Brosnan didn't want to see the face of anyone in a blue dress with a darker blue belt. Why? What did he think was going to happen? Even posing that question felt dangerous, so he turned away from that too.

★　　★　　★

"Here's what I would suggest…"

The next session with Dr. Andrews had come around, both too soon, and not soon enough. Brosnan wanted relief, but didn't want to experience what he might have to go through in order to get it. So, he found himself sitting there, in front of the doctor, hoping he wouldn't have to talk about very much at all. Maybe just the process of going to the psychiatrist's office would be enough to dislodge this stubborn anxiety.

After all, 80 per cent of success was simply showing up, according to
Woody Allen.

"We can bypass this stage – there's no need to get hung up on a
memory that won't come. We've gone back pretty far. Far enough for us
to move to the contemplation of what came before."

"But," said Brosnan, "I want to find out what—"

"It's not necessary. It's not what you're here for." The merest flicker
of impatience. "There's no need to get bogged down in examining these
memories, they were only a preliminary stage. And I feel you've entered
enough into the spirit of that hors d'oeuvres to allow us to move to the
main course, if you'll forgive the somewhat florid metaphor. So, I'd like
you to close your eyes, to relax—"

Brosnan found he was shaking his head. Disagreeing. Disobeying.

"No. There's something… I want to find out who this person was."

"But Jonathan, I think – I'm sure – that this is displacement activity.
Hmmm? Something you might be throwing up – albeit unconsciously –
as a means of avoiding the more necessary work we have to do?"

"No. That not right." Brosnan found himself burning with anger. He
was being patronised. It was Dr. Andrews who was avoiding the difficulty.
Well, Brosnan wasn't going to shirk from what was really necessary.
He was going to find out the meaning of that memory. The one Dr.
Andrews was determined to keep him away from. He wasn't the one who
was scared.

* * *

Dad had been in Hadleigh Court since before Mum died. He was eighty-
five and a combination of poor eyesight, arthritis and recurring UTIs
meant he simply couldn't manage on his own, even with a health visitor.
But his mind was okay. He remained relatively lucid. Enough to answer
questions about the nurse.

* * *

Brosnan had to prepare himself in order to go in to the care home. He did
not want to risk seeing a nurse. His aversion had worsened. It seemed to
have become something like a phobia. It was a relief to get inside the place

and remember that they all wore trousers. Trousers and tunics. Traditional nurses' dresses were rare.

★　　★　　★

Dad sat in his wheelchair, a large water bottle untouched in front of him. Brosnan's eye avoided, as it always did, the ballooning catheter bag that poked out from the bottom of Dad's trouser leg, full of urine the colour of Lucozade.

"Was there a nurse, Dad?

"You what?"

"Did I have a nurse, when I was young? I thought I remembered Mum mentioning it once or twice?"

Dad blinked slowly. "Oh aye. The Nurse. When you were a baby. Your grandma paid for her. We could never have afforded it."

"Can you remember anything about her?"

"She helped out. When you were a baby."

"What was her… What was her name?"

"Give over!" Dad laughed mirthlessly. The idea that he would be able to do anything as ridiculous as remember that.

"Did it rhyme with 'garden'? Do you think?"

Another smaller laugh – more like a dismissive exhalation.

"Can you remember anything about her?"

"She'd wheel you about a bit. Change your nappies. We didn't have disposables then. Everything went in the wash."

"Was there something wrong with her face?"

"Something wrong with her face? What you on about?" He waved his hand in the air. It was all too ludicrous and he didn't want to talk about it anymore.

★　　★　　★

Brosnan got a taxi home. He couldn't risk driving. He was too concerned about what would happen if he saw a nurse in a blue dress, with her face turned away, or worse, with her face turned towards him. He didn't want to own up to it, but he was aware he was scared of even looking out of the taxi window. He was staring at the floor, a flattened packet of Wotsits stuck to the carpet by dried mud. Not wanting the taxi driver to think there was something wrong with him, Brosnan lifted his head and stared intently at the headrest of the passenger seat. It required the expenditure of some willpower to keep his eyes locked there and not allow them to be drawn to the window on the left or the right.

It was only when traffic halted the car by the parade of shops at the top of Roundhay Road that Brosnan's will began to waver. His eyes flicked experimentally to his left. There was still a part of him that wanted to challenge his irrational fear, to stand up to its absurdity. But the moment he did so, he saw, right by the car – brightly lit by the harsh white light of one of the new LED streetlamps – a woman in a blue dress, with a darker blue belt around her middle. She was side on to Brosnan, her face angled away from him. It seemed as if he'd caught her in the act of turning towards him, very slowly, like a figure on top of a musical box. The hair, which was wet from the rain, hung in thick messy strands, concealing most of her face. But she was getting to the point where it was going to be exposed to him. His heart thumping, he moved his own head sharply away, not knowing where to put it. He willed the car to move on. For a moment, he feared she was going to lean forward, open the car door and get right in the back seat, revealing that terrible countenance – whatever it was. He didn't know what it would be like, but he feared that something about it would be so terrible that it would kill him. It would make him die. He pushed his feet downwards, tilting them into the dirty floor as if that would somehow move the traffic forward. Eventually it did.

★   ★   ★

That night he had the dream.

It was real. But then, of course, any dream is real when you're in it. He was lying down, staring through the pram hood, if that's what it was. It made a frame, or half a frame, across the right-hand side of what he could see. He couldn't move. He was tucked in tight. And there she was, her back towards him. But she was turning. Very slowly. Again, that mechanical feel, like something clockwork, inevitable, smooth and ordered. The pace of her turn was so slow. More like the hands of a clock than a musical box. It would be a while before her terrible countenance would come into vision, but there was no escape from it. Revealed it would be.

He wanted to move, to look away, to look down, to close his eyes, but none of these options were available to him. He could only lie there, tucked in tight, swaddled, the blackness of the pram around him, the drear light of the world outside, broken by the blue of her dress, the line of her belt, the slow rotation, the thin penumbra of her face, just coming into view. Wake up. Wake up. Wake up. He fought, he wrestled with all his will, because by now he knew it was a dream. Wake up.

He lay there sweating but there was no relief.

*   *   *

Brosnan paced the floor of his living room, waiting for the light to come, for the dawn to lessen his panic. He ran the rhyme over and over in his head.

Here she is, here she comes, standing out in the Garden
Waiting there, patiently. "Come and play with Nurse…"

Come and play with Nurse duh duh. Come and play with Nurse der der. Come and play with Nurse doo doo. Come and play with Nurse Varden. Come and play with Nurse Varden.

Nurse Varden. Nurse Varden. Nurse Varden. That was her name. Nurse Varden.

There was triumph in that moment. He had retrieved the name. The block was unblocked. Surely that was all he needed to move beyond this whole ridiculous obsession. He was elated with the relief of it.

*   *   *

He was supposed to go to Dr. Andrews this morning. He had an appointment at 10:15. And still carried by the euphoria of finally remembering the nurse's buried name he left his apartment early, with a lightness he'd not felt for weeks. Dr. Andrews' office was a fifteen-minute stroll away, and Brosnan was only five minutes into his journey when it occurred to him: 'Why do I even have to go? Surely I've achieved what I needed to achieve? Retrieved my earliest memory. Got back to the beginning. Contemplating what precedes that – well, that's just a formality. A thought experiment. I can do that in the bath. I'm going to text his office and cancel the appointment.' He pulled his phone from his trouser pocket. 'They'll charge me for it. Let them. I'll happily pay. I'm going to take the rest of the morning off. A leisurely breakfast, maybe a—'

There, directly in front of him, was the figure in the blue dress, darker blue belt around her midriff, face turned away, body curiously angled towards him, mimicking exactly the position of the figure in his dream last night. He was on a stretch of Princes Avenue where the grass banked up slightly on either side of the road as it passed through Roundhay Park, just ahead of Soldier's Field. There was no place of refuge. She was already turning, moving erratically, much faster than the dream. And suddenly her head jerked round, in little jolting movements, speeding faster, faster, faster. She was revealing herself to him and there was nowhere to hide.

Without thinking he ran across the road and everything slowed and went quiet as the car hit and threw him into the air. He saw the forty mph sign as he did so. Then he was on the tarmac – and he watched his phone land next to him, the screen shattering into little shards as he screamed and screamed and screamed.

★　★　★

What followed was a blur. He remembered the ambulance. Felt the straps around him. Then nothing. Then he was in the hospital. The General Infirmary. It was an LGI day.

Everything was red, coppery, like the taste in his mouth. There were figures standing over him. He wanted to ask, 'Will I be alright?' but his throat and mouth wouldn't respond to the urge. One of the figures must have seen something in him because it moved closer, turning towards him. It was a girl. She was young. Sweet looking. Brosnan thought of the Lenny Bruce joke about a man who's just had a heart attack trying to hit on the nurse in the ambulance. She smiled softly, reassuringly. She squeezed his hand. He could read the girl's blue hospital badge, though the red haze made it a muddy brown, the same colour as her dress and her darker belt. It stated simply her position, Staff Nurse, and her name, Julie Varden.

IF, THEN

Lisa L. Hannett

All is still quiet in the summer palace.

No silver-spun carriages jingle up the bailey's grand boulevard. No heralds announce any arrivals — feather-crested horses, footmen, fops. All are blind to the beauty of the avenue of linden trees dappling the cobblestones; the garlands swooping between gilt lantern-posts; the once-impeccable topiaries dotting once-immaculate lawns. No guards salute at the keep's high oak doors. No maids curtsey and whisk rich cloaks into richer cloakrooms. No stewards offer chilled wine in the atrium, nor usher ambassadors into passages burrowed behind cleverly damasked panels. No satin slippers skim over the ballroom's parquetry, no pampered toes splash in the quadrangle's merriest fountain. No cooks bellow at spit-boys and butchers and hearth hounds. No feasts boister the realm's dandified peers, those sun-starved aristocrats who swill and sup, their pale faces pink in the castle's blazing main hall. No grievances befoul the throne room, no peasant's complaints trundle past the queen's veiled hennin and into the seneschal's ears. No princess rings for her seamstress, her nine ladies-in-waiting, her cupbearer or personal taster. No gold clinks into the king's heavy coffers, no quills scritch across treaty parchments, no poisons plink into traitorous cups. No laughter burbles, true or hollow, in morning rooms, no evening arias float folk away to lands more magical even than this. No love is made here. No binding oaths sworn. None broken.

It's mostly quiet.

A low hum of bees follows the royal gardener through chambers and courtyards and corridors. Halls that once shimmered with mirrors and cut-glass chandeliers are now darkly tunnelled with vines, willow branches, tanglewoods, hellebore blossoms. Polished floors are carpeted with red feather clover. Marble ceilings, columns, walls — once white as pure cream — are all blue-black with *Hedera helix*, the dense creeper thriving in this floral twilight. Though humble, the gardener thinks, as he hurries through his rounds, the common ivy is remarkable for its rampant ambition, its complete lack of discrimination. It's steadfast, reliable. It does what it should. It grows fast, any and everywhere.

The truest plant he's ever known.

High above the gardener's salt-stained skullcap, the castle's twelve turrets are smothered in red *vitis coignetiae* – Crimson glory, a favourite for its resilience, its shades of perpetual autumn. Clematis Viticella, another strong climber, has infiltrated the balustrades and battlements, minstrels' galleries and fools' towers, gaps in the wainscoting and chinks between porcelain tiles. *Hydrangea petiolaris* blankets limestone façades and flying buttresses, filling endless rows of mullioned windows with its fragrant constellations. Bedchambers are shrouded in swathes of Albertine roses – a vigorous rambler with large apricot blooms – while, every day for months and months now, the hearty *Ipomoea purpurea* has unfurled its sweet morning glories in solars and staterooms alike.

Over it all, from bartizans to basements, finials to foundations, a mile-thick cage of briars keeps peace in the palace. Petals, vines and thorns hold everything in place – and in time.

Nan needs as much of *that* as he can get her.

Hurry, the gardener thinks. *Hurry.*

Birds warble in the distant, bright blue beyond the walls. From afar, but not far enough, comes a rhythmic clunking, a pendulum swing of a thousand ormolu clocks. A thousand hearts beating in time. A thousand woodpeckers jabbing for ants.

A thousand axes chopping the village woodsmen ever closer.

Too close, the gardener thinks, scurrying to outpace the lumberjacks' hatchets. And too soon. They're making headway now, these blade-thunking rustics – despite the toughness of his bespelled timbers, despite the haze drowsing from leaf and limb with each untiring blow – they're bashing through bramble and bark like a pack of wild boars. Tusks splintering all his hard, healing work.

Hurry.

He climbs to the second floor, then the third. Steps over a feather-capped messenger asleep on the landing. A skinny scrub-girl nestled in an alcove nearby. Halfway down this passage, the blacksmith's snoring apprentice clutches a clovered lump: a mallet, perhaps, or an unfitted wall sconce. There's a laundry maid with a basketful of linens under her steam-slicked head. Further down, a baby is tulip-twined in its nurse's arms. Sometimes, when the gardener navigates around these tendril-tied bodies, over mushroomed doublets and mossed skirts and lichen-clad legs, his boots will strike a clear patch of stone. In that moment there's a brief echo of his careful efforts, dull and damp, like pebbles dropped in a deep, dark well. No one stirs at the sound.

No one pays him any attention.

Everywhere, the sleepers sigh and dream-sputter. Their chests rise and fall. Behind closed lids, their irises rove this way and that. Nobody rouses – they simply lie where his plants and pollens have left them – though the gardener touches a cheek here, cups a chin there, leans forward to feel the stale breeze seeping from nostrils and gaping lips. He could climb atop any one of them any time, if he wanted to; strip off kirtles and garters and hose, have his way with lass or lady, duke or earl. He could do it right now. If he wanted.

After this long on his own – several months, probably, maybe a year and a day? Beyond the castle walls, the woodsmen will say they've battled his brambles for a century – after *this* long, no one would blame a man for being lonely. For taking small comforts wherever he finds them.

The royal gardener has found them all.

Kept a mental tally.

Who, what, where.

No one else is awake to blame him.

Still, he hasn't indulged, not even once, though he is a passionate man, though he *could*.

He hasn't.

Every part of him belongs to Nan.

Every part of her needs only him.

★　★　★

Others might think she's a bit on the plain side, his Nan, a stout little marigold next to the princess's peony perfection, but the gardener appreciates subtlety. He respects Nan's modesty. Her natural disavowal of ostentation. To spite the willow-wand women at court, Nan has remained small for her age. Her hair is more rust than bright copper, her complexion more peach than cream. For a woman in Nan's position – a noble lady attending the king's only daughter – to persist in plainness despite the court's frippery, its silks and spun gold and scandal, is a good mark of her character. It shows fortitude, the gardener thinks. Resilience. Stubbornness, even.

Admirable, necessary traits for people like them.

They're so alike in so many ways, he and his Nan.

At this court, they're the sturdy trellises supporting rich, delicate fruit. Vital, mostly invisible work. No one here wants to see the sorcerers behind the spells. Nobody wants the treat once they've seen the trick. He and Nan thrive in the shadows. They survive by disappearing.

His Nan will never outshine her mistress any more than he'll outmuscle the brutes hacking, hacking – closer now, *hacking* – at the tangleroot shield that's taken him a year's careful magic to grow. And that's fine, the gardener thinks. Just fine.

Sun-wrinkled and skinny, he's far from handsome but he *is* smart. Inventive. Observant. A master of timing. He knows just when to establish which seeds, how and where they'll most quickly spread. He hasn't pushed a barrow in years, but he's still strong. Every day, he wrestles unruly vines down corridors and through doorways. He drags the deadweight of knights and obese stewards away from the clinging suffocation of cobwebs. He saws boughs, snips offshoots, saps branches, desperate for new samples to splice, for new genera to graft, for new answers to Nan's illness, for a cure. He cuts and clips until his fingers cramp into claws.

At night, despite the bone-deep ache in his hands, he carries Nan between the divan and bed, peels the dried poultice from her fevered brow, gently tucks her under his mother's own wedding quilt. This is where all his strength has gone. This is how he loses it.

★   ★   ★

Forever in skullcap and mask, leather gloves and long smock, the gardener tends what he's sown, the enchantment he's nurtured, the time-stalling soporifics he's grown. Day in and out, he prunes the princess's sewing chamber, its embroidery hoops and loom, its untouched spinning wheel. He shakes the pain from his hands between chambers, kneading out knots between forefinger and thumb. He checks new and old growth, clips curiosities, *cramps*. Repeats. On and on, he forages concubines' boudoirs, the astronomer's study, the knights' chapel. On and on and on. Cellars, staircases, salons. Check, clip, cramp. Armories, pantries, attics. Check, clip, cramp. Slowly and thoroughly, he inspects every grove and holloway, though he just wants to run, just wants to find what Nan needs and get this over with, race back to his own small apartment in the south wing, where his melting pots overflow, his seeding pans sprout, and sunlight spills through the arched panes all year round.

His shears have never worked so hard for so little reward.

His hands have never so relentlessly ached.

In his rooms, the air is slightly more damp than dry: a calculated balance of mist and magic. Ideal for germination, propagation, grafting, regrowth. Perfect for repair and recovery. He has cultivated the time Nan needs to get well – all that's missing now is the right combination of plants for her treatment. The right tincture. The right extract.

Something.

Anything.

Hurry, his heart urges, loud as the axes storming against trunks outside. *Hurry.*

On and on the gardener goes through the castle, footsteps muffled on rugs turned to mulch. Again, he pictures Nan where he left her this morning, supine on the settee near his study window, her peach face angled to catch light that once fell on his desk, his scrolls and papers, his potions and cuttings, his calculations, recalculations, corrections. He sees her lying in his best chamber, eyes closed but not really resting. Still, a sickly verdigris creeps up her skin, a pond-scum hue shading her cheekbones, bruising her lips. It had taken other ladies of the court, this insidious illness, but few so well-ranked as his love.

None so shrewd, so proper, so sharp.

Nan! he'd called, weeks and months ago, noticing that algaeic tinge to her features before anyone else did. The lilac florets under her eyes. The slump in her attitude.

(Oh, how she used to scold him when he'd call out *Nan!* like that, brazenly across the princess's private courtyard. Oh, how he'd chuckle at her temper! She'd stomp right past the trefoil flowerbeds he pampered there, glance furtively around before hissing, *Please, good man*, as if this wasn't a years-long game, *Please call me Annette.*)

Nan! he'd called that day – the weeding can wait, he'd thought, while I'm helping her out – but she'd simply shuffled on by without so much as a glance. No banter, no lively debate. No averted gazes. No blushes.

Oh, how very ill.

Before planting the palace to sleep, the gardener had tried everything to cure her. He'd prescribed Nan all the nightshades – in measured doses, trickled into her lemon tea – then henbane and hay, lavender, wormwood, mint. He'd given her pills and powders. Brandied drips in her nightcaps. Syruped drops in her porridge. He'd drained countless phials, potions distilled and distributed week after week – all that and more, all for naught.

For almost six months, Nan's condition had worsened. She lost her bull's appetite, drank little, ate less. She paled and greened and weakened. She stopped collecting posies for her lady's dressing table, sending the new girl down for the meadowsweet instead. She rarely visited the east park with its brilliant amaryllis – alone, as was her wont – and hadn't once seen the lotus pond in its indigo glory. She politely declined the queen's invitations to seasonal galas. Time and again, she excused herself from the seneschal's evening salons, though she'd always had a weakness for tales of romance and heroic poetry.

I'm full enough already, she'd confessed to the princess in the secret garden – not to *him*, of course, but he didn't begrudge friendship between ladies – *I won't hear a single word more.*

Next day, the gardener had crafted a scented pomander to rebalance Nan's humours, but later found it untouched on her pillow. He'd raced out of her chamber, then, fearing the worst. He'd seen what Nan refused to admit. Just like the midden heaped beyond the king's stables, his poor love was composting. Decaying from the inside.

If he didn't intervene, and soon, she'd be nothing but dirt.

I can fix this, he'd said late that same awful night, perhaps a year and a day ago, before the household retired. He'd waited for her outside the privy, caught her by the arm, steered her into the queen's clock cabinet. *You know I can, Nan. Don't be stubborn. Let me help you. No one else will.*

She'd given him a long, hard look. Considering his offer, he'd thought. Accepting.

You forget yourself, gardener, she'd said at last.

Head, he'd quickly corrected, *gardener. Trust me, love. I know what I'm doing.*

Oh, what a violet flare there'd been in her nostrils! What a flytrap clamp to her lips.

I'm fine, Nan had said firmly.

I'm fine, she'd said. *Let me be.*

But she wasn't, and he couldn't.

★   ★   ★

Hurry.

On through the nursery, the library, the dairies and dovecotes, the gardener searches and snips, stepping over sleepers as he goes. Check, clip, cramp. Fresh samples go into his satchel, fresh fertiliser sprinkles out. Around him, the palace bristles with slumber, secrets, and growth. Beyond the limestone walls, a lumberjack shouts, *Getting there, lads!* The gardener snugs his mask, throws more powder, grasps for a solution among burgeoning leaves. He unclips his secateurs, snicks vine after vine, trims another handful of nothing. Jagged foliage crumbles in his palm. Shoots shrivel. He bags the dust. Continues.

It wasn't supposed to take this long.

This slumber was supposed to be a stopgap, not a last resort. While the gardener produced the ingredients to heal her, his Nan was to be like a bulb in winter. Dormant, pleasantly dreaming. Only for a while.

A temporary, desperate measure.

Please. The gardener pauses outside the king's chapel. A pockmarked summoner sleeps toes-up across the threshold, feet in God's house, head out here in the hall. He kneels beside the holy man, unsheathing a serrated knife, watching a cluster of gourds swell out of the black cassock. *Please*, he thinks. Let this work.

Let *something* work.

On the summoner's chest, the strange fruits are striped, trumpet-shaped. The tendrils winding around the single row of jet buttons are tougher than rawhide. Leaning in, the gardener saws until he sweats, until his clawed hands scream, but he barely gouges the cords. Changing tack, he slices the nearest squash, recoils from the rising stench. New buds quickly bulge in the spill of seeds and sour guts.

"Please," he growls, sitting back to shake some sensation back into his grip. He paws at the kerchief covering his mouth and nose. "Come *on.*"

Teeth clenched, he hacks at tiny pumpkins hemming the man's collar and cuffs, hacks and hacks like a spell-breaking brute, a woodsman bent on destruction. Until now, he's been gentle as a shepherd with his woolly-headed flock – and what good has it done? He's stalled time for his Nan, for the palace's courtiers and regents, and for what? His efforts have yielded nothing. His medicines are all benign, neutral as water. Yowling now, he hacks a gash at the base of his thumb, keeps hacking while the throbbing muscle bleeds. Gourds smash. Pulp and stinging juices fly. What else can he do? This unnatural sleep hasn't been restorative. Time isn't enough.

He hacks. Stabs. Weeps.

Nearly spent, he aims for a squash by the summoner's left wrist, its flesh grey and lurid skin mottled, but misses his target. With a swift childish slurp, his blade severs the man's little finger instead. Off it comes, clean as a buttercup! Without thinking, the gardener leans in and catches it. He bites back an oath – the thing is fat as a grub and now slimed with his own blood – and slams it between his two palms. Within seconds, there's a pinch. A sharp tingle. A prickling sensation in his wounded hand, the pins-and-needles of a deadened limb reviving. The gardener stiffens and peels his palms apart, tilting them toward his lantern's dim glow. On the flagstones, the summoner snores while in the gardener's grasp the stump of his digit oozes like a crushed aloe spear – not blood, but a clear viscous oil that both salves and secures, skin to skin. In a blink, one man's crooked finger grafts onto the other's seeping cut. Their ragged edges fuse together. Blood seals the wounds even as the balm heals them.

The gardener gapes, too stunned to breathe, not just at the appendage awkwardly jutting from his *opponens pollicis,* nor how its knuckle bends on its own as the base digs into its new home – but at the painlessness of it all. With a sigh, he flexes and relaxes his hand. Curls and straightens all six of its fingers. The movements are so fluid, so *easy.* For the first time in months, there are no spasms. No sudden contractions. No seizing.

At the end of one arm, an aching claw creaks and twitches for the lantern. But this other? It flutters and waggles and flicks! It squeezes secateurs with abandon. *Snick snick!* Thick tapestries of wisteria and ivy dampen the gardener's laughter, but not his spirits, as he stoops to examine the summoner. The pumpkin mess of his forearm and sleeve. The pink nubbin on his left hand, neatly poking above the gold band of his signet ring. No harm there, either. Only healing.

Only hope.

★ ★ ★

Experimentation is the lifeblood of any science: horticultural, medicinal, physical. There can be no sure answers without trial and error. Ifs that lead to thens.

After sharing the good news with Nan – *Hope, love! There's yet hope* – the gardener gently pinches her cheeks, prods her décolletage, walks his hands up and down the length of her forearms where they lay, exposed from elbow to wrist, atop his mother's patchwork. On her cool skin, the ovals of his fingermarks linger as he ponders the many variables, the complex conditions of his first, unforeseen, test. Amputation, he thinks. Grafting. And then? The conclusion is right there before them: the superfluous thumb jutting from a slash in his glove, wriggling as he hones his secateurs, adds pincers to his satchel, a dagger, one fine-toothed saw and another with a shark's jagged bite, a pot of lanolin and a roll of linen bandages. The *answer* is obvious, but what was the catalyst in this equation? Was it the pumpkins? The summoner's penitent flesh? The gardener's powders and petals scattered outside the chapel – or some combination thereof, or some lack? Was it the blade he'd used? The furious swiftness of the cut? Was his own blood the accelerant, the essential adherent? Was it his pain?

Outside, nightingales ratchet in the brambled forest, their stuttered alarms sharply insistent: *go go go! go go go! ch-ch-ch-ch-o-p!* The gardener has trained the vines to creep away from his study's large window, but tonight – above the countless white stars of *cestrum nocturnum*, the countless cream-pie faces of the *Ipomoea alba* – the moon is waning. Hoary light fogs into the room and settles on his Nan like ash. Every so often, her eyelids twitch, lashes dusted silver. Her bosom rises and falls.

Where there's breath, there's life, he thinks, straining to catch Nan's soft exhalations through the din in the forest outside. The birds relentlessly scolding. The nagging chatter of twigs and leaves. The village thugs, night and day, ruthlessly hacking. So close now he can clearly hear the scrape of their steel against his tangled stalks. The splinter of his spells tenderly wrought in wood.

Think of the princess, lads!

Think of the rewards.

The gardener tightens his fist, releases it. Still limber. Still mercifully hale.

Another glance at Nan – how he hates to leave her alone! – then on, and out, he goes.

To the grand hall and its feast of royal subjects. A fine assortment of men, women and children, all ages, all sizes, all slumbering in uncertain states of health. He paces between rows of heavily carved trestles, peering at jesters and judges asleep on the benches, cinched heiresses and suet-jowled peers, all fettered with foliage, all blubbing into stagnant bowls. Everywhere, the king's bounty has mouldered, maggoted, melted. Pewter goblets, iron brochettes and walnut trenchers are jewelled with aphids and ants. The undertable thickets are crawling with other invisible, mandibled life – but, the gardener reassures himself, at least *this* aspect of the experiment remains consistent. Beyond his own apartments, every inch of the castle is filthy. Every courtier is filthy. Both he and the summoner: *filthy.*

He cocks an ear – *Timber!* cries a hatchetman. At the moat? Already? – then the gardener commits to some chopping of his own.

Trials and errors.

Ifs, thens.

He nicks the webbing between two fingers on his near-crippled writing hand. Grunts through the pain. Breathing hard, he unsocks a toddler curled like a pup on the weed-covered floor. A quick *snick* and the child's tiny toe is free; translucent jelly seeps from its foot; the stub glistens a while, a miniature saliva-filled mouth, then scabs; sheathes itself; scars. Good, thinks the gardener, jamming the little toe into the bleeding crook of his fingers. As before, there's a pang, a tingle, a wave of relief as the pieces graft together. The torment subsides in his hand. His gestures are instantly sure. They're deft. Nimble.

Good.

Now to repeat the trial, again, again, again, changing one variable at a time to see what works, what fails. Now his own body is removed from the equation. Now a courtesan exchanges ears with a serving wench. Now a baron adopts a merchant's nose. Now a lutist's tune-strummers grip a carving knife. Now the harpist's string-pluckers cradle a cask of mead. Now a lawyer swaps tongues with the bishop. Now the second lady-in-waiting wears the falconer's whiskered lips.

Good, thinks the gardener, tools and smock smeared with gore, as he refines the formula.

Timber! at the postern gate as the portcullis surrenders, heavy oak shatters, and thick ivy portières give way. *Forward, men!*

Hurry.

He takes a deep breath. Quells the churn in his belly. Channels it into power. Pulse thundering, he trades coping saw for dagger. Now for the true test. A beggar's gangrenous cheek is carefully filleted. Purpled flesh separates, stinks, slides on the gardener's blade. He sets it on a plate, steadies his hand, then carves into the almoner's face.

Please work. The gardener transfers a healthy, kidney-shaped slab of meat onto the pauper's lice-ridden gouge, then takes the rancid chunk to bind the dignitary's wound. Please work.

Think of the prize! shouts a boor with an axe. Halfway, maybe, to the outer bailey.

There's no wondrous shimmer when the gardener presses down, holding the pieces together; no magic glow as rosy skin blends with putrid. Only a whiff of balsam – juniper, pine – and a slow suppuration of oil in the curved seams. Crouched close to his work, he rocks from tiptoes to heels as the unguent solidifies, sticks. Within minutes, the almoner's tone evens out, his high colour absorbing, diluting, neutralising the poor man's rot. Soon, little trace of the implant remains. A puckered outline around a slightly darker patch of cheek.

Beneath layers of grease and grime, the beggar's face pulsates from near-black to magenta to cerise, then to a respectable, rustic shade of fading sunburn. The gardener waits, watching, for the wellness to spread. He waits.

In his sleep, the vagabond smiles.

★   ★   ★

Quickly, quickly, the gardener harvests the castle's best snippets.

A handful from the princess's suite of chambers – including the lady's own fingertip, callused from spinning and dotted with spindle-pricks – another five from the throne room. Only the richest replacements for his Nan, he thinks, only the finest. Next, to the ballroom for ten sprightly toes. The cloisters and courtyard for pliable, fountain-dabbled soles.

Through the vestibule to claim astute ears. Through its secret passage to liberate palms lavishly crossed with gold.

His shears have never worked so little for so great a reward.

His hands have never felt so strong.

And yet.

The palace is vast and the gardener's apartments isolated. Before he can shortcut through the kitchens, much less return to Nan in the south wing, the cuttings in his satchel have healed shut. The stubs have sealed themselves off like segments of spade-split earthworms.

Panic punches his sternum as crude men holler triumph in too many directions. Are they in the outer bailey? Inner? Have they hacked past the stables? The storehouse? Chopped into his own secluded yard?

Not yet, he pleads, thinking, thinking as he runs, finally reaching the cook's coldest pantry and a possible solution. There, on a mulberry-bushed shelf, sits a crock covered in cheesecloth and twine. The gardener snatches it, pockets the cloth. Out pours the whey, in glugs a swilling of brine. That should do, he thinks, sloshing out to the kitchens.

No time now to be choosy. Into the pot go scullery-chapped fingers, blistered palms, crack-nailed toes that have never known shoes. *Plop plop plop*, every precious piece goes into water like so many scallions and leeks, their hairy ends soaking into new roots. Using the cloth to keep the whole lot from spilling, the gardener rushes through atrium and hall, hopping over heralds and pages, sidestepping chamberlains and masters of the hunt, shedding pollen and stress the closer he gets to his rooms. To his Nan.

As always, she's reclining on the divan when he arrives. Her forearms, bosom, throat and round face are translucent in the moon's glow, bone china blue. Hard to see the stain of sickness in this light, he thinks. Hard to believe she's so far gone.

"Not long now, my heart," the gardener says, raising his voice so Nan might hear him above the noise in the yard. *Over there, lads! There's a window!* A few more concise cuts, a few more moments, and they'll be through the worst of it. They'll be on their way. He draws the floor-length curtains, stokes the hearth, sets a brazier next to Nan's bed. Turns down the quilt, smoothing each fold as he uncovers Nan's embroidered stomacher, her nipped waist and wide farthingale, her heavy skirts, slender ankles, bare feet. With some effort, he suppresses the urge to mount her there and then, tear the pearls from her bodice, snap the strings on her slips. He's saved himself for this moment. Saved *her*.

"Not long now," he says again. What's another few minutes after so many years? The wait will be worth it. It will.

Can you see it? Keep those blades swinging, lads! We're nearly there!

"Brace yourself," the gardener mutters, setting the crock and its croppings on a sturdy plant-stand. He cleans and whets his sharpest shears.

Oh, how lithe his hands are now! How smoothly he squeezes the polished handles, how swiftly he scythes through sinew and bone. As he removes and replaces Nan's fingers and toes, dropping the diseased ones into a porcelain bowl, he imagines the offshoots of strength already veining through her body. With each amputation, each new application, his confidence grows. Soon enough, he thinks, she'll recuperate. She'll recover. She'll revive.

And while she mends – now he slices downward from arch to heel – he'll sweep her up, shepherd her to safety. Somewhere secret, just for them. *Hallo! D'you see that? A light within!* The woodsmen don't know the palace as he does, which twists to take in the tangled paths, which turns. They don't know its undercroft and storm tunnels, its hidden warrens and foxhole exits. He unfurls a rollmop of skin under her foot, holds it in place until it binds. When at last his Nan wakes, far beyond the dormant castle, beyond its vine-choked baileys and moat and imposing walls, she'll finally open her eyes and see what he's done. All of this, he'll boast. All for her.

Oh, how grateful she'll be then.

Oh, how she'll want him.

And then, he thinks, spooning the last little bit from the brine, *then* she'll accept what he's offered, again and again, ever since she was the lady's ninth maid and he an amateur soil-turner. A final cut and he lets the shears rest. As soon as it's healed – the gardener leans in, lining things up, assessing his handiwork – he'll slip his family ring onto Nan's third finger. As soon as she heals.

The gardener frowns.

Squints.

Starts to sweat.

Hold on if you can! We're coming!

Earlier, the bond was instantaneous. A snip and a tingle, a pinch and a press, then a swell of wellbeing, a flood of full health. What had he done differently this time? Why was his Nan still marbled like a wedge of *bleu de gex*? Each purloined digit was clearly at home on her hands, each toe aligned and perfectly curved, each fingerpad and ear attached *just so*. Perhaps the problem isn't the parts he's applied, but the process? Before, he'd firmly held the almoner's new face as it mended. He'd palmed the beggar's weal until it pieced into place. For strangers, his touch had been personal. Hand to hand. Skin to skin.

Intimate.

Why wasn't it so with Nan?

Why not.

Suddenly the study is stifling. The walls near the window shudder and thump. Forged metal shunks through vine and timber, strikes shingle and stone. Axes ring like church bells calling the faithful to prayer.

"By your leave," the gardener says before unlacing Nan's stomacher and setting it on the cushions. Trembling, he loosens her chemise. Peels her layered skirts and petticoats, hesitating at the needleworked bloomers. Stares at the thin beige linen between them. The triangular shadow between her legs. The barrow-mound rising just above it. The roundness of her navel. The horrible distention.

Gaze roving from Nan's mismatched toes to her varicosed shins, her swollen knees and pliable thighs, the gardener's frown deepens.

"Oh," he says around the ball-cactus in his throat. Reaching down, he places a hand on her belly. "Oh, Annette."

All together now, boys! Three, two—

Sliding an arm under the once-maid's back, the gardener sits her up. Braces her damp cheek against his shoulder, wriggles under her legs, lifts her like a sack of mulch. Holds her close. Swallows hard. Shuts his eyes against the tide rising hot inside him. Shudders. She smells of orange blossoms and loam. Lambs wool. Warm milk. Sleep.

Once more, lad! Once more!

"Wake up," the gardener says, shaking his head. Shaking. Holding this woman tight, tighter, they dash for the window, together, now and forever, they run headlong for it, tangled, together, they embrace as the twilit panes shatter, as the glass sings and slices and stings, as the woodsmen swing their ever-sharp axes, tireless, relentless, the senseless brutes shout, as they chop and chop and chop.

AQUARIUM WARD

Karter Mycroft

Take Jamie, for example. Jamie was dead when you got to her and alive twenty minutes later. It should have been impossible. When her eyes shot open and she gagged on the tube in her throat you thought you were dreaming, or you'd gotten too many huffs of crankbreath and lost your grip. But no, there she was, freaking out in real life to the tune of a hundred heartbeats a minute. Your first miracle.

You rushed to the monitors and did a happy scoff at the numbers. Then you spun round with a hand on her shoulder, a soft word in her ear, a quick drip of Dilaudid because at this point why the hell not? She calmed down some then, wiped her forehead with a bluish hand and made a face at the tube.

Try and relax, you told her. We have to make sure there's no residual serum in any of your fluids. You had a crooked thought that she maybe shouldn't trip about some oesophageal discomfort, that she maybe should be thankful to feel anything at all. But she hadn't seen what you'd seen. She didn't know the numbers. No one was saying things like *one hundred per cent case fatality rate* on the news; the Feds who prowled the hospital made sure of that. Probably all Jamie knew was she'd taken a hit, felt something like a hundred thousand orgasms blast through her skinny little body, then woken up choking on a Slinky. You could cut her some slack. Another drop of hydromorphone for Jamie, courtesy of the Good Doctor.

It took six hours for Jamie's readings to come back clear. In that time you operated on four others, maybe five, trying to replicate the procedure that had worked on her: the quadruple dose of verapamil, cyproheptadine and whateverazepam, the hasty microincision above the renal artery, the modified dialysis to extract serum from the blood. None pulled through. None came close. Either they were dead on arrival and stayed that way, or their hearts gave out from adrenergic storm during operation. This cyclical devastation had been your routine for months and you tanked it with a shot of vodka and a long sigh. Was the drinking making you sloppy? Did anyone notice? It was hard to tell who cared anymore. The bugs certainly didn't.

When it was time to check on Jamie you collapsed the tube, removed it, told her not to talk and felt excited when she did anyway. She said she needed to piss. By all means. While she shuffled to the toilet you peered at the bag of aquamarine serum you'd filtered out of her while she was dead. Little shimmers in there. Bioluminescent. You squeezed the bag and they brightened even more, dashed at your thumb from inside the plastic like one of those plasma ball toys. Bioluminescent and hungry. A few more minutes and they'd have eaten Jamie's entire bloodstream.

Sometimes you wondered what it felt like. You'd cut open plenty of corpses who'd found out. The bag of blue felt warmer the more you squeezed it. You filled a syringe with the glittering serum, slipped the vial into your coat pocket for later testing. Can't let the Feds have all the fun.

You heard a skittering over your shoulder, turned and saw a cluster of bugs on the threshold of the open doorway. Howdy, friends. Their antennae twitched with excitement and they gave a little hum that changed its tone when you let go of the serum. They scattered as Jamie returned from the restroom, almost running one over with her IV stand. She slid back into bed and asked for more Dilaudid. Then she got to talking.

*　　*　　*

Jamie Marguerite Aster was twenty-two years old and had spent most of her life training to become a professional dancer. She'd never tried drugs until recently, but she'd given several acclaimed performances in both classical and modern styles as a member of an East Hollywood theatre company, and was well on her way to beating the odds and making a living off her craft. Almost exactly one year ago, she had gotten in an argument with her ex-boyfriend which resulted in her spilling down a flight of stairs and breaking her ankle. By the time she moved in with her new boyfriend the theatre company had replaced her. The world turned too fast for a dancer who couldn't dance. So she started doing coke and painting instead. Her new boyfriend was very kind but also very into coke and things got out of hand fast.

(You noted to yourself, with a glance at the dangling serum bag, that it was also right around a year ago that UCLA scientists first reported the discovery of a new species of fist-sized, deep sea arthropod with the apparent ability to survive indefinitely on the surface. Jamie paused, maybe noticing your inattention, and you pretended to jot something on your clipboard. Yeah. Go on. What do you mean by out of hand?)

The first time they did meth together was like the first day of her life she'd actually been awake. Well. Three or four days. No sleep, no food, just painting and smoking and unbelievably passionate, if somewhat repetitive, fucking. And so much talking. They solved the mysteries of religion and unravelled conspiracies that spanned the cosmos. When they finally collapsed into an afterglow of giggles and naps, she'd wanted nothing more than to do it all again.

(You fidgeted in your seat at all the details, but you'd treated her type enough to know how to roll with it.)

So they did it again. Of course they did. Why wouldn't they? She couldn't dance, her boyfriend was out of work, the economy was dogshit and the government was beginning to limit travel into and out of Southern California for reasons that were never entirely clear. Jamie was painting a lot then, mostly landscapes and seascapes, in both classical and modern styles, her abstract touch lending a hint of the uncanny to otherwise realist compositions. She even sold a couple. And they were always on meth, just the two of them at first, then with others, new friends of her boyfriend who came over and eventually stopped leaving. They were nice enough. Interesting enough, anyway.

(You blinked at your clipboard, at the bug you'd been doodling without realising it.)

Before long things got blurry and she stopped paying attention to who exactly was living at their house at any given time. People change, after all, every minute of every day. Every time she talked to someone it was a new surprise. She slept very little and painted often. She mostly remembered feeling hungry and itchy. She lost all interest in sex but did not stop having sex, and not only with her boyfriend. Sometimes there were people in her bed and she had no idea how she knew them. It was one of these, a girl with blue hair named Bell, who brought her the crank.

(You took a deep breath and tapped your pencil. You knew how the rest went. For some reason you scribbled down *blue hair*. You thought you knew, anyway.)

* * *

The first scientific article describing the blue-eyed isopod (*Bathynomus azurocula*) made no speculations about their ecology, range, reproductive characteristics, or life history. It simply reported the discovery of several large, colonial invertebrates at a depth of 2,800 metres on a previously-unmapped slope of the Davidson Seamount. The submersible making the initial survey did not have adequate sampling capabilities, so a second vehicle was sent by UCLA which collected seven specimens. The animals were found to be a new species in the genus *Bathynomus*, the giant isopod. They were smaller than the other known species but potentially more numerous, given the high concentration of individuals in a relatively small sampling area. The authors noted the species showed remarkable resilience to changes in pressure, light, salinity, and even medium, seeming to thrive equally well out of water as in it.

The new isopods were named for their radiant, jewel-like compound eyes which sat between two pairs of antennae. They arrived onshore *en masse* three weeks later.

Jamie first mentioned the bugs after the nurse came to tell you in panicked tones there were more patients needing attention. I know, I know, you barked, sounding harrowed, sounding old and suddenly aware of it. How long had your voice been this way? Like a mouthful of sand. You told the nurse to please get another doctor, that you were with a responsive patient and needed to make thorough notes. The nurse frowned and split and you wondered if she knew that no one should have to go through what she was going through in a million years.

That's when Jamie coughed and said, Are they always watching?

What?

Can I have a glass of water?

You got her some water. Thanks, she said, then pointed at the vent on the ceiling. But yeah, so, they watch you too, huh?

You glanced to find three up there, spindly feet dangling through the grates, antennae flitting excitedly.

How much did Jamie know? As far as you were aware, the public hadn't connected the arrival of the bugs to the influx of superpowered meth that had swept through the county. People are good at compartmentalising, and freak-giant scuttlers are nothing new in Los Angeles, California. The blue-eyes avoided crowds and buildings for the most part, though you could see them all over outside, slipping down a storm drain or up a tree, darting under cars at the stop light. Aside from environmentalists raising invasive species concerns, most people ignored them. You did too, for a while. Jamie was the first person you met who seemed to know what they were up to.

They sure do look like they're watching, don't they, you asked, trying to play it casual in case she was just rambling.

Oh, they've been into me for a while. They started watching around when Bell brought the first crank. They wanted to get into my skin and I think maybe some of them did. I don't think they mean any harm by it though. Also a lot of them were there tonight, when we went to get the pure stuff.

You turned in your chair to face the bugs. Your legs were bouncing. The bugs seemed much more casual than you did. You took a pull from your flask, deciding you didn't care if Jamie saw, then turned to her and leaned in close.

Look, you whispered, right now only my staff knows you made it. But there will be more soon. People in suits. Cops. You *cannot* tell them anything you're telling me now, you understand? Anybody besides me asks, you did a hit and passed out and you don't know jack shit besides that.

Jamie squinted. You realised you were squeezing her wrist. Jamie, you got it?

She looked up and waved to the bugs, a smile leaking off her lips, and made a *shh* gesture with her finger.

She got it.

★   ★   ★

Once Jamie got her first taste of Bell's crank she immediately took measures to ensure she was on it at all times. There were no doubts, no second thoughts, no addict's pillow-squeezing guilt. There was only Bell and Bell's mysterious, magical, unfathomably powerful blue shards. Time passed or it didn't. Jamie's house became a living toilet where people and their detritus swirled together, collected in corners, left skid marks wherever they went. The crank, or some said *sparkle*, was the only constant. Her paintings transmogrified into wild distortions of the vistas they once depicted. Colours bled out of inverse mountains, a cubical sea swallowed the moon, sabretooth trees disembowelled the sky. She couldn't be stopped. She painted with chalk, dirt, jizz, her own blood, whatever the drug led her to. She lost track of her boyfriend. Someone said he'd left, someone said died, someone said he was just in the other room. It was a silly thing to worry about either way. She started noticing the bugs around that time, but didn't bother shooing them out. All that mattered was the crank. And the only thing more compelling than the crank itself was Bell's insistence that this stuff was mostly filler.

(You'd heard similar stories. Sometimes you'd get a patient who had just barely edged an overdose; their supply had been cut with pseudoephedrine or farm fertiliser by some enterprising and merciful dealer. The critical blue serum only overtook the circulatory system upon end-stage heart failure, so these lucky dabblers didn't even need dialysis. Once they were stable they got to go home, instead of the crematorium.)

It was something like 4:00 a.m. yesterday when Bell told Jamie they could go to the Source together. Bell said it was where all the sparkle came from. Of course Jamie had been thrilled. She didn't waste a second. They went outside without locking the house and walked seven miles on foot from East Hollywood to Vernon. How long had it been since she'd actually gone outside? Along the way she caught the sapphire eyes of bugs at every corner, and wondered whether it was the same bugs following them from home, or different bugs who happened to be everywhere.

They arrived at a crumbling old textile factory that had been converted to lockouts for bands to rehearse in. Bass oppressed the dim halls, fat and noteless, carrying the stench of spilled beer and cigarettes out from the practice rooms. Bell led Jamie to door #381 and paused.

Okay, Bell said to Jamie. I should tell you now that we aren't supposed to be here. She reached in her tight pants and handed Jamie a switchblade and said, You cool? And Jamie was cool. She'd never used a weapon before but her whole life had led to this moment and she liked how the blade looked in her skinny fingers, next to the scabs where the bugs had been trying to get in. She nodded to Bell and Bell began sticking keys into the many locks on door #381.

(You made a face at Jamie and stood. Checked the hallway. At the far end, three Feds in hazmat suits were wheeling out a body and packaging the serum that'd been collected from it. You hoped to God they hadn't heard about Jamie yet. You closed the door and three bugs scuttled in through the crack before you shut it. Oh, sure. Make yourselves at home.)

It took Bell a long time to get the door open. There were at least ten padlocks and while Bell had all the keys, she said half were stolen and the other half were forged. All Jamie could think about was how badly she wanted the Source. They were so close she could feel it. At one point she grabbed the keys from Bell and started on the locks herself because it was taking too long. The band practising down the hall started an extra-fast cover of 'Rise Above' just before the final lock clicked open.

Bell gave Jamie a final nod and they pushed inside. Hundreds of bugs swarmed out, so many they must have been piled on top of each other in there.

Then they saw it.

(A bead of sweat hit your clipboard as Jamie paused. She seemed to zone out, slumped back in bed with a glaze on her eyes. Was it the Dilaudid? You checked her vitals, all good. She was simply done talking. The tweaker evaporated out of her and you found yourself staring at a twenty-two-year-old girl from Glendale who wanted to be a dancer. You scanned through your notes. *Blue hair. Sparkle. Vernon. The Source.* There was blood crusted on your hands. Whose blood? How long since you'd slept? How many deaths for this one miracle? Where would it end? There were bugs under your chair, wiggling their antennae up at the bag of Jamie's serum.)

Jamie?

Yeah?

Are you feeling okay?

I'm fine. Actually, I feel pretty good.

Can you tell me what happened inside that room?

Her breath whistled up her nose. She giggled, almost sweetly. What do you mean, can I tell you?

You leaned in close, voice hoarse and thin. I mean what did you find? A stash, a dealer, a lab? You gotta understand, I've been at this for months. Even when we find traces of the drug we can't sequence it. Our shit breaks when we try to analyse it. All we have to go on is this.

You grabbed the dangling serum bag and shook it and one of the bugs hissed.

Jamie. Do you know what this stuff does? Do you know what happens to the corpses?

She moved her head a little, might have been a nod or something else.

These little shimmers. The *sparkles*. They aren't bacterial or animal or fungal, honestly no one knows what they are but they're alive. They permeate the bloodstream once the heart stops. They get bigger. They start breaching the skin. The Feds make us incinerate every body and every drop of serum, so we don't know what they grow *into*, but... Do you get what I'm saying, Jamie? The Feds think it'll be self-limiting; they think they can just deep-fry the victims and keep it all hush-hush but they're wrong. It's spreading. Unless we can figure out where it's coming from and what the fuck it *is*, we'll never stop it. Pretty soon there will be too many for us to handle. Do you understand? You gotta tell me, Jamie. Please! What was the Source? What did you find in that room?

Jamie looked you in the eyes, calm and unfazed. You knew you sounded completely unhinged but to Jamie you might as well have been reading the phonebook. You finished off your flask and tossed it to the ground, scattering the bugs. Fuck them.

Jamie smiled. You saved my life, Doc. If I could tell you, I would. It's just, I just, I don't know the words. She leaned over the side of the bed, rested her cheek on yours, whispered in your ear. Why don't you go and see for yourself?

The door flung open. On the threshold stood three Feds, suited up and gawking like they'd just found life on Mars.

★   ★   ★

Oh, said the one in front.

Sorry about that, said another.

Goddamn bugs, said the third as a few blue-eyes darted out between his legs.

We didn't realise anyone was, uh. Is she in the wrong ward?

You stood, pushed up your glasses. She's in the correct ward. She's a survivor.

There was a bloated silence.

Front Helmet spoke again. We're going to step out to confer with our branch chief. Don't go anywhere.

You nodded. Of course not.

Front Helmet pointed to the bag of serum. This is hers?

Yes.

She survived a full extraction?

Yes.

Standard procedure?

No. My procedure.

More silence. Front Helmet paced across the room and unhooked the bag. The door slammed behind them as they returned to the hall.

You spoke to Jamie out the side of your face. Remember what I told you.

She nodded, brought a finger to her lips. *Shh.*

Chances are they'll just ask some questions. Don't give them a reason not to. You don't know anything, you don't remember anything, you're just another tweaker who took a hit from somebody you don't know and now you're here.

You got it, Doc.

She still looked calm. That was good. You thought about saying something like *Once you're out of here, I'll come find you,* but before you made up your mind the door opened again and the helmets came in hot.

All right. We'll take the patient with us now.

Your heart slammed into your stomach. Excuse me?

They didn't answer. Just walked over to Jamie's bed and started rolling it out. Her calmness vanished the second she saw your expression.

This is my patient. You positioned yourself between the bed and the door. You're not taking her anywhere unless I say so.

In fact, said Front Helmet, we are.

Take her where? How will I follow up on her recovery?

The Department of Health has authority on this matter, Doctor. You can contact your ward liaison with any questions.

You found yourself leaning on the foot of the bed, pushing against them.

Sir, please don't make me call the security team,

You think you can just fucking roast her, is that it? You don't care about stopping this shit as long as you can keep it quiet. You want to murder our first survivor.

He scowled inside his helmet, held up his hands, glanced to the floor, saw the flask.

Sir, I believe you are not thinking clearly—

Bullshit.

You looked Jamie in the eyes. You saw her fear and matched it. Your heart was fucking pounding. You communicated without words and somehow she heard you. You watched as she slowly, surreptitiously slid the IV out of her arm.

The rest happened in about six seconds. You reached into your coat and pulled out the vial you'd taken of Jamie's serum. All three Feds lunged at you as you plunged the stopper, painting them in thin streaks of gleaming blue.

And the bugs were on them. Dozens, maybe hundreds, of blue-eyed isopods swarmed in from the vent and the hallway and smothered the three helmets, darting over one another in mad bursts of insectoid speed, sharp legs ripping holes in the hazmats, armoured bodies obscuring the Feds entirely. You might have yelled *Run!* Or you might not have had to. Either way, Jamie was out the door, down the hall, past the stairwell. From the window you saw her vanish behind traffic, pursued by three security guards but with a good lead on them. One of the helmets shoved you over in his frantic attempt to get free of the bugs. You cracked your head on the floor, and for the first time in ages you got some sleep.

★   ★   ★

It's your first night off in weeks, and Jamie's a heavy memory. Maybe you've been daydreaming for hours, maybe it all flashed by in a second. There are scuttling sounds beneath your car and the rumble of bass up above. Maybe you've cruised past this spot a few times, this old cracked factory by the Vernon train tracks. Maybe you've almost gone inside once or twice.

This time you're ready.

The garage is unlit and you fumble through the glovebox, past your car registration and your handscrawled notes and all the court papers. You can't help smirking when you think of the trial. The helmets gave damning testimony, but the Department of Health couldn't risk losing a good doctor, especially not one who pioneered a successful treatment procedure. In a twisted way you feel thankful for the rapidly increasing caseload and resulting shortage of medical personnel. A hefty fine and a transfer to a different hospital is a small price to pay for biologically assaulting three federal agents.

You find your flask. Hot vodka smooths your nerves, keeps you in focus despite all the sleep deprivation, the endless nights at the hospital and the long mornings at home testing the serum however you can, trying to learn something, anything. You wonder if there will ever be any answers and you tell yourself if there are, they'll be here. Then back into the glovebox for the keyring you swiped off Jamie's hoodie after she'd escaped in her gown. You step out the car.

Hey, little guys.

A dozen blue-eyes watch from the corners as you head from your car to the stairway. The bugs have been following you lately, you're sure of it. Maybe you smell like serum all the time now, or maybe they're upset you keep saving people. Jamie was the first, but not the last. You're up to fourteen now. The Feds leave the survivors alone now that there are too many cases to keep secret. Maybe they would have let Jamie go, too. You're glad you didn't risk it.

The lockout halls are all sweat and drum thunder, the shrieks and croons of vocalists coming muted through the concrete walls. A girl with a guitar case and pink hair brushes past and says she likes your scrubs. Thanks. Did you really forget to change?

Door #381 lies at the end of an especially dim corridor. You feel the bugs eyeing you as you approach, put your ear to the cold door and hear nothing. You examine the many padlocks, just like Jamie had described.

You start trying keys. Your heart beats faster with each click. This must be how Jamie felt when she and Bell were this close. Your phone rings and you ignore it. The band down the hall starts a song. Maybe you recognise it. *Rise above, we're gonna rise above.* No, that was Jamie's story. This is something else. Probably an original.

The final lock clicks, slides off and hits the floor. You take a deep breath. The Source, that's what Jamie called it. The place where all the sparkle came from. You realise, for all your research, all your frontline toil and testing and notetaking and endless, unrelenting contemplation, you have no idea what you expect to find in here. Some mad-science meth lab, maybe, or an isopod the size of a truck. A pile of corpses covered in tiny, wiggling cilia, thousands of them growing from every pore, pulsing in odd patterns, sparkling with a bluish glow. Anything is possible, and also nothing is. That's the way you've started to think.

You hear the bugs in the hall right behind you. Skittering, humming, excited. You press on the door. It's heavy. You shove again. It budges a little. A cluster of bugs scurry over your feet. Maybe you gasp, maybe it doesn't even surprise you. You brace yourself, throw your shoulder into the door and then you're inside.

Dark. Your eyes adjust, heart pounding so hard it'd break an EKG. Your stomach flips when you see it.

Or don't see it. The room is empty. Immaculate, even. Fresh white paint on the walls, dull red carpet with vacuum lines up and down it. No bugs except the few who followed you inside. You scour the vacant cube, squint at the ceiling and kneel to the baseboards. Nothing.

One thing.

Near the doorway, on the carpet, you find a single strand of long, blue hair. You pick it up, twirl it in your fingers.

Your phone rings again, and without thinking, you answer.

Hey, Doc.

It's one of your nurses. Your reply is a parched whisper. Evening.

Look, I know this is terrible, but is there any possible way you can come in tonight? We just got fucking slammed. A whole party, seventeen of them. Some are barely still breathing.

You stare at the strand of hair. Did you ever get Jamie's address?

The nurse continues, through tears this time. They're teenagers, Doc. Kids. And no meth. It got into them some other way. We're trying to stabilise them, but the dialysis machines are all in use and... Hello? Are you there?

Everything feels blurry then. You squeeze a hand over your eyes, wipe your forehead. You turn to the doorway, see the blue-eyes creeping around the corners, watching and waiting. You guess they'll always be watching. Always waiting. For what?

Doc? Say something.

You raise the phone to your lips, croak out a response. Had the original Source been moved? Was there even a Source to begin with?

You take out your flask, swish it around. You start to polish it off. Before the booze hits your lips you toss it away, let it spill out onto the carpet. Where is Jamie now? Who is Bell? What are those sparkles in the serum, and what happens to the victims who aren't incinerated? So many questions. No one to answer them but you. Meanwhile, seventeen kids need a miracle.

You've got work to do.

A MYSTERY FOR JULIE CHU
Stephen Gallagher

It was a ramshackle acre of iron rails and wooden pens with a corrugated tin roof to keep off the rain. Midweek, it was the biggest livestock auction yard in the county. Tuesdays were sheep, Thursdays were cattle. On the seventh day they opened up the parking lot and ran a car boot sale right there in the stalls.

Julie Chu rarely missed a weekend.

In a perfect world she'd get there early to scout for cast-off treasures, but at weekends her housemates liked to sleep in late. She'd no car and didn't drive, so she relied on them for rides. Trading in recent memorabilia gave her a living; not a great one, but it kept her afloat. Julie Chu had an instinct for neglected value.

With Natalie and Gemma off on the hunt for vintage clothing, Julie did her scouting alone. A good Sunday might see a couple of thousand visitors shuffling through the pens, back and forth like an airport line, following the cattle route around the sale ring. People from the area ransacked garages and attics for goods they could sell; old clothes, old books, picture frames, glassware, wedding china, *stuff*. Families from town made a day of it and came out to browse, with social distancing a dim memory.

Among the weekend dealers and part-time traders she was drawn mainly to those who were simply clearing house; toys and games and plastic jewellery, jigsaws and snow globes, grandma's clock and grandpa's buttons. It was here that discoveries could be made.

Toward the end of a fruitless hour she stopped before a picnic table with three open suitcases displaying bric-a-brac, and immediately her senses flared.

She picked up a boxed doll and turned it for the stallholder to see. She said, "How much for this?"

The stallholder was a woman in her 50s, bundled up in several coats and sitting low in a folding chair. She'd been reading a fat paperback. Beside her were a Thermos flask and a small dog on a blanket.

She said, "Call it five pounds?"

"Can I see it out of the box?"

The woman shrugged in agreement, so Julie opened the box. The doll was loose inside. She tipped it out for a closer look.

The woman said, "All the bits are there, I think. I've had it in a cupboard for years."

Now the little dog had raised its head and was taking an interest too. Fighting the urge simply to throw down the money and run with the goods, Julie said, "So it's not been played with in all that time?"

"I offered her to our Chloe. She was all, '*Ooh, thank you, Grandma, she's lovely,*' but then she didn't take it with her. You have your memories but you can't hang on to everything. Times are tight. I lost my husband last year."

Julie slid the doll back into its box. She didn't set it down while she fumbled out her purse, but guarded it as if some other scavenger might swoop in like a gull and snatch it like a toddler's chips.

As she sorted out a banknote, she continued to glance over the stall. She saw a souvenir tea towel, some coasters. A selection of ties. Cufflinks. Who wore cufflinks anymore? A gents' wristwatch, nothing expensive, still in its box.

I lost my husband last year.

She stopped with the money in her hand.

"I can't do this," she said.

"I'll take four," the woman said.

"No, I mean…" Julie stopped, and then went on. "Do you know what you've got here?" The woman looked blank. "It's a Brunette No-Bangs Francie from the Barbie range. Before you sell it you need to get it valued."

"I'm not daft," the woman said. "I showed it to a friend who knows about these things."

"And?"

"It's not a proper Barbie. They're the ones that are worth the money. Do you want it or not?

"I absolutely should, but I could be robbing you."

"Fine," the woman said, "I'll get it looked at," in a tone that seemed anything but grateful. She reached across and removed the box from the hands of the trader's nemesis, the time-waster.

She said, "Satisfied?" and set the box at the back of the stall, out of Julie's reach.

Julie wanted to say something. But there was no rescuing the situation.

So she moved on.

She took in nothing of the next two or three stalls. She was too busy cursing herself. Empathy was a weakness in this trade, and she knew it. In the right condition a No-Bangs Francie NRFB – Never Removed from Box – could fetch three times the price of a 1912 Meissen figurine. The one she'd just handled was less than fine, but it was a good example and the box was original.

She was still brooding over it when something else caught her eye.

She'd reached the worst-lit and least-frequented end of the shed. All of the livestock pens beyond this point were empty. Behind his table in this last enclosure sat a grim-faced man in a canvas chair with his arms folded, staring ahead, mind adrift. Spread out before him was an odd selection of used garden tools and teen bedroom clutter.

"Hi," Julie said. "Having a good day?"

This drew from him a grudging, "I've had better."

One item had drawn her interest. Between a set of hair straighteners and the usual stack of Harry Potters was a squat figure in dark blue plastic, roughly the size and shape of a small biscuit barrel.

She took a closer look. It was a novelty radio in the form of a cartoon robot. It had a wide frog-mouthed head, a speaker with two tuner buttons on its chest, and two useless spindly arms with oversized hands.

She began to reach for it, then paused.

"Can I?" she said.

"Go ahead," he said. "But there's no batteries."

"Does it work?"

"Far as I know. Sold as seen. That means you take your chances."

"I know what it means."

She'd never seen a piece like it before. It might be of interest, it might be worthless. Novelty radios, like novelty teapots, were unpredictable sellers. The brand was a minor collectable name. Not in the Disney class, but recognisable. The logo on the chest read *Mr. Disco*. He had a telescoping FM aerial and he was accessorised with a little microphone headset, like Madonna's.

When she picked him up there wasn't much weight to him. The knobs clicked when turned. The battery cover was present and the compartment clean.

She said, "How much?"

"Make me an offer."

"Will you take four?"

"It's yours."

She paid with a couple of two-pound coins and stowed the radio in her satchel. Not an exciting find, more a consolation purchase.

"Thanks," she said.

The man only grunted.

She moved on, nodded to the Rug Man further along, and began giving a second look to some of the stands she'd skimmed. But her heart wasn't in it now. She was trying to think of some way to go back and rescue the Francie sale, given that the woman hadn't cared for her advice and almost certainly wouldn't follow it.

Truly, she thought, no good deed ever goes unpunished.

Julie needed the money. These weekend expeditions supported her studies; Medieval History, postgrad, UCL. She'd originally envisaged herself ferreting out antiquities, only to find that her real talent lay elsewhere. Most of her finds she'd sell on eBay, but any rarities went to a big-name auction saleroom in London. Julie's kind of low pop culture would never be their core business, but they couldn't afford to ignore it. They ran a regular online sale in which a Steiff bear or a Beatle signature would appear with a provenance as meticulous as any Rodin or Rubens.

Maybe she could go back and offer a tenner?

But no. When she went by the stall again, the woman was talking to someone and the doll was gone.

Outside the covered area stood an enclosure with food trucks and picnic tables and a First Aid post. Julie's gloom must have been apparent when she met up with Natalie by the refreshment van.

"Hey," Natalie said.

"Hey yourself," Julie said.

"Got something that might cheer you up," her housemate said, and presented Julie with a box.

It was Brunette No-Bangs Francie.

"You owe me three pounds," Natalie said. "Pay for the coffee and we'll call it quits."

"How did you—"

"I saw it and wondered if it was your kind of thing. But I knew you'd been by, so I assumed you didn't want it. Then the woman told me about this pushy Chinese girl who tried to fool her into thinking it was some rare antique."

"I was trying to do her a good turn!"

"She also said, 'I don't know what her game was, but I don't trust any of those people after they gave us that virus.'"

"Well, fuck her then. Three pounds?"

"After what she said about you I beat her down from five."

"Good," Julie said, feeling significantly better.

They drank scalding coffee from eco-unfriendly cups, waited for Gemma who didn't appear, and then separated for one last go-around. It was early afternoon but some of the stallholders were already packing up to leave. In her brightened mood Julie bought a knitted hat that took her fancy and said hello to a few of the regulars, including the seller of old Belgian film posters and the man who did a thriving trade in obscure parts and trim for classic cars.

"Hi Maurice," she said to Car Parts Guy. "What's new?"

"Nothing here, and I'll sue anyone who says different," Maurice said. Same joke, every week.

The quiet part of the shed was even quieter now. The grumpy man who'd sold her the novelty radio was gone, and the site manager had come down to clear his stall. She saw him bend to reach for something on the concrete floor, picking it out of the last week's unswept straw.

"Cheers, John," she called out. "See you next Sunday."

"Look at this," the site manager said. "Who throws money away?"

He held out his hand for her to see.

On his palm lay a pair of two-pound coins.

★   ★   ★

They found Gemma, and all three of them squeezed into Natalie's black Yaris for the drive back to Ealing. Gemma had spent the morning hovering and hesitating over an Italian designer jacket, sold as new-without-tags at a price that was too good to be true. In the end she caved and bought it anyway.

"I know it has to be a fake," she said as they were reaching the motorway. "But I still like it."

"Let me have a look," Julie said, and Gemma passed the carrier bag over into the back of the car.

"The label's Italian," she said. "But it has to be a knock-off. Doesn't it?"

Julie pulled the jacket partway out of the bag, checked the label, felt the material, looked at the lining.

She said, "Don't quote me on this, it's not my field. But looking at the quality I'd say, yes and no."

Natalie, from the wheel, said, "What does that mean?"

Julie said, "Every season the Milan fashion houses take their designs down to Naples. They put on a presentation for the tailoring workshops and invite them to bid on the jobs. So many pieces, at such a price, by such a date. Every bidder's given a supply of fabric. They're taking a risk because only the first one to meet the target will be paid. But the others get to keep the free cloth and sell off what they made."

"And my jacket could be one of theirs?"

"It's how the system works. The big labels turn a blind eye."

Gemma said, "How do you know so much about stuff?"

"The girl has a gift," Natalie said.

An hour later, they were home. Home was a shared house on a quiet North Ealing street. Julie's housemates were all smart young women of a similar age; flighty Gemma, fearless Natalie, and serious Victoria who'd stayed behind that morning to work on her dissertation. Natalie dropped off her passengers and went cruising for a parking spot.

Julie's room was one floor up at the back, with a view over railway lines. She threw her coat on the bed, kicked her shoes under it, and turned her attention to the day's haul.

She took the doll from its box and held it for a while, feeling the thrill of its rarity. The lesser items included a couple of pieces of paste jewellery with Suffragette associations, a tortoiseshell fountain pen, and a badly stained copy of *The Lost World* that might be a useful source of plates.

Finally, Mr. Disco. She needed to see if he was in working order.

Natalie wasn't back yet and Gemma was in her room with music turned up loud, so she went upstairs and knocked on Victoria's door.

Victoria was working but seemed to welcome the interruption. Julie held up the toy and said "Do you have a nine-volt battery? I need to test this."

"Nine-volt battery," Victoria said. "That we can do."

She dragged the chair from her desk and out onto the landing. There she climbed onto it to reach the smoke alarm. She popped open the alarm cover and took out the cell.

"There you go."

Curious, she followed Julie back down to her room and watched from the doorway. Julie installed the battery and then used the knobs on the robot's chest to tune the radio to a music station.

Out came Elton John. 'Crocodile Rock'.

Mr. Disco had begun to sing and dance.

With no legs to speak of, a motor lurched the stumpy body from side to side like a bucket on a rolling deck. Some internal sensor was flapping the mouth in perfect synchronisation with the vocal, to hypnotic effect.

After a while Victoria said, "That is… bizarre."

"Isn't it?" Julie said.

When the track ended and music gave way to radio ads, Mr. Disco mimed along with those voices too.

"Is it worth anything?" Victoria said.

"I'm looking now." Julie was on her phone, searching eBay. If there were other examples out there, she could get an idea of the going rate.

By the time she'd found it Mr. Disco was dancing along to the news, accompanying the broadcast with the whirring of his motors and the clack-clack-clack of his wide plastic mouth, opening and closing like a letter flap.

"Not much," she said, disappointed. There were three on offer, two with no bids and the third with a *Buy It Now* price of twenty-five pounds and no takers. Victoria detached herself from the doorway, to head back upstairs.

"Don't forget to put the battery back in the alarm," she said. "Lest we all die in our beds."

With her attention still on her phone, Julie reached to turn off the radio. She heard something addressed to her and replied, "Why not?"

Victoria reappeared in the doorway. "Sorry?"

Julie looked back over her shoulder. "You just said, '*No, Julie*'."

"Not me."

There was an awkward moment.

Then Julie said, "Oh. Okay."

Strange.

When Victoria had gone, Julie shut off all switches and removed the battery. After restoring the smoke alarm she came back and placed Mr. Disco on her shelf with the books.

She wouldn't lose money on him, but he wasn't the prize he might have been. She should have known.

That was the point, she realised. She *should* have known. For once her instincts had steered her wrong.

Well, it was bound to happen.

Sometime.

★   ★   ★

The next day, Monday morning, she carefully packed the weekend's more promising finds into her satchel and took the Piccadilly Line into town, nursing the bag on her knees. First she had to make a stop at the University College campus in Bloomsbury, where she checked her History Department pigeonhole for any flyers or mail. Then to her supervisor's office, which was locked and empty. She'd been hoping to ask about the possibility of making some extra money with a teaching assignment or two. He was supposed to be in his office and available, but he wasn't.

On the way out she saw a few faces, all young, all strangers. She'd been around longer than any of them, but she felt like the outsider. Her own cohort had moved on and out into the world. Of them, only Julie remained.

She took the long way around to avoid the biosciences building, the sight of which was still hard to bear. It would always remind her of Sean. Dear Sean. The rotten, selfish bastard.

Next, the Tube to South Kensington and the salerooms.

The auction house had been in business at the same address for over two hundred years. Its fortunes were built on the contents of Great Houses and the gambling debts of those eighteenth-century gentlemen who married into money and then burned right through it. Behind its understated frontage stretched an off-street warren stuffed with riches and with labyrinthine internal geography. The public areas were open for viewing of the upcoming Modern Masters sale, but Julie signed in at the desk and then headed backstage into Storage and Conservation.

"Mac," she said, "have you got a minute?"

'Mac' Matheson was Julie's regular point of contact. Not an executive but the longest-serving of the saleroom porters, the men in brown coats and white gloves who handled all the objects and brought them out for display. Mac had been with the company for forty years, much longer than the current owners. He despised everyone in the place, but he seemed to have a soft spot for Julie.

"Don't tell me," he said. "Another of your car boot weekends."

"I think I found something good."

She laid out her goods on his big table. The No Bangs Francie first.

"Dolls aren't really my field," Mac said, but he took a look. In his time he'd handled everything from mummy fragments to Dresden porcelain. Julie always noticed a slight tremor in his hands when he examined her latest finds, but she never said anything.

He said, "Good to Very Good for its age. Say VG minus. Playworn and collectable. Is it complete?"

"Seems to be."

"Bit of restoration needed on the corners of the box, nothing too invasive."

She said, "A 1971 example went for fifteen hundred dollars in New York. But that was still in its box and sealed."

"You won't make half of that. But still not to be sneezed at."

He looked through the rest. One brooch he reckoned worthless, the other might make ninety, maybe a hundred on a good day. The damaged *Lost World* would go into stock, like a broken machine kept for parts.

Mac said, "Anything else?"

The bag was now empty. Julie said, "Just a dancing robot radio. Not the find I thought it was."

Mac's eyes narrowed.

"Dancing robot radio?" he said. "Would that be a Mr. Disco?"

"I checked online. They're ten a penny."

"Bring it next time," Mac said. "Let's have a look at it."

It was an interesting reaction. He wouldn't say more. He wrote a receipt for the goods and as she made to leave, he said, "See Mister Fisher before you go. He's got something for you."

Philip Fisher was the acquisitions manager. She knocked on his door, and entered when he called.

"Julie," he said, all languid charm and good manners. Fisher was entering middle age with his chiselled looks largely intact, though anyone could tell he'd had some eye work done.

"Mac said you had something for me?"

"I do. You're due some commission." He pushed an envelope across the desk. "As my old dad used to say, don't spend it all at once."

It would have been indecorous to look at the amount there and then, so she waited until she was five steps away from the door and then destroyed the envelope in her haste to get it open.

A cheque, as expected. She looked at the amount.

She blinked.

And then she went back in, forgetting to knock.

"There's been a mistake," she said.

"Let me see." Fisher took a look. Then he handed it back and said, "Don't panic, there's no mistake. You're too honest for your own good, Julie. That can set you back in this game."

"But it was just a toy gun," she said, recalling the rusty replica fit for little more than pirate cosplay. She'd almost let it pass, until some small internal voice had prompted her to haggle.

Fisher said, "Clearly we did rather well with it."

"Who paid that much?"

"I have two words for you. Don't ask. Just enjoy."

He wasn't joking. So this wasn't really the time to point out that he'd used four words.

She went looking for Mac to see if he could tell her more, but he'd been called down to the loading bay for an all-hands on a statue. So then she went straight to the nearest branch of her bank to pay the money into her account.

Back in Ealing she called by the Polish minimarket on her way from the station. She'd thesis notes to write up that evening, so a G&T in a can was as much celebration as she dared risk. At the same time she picked up an unbranded nine-volt battery. She couldn't keep stealing from the smoke alarm and Mac would no doubt want to see Mr. Disco in action, for no reason she could fathom.

But then, what did she know? That toy pistol. God Almighty. Picked up on an impulse, sold for a fortune.

How had she done that? Maybe she *did* have a gift.

If that's what you could call it.

★   ★   ★

At the house, in her room, she cleared her table and set a light for the evening's work. Laptop, books, notepad. She took her toothbrush out of its glass and rinsed the glass for her cocktail. Just to be posh.

It was tough to get going. She loved her subject, loved the work. But she spent so much of her daily life on the move that whenever she settled to it, exhaustion caught up with her. The gin probably wouldn't help with that, but what the hey.

She was fine for almost an hour. Then she began to wilt. Then Gemma put her music on. Julie wished she could be like Gemma, who bounced her way through a series of temp jobs and an equally rapid-fire turnover of boyfriends, sometimes using the music to cover their noisy sex.

The walls muffled the noise. Drowsiness rose in Julie like a fog. She tipped forward and rested her forehead on the desk, just for a few moments.

A brief darkness closed in. Just for one second.

She heard Sean's voice saying, "*Listen, Julie*".

What?

She sat upright and looked around and of course there was no one there. Certainly not Sean, whose voice would never be heard again. Still, for a moment she was uncertain. She'd been sure someone had spoken.

But no, it was just a brainfart in a microsleep. Such things happen when you're tired.

Her eye was caught by Mr. Disco, there on her shelf.

She tried to get back to work. But now she was aware of him. She got up and switched him on and off a couple of times, to be sure. When she put him back, she turned him around to face the wall. That didn't seem to help so after a while she stood up again and took him down and set him on the desk.

"Well?" she challenged him.

He'd been stopped in mid-rock, so he didn't sit straight. Now something gave way and he slowly settled into a resting pose, his mouth shutting with a click.

He seemed to be watching her, waiting for her next move.

She was going to say something else.

But instead she took out the cheap battery and he stayed under the bed for the rest of the night.

★   ★   ★

Before the end of the week she packed Mr. Disco in her satchel and set out for town. She found Mac in the saleroom porters' workshop. He had a stack of old books on his table where he'd been cutting mylar sleeves for their protection.

"I believe someone came into some money," he said, laying his craft knife down.

"I did," she said. "And it's all from that one commission. I've cleared my card bill and my rent's paid for the next six months."

"And you're not happy?"

"I just don't get it."

"We're talking about the duelling pistol?"

"Is that what it was? I picked it up for almost nothing. They said it was one of a pair."

"That can be a plus. Have a guess why."

"Because the buyer already had the other gun?"

"A collector will pay a lot of money to complete a set."

"A lot of money, I can understand. But this must have been a fortune. How could it be worth that much?"

Mac said, "Close the door."

She sensed something serious. She closed the door.

"Take a chair."

She sat.

He said, "Number one, those guns were not toys. And secondly... do you believe in magic, Julie?"

"No."

"And yet here you are, in the magic business." He slid over two identical-looking volumes in blue cloth binding with pictorial boards.

"Wells," he said. "*The First Men in the Moon*. Both are first edition, one of them a first printing. The other's first printing, but second state. That means…"

"They print all the pages in a single run and bind them as they sell."

"This one with the black endpapers, it's the first state. At some point the bindery switched to plain white. It's the only difference but collectors will pay thousands more for a first state copy. They're definitely paying for something. But what? Coloured paper?"

"What's your point?"

"You know my point. Two identical dinner plates. One's worthless, the other was on the *Titanic*. You, Julie, you can pick out the winner without knowing. I know, I've seen you do it."

"That was luck."

"It's consistent. What you can sense is real. It's why they keep you on."

She began to see what he was getting at.

What he was calling magic – it was the very engine of the trade, the invisible quality that drove desire.

He said, "The memorabilia you deal in, it has the purest magic because there's no other value to it. No precious materials, no craftsman's touch. It waits for the right person to come along and feel its pull. Tricky stuff, magic. Remember those X-ray specs you brought in? Did you ever try them?"

"No."

"Good. They'll give you a peek inside a person's soul. They'll also give you a brain tumour. That's why Philip Fisher's got them in his safe."

"But… What?"

"Magic can go wrong. Something can happen to bend it out of shape. There's a certain kind of collector who'll pay way over the odds for the aberrations. Fisher will sell those glasses when he finds the right buyer. When he does, you can cover your rent for the other half of the year."

"Come on, Mac," she said. "Am I supposed to believe that?"

"*You* come on, Julie," Mac said. "In your heart you know it's true. Like you suspected that rusty pistol was more than just a replica."

"I did get a buzz," she conceded.

"The original set was known as the Radetsky Pair. They were split up in the 1850s after six duels with five woundings and three fatal outcomes. By then the pistols had acquired a taste for blood. They'll always drive their new owners to seek each other out. Angry people stalking total strangers without knowing why."

"And I brought the set back together."

"Probably not for long. The guns enjoy the game too much."

"Okay then," Julie said, lifting her satchel onto the table. "Say that was so. What about this?" She brought out the novelty radio and placed it before him.

"Ah," Mac said, "your Mr. Disco."

"What you're calling magic," she said. "I mean, the bent out of shape kind. What if someone were to hear it speak? Would that count?"

"They all speak," Mac said. "It's what they do."

"But if it was speaking to *me*. And if it sounded like Sean."

"Sean?"

"We were together. He died."

Mac took the plastic radio and held it before him in his two hands, looking down on it like the face of a devoted dog. The googly eyes of the cartoon robot returned his gaze.

"Explain it to me, Mac," Julie said. "Or tell me it's a wind-up and let me off the hook."

Mac said, "All kinds of things can make the magic go wrong. None of them good. With Mr. Disco it was a workplace massacre at a warehouse in Leith. A forklift driver – he must have been unhinged or on crack or something, I really don't know. He went berserk, trapped his boss and three of his co-workers in a container, and set it on fire. A case of toys survived the blaze and some of them got onto the market. Rumours went around."

He looked up at her. "People swore they were hearing final messages from the dead."

"From the—"

"From the dead." He wasn't smiling. "Find a meaningful spot and you can pick up their signal. Imagine that. Personally I wouldn't try it. But in the market we're talking about, a working-order Mr. Disco from that tragedy in Leith now goes for serious money."

"X-ray specs that really work. Two pistols that pick a fight. And now a case of radio toys that can speak for the dead."

"Correct."

"And this could be one of them?"

"Sounds like it. Much depends on whether we can offer provenance. Are you putting it in for sale?"

She was silent for a while.

Then she said, "Not just yet."

He handed the radio back.

"Be careful, Julie," was all he said to her.

She put the toy into her satchel. Mac said nothing more as she let herself out.

Julie made her way to the street, her head reeling. It was mad stuff. Mad, mad stuff.

★   ★   ★

Whatever she tried, spinning the dial, moving the radio around her room, Julie couldn't get it to repeat the moment. So on Sunday she went looking for the man who'd sold Mr. Disco. He'd unloaded the item like a piece of bad luck and then thrown her money away, and there had to be a reason. She made her way to the unpopular corner, but he wasn't there.

So then she went to find John, the site manager, in his office overlooking the sale ring. As a county auctioneer he sometimes handled estate sales and brokered deals for the London houses. He'd known Julie for a while. Sometimes he'd give her a heads-up if he'd spotted something of special interest.

She explained her quest, or as much of it as she could sanely repeat. She said, "You might remember him, John. He left money on the ground."

"I know the one," John said. "He was a one-off. Long-faced miserable bugger."

"Have you got any contact details?"

"Are you after a refund?"

"I need some history."

John consulted his screen and called up the previous week's records. The man had paid for his pitch in cash and left no personal information, but he'd given his car registration for dealer parking.

"Now I feel bad," John said, still looking at the screen. "I've remembered him. He's the one whose daughter died. He was selling off her stuff because his wife couldn't move on."

"Worth knowing," Julie said.

Then she took the registration number to Maurice, the vintage car parts stallholder.

Maurice said, "You can get a vehicle history from a plate but they won't disclose owner details to the public."

"But you're not the public," Julie said. "You're in the trade. Yes?"

He'd seen this coming. "Leave me your number," he said.

"Thanks."

"No promises."

★   ★   ★

It was almost two years since Sean had made his way up to the roof of the university's Rockefeller building and stepped off. She didn't know if he'd planned it, or if it was an impulse. When he'd left her that morning, he'd given her no hint of what he'd intended.

In the movies they always land on a car. Sean had jumped into the narrow service courtyard behind the building and hit dumpsters and concrete. If he'd planned for instant oblivion, he didn't get it. He was conscious when the paramedics reached him, though he faded very soon after.

She was alone down here, in this deep narrow well of brick and cement that echoed with a constant roar of industrial strength cooling fans. None of the windows above had been cleaned in some time. But there was recent trash and there were empty gas cylinders, so the area was in use. She couldn't linger.

She felt foolish. She felt scared. But *find a meaningful spot*, Mac had said. What place could be more charged with meaning than this? She took out Mr. Disco and extended the antenna.

She spun the tuner all the way through the FM waveband, and heard nothing but static. Not Capital, not LBC, nor anything from the BBC. The buildings all around her must be blocking the signal.

But what should it matter, if that wasn't the kind of signal she was looking for? So she began again, turning the small plastic button more slowly this time.

Back then, the police had come to visit and they'd given her a hard time. Had she and Sean argued that morning? What had they argued about? In the absence of a note or any kind of a farewell, they clearly had a narrative that they were looking to prove. The narrative being that someone – Julie, it could only be Julie – must have driven him to it.

But there had been no argument, there'd been no sign. She'd known that he had a history, that at the age of fifteen he'd tried to overdose on his mother's prescription meds. He'd had help for that, and could joke about it with her. Whatever his darkness, he'd kept it well hidden.

The static faded, and Mr. Disco turned his head to look at her.

She took her hand from the button. For a moment she held her breath. Then—

"Sean?" she ventured.

"*Julie,*" the little robot said, letterbox mouth clacking. "*I've missed you.*"

Her pulse was racing. Somehow this didn't feel absurd. Although she couldn't imagine how it must look to anyone who might glance down from one of those dusty windows.

"Is it you?" she said.

"*Yes. Yes it is.*"

"You broke me," she said.

"*I'm so sorry.*"

"What did I do wrong?"

"*Nothing! You held off the pain for so long. But my destination was always the same. I fought with life. Life won. I loved you. Forgive me. Please.*"

In her mind she was composed but she could feel the tears running down her face.

"They said it had to be my fault."

"*It's not all about you, Julie.*"

"Fuck's sake, Sean," she said. "You selfish bastard."

"*I know,*" the wee chap said. "*But what can you do?*"

And slowly, too soon, the music faded in.

★　　★　　★

She waited at the end of the close until the man came out of the house and got into his car. His head was down and she didn't get a good look at his face, but it had to be him. The car's plate matched the number from the boot sale records. Maurice had finally come through with the address.

She'd been hanging around for more than an hour. A convenient bus stop on the far side of the road had provided both shelter and an excuse, but after letting five buses go by she'd begun to feel conspicuous.

With the car gone, she crossed to the house and rang the doorbell.

The woman who opened the door was as washed-out as the flowers on a thrift shop summer dress. Julie needed no special intuition here. She recognised the draining effects of grief well enough.

The woman said, "Yes?"

Julie reached into her satchel and said, "You'll remember this."

The woman looked down at Mr. Disco.

"Oh God," she said.

"I bought it at the boot sale. I need you to tell me why your husband got rid of it."

"He cleared everything out," she said. "Even though I said no."

"Because you told him your daughter was trying to speak to you."

The woman tensed, and stared at Julie.

Julie said, "She was, wasn't she?"

The woman glanced around for watching neighbours, and then curtly beckoned Julie into the hallway. It wasn't an invitation, she just didn't want to risk being overheard. She held on to the door without closing it all the way, ready to push Julie out if she had to.

She said, "Who put you up to this?"

"Nobody," Julie said. "I lost someone too."

"He said it was for my own good. He thinks I'm going insane."

"You're not," Julie said. "You're in pain. Maybe your daughter knows it and she wants to help. Either way. Don't you want to hear?"

"Don't play with me."

"I can show you if you'll let me."

The woman took a moment. Then she closed the front door and beckoned for Julie to follow her upstairs.

The room that they entered was furnished but stripped bare. No sheets on the single bed, no clutter on the dresser, a few marks on the walls where posters had been.

"He did it while I was out," she said. "Everything's gone."

And then, "She was only thirteen."

"This works best if you can find the sweet spot. Where did she die?"

"We found her in bed."

"Has the bed been moved?"

The woman shook her head. Julie had expected more resistance, some disbelief. But it was as if she'd brought bread to the starving.

Once more Julie drew out the antenna and then placed Mr. Disco on the mattress. The woman asked nothing. Just held her breath and stared hard, as if willing her daughter's voice to come.

Julie turned the knob and searched through the airwaves. There was music. Then static. Then other music.

Then suddenly—

"*Mum?*"

There was silence in the room.

"*Are you there?*"

"Say something," Julie urged.

"I'm here," the woman managed.

"*There's something I should have told you. But I didn't know how.*"

"Tell me anything," the woman said. "Tell me now."

She leaned in to listen as Mr. Disco continued to speak with the dead child's voice, and at that moment Julie heard a car door slam outside. She looked out of the window and saw the woman's husband about to re-enter the house.

"Shit," she said.

The dead child was still talking and now the woman was crying while from downstairs came the sound of the front door being opened. Julie heard the man call out just as his wife let out an agonised wail, and that was it. Julie grabbed up Mr. Disco and headed for the door.

They met on the landing, but he was too surprised to stop her as she pushed by to get to the stairs. He caught sight of the robot radio clutched under her arm, antenna still extended, the child's voice gone and some shadow of a music station now struggling to come through. His response was one of horror.

"What did you do?" he called down after her.

He was still calling over the sound of his wife's screaming as Julie made her escape.

"What did you *do?*"

*   *   *

"What *did* you do?" Mac said.

"I blew his cover," Julie said. "Or his daughter did. She took her own life because he'd been touching her since she was small. Now she was growing up and it was getting worse. The mother knew nothing about it."

"And now she does."

"Now she does. So that turned out well."

"You shouldn't feel bad," Mac said.

"I don't," Julie said. "I got what I went for. What will happen now?"

Mr. Disco sat on the table between them. Under Mac's inspection lamp he showed a lot of wear and scratches, none of which would affect his value.

Mac said, "There's one of the Midnight Auctions next month. Selected private clients only. He'll be very sought after."

"Good to know," she said.

Maybe his next owner would use him better. With everything from the child's bedroom captured on her phone, the recording would serve as both provenance and a warning.

Mr. Disco. She wouldn't be sorry to see him go.

"I've found my niche, Mac," she said. "Tainted magic. What's not to love?"

Empathy was a weakness in this trade, and she knew it.

AWAY DAY

Lisa Tuttle

The email from headquarters announced an away day for members of staff to attend a special training course in Inverness at the end of January. It was the first such invitation Kirsty had received, and although she did not like the sound of "a series of tough mental and physical challenges that will boost morale and create team unity", her spirits lifted. She felt even happier when her line manager, Val, offered to take the lot of them in her car, so long as nobody bitched about her choice of music. After a year on the team Kirsty was still the outsider who didn't get invited out, or understand her colleagues' in-jokes, but that would surely change after four hours in a car together.

But on the day before they were to go, Val took Kirsty aside, a solemn expression on her narrow pixie face, and said, "I'm sorry, hen, but plans have changed. There's no room for you in my car. But you've got your own, so no problem, yeah?"

"You said we'd all go together."

"There's no' enough room."

"Two in front, three in the back?"

"That's right: Les and Fee and Annie in the back, Bob in front with me. See?"

"Bob?"

Val rolled her eyes. "*Bob.* My man."

She knew Val was married, but what did that have to do with their job? "Does he work here now?"

Val frowned. "Don't be daft. He's not going on the course. He'll play golf."

"I didn't know we could bring our husbands."

"Why not? The rooms are all doubles anyway. You can bring your – Barry, is it?"

"Gary."

"Does he play golf?"

"No."

"Never mind. He can do what he likes, and share the driving. So much nicer for you, and he'll be pleased, won't he?"

There was no use arguing, or asking if she could change places with one of the others: she had her own car, and they were all friends.

When Gary got home, she tried to make it sound like a great opportunity for a mini-break, but he was not fooled.

"You *know* I have to work tomorrow."

"I know, but—"

"But I should pretend I'm sick so I can drive you to the other side of the country?"

He scared her a little when he glared like that. "No, but we could leave *after* your work, and stay over Saturday night. You were just saying that we never go anywhere. I thought it would be nice for us to have a weekend away."

"Yeah, maybe it would, but that's not what this is, is it? I'd work all day, drive half the night, so you can have fun and games with your workmates while I hang around in freezing bloody Inverness on my tod."

"I thought—"

"You didn't think. You never do. You live in your own little dream."

Once upon a time he had liked her dreaminess, had laughed fondly at her naive and unrealistic ideas, and would have jumped at the chance to spend a night with her in a hotel room anywhere. Once upon a time, they had lived in the same dream. When had that changed? "I'm sorry," she said in a small voice.

"Forget it."

★   ★   ★

All her life, Kirsty had had a tendency to get lost. People told her it was because she didn't pay attention. Luckily, her car had come with a built-in navigation system. Gary thought it pointless, and it was true she had hardly ever used it – but she needed it now. She had never been to Inverness, and although the map revealed just one obvious route –

Lochgilphead to Oban to Fort William to Inverness – and practically nowhere to take a wrong turning, she was grateful to have a guide.

She entered the postcode for the hotel and the one for the conference centre, and knew she wouldn't have to worry: the system would tell her where she needed to go.

The weather was perfect. There had been no snow yet this year, and even the tops of the hills were bare and brown, outlined starkly against the clear blue winter sky. The beautiful, open landscape lifted her spirits, and her worries about her marriage and work evaporated as she drove.

She was the first to arrive at the hotel. Rather than waste what remained of the glorious daylight, she went for a wander, intending to meet up with the others by six o'clock.

Darkness fell quickly, but there was plenty to explore, including the biggest secondhand bookshop she'd ever seen, inside an old church. She was quite content until the shop closed and she remembered she didn't know where the restaurant was.

"Six o'clock at the Italian," Val had said. In her small-town naivete, Kirsty had imagined there was only one, and that any passing resident would point it out to her.

But the people she asked – most of them visitors – wanted to know *which* Italian. TripAdvisor listed a dozen. And when she tried to phone Val, she got her voicemail. She left a message and made her way back to the hotel, to find her colleagues had all gone out together, without leaving a message.

Of course they hadn't done it on purpose, Kirsty told herself, but her eyes stung as she envisioned them sitting around a table drinking wine and laughing. Were they laughing about *her*? Had they even noticed she was missing? She had not eaten since breakfast. She had to eat something. Leaving the hotel again she decided to get a meal at the first place that looked promising – anything but Italian.

★   ★   ★

At breakfast next morning Val was sitting with a man at a table set for two, and looked startled when Kirsty approached. "Ah, good, you made it," she said.

"Didn't you get my message?"

"What message? When?"

"Yesterday. You didn't answer your phone."

Val's eyes widened. "*My* phone?"

"Who else would I call?"

"Oh. I am so sorry. I left it in my other bag. When you didn't turn up, we guessed you and Barry must have stopped for a meal on your way."

This remark shattered her cool. "I never said *Gary* was coming. Didn't you see my car? I saw yours. I didn't know where to go. You never told me the name of the restaurant."

"Of course I did. Don't be daft. I told *everybody*: half past six at Bella Italia."

It was almost plausible. Only the malicious sparkle in Val's eyes said otherwise.

★   ★   ★

The training course was being held in another location, on the far edge of the city, so Kirsty was happy to let the navigation system take charge.

"Prepare to turn left. Take the second left. Turn left immediately.

"Take the second turn at the roundabout.

"Take the first turn at the roundabout.

"Prepare to turn right.

"Follow the road for two kilometres."

Something about the disembodied voice's inflections reminded her uneasily of Val, but the directions proved true, and she arrived without a hitch.

About the course, the least said, the better. Afterwards, Kirsty was not inclined to linger. She hurried out to her car, eager to get a start while some daylight remained. She selected New Destination and entered Fort William, thinking that would be a good place to stop for a break.

"Please wait while the route is calculated."

Imperceptibly the tension in her back and shoulders eased. Although not as good as being driven, this was the next best thing: like having a confident guide in the car to see her safely home.

"The route has been calculated. Please drive onto a digitised road.

"Prepare to turn right.

"At the roundabout, take the second exit.

"Please take the second exit.

"At the roundabout, take the second exit.

"Prepare to turn left.

"Turn left.

"Continue on this road until further instruction."

Not really paying attention, she had been travelling further into the countryside. She gripped the steering wheel more tightly and frowned, certain that this was not the same route she had taken in the morning. But of course not; why should it be, when she did not wish to return to the hotel? Likely she was being sent around the city rather than through it, to avoid the worst traffic.

But her journey dragged on, and she wondered why it was taking so long to get back to the A82. Even at sixty mph, without a single set of traffic lights to slow her down, she seemed to be getting nowhere. At last, after a long silence, the voice of the system spoke again:

"Prepare to turn left.

"Turn left in two hundred metres. Take the next left. Turn left now.

"Continue to follow the road."

In silence, she passed through a forest that seemed familiar. The road grew ever more narrow and winding in the gathering dusk, and she was forced to travel at half her previous speed, and pray she would not meet any oncoming traffic. After another turn, she realised she was driving alongside a large body of water.

She was alarmed by this. It could only be Loch Ness, yet her memory of the map insisted that there was only one road that ran along the loch side from Inverness on the way to Fort William, and that was the A82.

But the A82 was a trunk road. This was a single track.

She tamped down a rising feeling of panic. She told herself she was not lost, she could not be lost. The navigation system would not let her down. It was taking her by an alternative route, but still taking her where she wanted to go. She had to believe that. She could not bear the thought of turning around and going back to Inverness to start again.

"Prepare to turn left."

She sighed with relief.

"Turn left, after two hundred and fifty metres.

"Turn left now."

The turn was a tight one, onto another single track. No lights, no signposts – she was in the middle of nowhere, and it was almost full dark.

"Continue on the road until further instruction."

She drove grimly into the night, almost hypnotised by the moving patch of light against the narrow, dark winding road until the voice brought her out of a semi-trance:

"Prepare to turn left.

"Turn left now."

She turned, and felt the car wheels bump over a rough, loose surface, and realised she had come off the road. She stomped on the brake as the headlights swept across a white building – a big house, or maybe a hotel – directly ahead.

"You have reached your destination."

"What?"

The engine died and the headlights faded, leaving her plunged into darkness.

"Hey!"

Nothing happened when she tried to start the car. Even the internal lights were dead. Shaking, Kirsty grabbed her bag and scrabbled inside for the smooth, comforting shape of her phone. But no matter how she jabbed and pressed, it lay inertly unresponsive.

There was a miniature LED flashlight attached to her keyring – she'd had it for years, and used it so seldom that she'd never even thought of replacing the batteries. And, clearly, she should have, for it wasn't working.

For a moment she wondered if she was dreaming. Maybe she was safe in her bed at home. She shut her eyes tight and breathed slowly in and out, a silent prayer to a nameless force. When she opened her eyes she was still sitting behind the wheel of her car in the dark, but now, through the windscreen she saw a faint, distant yellow glow.

Concentrating, she realised a flickering light was coming from the building she had so briefly glimpsed, and her heart beat faster as she seized upon the idea of light and warmth and someone who could help.

Clutching her handbag, Kirsty almost fell out of the car. It was hard to get her bearings in the darkness all around; she tried to keep her eyes fixed on the light, but its flickering made that difficult. Either the house was farther away than it had first seemed, or she was walking even more slowly than she realised, for it took an agonisingly long time to arrive, and she felt dizzy and disoriented when she located a door, which opened just as she was raising her hand to knock.

A small figure wrapped in a shawl stood there, holding a lantern, and spoke a traditional Gaelic greeting in a soft, lilting voice that swept Kirsty back in memory to childhood visits to her grandmother, and she knew this must be a dream. She could only pray she had not fallen asleep at the wheel, or she really might be about to join her departed grandmother – someone she had thought of, and missed, every day of the past three years.

But then the woman in the house lifted her lamp, and Kirsty saw her face, and saw a stranger in early middle age who did not resemble her grandmother at all. "Come in, my dear," the woman said, in English. "Come in and warm yourself by our fire."

"Thank you." Kirsty followed her inside, trying to explain her plight: "My car broke down, and I have no idea where I am. I wanted to call for help, but my phone is dead. I wondered if I could use yours to call—"

"I would not deny you anything, but those things won't work here."

"You don't have a landline?" Kirsty tried to imagine being so cut off. "What about your neighbours? There must be someone living nearby."

"Come and sit by the fire," the woman coaxed. "And will you have something to eat?"

"I don't want to put you to any trouble."

"It is no trouble at all." She led her towards the fireplace, and Kirsty saw there was a table, and someone sitting there.

"My son," said the woman, as the handsomest man Kirsty had ever seen rose to his feet and put out his hand to take hers.

She gave him her hand. He held it only for a moment, but that was time enough for her to fall in love.

She no longer had any wish to leave. She only wanted to be near him.

Out of courtesy rather than hunger she accepted the delicious broth and fresh brown bread the woman served, and drank the dark red wine the handsome, smiling man poured into a glass, happy to feel the touch of his fingers on hers when she took the glass.

After they dined, the young man fetched a fiddle and played. The music was at once familiar and strange, and she thought she would never tire of listening to it.

Later, when his mother had left them alone, he set the fiddle aside, moved closer, and kissed her. She thought she might die with happiness.

But there was even more intense joy to come, when he took her to bed. And later still, as she lay drowsy and contented in his arms, she knew that she was where she belonged. As she drifted on the edge of sleep she remembered something people had used to say about her, from childhood on, an old-fashioned phrase applied to her in fond exasperation, resignation or annoyance – only her grandmother had said it always with affection – and realised that now, at last, it was actually true.

Kirsty was away with the fairies.

POLAROID AND SEAWEED

Peter Harness

Daniel Shirt was teased at school. He was an intelligent boy with an unhappy life, and for both of these things he was made to suffer.

His parents were divorced and he lived with his father and his father's new wife. The divorce had come because his mother changed in some way after Daniel's birth. She became very sad and was unable to properly take care of him or herself.

On several occasions during the first few years of Daniel's life, his mother had pushed him down to the beach in his pushchair, filled the pockets of her coat with stones, and walked into the sea. Daniel had sat on the seashore, straining against the straps of his buggy, watching his sad, wet mother, and knowing that something was desperately wrong. On each occasion, his red-faced, throat-sore, inchoate screams and heartbroken calls for Mummy to come back, had made her turn around. She had slowly walked, step by painful, frozen step, back to land and child; wrapped her fingers around the handles of the pushchair, and trundled home again without a word.

As one might imagine, Daniel never forgot what it felt like to yell after his mother, about to take her own life. The recollection of it was never more than an eye-blink away. He knew every step of the silent walks home after he had called her back from leaving him. He remembered every second of the deathly, empty hours until his father came home, and saw her, still soaking wet and unmoving, and looked at both mother and son with fury and disappointment. Once Daniel had been put to bed, he could always hear the unravelled, screaming voice of his father echoing up the stairs. And the process of his thoughts went through this story over and over again. He was angry at himself because he never knew what to say to his mother to make her better, or to encourage her to like him. It was his fault that his mother was unhappy; and, despite all of his best efforts to cheer her up with pictures, with toys and with softly-held hands, Daniel never managed to raise anything more than a blank smile, which even a very young child could see was just for show.

When Daniel was six years old, his mummy left home without any warning and went to live with her sister, a nun. Daniel took himself off to school in the morning, and when he came back, carrying that year's class photo to show her, there was no longer a mother at home to see it. His father explained that Mummy was poorly, and that she needed some time away in order to get better.

Daniel knew that "poorly" only tended to last a couple of days or a week at most, so to begin with, he wasn't unduly concerned. But soon Christmas came and she wasn't there. Then Daddy started going out in the evenings with a woman called Miriam from work. And at last, Daniel started to receive postcards and small gifts from his mother now and then, through the post; and it became clear to him that, without his knowledge, the status quo had shifted beneath him, and Mummy was not coming home any time soon.

After this realisation had crystallised within him, Daniel wrote to her every day. His handwriting got better and better. He spent his hours working out what he could say to her in these letters. He saved up his pocket money and spent it on stamps. But every morning he woke to the sound of the letterbox rattling against the door and the whack of post on the hall carpet, and shuttled down the stairs, only to find nothing for him there. She still only wrote to him every now and then. And shortly, Daniel began to realise that he was forgetting what she looked like.

When he pictured her, the clearest image that came was of her standing beside his dad, as in one particular Polaroid that he had pinned to a noticeboard above his little desk. This was the only photograph he had of her. On it, she was wearing make-up, purple and pink. Her hair was tightly curled, and she was wearing large glasses and holding a cigarette. His dad was suited, bearded, and with more head-hair than he'd ever had in Daniel's recollection. They were out at a party. They looked happy. This was before Daniel had been born.

He had never seen his mother looking like this. Not in real life. And it made him realise somehow, that *he* must have been the factor: the thing that changed her, that broke her. That it must have been *him*, when he came along, squealing and shitting into the world, that caused his mother to fail like she had. In some way, he had killed the laughing, curly-haired lady in purple and pink.

After a year or so, Daniel started being taken to visit his mother during the school holidays. To the nunnery in Lincoln where she stayed. He would visit her for four or five days. She would buy him a jigsaw. Sister Matthew would take them both out for ice cream. That was it.

Despite this, he looked forward to those visits with a burning and clear passion, with a wide, boundless, optimistic imagination of how it would be. He came home on the train each time, ready for a new term of bullying and teasing, heartbroken beyond his years and each time a little more wounded by her indifference.

Eventually, the pressure in his head of grief and disappointment became too much to contain, and Daniel developed ways of behaving which his classmates found hysterically funny. Every few steps, he began to have to bob down and touch the ground to make sure it was still there. And after he'd been bobbing for a couple of months, he started having to contort his face after every few words, pulling it into an uncontrollable grimace that made him look like a desperately offended Kenneth Williams. And after the bobbing and the grimacing, he started having to repeat everything he had just said, underneath his breath as if to make sure he had said it right. He became a strange and guttural echo of himself.

These strangenesses, and the fact that his own mother had abandoned him, marked him out as the school's number one target for being teased. The lack of empathy and instinct for butchery that any group of seven or eight-year-olds naturally has, informed Daniel's classmates that any kid whose mother tries to kill herself rather than stay home and make fish fingers, must clearly have something very wrong with it. A motherless kid could never fit in. A motherless kid must be the lagging runt at the back of the pack, easily picked off and torn to pieces. A motherless kid is one of the funniest things one could think of: funnier than having big ears, dirty clothes, or being called anything other than Mark, John or James. Funnier even than calling the teacher "Dad".

So it happened that everything that was wrong with Daniel, every bursting psychological boil on the surface of his personality, was mercilessly, cheerfully, and relentlessly exploited for the purposes of taking the piss. The other children did comic vignettes of his mother walking into the sea, with Daniel, the figure of fun, the baby in a pushchair, crying there on the beach. They repeated these shows again and again, every day. They dramatised her leaving him. They made great sport of the fact that she lived with a nun. And not only a nun, but a nun with the ridiculous name of Sister Matthew. They imitated his tics. Until eventually, not every day, but once or twice a week without fail (and often on Thursdays), it would reach unbearable proportions, and Daniel would boil and blaze, and run at his tormentors, limbs flailing, kicking and punching at the air, before sinking down to his chair and sobbing his eyes out. Then the other children would regroup and squeal with laughter at the fact that he was crying. And it became a competition amongst them to see who could provoke such an eppy from him in the shortest time.

Every night, before he went to sleep, and was consumed by nightmares in which Mummy would sometimes drown, and sometimes walk back, Daniel enjoyed five minutes of calm, in which he was able to find a still point in the turmoil in his head. In those few minutes, he was able to conjure an imperfect vision of his Polaroid mother coming to his bedside in the soft light, stroking his hair and smiling at him with sparkling, back-to-life eyes. His happiness shrunk to those unassailed minutes, after school and stepmother had retreated. To a few moments before bad dreams, pissed beds, the distant disappointment of nothing in the post and the terror of school. Each night he would summon her to him to give him the strength to carry on. But she was never fully in focus. He could never visualise her properly. And he could never hear her voice.

Another boy in his class was called Carl. Carl was the other intelligent boy in the school. He was also bullied and Daniel was jealous of him. They weren't friends but sometimes they played together out of mutual loneliness. Occasionally they would take their clothes off and look at each other's penises, but they weren't friends.

Carl's parents spoiled him. They didn't seem to be rich. Their house was small and old and it smelled of dogs, yet somehow Carl got everything he wanted. He had remote control cars. All the Christmas toys that had the most enticing adverts: Mister Frosty, disco lights, Simon Says. Disregarded treasures that lay half played-with and batteryless, strewn over the floor of his room. Carl's mother loved him very much. She was always calling upstairs to check he was okay. She was always bringing sandwiches and fizzy drinks and looking at him as though she was worried.

Daniel's dad said that Carl's parents spoilt him so much because Carl had been born with a hole in his heart.

Daniel thought about this. He felt that he had also been born with a hole in his heart. He had been born with a dark, empty cave in his heart. He could feel it all the time. The wind whistled coldly through it and crabs lived there. But no one bought Daniel remote control cars. No one bought him Mister Frostys or disco lights. No fucker ever came upstairs to him with a plate of corned beef sandwiches and strawberry pop.

As he thought through these things, Daniel went down to the sea. He went to the spot where his mother used to park the pushchair, and looked out over the roiling brown mass. The town pumped its sewage out there. And sometimes at the turn of the tide, it washed back up on the shore. You weren't supposed to swim in it, even though the town thought of itself as a place for holidaymakers.

Daniel looked around him. It was a cold afternoon, but there were others on the sand. A few dog-walkers. Two families with young children. Six fat men fishing at the far end.

Daniel removed his school blazer, took one step into the sea and looked back.

Nobody was watching. Nobody was paying attention.

He took another step.

His plimsolls were wet now, and his thick woollen socks starting to feel heavy.

Another step, and another.

The cold water was biting at his bare legs, lapping up towards his shorts. He walked on.

People on the beach had started to notice.

There were shouts.

He walked on. The brown water was up to his stomach. He could feel the tug of the tide, drawing him further and further into itself.

People started running towards the water.

Daniel's heart beat hard in his ears.

The people on the sand were standing there. He couldn't make out what they were doing.

But the sounds slowly started to resolve into something that made sense. The people were laughing at him. He glanced over his shoulder again. The fat fishermen and a couple of the dads were standing there,

218 • BEYOND THE VEIL

laughing at him. One of them yelled, "Come out, you silly little bastard. You're covered in shite."

Daniel looked down at his body. He was indeed coated with flecks of toilet paper and sewage. The men laughed. Daniel stood still, the tide still tugging at him.

He walked slowly back to shore, dried himself off on his blazer and went home.

And that night the vision of his mother said to him in a soft, truthful voice, "I am your *real* Mummy, Daniel. I am your *real* Mummy who loves you with all of her heart."

Daniel looked up at her, shocked. This voice had come unbidden into his thoughts, with a clarity and certainty that his dream mother never had. And she swam into focus at last.

This wasn't the woman from the Polaroid. This was a different character. She smelled of brine. Her clothes were damp. But she was terribly, primally familiar. Daniel's skin tingled and his heart responded to her voice. His whole body leapt up in excitement, and he suddenly felt very alive. She leant into him, and with a salty hiss that was suddenly cold as the wind that blew all the way from Holland, she said, "The woman who you call Mummy is really an impostor, who has taken my place and trapped me under the sea."

★   ★   ★

Daniel did not know what to do with this information. At first, he ignored it. He kept both mothers in his head at once, examining each and working out which one was which.

The first mother. The one who lived with Sister Matthew. Who was she? Daniel tried to think of his thoughts about her. How did he feel when he held her in his mind? What images did she bring?

He realised that he thought of her as a photograph. As the Polaroid from the time when he did not yet exist. That was who she was when he thought of her.

But this Polaroid, he decided, was a false image. It was of a normal woman, capable of laughter. A simulacrum of a functioning human being. The mother who lived with Sister Matthew had never been like that. Not in his experience.

The mother who came to him before he went to sleep looked different. When he thought of her, he thought of her smiling eyes. But that wasn't right. Yes, she did smile. But as she combed her fingers through his hair, he could see the marks of claws around her eyes. Her eyes were not normal. They were not really there. They had been removed and eaten by birds.

★　　★　　★

At half term, Daniel took the train to Lincoln.

Sister Matthew was there at the station, waiting for him as usual. Like a strange grey ghost: another pretend woman. As they walked through the town, and Sister Matthew gradually ran out of questions to ask a little boy, Daniel thought through all of the swearwords he knew, and wondered what would happen if he said "fuck" to the nun. Would she explode? Would she cry? Would she strap him to a bed and have someone come to take the demons out of him? It occurred to Daniel that he could command Sister Matthew to kiss his tadger, and he suddenly burst out laughing and had to bob down to check if the ground was still there.

The woman who said she was his mummy – the Polaroid Mother – was standing at the lodge of the nunnery, waiting for them, wearing an old brown dress and a watercolour smile. Who was she, thought Daniel, as he looked at her. She didn't *look* like a mother. She didn't look like the other mothers who waited for their sons at the school fence. When she limply hugged him, she didn't smell reassuring. She didn't smell like the other mothers: of perfume or cigarettes. She smelled of Savlon. She smelled as though she covered herself in Savlon and disinfectant to get rid of whatever she *really* smelled of.

They had no connection, he decided, as they walked quietly towards her room, where he would sleep on a thin mattress on the cold floor. She had bought him some board games. He didn't like board games. The board games she bought him were shit. She was a prick. She was an impostor and he hated her for what she had done.

Before eating dinner with the nuns, Daniel had to go through the ridiculous ritual of saying grace. All these strange grey women giving warbling thanks to God for the colourless tubular meat on the chipped plates in front of them. They had to say thank you to God for the abundance of His sprouts and watery sauce. Daniel had to give thanks too, even if his natural instinct was to yell instead, "What is this crap?"

He took to unclasping his hands and opening his eyes during the prayer, and looking at the daylight-starved, unhealthy faces of the women around him. They were disgusting. They looked like old biscuits and they too smelled of Savlon.

On the evening of his third day there, it occurred to him that he should shit himself as the nuns said their collective grace. He looked furtively around him as the Mother Superior murmured her fluty thanks, and squeezed as hard as he could. He managed a loud fart, which was ignored; and he pushed again. This time he was lucky. He pushed and pushed until finally he had filled his pants. After the prayer was over, and the nuns relaxed into their meal, Daniel turned to his mother just as she hovered over her first bite, and, trying not to laugh, said, "Mummy, I've had an accident."

She took him to the cold lavatories. Clearly, she expected him to sort himself out. But he just stood there, and repeated, "I've had an accident in my bottom." She looked at him for a moment, and then undid his shorts and took down his underpants. He enjoyed how she gagged as she wiped the stinking mess off his buttocks and thighs, and rinsed his red Y-fronts in one of the ancient communal sinks. He enjoyed the sensation of the cold air around his private parts as he stood in the bathroom and waited for her to return with new clothes. He was making her do the kind of things that a mother should do, and she was a total failure at it.

Every night that week he shat himself during grace. He became very good at it. He would save up a bowel movement for the whole of the day, so that he was ready to go when they sat down on the long wooden benches in the dining hall. As soon as the Mother Superior said, "Dear Father," he would race to crap his pants in the thirty or so seconds before the Amen came. He tried to ensure that he never finished too early or too late. He wanted to fill the entirety of the prayer with defecation, and be ready, as soon as the nuns started eating, to turn to the woman who called herself his mother, and say, "Mummy, I shat myself in an accident."

On the fourth night, the evening before he was due to go home, she cried. He had made her clean up his mess, and he'd made it as difficult as possible by kicking his legs and squirming, and trying to wipe as much of it as possible on her as she took down his pants and cleaned him with her flannel. She didn't know what to do. She couldn't discipline him, she didn't know how to speak harshly or kindly to him. She just took it. And then sobbed over the sink.

And she didn't just sob a little bit. She wailed and wept with the kind of insane, choking abandon that Daniel gave himself over to when the bullying reached its critical mass at school. She became a flailing, useless bubble of emotion. And once upon a time, Daniel would have been upset by this. But here, on the cold wooden seat in the dark lavatory cubicle at the Church of Saint Agatha, Daniel realised how much fun it was to subject and degrade the hideous impostor.

He thought that he would like to see her sob herself to death.

He asked her, "Are you really my mum?"

She looked at him for one sad, long moment, and murmured, "I don't know, Daniel. I can't say if I am or not. Maybe I'm something different."

On his first night back home, his *real* mummy came again, climbing spikily into his dreams. He could see her clearly now. She had been in the sea a long time. The Polaroid Mother must have trapped her there a long time ago. Her dress was ragged. There was seaweed growing on her. Her skin was bleached and salted, and there were the marks of bird claws all about her.

"How do I get you back out of the sea?" asked Daniel.

"You can't," said the Seaweed Mother.

Daniel's heart went cold. He had been hoping that, since the situation was now acknowledged, it could be rectified. Did this mean that he would have to live forever like this, the child of a fake mother, living a compromised life?

"It doesn't matter, Daniel," said the Seaweed Mother, hearing his thoughts. "If you like, Mummy can live inside your head from now on. And Mummy can make a new little boy out of you."

Daniel wanted it. He wanted his real mummy to live inside him and make him into a new little boy. He wanted his life to start again and go on as it was meant to.

"Would you like that?" said the Seaweed Mother.

Daniel nodded. He was crying.

The Seaweed Mother pulled down her dress and exposed her breasts. She took Daniel by his hair and guided his head to her nipples. He sucked.

The milk was gloopy and sour. And overpoweringly salty.

But it was filling the empty cave inside his heart. He could feel the cave filling faster and faster with sour milk until his chest was almost bursting.

As he drank, he saw images in his mind.

★   ★   ★

He was in a green-painted room. It smelled medicinal. There were machines that he didn't understand. It was a room in a hospital.

His mother was on the bed. It was the mother from the photograph, the Polaroid Mother. She wore large glasses and had curly hair. She had a cigarette in one hand and a glass of wine in the other. Her skirt was hitched up and her private parts were visible. Her private parts were huge and hairy and bloody and there was a bump coming out of the middle of them.

A nurse of some kind was looking up into the mother's private parts. Suddenly, the mother screamed. Her glass of wine fell onto the floor and smashed.

"That's it, come on, love," said the nurse, as the Polaroid Mother clenched her teeth and screamed again.

"My glass of wine!" yelled the mother. "My glass of *wine!*"

Something gave way. The Polaroid Mother's private parts distended and bulged and the lump in the middle flopped out and started crying. It was a small human being. A baby.

Himself. Baby Daniel.

The child was attached to the Polaroid Mother by a red rope.

"Give us your cigarette," said the nurse.

The Polaroid Mother handed over the cigarette. The nurse carefully pinched the lit end down onto the red rope, and burned it through. There was a terrible stink of tobacco and cooked flesh. The baby screamed and it was free.

The nurse handed the baby to the Polaroid Mother.

"What am I supposed to do with this?" said the Polaroid Mother.

"Don't you know?" asked the nurse.

"This isn't my baby," said the Polaroid Mother. "Has it got a hole in its heart?"

"Not yet," said the nurse.

Then he was in another room. He recognised it. He was in his own bedroom. But there was a cot in it and a baby in the cot.

The Polaroid Mother was there, although her hair had gone flat and she didn't look like she was any longer in the mood for a party. The baby was crying. There was no glass of wine.

His father was there, with more hair. "Don't pick it up," said his father. "Let it cry itself out. It doesn't want learning that it can get everything it wants."

The Polaroid Mother looked down for a few moments, as if trying to work out where she might have seen the child before. Then she leant down into the cot and stubbed her cigarette out on the baby's chest.

"Now it's got a hole in its heart," she said, happily.

"She's always been like this," thought Daniel vaguely to himself. "When did she do the swap?"

★　　★　　★

After he had suckled, the Seaweed Mother drew back Daniel's head. He was numb and sleepy. He felt like the cave in his chest had been filled almost to bursting. The sour milk lined his throat and made it hard to breathe. But he felt something like happiness. A numb kind of feeling, like when you've been out walking on the beach too long on a winter's day. A cold, numb kind of happiness.

His Seaweed Mother looked down on him with her empty eyes.

"Now let's get you comfy," she said.

She lifted him off the bed, and started fluffing out the covers, ripping at his pillows with her sharp, broken fingernails.

He watched as his mother ripped up the mattress, and began stuffing it with things that she took out from under her dress.

When she was gone, Daniel looked into the mattress. It was filled with seaweed, crabs' claws, pieces of thread, broken glass that had been sanded smooth by the motion of the water, tufts of what looked like hair, slivers of wood and iron, pebbles, faeces, small effigies that were made of knotted seagrass, and clots of blood.

★　　★　　★

Daniel went back to school the following week. On the morning of the first day, he woke up with a pain beneath his sternum and a feeling like he'd been punched in the stomach. He found himself hunched over the toilet, being sick. He was more terrified than ever by the thought of his classmates and the horror that awaited him there. As he walked down the quieter paths, his fists pre-clenched, he heard, as he neared his school, the slowly increasing roar of other children's voices, the appalling clamour of a many-headed beast. He could hear it echoing off the walls of the houses. The baying of a mad creature that was going to devour him.

He couldn't learn. He found that he could no longer learn. He was a clever boy. But the knowledge wouldn't go in. There was something guarding the doors of his mind. Despite the bullying, he had always been good, conscientious. Yet all of a sudden, he felt it slipping away. Within a day or two, there was just blankness there when he was supposed to get his head down and work.

He sat in his classroom, staring ahead at the blackboard, covered with words and images that he could no longer understand. He felt very different. There was something changing inside him. Perhaps he was becoming the new little boy that his Seaweed Mother had talked about.

At playtime on Wednesday, he went into the yard, bracing himself vaguely for the teasing and scorn. But none came. He was being ignored.

He wondered why this was. And it occurred to him that he wasn't twitching anymore. The facial contortions had ceased. He didn't need to bob down to the earth. It didn't matter whether it was there or not. He wasn't a creature of earth anymore, but of sea.

The thought of the sea made him need to go to the toilet.

He walked into the boys' lavatories and stood at the urinals. His friend Carl was standing there already, peeing into the bowl. Carl smiled at Daniel. Daniel looked down at Carl's penis.

Daniel wanted to piss on Carl's penis.

Something not quite within himself made a decision, something moved in his chest; and Daniel backed away from the urinal, holding the tip of his penis very tightly. He backed away until he was behind the other boy, and then he let go. He pissed all over the other boy, all over his trousers and his shirt and shoes. Then he pissed on another boy who was just coming out of the toilet cubicle.

Then he ran into the girls' lavatories and pissed on some of them too.

When he'd stopped, a crowd was gathered, yelling in disgust and disbelief. Laughing.

Daniel looked calmly at the children gathered around him. He reached out his hand, and grabbed one of them by the hair. A boy called Christian. With strength that he didn't know he possessed, Daniel yanked Christian's head down and smashed it into the ground. He then stamped on Christian's head, over and over, until he felt himself being picked up and carried away by Mr. Ellis, who mostly taught P.E.

★   ★   ★

Daniel could feel the child moving in his head.

He hadn't been to school for several days. He felt unwell and there were questions to be answered. He was sick in the mornings. He had a headache. He found it hard to breathe. He tried to conjure the Seaweed Mother to him but she didn't come. He snuck out to the beach and tried to look for her, but the sea was still and motherless. He wanted to know if the change in him was a sign that his transformation was under way.

He looked inside his mattress and examined the artefacts that the Seaweed Mother had left there. Hair, pebbles, little effigies.

And he found himself wondering again, when did my *real* mother go into the sea? When was the swap made? What's going to happen when I'm a new little boy?

That was when he felt it for the first time. A distinct kick.

Something moved in his throat. Some limb flailed and knocked against his windpipe, taking the breath out of his body.

He froze, trying to understand the unfamiliar and terrifying sensation.

It came again. A movement. A definite, independent movement. A kick.

There was something *alive* inside him. Somewhere between his throat and his chest. There was something moving in there. Something growing, trying to make space for itself.

He remembered the night when he'd suckled at the Seaweed Mother's breast and she had filled the hole in his heart with salty, viscous milk. It had made him feel satiated and complete. But ever since, it had felt as though whatever she had left there had been getting bigger: pressing against the walls and fibres of his body. Pushing aside his thoughts, growing and strengthening rather than dissipating.

And Mummy can make a new little boy out of you.

Suddenly, Daniel was very scared. He wasn't ready to have a child. He didn't want there to be something growing inside him, moving and kicking. He didn't know what he was supposed to do. He couldn't think of who he should ask or tell. The Seaweed Mother wasn't there, and perhaps she wasn't who she had told him she was at all.

In the middle of the night, a sudden searing pain ripped through his neck and upper body and he just had time to get to the bathroom before he unleashed a torrent of vomit onto the floor. The vomit tasted of salt.

He leaned back and looked at himself in the mirror. He looked down at what had just gushed out through his mouth. It didn't look like normal puke. He couldn't see anything that he'd eaten in it. It was clear, tinged with bubbles of froth. Seawater.

The waters have broken, he thought dimly.

Another great burst of pain hit him. He gripped the sink until his knuckles whitened, and angled his stepmother's blackhead mirror so that he could see a huge reflection of the inside of his mouth.

Sure enough, there was something in there.

Something unfamiliar and alien, stuffed there behind his tonsils.

A hairy ball.

No, not a hairy ball. A *head*.

Daniel looked at it for a long moment.

There was another human being emerging from him. Another human being squeezing its painful way up through his throat.

It was huge. It was far too huge to come out through his mouth. It was far too huge to travel up the inside of his neck.

This was going to be agony. Surely this was going to kill one of them. Surely it was going to kill them both. He was only eight years old. He was much too small to give birth.

He was stopped in his thoughts by another massive, wracking spasm of pain. It was so terrible and so new that it was impossible for him to think, impossible for him to see or hear, and impossible for him to breathe. The pain screeched in his blood. It stretched the fibres of his body until it felt that the whole of him would burst.

How long was this going to last? How much could this possibly hurt?

This pain was going to stay with him forever. His body would never forget. It would never be the same again. The damage that had been done by that writhing, bony lump as it pushed itself up his windpipe would never be repaired. He would be irreparably broken.

The first wave of pain subsided. It could have lasted for twenty seconds or twenty minutes. And it was gone as swiftly as it came. A massive wave of relief crashed upon his body, cooling him, calming him. He felt a kind of joy.

When he looked at himself again, he could see that the head had forced itself further into his mouth. The crown of the head, clotted with thick blood and wet, straggly hair sat there at the top of his throat like a fat, evil spider. It was moving vaguely from side to side.

It was now impossible for him to close his mouth. His jaw was forced open to almost its fullest extent, so that his chin almost rested on his sternum. He looked as though he was emitting a permanent, silent scream of surprise. Daniel thought that he looked like the ghost of Jacob Marley. He looked like Marley's ghost after it had released the bandage that kept its broken jaw from falling. Daniel had a talking book of *A Christmas Carol* read by Leonard Rossiter. He liked listening to it under his bedcovers. He wished he was doing that now.

Then it occurred to Daniel that sooner or later in this process, the baby would break his own jaw. His jaw would have to dislocate from its joint and dangle uselessly below. His teeth would probably have to come out too.

He didn't want this to go any further.

But he was committed. His body was committed, and acting outside of his own control. This creature was breaking its way out and there was nothing he could do to stop it.

It was least painful for Daniel to bend over on all fours over the toilet, as though he was vomiting.

Another inferno of pain exploded in his head and he couldn't think coherently for some considerable time.

The baby came in a salty tidal wave of relief and the last of Daniel's milk teeth.

It was like his mother. It was like his Seaweed Mother.

But most of all, it was like *him*. It looked like him.

He didn't know what to do with it.

It lay there, furled up in the bowl of the toilet.

He didn't want to pick it up.

For a moment, he considered flushing it away, flushing it away so that it would go out to sea in the sewage outlet pipe. But it was far too big. And he suspected that his Seaweed Mother would be angry with him.

Because this was *her* child. This was the child that she and he had made together. She had fed it into him through her milk, and he had nurtured it in his heart and his brain until finally expressing it into the world in a series of painful spasms. This child was the fruit of their union.

The bathroom door opened, and the Seaweed Mother was standing there. Under the unforgiving glare of the fluorescent light, she looked hideous. Her eye sockets dark and dead, the skin around them tattered and clawed, a hermit crab living in one of the holes. Her mouth, lipless and without teeth. Her hair long and tangled, only half attached to her head. She stood there like a ghost and finally reached out her arms. She wanted to take the baby.

"What should we call it?" he asked.

"Its name is Daniel," his Seaweed Mother said simply.

"But that's my name," said Daniel.

"*Its* name is Daniel," she said again. "Baby Daniel."

The Seaweed Mother lifted Baby Daniel to her breast, and it sucked eagerly.

She walked with it through the silent house towards Daniel's bedroom. As he followed her, Daniel saw his father and stepmother sleeping in their bed, and wondered whether he should wake them and ask what to do.

The Seaweed Mother reached Daniel's bedroom, pulled back the covers, and laid Baby Daniel down. Baby Daniel was sleeping soundly. He was very big. Daniel thought again how similar the child was to himself. And how grown-up it looked, scarcely like a baby at all.

The Seaweed Mother looked down at Baby Daniel, and crooned something that sounded like a broken lullaby made of ship's nails and broken bottles.

When she had finished, Daniel asked, "What do I do now, Mummy?"

"You can fuck off," she replied, pushing him out of the room, and closing the door.

★   ★   ★

By now, the dawn was breaking and the day was about to start. Daniel didn't want to be in the house to have to answer more of his father's questions. He couldn't think of an explanation for there being another Daniel there, he couldn't frame a story to explain the mess in the bathroom. He was in enough trouble as it was.

Daniel put his coat on, closed the door softly, and walked down to the sea.

He felt much lighter than he had ever felt before. The pressure of the baby had gone, of course, but so had much of the other weight that he seemed to have been carrying around with him all this time. He could think clearly again. His intelligence was returning to him. The pain of the birth was diminishing, and he hadn't died, as he had thought.

It was a lovely morning. The sun was rising over the sea, which was calm and reasonably clear.

Daniel was still covered in blood and salty detritus, which was caking to his skin and starting to smell. He took off his coat and his pyjamas and walked briskly into the water.

The water wasn't too cold. The sun was warming it. Daniel washed off the blood and the shit and the seaweed, and got himself nice and clean.

He plunged into the water, ducking himself under, holding his breath, and swimming out a little way. He opened his eyes and could vaguely see the sand shifting underneath him, and the fresh pinkness of his hands in front of his eyes.

He swam up towards the surface.

But he couldn't break through.

He swam harder, but the more he struggled, the harder it became to move.

The sunlight rippled above him. He tried to reach it. But he was being held back. The sea was refusing to let him go.

Then he saw a brief vision of the other Baby Daniel, now looking just the same as himself, riding quietly on the train to Lincoln.

Daniel struggled. Suddenly very sure that he didn't want to swim any more. That he wanted to be on the train to Lincoln himself. He managed to break the surface of the sea for a few moments, and take a hoarse, whooping breath until he was pulled back under again.

But he was sinking deeper and deeper, and the sunlight was becoming less and less possible to attain.

He saw the Baby Daniel meeting Sister Matthew at the station, and walking happily to the nunnery, chatting animatedly. He saw the other Daniel meeting the Polaroid Mother at the nunnery door, and the Polaroid Mother hugging him warmly, ruffling his hair, and giving him a brand new Simon Says.

Under the water, Daniel gulped in a lungful of brine, out of shock that the horrible, twisted version of himself should be given a Simon Says by his mother when he himself never got one. He broke the surface once more, trying to cry out for help but lacking any air with which to do so, before sinking again into the rapidly cooling tide.

He saw the other Daniel being tucked into bed by the Polaroid Mother, who suddenly seemed so much better, so much happier than he had ever made her. She seemed kind and at peace. The other Daniel had clearly never shat himself at dinner on purpose. He had never pissed on other children or fractured Christian's skull.

But couldn't she see that Baby Daniel wasn't a proper little boy? Couldn't she see what he was made of? Couldn't his mummy recognise an imposter?

Baby Daniel looked up at the Polaroid Mother and whispered, "Are you really my mum?"

Daniel saw the Polaroid Mother's eye glisten, and a warm smile break over her face. "Of course I am, Daniel. Of course I am."

So this grotesque little parody of a child was the one who would be known as him.

This approximation of a life, this half-child, would be the one who would bear *his* name and take *his* place forever. This thing made of salt and sewage and debris, vomited up into a toilet and sired by a witch. That would be him from now on, and forever.

A few moments after he realised this, Daniel Shirt disappeared under the water for the third and final time.

Perhaps, he thought, this was all for the best.

DER GEISTERBAHNHOF

Lynda E. Rucker

The other day, I saw C— on the cover of another magazine.

Someone had left it lying on the table at a currywurst stand. When I saw it, I went cold, even though it was a warm day. I lost my appetite. I thought maybe it was time to leave Berlin, but what good would it do? Where would I go?

He looked handsome, of course. I don't remember the magazine, but it was in English. The phrase 'Generation Excess' was scrawled across his chest, only the 'Ex' was crossed out in print that was made to look like a handwritten Sharpie, and a carat inserted the letters 'Suc' above it so that it said 'Generation Success' instead. I didn't need to look at the article to guess its genre: privileged wild child makes good. Founded a startup making extraordinary discoveries in the field of machine learning and artificial intelligence, strides that just a few short years ago experts would have said would not have been possible for a very long time, if ever. It would not be an exaggeration to say that C— was changing the world.

I had only taken two bites of my currywurst and there was a pile of crisp fries and creamy mayo alongside it. It seemed a shame to throw it away even if I could no longer eat it. I took it with me with a vague thought of giving it to a homeless person or maybe walking down to the canal and feeding some birds, but in the end I went a few blocks with it and then I stuffed it into one of the orange trash receptacles. A sticker on the side of it lamented in a Gothic font 'I miss the old Berlin'. I wondered what old Berlin they were thinking of: before the 2010s, when the digital nomads and hot young entrepreneurs hadn't yet colonised the entire city; before the 2000s, when you could still get a flat in Prenzlauer Berg for next to nothing even if it did mean your bathtub was in your kitchen and you heated the place with coal; before the 1990s, when the city was riven with walls and barbed wire; before that, when the city was rubble;

before that, going back, back, like a silent movie in reverse, bombed-out remains rebuilding themselves, moving slowly but inexorably beyond living memory until only names were left: Weimar, Bismarck, Germania.

Their ghosts are everywhere.

★   ★   ★

The last time I saw C—, or the last time before the time I mean to tell you about here, it was autumn in Berlin, an autumn that came at last on the heels of what had seemed an endless sweltering summer of thirty-five degree days that left the entire city limp and defenceless. Germany is a cold country, but Berliners relish the heat when it comes, disrobing in local parks, diving into one of the dozens of lakes all around the city and its outskirts. This, however, was too much. Summers in Berlin usually feel freeing, but this one was oppressive.

So autumn, when it finally came, was welcomed even by me, and even though I knew it heralded the inevitable descent into darkness: the long, grey winter months that would drag me with them into the underworld. Every winter felt like that to me, like a real death, not just a seasonal or metaphorical one. I was always somehow certain that I would not survive each one. Sometimes I imagined that I didn't, that on the darkest or coldest night of the year I had perished in my sleep, leaving behind this carapace that another soul crept into sometime in the wee hours. The *I* becomes another, different *I*. When I used to live with Julian, I once told him this and begged him to keep watch over me, to wake me frequently and make sure I was still *me*. He thought I was joking and then he said I was mad.

At any rate, autumn that year seemed suffused with a particular clarity, an unprecedented crispness and an even more glorious than usual afternoon light that washed everything golden. Berlin, you think, is an unbeautiful city, but it is like one of those women – the kind I always aspired to be, actually, and never have been – one of those women who has such unconventional features you think she can never be beautiful, you might even call her ugly. And then you catch a glimpse of her at some angle or in some lighting and you realise there are words beyond *beautiful* and *ugly*, you realise that there are far more powerful things like *mesmerising* and *spellbinding*, and that is what Berlin is like. It seduces you with its ugliness, its filth: its grim uncompromising modern buildings and graffiti, the reek of urine in the U-bahn stations, its steely determination to survive. And when you are walking on a path along the canal or past a block of flats that weren't bombed to oblivion seventy-five years ago, sometimes that golden light steals in to splash a more conventional beauty around as well, one that is all the more breath-taking for its rarity.

It was on one of those blessed autumn days that I ran into C—, in my neighbourhood Lidl of all places, staring at a stack of 'American-style' branded snacks that were just a little off, like there was some America where people routinely ate sugar on their popcorn. At first I thought it wasn't him because he lived across town in Neukölln, but just as I was turning away, he saw me.

"Abby!" he said, and came over to me.

I'm already lying to you. I saw him and I knew it was him, but I didn't want to talk to him. I was going to walk away quietly. When he said my name, I felt a little stab of what I can only call panic. Why had I stopped in this store, at this time, and turned onto this aisle? Of all the gin joints in all the world, etc.

"How have you been?" he said.

I tried to keep things light. "Oh fine," I said. "Been working a lot. You know." I tried to push past him, like I could get away with just a casual greeting and go on with my shopping.

He grabbed my arm. "Are you sure?" he said. "Do you want to get a drink?"

My excuse, "I've got a lot to do," died on my lips. I don't know why I said okay.

No, I know why.

*   *   *

I don't actually know where C— was from. He had a vague unplaceable accent that I thought of as 'European'. He'd grown up rootless, with a diplomat dad and an artist mom. You might have heard of her. She mostly does temporary installation-type stuff but one of her paintings hangs in the Met, or so C— said. They were divorced, so he'd bounce between their homes, which were always in far-flung places. About his past, he'd drop vague references – 'Oh, that was when we were wintering in Dharamsala' or 'when I was at school in Botswana' or 'the summer camp in Italy'. It seemed like there was nowhere that he hadn't been but he was so blasé about it, as if he had in fact never gone anywhere at all, and it was all unimaginable to me. Where I came from, in rural Tennessee, C— would have seemed like a creature out of a fairy tale, and I guess he kind of still was to me.

He was beautiful, too, in that sort of rugged but dying poet kind of way, dark waves of hair, too thin, eyes that changed colour with his surroundings from blue to green to grey and back again, not that whatever was between us or at least what went from me to him – I'm not sure anything ever went from him back to the other person – was sexual in nature. We'd slept together a couple of times and it hadn't even been especially memorable. Sex for C— was as perfunctory as attending to any other bodily function; it hardly held the potential for transcendence and was barely even pleasurable. He had his mind on other things.

I can't remember how I'd first met him – a warehouse party, a nightclub, an art opening? It's weird that I can't remember because I didn't actually go out that much. I didn't like crowds of people. They made me anxious; when people are in a crowd, I am not sure that they are fully human. Do you know that Ray Bradbury story 'The Crowd'? It's about that group of people you always see gathering at accidents, rubberneckers, only it gradually becomes clear that it's the same group of people, like there is some demonic entity moving from tragedy to tragedy and feeding from it. I don't think of crowds in quite that way, but close. I think humans en masse can be a dangerous sort of conduit.

I told C— this once, and he really liked that idea. I think it was when he first took an interest in me. That was what you wanted with C—, for him to take an interest in you, to find you intriguing enough to spend time with. I know how pathetic that sounds, but he had that effect on everyone. Things *happened* around C—. C— had answers, or at the very least, he had interesting questions.

When you met C—, if you were the right sort of person, you knew he was someone who could show you the sublime.

I didn't say any of this to him when we went for our drink. Wedding, Berlin's next up and coming neighbourhood for at least a decade now, has yet to up and come, and it's still light on the hipster establishments jammed all over places like Kreuzberg and Friedrichshain. But a cosy little wine bar had just opened on the corner down from my place and we went there. C— said, "I wanted to talk to you about the last time we saw each other."

I said "Mmmhmm" into my glass of red wine.

"Things didn't really go as planned," said C—.

I drank more wine so as not to say something like, "You can say that again."

"That girl wasn't hurt," he said. "I know it looked like she was. I just wanted to make sure you knew that. It was all part of the – well, it's complicated to explain."

I put down my wine glass and said, "It's not complicated, C—, and I want nothing to do with any of it," and I left.

I'm lying again. I didn't.

I stayed, and I listened to his explanation.

C— repeated again that the girl was fine, and he said I could even meet with her if I liked. It sounded like he doth protest too much, but I didn't say that. I wondered if he was doing this with everyone else, going round to the dozen or so other people who had been there that night and proffering this explanation. If so, he didn't need to. As far as I know, I am the only person who had found the whole thing off-putting enough to start avoiding C—, and I am, well, a timid sort, and this is not, by and large, a city of the timid.

As I was leaving, C— pressed something into my hand. I was telling myself it was the last time I would ever see him, or that if I did, again, by accident like that day, I would not go with him for a drink. I would say hello if I had to and move on.

I didn't look at what he had given me until I was outside and halfway up the block to my own flat.

It was an invitation.

*　　*　　*

The envelope was black, with no markings. I opened it to find a piece of paper inside, thin as tissue, words debossed on it in gold.

There were only a few words on it: my name, first and last. A word: *Geisterbahnhof*. A date, a few nights later. 'Wear black', it instructed me. A place name, and an address. I am not going to tell you what they were.

They were both things that had been lost and that ought to have stayed that way.

I have wondered since about how we came to meet that day, C— and I, when he happened to be carrying an invitation with my name on it. As far as I'd been aware, if he had any idea at all where I lived, it was only in the vaguest way.

Perhaps it was a coincidence. Maybe he carried a packet of invitations with him everywhere, in case he ran into the intended recipient. Yet I believe he came looking for me. I suspect he knew that if he rang my apartment directly, I might not have let him in. I imagine him standing across the street from my place, waiting to stage a casual encounter. Following me to the Lidl round the corner at a safe distance, me swinging my bag, scuffing yellow leaves up the pavement, buds stuffed in my ears so I could listen to a podcast, all unawares. I hated the idea of it all.

I suppose I could have thrown the invitation away and forgotten about it all. And yet I couldn't. I have already described myself here as timid, which is perhaps misleading, or maybe just another lie. Timidity has not got me where I am. Cautious, maybe; but not cautious enough to stifle my curiosity.

I went because C— saw in me what I can barely see in myself: a burning curiosity, an unceasing and implacable desire for knowledge. That is what drives me, it's why C— was drawn to me, it's my best and worst quality.

★   ★   ★

C— once told me that I was a naif. It was one of those words I knew, of course, but it was the kind of word you read without ever actually hearing someone say it in conversation.

"It's like you were raised in another time or something. Some people have this kind of faux naivete, but with you it's real."

Of course it's real. I am the home-schooled daughter of a preacher. I once thought that, always and forever, I would be trying to catch up with the world and I never would. The funny thing is how quickly I stopped caring once I was actually out in the world. My eccentric parents had perhaps done me a favour: I might not have read any fiction written after the nineteenth century until I was eighteen, but I had taught myself Latin and German and rudimentary physics; I had barely seen any TV shows, but I could give you a potted history of the pre-Socratic philosophers and recite long passages of *Paradise Lost*. My childhood had been awash in mysticism, a sense of Gnostic knowledge-seeking. To be brought up, as I was, in an environment so steeped in religiosity might, I suppose, seem repressive, but for a child like I was, it had been revelatory, a sense of constant engagement with the mystic.

We were polar opposites, C— and I: he once told me that by the time he was twenty he had indulged in every kind of drug and sexual experience that he could find. By comparison my own world might have seemed narrow and barren, but he said that was not the case at all, that in fact the opposite was true.

We were also twins: because we shared an identical and unslakeable thirst. The ordinary was both inexplicable and repellent to us. We longed instead for the esoteric. I no longer believed in the religion of my upbringing but my conviction that there was a way to access the transcendent remained unshaken.

★   ★   ★

Here I need to tell you about the Geisterbahnhöfe, the ghost stations.

When Berlin was divided, there were U-Bahn and S-Bahn lines that largely travelled through the West but that crossed over into the East a few times. The solution was to simply have the trains pass through without stopping. They put up guards and fences at those stations, where the trains slowed but never stopped; there was a rule, I once heard, that any work done was required to be performed by pairs who did not know one another, to prevent a lone guard or repair person from escaping, or the hatching of a plan between co-conspirators.

After the Wall fell, the ghost stations were brought back into use. There's nothing today to tell you that Stadtmitte or Potsdamer Platz or any of the others were ever a forbidden zone. There are still a few disused lines, I think, and some stations that fell into neglect and became new ghost stations after the old, divided Berlin and the Cold War retreated into history, shifting the city into new configurations.

C— thought cities were themselves magical, or had the potential to be, and Berlin especially so. He once gave me a novel to read, a little paperback called *Our Lady of Darkness*. C— swore that it wasn't really fiction, that it was a thinly disguised autobiographical account by the author, Fritz Leiber, of this occult science he had uncovered called megapolisomancy. If ley lines and megalithic structures were the way the ancients harnessed magic, C— claimed, then why should contemporary people not use urban landscapes, the buildings, the layout of the streets, in the same way? And what could be more powerful than the cities underneath cities: the underground networks?

C— used to talk about the ghost stations a lot. They were, he said, a fabulous metaphor although I'm not sure for what. But he'd also become convinced there was a missing station – not just one that had never been reopened, but one that had been entirely forgotten. It was nonsense, of course. You couldn't forget a whole station, there would be records and maps – especially, goodness knows, in Germany, where they keep records of *everything* – and of course there would be its undeniable physical existence: presumably trains that still passed through it many times per day even if they never stopped, or, at minimum, tracks that led to it if it was at the end of a line.

No, no, no. None of that. According to C—, we were missing the point. This was a genuine *Geisterbahnhof*. A ghost of a place. A station that, like a ghost, was sometimes there and sometimes not there and only ever there for certain people.

When everyone starts to forget a thing, C— said, it begins to forget itself as well, and stops *being*, at least in the way we think of it.

It was, of course, a kind of madness, but that is Berlin – a mad place, a place where anything can happen. Probably C— was talking shit, but what if he wasn't? What if C— tapped into the Great Mystery and I wasn't there for it because I was at home finishing a document for a client, so swayed by the banality of everything around me that I could no longer believe?

Of course I was going, even though I anticipated a cold and uncomfortable night ahead in which nothing happened. That at least would be an improvement on C—'s last so-called experiment where I really do believe that girl was seriously hurt, however much he bluffed about putting me in touch with her so I could see for myself that she was *just fine*. That was the other thing about C—: he scared me, he didn't seem to have any limits. You had to pay a price to connect with the divine, C— said once, but it never seemed like *his* price. C— always made sure it was someone else.

★   ★   ★

I was still with Julian when I first met C—, and not long after, I introduced them. All the way home Julian couldn't stop talking about how much he disliked him. "Dangerous", that was the word he used. "That guy's dangerous, Abby." He said it like it was a bad trait.

Julian was from a well-off family in southeast England and liked me because I was weird, or so he thought. A lot of men are like that; they start to hate you for the thing that originally attracted them to you. It was bound to end. Julian should have been dating posh girls with names like Olivia and Philippa, and indeed, right after we split up, he went back home to work in the family business and, I heard, married someone named Xanthe a few months later. A childhood sweetheart, I think.

I often wished I could be her, even though I didn't love Julian and maybe never had. Or that I could be one of my sisters, or like my mother: *content.*

But I wasn't, and I couldn't, and this is why I found myself, on a freezing cold late autumn night, clambering across an industrial landscape on the eastern outskirts of Berlin. I remember that there weren't any stars at all, nor any moon, and although I'm sure it was just an overcast sky, it didn't seem that way. Instead, I imagined that they had been snuffed out because of what we were going to do, by what C— had already set in motion.

We'd met on a street corner, at the address specified on the invitation, nine of us in all, dressed in the dark colours requested. I didn't know any of the others besides C—, which wasn't unexpected; my world was a small one while C— moved in all kinds of circles.

If we'd been with anyone but C—, I'd have been anticipating, at best, a bit of urban exploration: some atmospheric photo ops for our Instagrams. This was different. While I was apprehensive, because of the last time, I could also feel something swelling inside me that I couldn't quite name. My breath came in short, tight gasps, and I was struggling to keep up with the others. Beneath my right foot, ice cracked, and suddenly I was ankle-deep in cold water; I'd stepped into a frozen puddle. At two separate points we had to cross metal fences; one had a people-sized hole in it but we had to clamber over the other one, and I felt my thick winter tights snag as a bit of metal sliced my leg.

There were places like this all over Berlin, still, despite all the rebuilding and gentrification: sprawling complexes that had once been factories or offices, and I guess all of them were occult, in a way, if you go back to the old root of the word meaning hidden; they weren't hidden from sight but nobody saw them any longer, the way you stop seeing things and even people when they don't have a purpose.

Ahead of me, the others had all stopped abruptly, and as I came nearer I saw that they were gathered on a stretch of pavement. There was a short set of steps leading down to a black square of an entranceway, only it was blocked by a metal grating.

It looked so ordinary. I wondered if C— had got it wrong. I don't know what I expected, but although we were in the middle of nowhere, surely nothing so solid and prosaic could be the kind of thing he spoke of, a place that flickered in and out of existence.

And if it was such a place, surely you would not need the hacksaw someone produced from their rucksack, which they then used to begin sawing vigorously away at the bars.

It felt like the sawing took a very long time, but it's hard to say. It might have only been because I was so cold. Nobody talked, to me or to one another. I tried doing jumping jacks to stay warm but it was difficult as I couldn't really feel my feet any longer.

At last there was a square cut in the bars that was big enough for each of us to worm through. I hung back. I was going to say no, that I had changed my mind, but somehow I didn't. Instead I followed the other eight silent figures into the underworld.

*   *   *

It's hard for me to remember, even now, what we did there. What was done to me. It comes to me in flashes, mostly as parts of nightmares. In the manner of dreams, I mercifully forget the details.

I can tell you this much. It was even colder underground. Beneath our feet, old tile, slick with water and sticky with debris. C— had the only torch – the rest of us were forbidden to use one, or our phones – and played it minimally about the walls and floor as we went, just enough light to allow us to keep moving. Perhaps the strangest thing about it was that from what I could see of it, in that meagre light, it looked so much like so many other stations in Berlin. I don't know what I expected or why that surprised me. The city's transportation system shows its age, and it feels like some of the stations have barely changed in decades.

We went down a set of stairs, and then another.

Somewhere, water was dripping, a slow, maddening sound. I imagined I heard the rumbling of distant trains as well, but it might have been my imagination.

Once or twice C—'s torch would glide over a faded, illegible advertisement, forgotten across more than fifty years. The Wall, not immediately literal but good as, had gone up overnight. Everything had changed abruptly, people going to sleep in one world and waking up in another one. Mid-conversation, the city had been halted, its veins, these underground passages, severed. I tried to imagine it, what it would have looked like on that last day it was in operation. It would have been teeming with people headed to school or work, to see family, to visit a dying loved one, to an illicit rendezvous with a lover, all unaware that they would never set foot here again.

That sudden truncation: could a place be said to grieve? The atmosphere heaved with the unlived possibilities. I wanted to say something to the others because I couldn't believe that they couldn't sense it as well, but I didn't know if we were allowed to speak. I didn't know why I was down there. I didn't know anything except that I was suddenly and acutely aware that I was the outsider.

I felt the weight of the earth on us all. I thought of old myths, about women lured into the underworld and then tricked into remaining there. I thought about the nightmares I used to have when I was with Julian, how I would wake up thrashing in bed with dreams of being buried alive and replaced with a me that was not me. I wondered who these people were in that terrible place with me. Why had I come here with these strangers? What was wrong with me?

From there, my memory is hazy. It's hard for me to remember which parts really happened and which parts are just remnants of my bad dreams, and ultimately, the loss was so gutting that it blocks everything else out. Unlike the girl from the earlier 'experiment' of C—'s that I had attended,

I wasn't physically harmed or even touched, but what they took from me was worse.

I tried to go back there, days later. I thought if I could retrace my steps, I could harness the power there just as C— had, and put myself back together again.

I have an unerring sense of direction, and on a bleak afternoon that portended the grim winter ahead, I picked my way back across that industrial landscape, but of course, I found nothing. Where we had descended the short flight of steps to the barred entranceway was simply a stretch of pavement. I paced up and down and I sat for a short while, as though it might appear to me, and I wanted to cry but I had lost the ability. I had already started to come apart.

I have never seen C— again except in the way that everyone has, as part of his meteoric public rise, building his empire while my soul ebbs and is scattered to the wind.

★   ★   ★

In the old West Berlin, the shuttered stations still appeared on maps. As for those produced in East Berlin, it was as though they had never existed. I said before that Germans were diligent in their record-keeping, and they are, but when human ideology clashes with reality, it is surprising how often ideology wins. This is also the essence of magic, the power that C— sought to harness: forging reality by force of will.

I am becoming a ghost like them. I know this because the ghosts speak to me, in the only ways they can: in baroque graffiti, in reflections in the windows on S-Bahn trains, in the low hum of vanished buildings and lost places.

They tell me that the long-dead and the not-dead but forgotten are one and the same. It is, they say, only a matter of time before I join them. They try to soothe me; they say it hurts less once you have crossed over. Yet I keep resisting them, endeavouring to physically imprint myself on the world. I have taken to carving my initials into wooden surfaces. *I was here. I was real.* One Sunday afternoon I took cans of paint to Mauerpark and sprayed bold designs on segments of the Wall, but they wouldn't stop: *don't you know those will be ghosts one day too?*

I can't stop them talking to me, but I can refuse to listen.

C— and I believed there were many doorways to the numinous. I only need to find and open one. I only need to have the light of the living spilling on my face to start climbing upwards again, to find my way back out of the underworld.

I only need the right map.

I only need someone to remember me.

ARNIE'S ASHES

John Everson

Arnie's ashes were hidden in a silver canister meant to hold flour inside a wall near Sibley Boulevard and Dixie Highway.

We never thought we'd need to worry about them being found. The building was not exactly ripe for new development. There was a quarry to the west and an expressway to the east. Weeds and scrub trees grew to the north and south. The building itself had been there since the Fifties... it was made of concrete blocks and plastic siding and I'd guess the roof leaked since it was flat and sagging and old... but nobody was going to worry too much given its use. The place stood at the end of a row of potholes broken by occasional nubs of asphalt surrounded by an area that was about as undesirable as it got. This was a no man's land at the ass-end of three low-rent municipalities.

The sign out front along Dixie Highway read 'Adult Arcade, open 24 hours'. Carl and I knew it was a place that Arnie had frequented often, so when we decided to get rid of them, it made sense to secrete his ashes in a wall of the seedy joint. Based on the bizarre circumstances of his demise, that same joint, I assumed, was the reason Arnie was now sitting inside a canister instead of holding loquacious court at a bar on 147th Street, so... it seemed right. The place had been there for decades and was likely to be there for another century.

Nobody would admit it was there. Nobody would admit going there. Men parked in the gravel lot and walked around the side of the building as fast as they could, heads down whether in fair weather or foul.

We figured hiding the canister in the wall was a much safer way to dispose of Arnie's ashes than throwing them off a cliff or out into Lake Michigan. God knew what would happen if we did something like that.

That's what we'd thought, anyway.

Until the day they began coming home.

*   *   *

Carl answered the door the first time one of them showed up. I heard the brittle crack of his coffee mug hit the front foyer tile.

"What the…" he yelped. And then a moment later he called, "Darnell!!!"

*   *   *

I heard the panic in his tone and jumped up from the kitchen table we had once shared with Arnie. It had been the perfect bachelor pad for three divorced men; a three-bedroom house with a full finished basement and a stand up attic. We all had had plenty of space.

At that moment, it was *too* big. By the time I reached the foyer, Carl had slammed the door shut.

When he turned, his face was white. I reached for the door but he grabbed my arm.

"Don't," he said.

"Who was at the door?" I tried to move past him.

"Seriously," he said.

Just then, a fist pounded on the door. Slow but rhythmic. I reached to open it, and Carl grabbed my wrist.

"I mean it," he said.

I turned the knob anyway. The door squealed open and I saw the heavyset man standing just inches away from the glass of the storm door.

His body looked nothing like my old friend. But his face was Arnie's.

I did a double take, because Arnie had been skinny. This guy had to top 250.

Plus, Arnie was dead.

Minor detail.

Without thinking, I slammed the door shut.

"Did Arnie have a brother?" I asked Carl.

He shook his head.

"Maybe a cousin?" I suggested.

He shook his head again. Carl still looked sheet-white.

That's when the pounding really began at the door. The glass rattled. Hell, the wooden frame inside rattled. Dust fell from the lintel.

"Well then, who is at the door?" I asked.

Something in the doorframe cracked. It was an old house.

"I think we're going to find out," Carl said. He backed away toward the kitchen.

And then the door burst open.

Carl darted for the kitchen, while I began to back my way towards it.

"Arnie," I said. "We missed you."

The man who looked like my dead friend... with an extra two hundred pounds... only grunted and lunged at me. I abandoned bravery and followed Carl into the kitchen.

Okay, I didn't follow, I *dove* for the kitchen.

When I got there, Carl was crouched by the table, holding a knife.

"What are you..." I began. But I never completed the sentence. Because a second later, the football player who looked like Arnie burst into the space and lunged at Carl. I was on the floor.

I watched the unthinkable happen.

The man rushed at Carl, and Carl screamed like some kind of mad samurai and held the knife in front of him. And not-Arnie ran right into it. Skewered like a bell pepper.

There was red. In the air. On the counters. On the cabinets.

And then Not-Arnie was down on the floor, squirming and moaning and spinning a smeary crimson pattern on the kitchen tile. A few minutes later he stopped moving, and Carl stood over him, the blade of the knife dripping the man's blood back down on his shirt.

"Okay," I said. "Now what?"

There was a dead man who looked like Arnie lying on our kitchen floor.

Blood seeped from the wound in the man's chest. It quickly puddled around his arms on the floor.

"I killed Arnie," Carl whispered. The knife dropped to the floor with a clatter.

"Arnie was already dead," I pointed out.

*   *   *

We took the body into the basement and laid it out on the concrete floor. We didn't know what to do, really, but we knew we couldn't call the police. They wouldn't see this as a monster with our friend's face... they'd see this as a murder. So we laid the body out downstairs until we could figure out a plan.

The problem was, before we figured out what to do, there was another knock at the door.

The two of us looked at each other in panic. "I'm not getting it," I said.

Carl shook his head vehemently. "Well I'm not either."

The knocks on the door only grew louder. We stared at each other for what felt like an hour.

The pounding grew more forceful.

I finally caved in. "All right," I said. "But you're coming with me." I grabbed him by the arm and dragged him along as I walked up the stairs.

It was bound to be the police. I didn't know how they'd know, but I figured someone had reported Not-Arnie's murder already. Anticipating a blue uniform and a quick ride to jail, I took a breath, held it, and turned the knob on the door.

The guy on the other side was not wearing a blue uniform.

Once again, the visitor looked exactly like Arnie.

Only this guy was tall and gangly. And dark-skinned. So... I guess, really, outside of the face, he looked nothing like Arnie. Arnie had been solid. And shorter.

But... the body is never the first thing we see. When I opened the door, I saw my friend's face. And this time, instead of slamming the door, I screamed.

While I was busy freaking out, the guy walked right past me and into the house. He turned and took the stairs to the bedrooms, and disappeared.

I looked at Carl, who only cowered against the hallway wall.

"What the hell was that?" I asked. "*Who* the hell was that?"

His arm only pointed at the door.

Another guy stood there, in faded jeans and a dark T-shirt. His complexion was Latino. Yet he had Arnie's face.

Arnie had been Irish.

I stepped away from the door and pointed towards the stairs. "That way," I said.

He didn't wait for pleasantries, any more than the last Arnie had. Instead he ascended the stairs towards Arnie's old room.

I followed him up, and saw that the first Arnie was already in the room, standing near the closet. I couldn't tell if he was looking for something, or simply frozen in place, but I didn't stick around to find out. As soon as Arnie2 entered the room, I pulled the door shut behind him. When I went down the stairs, Carl's face was white.

"What is going on?" he wheezed. I thought he might be hyperventilating. A theory had already been brewing in my head since the first Arnie had ploughed through our broken doorway.

"Somebody found Arnie's ashes," I said.

His eyes screwed up, and he looked at me as if he'd just chewed a sour apple. "Huh?"

"What happened when Arnie came home that night from the smut store?"

"I don't want to talk about that."

"I don't either. But... I want you to say it. What happened?"

Carl shook his head, refusing to speak.

"You tried to kiss him," I said finally. "Because when he walked into this house that night, he had the face of a beautiful girl."

"Shut up."

"And why did he look like a girl?"

"Stop talking about it."

I shook my head. "I can't... just answer me."

"Because he did it with that girl at the smut shack? That's what you figured."

I nodded. "He admitted that much before..."

"Don't say it!"

Carl had been in denial since the day that Arnie died. But the appearance of two Arnies upstairs plus the dead one in the basement was a sure sign that denial wasn't going to cut it anymore. We had to face this thing head on. So to speak.

"Someone found Arnie's ashes," I said. "Whatever made *him* turn into that... thing... has done the same to the guys at our door."

"Why are they here?" Carl asked.

I shrugged. "Same reason Arnie took your truck and drove to that mobile home in Indiana."

Carl shivered.

"It's like salmon going home to spawn," I said.

Finally, I got the reaction I had been waiting for. It all clicked, and Carl's eyes shot open. "You mean, those things upstairs…"

Just then, something crashed in Arnie's former bedroom.

"Exactly," I said.

"Oh shit," he said. "What are we going to do?"

"Go to the utility room and grab the hammers," I said.

He shook his head. "I can't do that again."

Something screeched upstairs… a cross between a hawk's kill cry and the howl of an animal stabbed in the heart.

"No choice," I said.

Carl ran to the basement, as I took position at the base of the stairs. Hopefully they wouldn't try to come down before he returned. I didn't know what I'd do to stop them if so. I couldn't take them both myself.

The landing filled with the sounds of things falling upstairs. The crash of a lamp, the thump of things leaving the walls to hit the floor.

Carl returned before the noises left Arnie's room. I took the small sledge from him. Carl kept the normal hammer.

"Ready?" I asked.

He shook his head no. I took that as a yes, and began to ascend the stairs.

* * *

Arnie's room was a disaster area. The top of one dresser was wiped clean of all his junk, while the highboy had been toppled over. The edge of it rested on the bed, drawers hung partially open to spill pairs of faded jeans and moth-eaten underwear to the floor.

One Arnie was facing the corner of the room, slowly knocking his head against the wall. The other appeared to be waiting for someone to let him out. As soon as I stepped inside, he lunged, long dark fingers scrabbling to grab at my face or neck.

I didn't wait to find out which.

With one fast stroke I brought the sledge down on the top of his skull, and his body collapsed instantly to the floor.

"Jesus," Carl whispered at my shoulder.

"I don't think so," I said, not taking my eyes off the place where my hammer had fallen. The blood flowed dark and fast, but that wasn't what I was looking for. My gaze strayed to the other Arnie, who didn't appear to have noticed that his doppelgänger had been felled. When I looked back at the body at my feet, I saw just what I'd been dreading.

It was tiny, at first. But then it grew, like a corn sprout captured in time-lapse video. A thin silver tendril expanded from the heart of the gore and reached past the man's black hair to clutch at the air.

I brought the sledge down and smashed the bastard.

Hot blood sprayed my face, but I didn't have time to wipe it off, because for some reason the other Arnie finally realised that it had company. He was climbing across the bed as I yelled at Carl.

"Get him!"

"I don't…" he started to complain. But then it was too late. The guy's hands had already fastened around Carl's neck. My friend's eyes bulged and instead of striking out, I heard the thump of his hammer as it fell to the floor.

"Dammit, Carl," I complained, and lifted my arm. The sledge connected with the side of this Arnie's head, just above the ear. The blow wasn't enough. The thing shifted its attention from Carl to me, and suddenly I was lying on the floor, with the angry body of a guy who looked like my best friend on top of me. Only my friend had weighed about one hundred pounds less and had never tried to throttle the life out of me.

I called for Carl's help, but all that got past my lips was a wheeze.

Arnie gripped my neck like he was trying to hold on to a noodle. He lifted my head up and slammed it back repeatedly on the leg of the fallen Arnie. I pounded at his back with my fists, but it didn't seem to make any difference. Arnie was going to crush the life out of me anyway.

"Carl," I tried to call… but I still couldn't make a sound. There were stars exploding in my eyes, as Arnie's normally gentle face stared blankly down at mine.

And then… the pressure and Arnie's head suddenly disappeared. Carl's face took its place. A hand reached behind my neck and yanked me up. Carl pulled me back towards the door, and I saw that the second Arnie was now spasming on the bed. A dark stain spread across the peach bedspread.

I held on to Carl's arm and finally pulled myself fully to my feet. My vision still strobed with stars and fog, and my breath came in gasps. But slowly I got my legs beneath me. The body on the bed stilled as we stepped backwards into the hall. But not before I saw the silver worm slip from the man's head to swim across the pool of blood on the comforter.

I could have gone back to kill it, but it wouldn't have mattered. There were dozens of them scattering across the hardwood floor already, slipping with wet plops from the wound in Arnie1's head. I knew that the tiniest ones, maggot-sized, had already slid between the cracks in the hardwood floor.

"What are we going to do," Carl asked. "We can't take all these to Fulton's!"

Fulton's was the funeral home a couple blocks away owned by a friend of ours. When he'd seen the wrong face on the real Arnie, as well as the tattoo on Arnie's arm which clearly demonstrated that the hairy body with the pretty woman's face really *was* that of the man we said it was... he'd helped us out, and put the corpse through his crematorium. But three more bodies?

No. You could only stretch friendship favours so far. And then the police were bound to show up.

"Grab whatever you want to keep," I said, still catching my breath. "And then get the gasoline can. Those things are probably already in the walls by now. We can't stay here."

⋆　　⋆　　⋆

Moving out of a place you've lived in for years is definitely an easier thing when you know that there are monster worms potentially lurking in every corner prepared to turn you into a ghoul with someone else's face. And for all I knew, there were more Arnies on the way to boot.

I didn't want to stick around to find out. The first time around, I'd been careful to try to fully destroy whatever it was that had killed my friend. This time I just wanted to get away... and hopefully mask the evidence of what we'd been forced to do.

⋆　　⋆　　⋆

The old house burned fast and hot.

Carl and I left most of the meagre things we owned behind, but we took a couple suitcases. I suggested that maybe now would be a good time for us to head south, like we'd always talked about. I hated the Chicago winters, and, well… now we had no place to live through them.

I headed up Sibley Blvd. toward the I-57 Interchange. Carl sat silent beside me. But instead of getting on the expressway, I turned left and then right, into a gravel parking lot with more potholes than level surface.

"What the hell are you doing?" Carl said when he realised where I'd gone.

"I want to see what's happened to Arnie's ashes," I said.

"I think we've already seen," Carl said. "I don't want to see him anymore."

"Neither do I," I said. "That's why we're here."

I opened the door and stepped out onto the lot. Carl didn't move.

"You coming?" I asked.

He shook his head. I noticed his face looked pale. I realised that at some point in the past twelve hours, Carl had passed his limits. I decided not to push them any further. I just nodded and closed the door. Then I walked up the broken sidewalk to the old wooden door that marked the entrance to the adult peep show building. The faded red paint peeled away from the wood like old tree bark, and a sign tacked in the middle simply read 'Must be 21 or Over'.

I was long past twenty-one, and I pushed the old door open and stepped inside.

It was just as I remembered it. The place probably hadn't changed in thirty years. The entry foyer was dim and dingy; faded brown linoleum covered the floor and the walls were covered in panelling that had gone out of style in 1975. A thin man with thin hair but a solid bush of salt-and-pepper beard sat reading a magazine behind a glass counter with a cash register on one corner. The glass shelves beneath the counter featured a number of sexual aids: lotions, pills, rubber rings, rainbow-coloured condoms.

I dug into my wallet for a ten-dollar bill and offered it to him. He nodded, and slipped it into the drawer of the cash register. I already knew the drill, but a sign next to the cash register told the story: '$10 per half hour. Clock starts when you turn on the TV.'

I walked past the counter and turned down a narrow hallway. The walls were plastered with posters advertising porno films, and every few feet there was a door to a private viewing room. I passed two that were closed, with the sounds of human copulation bleating in exaggerated, escalating rhythms. I say exaggerated, because I don't believe regular people ever sound like that. Neighbours would never get any sleep if they did.

As I'd hoped, Room 7 at the end of the hall was vacant. I stepped inside, and closed and locked the door. The room was too dark to see anything, with no window. I fumbled for the TV switch, and the space suddenly came alive with the display of a pair of big bouncing breasts. But I only spared one glance at the screen, and then turned my attention instead to the wall above the white sheet-covered couch on the opposite side of the room.

I had stood on that couch, and lowered Arnie's urn into the wall behind it, thanks to the removeable white tiles in the ceiling. The drop ceiling was low, allowing easy access to the TV wiring that snaked from room to room.

There was a jagged hole in the wall just behind the back of the couch. It looked as if someone had slammed the couch into – and through – the drywall. Had someone gotten too excited while enjoying the, shall we say, naturalistic expressionism onscreen?

I knelt on the couch and examined the gash in the flickering light of the TV. The lip of the broken drywall was covered with something dark. Dirt? Ash? I frowned. If that was what I thought it was…

I climbed onto the couch and stood on the arm to pop the drop ceiling tile. Then I pulled myself up on the beam and looked down. The silver urn was there, on the wooden ledge just a couple feet below, right where I'd left it the last time I'd been here.

Only… now it was tipped over.

A small pile of dark ash lay next to the lid, and I could see where Arnie's remains had cascaded down the inner wall to find the ragged gap in the wall. Maybe whoever had slammed the couch through the drywall had knocked the urn over and spilled some of Arnie's remains out.

Since then… it wasn't hard to imagine that men who'd sat on this couch and watched the bouncing breasts on the screen behind me had periodically bumped the wall and breathed in the resulting dust that carried the black bits of burnt flesh that had once been my friend.

Apparently burning him hadn't been enough.

I pulled out my cellphone and texted Carl. Limits or not, I needed his help.

Bring me a coat and a bottle of water. Room 7, I wrote.

Water? he answered.

From the cooler in the trunk, I texted. We'd packed some basics from the refrigerator before we'd torched the house.

A few minutes later the door to the room opened and Carl stepped inside. He handed me the bottle of water, but looked confused.

"Arnie got out," I said, and pointed at the hole in the wall. Then I explained.

"So what do we do?" he asked.

"We get him out of here."

I pulled the sheet off the couch, and wrapped it around my arm. Then I stood back on the couch and pulled myself up into the ceiling. Hanging over the edge, I pulled out my cell phone and triggered the flashlight app so that I could really see what we were dealing with. Then I reached down with the sheet-protected hand, and righted the urn. Once I had carefully pressed the lid back on it, I lifted the canister up and slid my body down from halfway through the ceiling back into the room.

Carefully I set the urn in the corner, and then knelt on the couch. I blew gently into the hole in the wall… and then slowly increased the force of air. I turned away, took a breath, and blew again. Hopefully, all of Arnie's ashes were now on the dead side of the wall.

I picked up the bottle of water and pulled myself into the ceiling again. Using my cell phone light as a guide, I carefully poured the water down the wall, washing what remained of Arnie's ashes to the building's foundations.

It was all I could think to do, short of trying to smuggle a vacuum into the place.

When I was done, I slid the ceiling tile back into place, and tossed the sheet back over the couch, making sure the part that my hand had touched was in the back on the floor. I didn't think there was really any ash on it, but I hadn't been willing to risk my hand.

I pulled a tissue from the pocket of my jacket and stuffed it into the hole where Arnie's ashes had sifted through and into the lungs of some poor fools who'd come here looking for a quick, harmless release. A respite. Guys who'd looked for a private 'little death' and gotten the big one instead.

"Go back to the car," I told Carl. He nodded, and slipped back out the door. I pulled on the jacket, and then tucked the urn under my arm, draping the front of the jacket over it. I looked once at the white of the tissue stuffed into the gap in the white wall.

It seemed enough. Even if someone pulled it out, I'd washed away all that I could see of the ashes.

I followed Carl out the door.

The guy at the front didn't look up from his magazine as I passed. If he had, I wondered if he would have noticed I was wearing a coat that I hadn't been on the way in.

Why would he care? All he was here to do was to make sure there was no trouble while people fulfilled needs they couldn't talk about in public conversation. While people were actually being themselves.

Which made me smile, grimly. We never admitted publicly who we were, not really.

Not to anyone. These faces we show outside our caves... they're just masks to hide the real us.

Who were you really? I asked, as I carried Arnie's urn back to the car.

For just a second, I could have sworn I heard Arnie ask right back, "Who are *you*, really?"

★　★　★

Carl held Arnie as I drove to a Walgreens and bought some packing tape. Once I'd done that, and securely taped the lid of the urn shut so that the rest of the remains couldn't spill out again, we got on the road. It was long, and we made several stops at roadside bars, hoping to wash away the memories.

Memories of Arnie as he'd once been, loud and boisterous and funny and kind. Memories of Arnie who was not Arnie, but rather, someone else. Someone who wore Arnie's face like a curse. Someone who only existed to remind us of the person who was now gone. Shadows of a man we'd loved but probably never really known.

Who ever really knows anyone? Behind the disguise of a smile, there is really only a cipher. And the hope that the words you hear from those lips are in some way real.

You just never know.

I looked at Carl, and thought of all the things I knew of him. All of the heartaches he had confessed, and the anger and the humour, the laughter and the tears. What really lurked behind his eyes?

I would never know, even though I thought I did. But at least he looked like Carl, and not Arnie.

★   ★   ★

We rented a shitty apartment in Chattanooga, and took shitty jobs to pay the rent. I didn't care. It was warmer there, all the time, than in Chicago. And life was quieter. Less stress. Even though what I did every day was clean up the foul messes that people on their way out left in the hospital.

I convinced myself that cleaning up the messes was better than being on the way out myself.

Carl ended up with a job at a grocery store, bagging groceries. Something I'd done in high school to pay for the beer I wasn't supposed to drink.

Whatever.

You do what you have to do to make ends meet, and when you're done doing it, you sit back in your little man-made cave, your hideout, your mask between you and the world and think about it all. Sometimes not much at all, but sometimes a lot.

I thought a lot about Arnie. Maybe because his ashes sat on a shelf above our TV. I wondered how much I'd ever known about him, really.

What did you really know about someone beyond the expressions on their face?

When Carl and I had unpacked and moved into this little apartment, we'd found a picture of Arnie from a few years back. It showed the three of us, mugging for the camera at a sports bar somewhere, raising three glasses in the air. He'd been smiling, and looked in that moment, as happy as I'd ever seen him.

I taped that photo to his urn. It's how I really wanted to remember him.

But then I turned the urn, so that the photo faced the wall.

Because as much as I'd loved Arnie, I really didn't want to see his face ever again.

For Bob Weinberg

A BRIEF TOUR OF THE NIGHT

Nathan Ballingrud

Allen turned off the road and walked up to the Mountain Laurel Motel, a two-storey strip of dingy concrete with a row of faded red doors top and bottom, abutting a parking lot that was never full. Rusted bars protected the windows on the bottom floor. He'd just finished his dishwasher shift at the restaurant and his white clothes were soiled and damp. A nearby dumpster exuded a complex reek. Trash had accumulated around it like supplicants at an altar. The motel was located on the outskirts of Asheville, close enough to where you could look out one of the windows and see all the city lights filling the valley.

Frankie was waiting for him at the rear entrance, as usual.

"She's been asking for you," he said. He held the door open for him like some fallen bellboy. Frankie was considerably smaller than Allen. He had the dead-air stench of a chain smoker, and his boozy swamp breath passed over Allen as he squeezed past him.

Allen experienced a brief flare of emotion, something strange and giddy. Was she really asking for him? What would that mean? But one glance at Frankie's stupid grin told him it wasn't true.

"Don't make fun of her, Frankie," he said.

"No, hey, not me man. You know I wouldn't do that."

Frankie was the night manager at the Mountain Laurel. He lived in a trailer park not too far from here, owned by the same folks who owned the motel. They let him stay there for reduced rent as long as he kept the place in working order, which he did more or less successfully.

They ventured up the narrow, piss-smelling stairs, both of them breathing heavily from the exertion. "Truth is she quiets down after you visit," Frankie said. "It's good for her. She's just lonely, I guess."

Allen knew that Frankie was married, and that he had two kids of recent vintage. He talked about them with the affectionate disdain some men use to express their love. So he wondered with what authority Frankie could diagnose loneliness or even comprehend it. It was an unkind thought; of course there could be loneliness in community. But as long as Frankie had a warm hand to touch his cheek or to push back a lock of his greying hair, he would always have a buffer against the absolute value of human disconnection. Allen was willing to bet the woman upstairs had not known one of these things even once in her whole life, and it was damn sure now that she never would.

They entered a vacant room on the second floor: untenanted and cold, with the indifferent tidiness of a long-unoccupied space. They didn't even try to rent it out anymore. Nobody stayed a full night without complaining. The light was on in the bathroom, a low forty-watt glow pushing a polite wedge into the room. The blinds were up, giving them a view of the city nestled in the dark Appalachians.

The woman leaned her left shoulder and her head against the window, staring into empty space. She was dressed in a ratty sweater and a pair of jeans, and her hands were tucked beneath her armpits, as though she was trying to conserve warmth. A plain silver chain decorated her neck. She was overweight, the whites of her eyes yellowing mildly. Her hands were calloused. She might have been a housekeeper at this very motel, or a dishwasher at a restaurant, like himself. She had the beleaguered look of someone who'd spent a long time being poor and working hard: premature aging lines on her face, springs of grey hair nestled in the black, and a look in her eyes like something was frying inside her head.

Allen lit a cigarette and leaned against the wall in front of her, close enough that their foreheads almost touched. She gave no acknowledgement. She never did.

"Hey darling," he said. "It's me again. Three days in a row now, how about that. People are gonna start talking." He paused. This was all rote by now, but he liked to give her a chance to respond, just in case she said something new.

"Turn it off, please," she said.

"Okay, I'll turn it off for you." He walked to the bathroom and switched off the light. Darkness filled the room. Frankie, hovering at the entrance, retreated a step into the hallway. Normally he didn't stay for this part, and his presence this time felt like an intrusion. Allen resisted the impulse to shut the door on him.

He turned off the light every time he came up here. Not because it made a damn bit of difference to what she said, but because he thought it might be nice if every once in a while someone actually did as she asked. He resumed his position at her side.

"Turn it off, please," she said.

"Maybe one of these times you'll say something different. What do you think? Maybe a new request. We'll take them one at a time and eventually we'll get to where you need to go."

He waited.

"Give it a try," he said.

For a while she was silent. A bar of light roamed across the wall and onto the ceiling as a car passed by outside. He thought he could see the sparkle of downtown lights through her face, as though her last anchor to the world was beginning to fade.

"There's no one left to remember you except yourself," he said. "It's time to forget, sweetheart."

Allen stood with her, smoking his cigarette, while the city whispered beyond the window. Frankie eventually ambled off, attending to his own purposes. Allen kept her company for a little while and then he left.

★   ★   ★

Frankie kept an office on the bottom floor. With the help of a small desk, a filing cabinet and a radio, he'd converted a storage room into a refuge from the battery of obligations visited upon him by an unkind world. Allen unfolded the metal chair Frankie kept behind the door and waited for his measure of cheap bourbon, poured from a bottle kept in the lowest drawer of the filing cabinet.

"The thing about it is, she don't know what I have to do every night, you know?" Frankie was talking about his wife. "I mean yeah, mostly people are asleep on my shift, but that doesn't mean I get to sit on my ass all night. The building manager has a list for me. He spends all day just thinking of shit for me to do."

Allen offered him a nod of solidarity. A cigarette burned in his left hand and smoke curled over his face.

"Every day it's a new thing. Fix the water heater. Check Unit 4 for a leak. Unclog the toilet in 23. Clean up the trash. You know what it was tonight?"

"What," said Allen.

"Painting. He wants me to paint the base moulding on the walls in the whole goddamned building. You know what base moulding is?"

"Nope."

"It's those boards that run along the bottom of the walls. Why do you think they call them moulding? I don't think that's a word you want to associate with domestic structures."

"I don't know, Frankie."

"It's like to take me all month. And after that I have to do the crown moulding. You know what that is?"

"Is it the little boards that run along the top of the walls?"

"Yeah, that's right. It's like I'm a mule. Just work all night, every night. Like a damn mule."

Allen stubbed out his cigarette. "Well, I guess I gotta go."

"You gonna go talk to another one?"

"Yeah. There's a few."

"Does any one of 'em ever talk back to you?"

"Some of 'em say stuff, but they're not really saying it to me." Allen finished what was left in his glass and set it down softly on the desk. "Thanks for the drink, Frankie."

"Glad to share it with you. See you tomorrow night?"

"I'm not at the restaurant tomorrow night, so I guess I'll stay home."

"Oh. Well, okay. Friday then." The door was open and Allen was halfway through it when Frankie started talking again. "Why do you feel like you gotta talk to all these creepy fuckers?"

"I don't think they're creepy. At least not most of them."

"This is the only one I have to see regular. It's bad enough. I can't imagine seeking 'em out. I don't think it's good for you. You know, you can come by sometime and meet my wife and kids. Her idea. She said she'll cook you a homemade meal. When's the last time you had one of those?"

Allen didn't like these moments. "I appreciate it, man. I'm okay though."

"I worry about you sometimes."

Allen stood there silently, nerves jangling with discomfort.

"Well anyway. Good night, Al."

Allen closed the door and started the long walk into town. Asheville glimmered brightly in the valley, open to what Allen thought of as the cool avenues, the cold blue roads the ghosts used to make their visitations. The notion soothed him. It was possible, walking at night with a light breeze blowing through your hair, to believe that there was an underlying kindness to the world's order. To believe that with terrible patience and a willingness to listen through silence one might come to the attention of God. He closed his eyes and believed in it for a little while.

★   ★   ★

The next one was in a shallow creek just a few dozen yards from the Wild Acre housing community. Seventeen or eighteen years old, probably. Sometimes you could see him, sometimes you couldn't. He was hard to spot unless you knew what you were looking for. He lay face down in the creek, head underwater and legs on dry land, the water sliding right through him. He wore a thin green jacket and blue jeans; his hair was longish, blond and unwashed. Both his arms lay at his sides, as though he'd been gently placed there. Allen didn't think it had been gentle, though. It was too easy to imagine the knee in the young man's back, the strong hand gripping the back of his neck, keeping him under until the struggling stopped. He wondered if the person who did it had ever been caught; or if he lived close by, maybe in one of those cheap new houses, staring out each night at the stream which carried this dead boy's ghost.

He scooted down the embankment until his own shoes were only an inch or so away from the water. In the summer he sometimes came wearing swimming trunks, getting down close and crouching in the cold stream. Not now though. Now he sat on the edge. The earth was cold enough.

"Well, I'm here. Talk to me if you want to talk."

The boy in the creek turned his head a little bit, and Allen could see the jaw muscles work. No telling what he was trying to say. Early on, Allen had tried to get the boy's mouth clear of the water in an effort to hear him. He'd tried lifting him up, which was no good – his hands passed right through. He'd tried damming the water upstream, but some homeowner had noticed and chased him off with a brandished gun. He kept a low profile after that.

Since then, he'd made peace with the fact that he would never know. Who knows, maybe the kid was just asking to be left alone.

Visiting this one was tougher, because he started to wonder what Charlie would have been like if he'd made it to seventeen. Would he have been strong and athletic, like this kid was? Would he have fallen in love? Would he have inspired the same dangerous emotion this one had, that led him to this? And yet he felt no curiosity about this boy's life. He was just here. Dead, face down in a creek, speaking into the mud.

"Cold is coming in early," he said. "We might even get snow for once. Maybe some ice in the creek. Would you be able to feel that?"

The boy's mouth opened and closed, opened and closed.

"I don't like visiting you. I don't like visiting any of you, but I think you're the worst."

He pressed the heels of his hands into his eyes, felt the black wave rising inside him.

"Did you deserve it? I bet you fucking deserved it."

That afternoon, before work, he'd woken up and stared at the water stains on the ceiling for too long, ignoring the clock, ignoring the crawl of sunlight across the floor. What if he laid there in the warmth and let the world move on. What if he opened every vein in his body. He imagined all the blood flowing from him, saturating his mattress until it was sodden with gore, until it dripped through the floorboards and soaked the dark earth with his poison, fattening the spiders and the earthworms and everything that crawled and thrived in the dark. How the world would celebrate. How it would rejoice.

The relief of it.

His mouth opened and closed.

Allen took off his jacket, got on his hands and knees, and crept into the water. It was shockingly cold. He inched forward until he was next to the dead boy. He leaned in close. The boy's eyes were white and empty. His mouth kept moving.

Allen dunked his head under the water. He heard the boy's voice, muffled and distant. He opened his eyes and looked around. He wanted to see what the boy saw.

Rocks, silt, tumultuous murk. A cold rushing. A black torrent.

⋆ ⋆ ⋆

He was on his way to his third stop when the police cruiser speared him into place with its spotlight. The siren gave a single low *whoop*. He stopped where he was, hands at his sides. His silhouette was splashed on the wall of a gas station convenience store, tall and hulking. He moved his arms, entranced by the strange, dancing image he produced.

A voice barked at him over a loudspeaker. "Don't move."

Allen stopped moving. He couldn't be sure his shadow did.

"Turn around."

He turned, blinded by twenty thousand lumens. Reflexively, he blocked the light with his hand.

"I said don't move, asshole."

Allen dropped his hands, eyes squeezed shut.

"Well, holy shit. It's Allen Tucker."

The cop opened his door. Allen could hear the sound of the cop's boots scuffing onto the pavement, but he couldn't see anything around the glare of light. Cars hissed by on the highway, oblivious to the small drama on the roadside. They might as well have been invisible. The door of the convenience store jingled as someone went in or came out.

"Did I do something wrong, Officer?"

"Well ain't that a loaded question. I hadn't seen you out on your route for a little while, Allen."

"I was taking a different one the last couple weeks. Switching things up." The truth was that the ghost he was on his way to see was only visible in moonlight, and he'd been waiting for the moon to grow full.

"Uh huh. Thought maybe you did us all a favour and got hit by a car or something. Though I guess we woulda smelled you stinking up the road by now."

"Sorry to disappoint."

"Yeah, I bet you say that a lot."

The cop came closer, his hands hitched on his belt, the light a blinding halo around him. He stopped close enough that Allen could smell Doritos on his breath. "Keep creeping around, somebody's gonna put a bullet in you. And I hope when it happens I'm the one who gets the call, because if I do? I'm gonna piss on your fucking corpse. My report's gonna make whoever does it look like a fucking hero, I don't care if you were planting

264 • BEYOND THE VEIL

flowers across the street and they shoot you from their BarcaLounger. It's gonna be a good day, when it comes."

Allen said nothing. His heart was beating hard. He wondered if this cop – a man he did not even recognise, but he'd seen so many of them in the years since The Day – would pull his gun and put a hole through his heart right there in the street, in front of the oblivious drivers and whatever human flotsam drifted through the convenience store parking lot. He felt the crackling electricity of possibility, the vertigo of standing so close to extinction.

The spotlight went out, the cruiser's engine roared, and the cop was gone, sliding back onto the silent black road and out of his world. He must have said something else before he left, dropped some final cutting remark, but Allen couldn't bring it up.

The sudden darkness felt heavy and absolute. It was as though God had opened His eye and regarded him for one incandescent moment, only to close it again, leaving him in his exile.

Somebody at the convenience store shouted "ACAB!" like it was a word, in an apparent show of solidarity. Allen ignored it and resumed his walk. The dead were waiting.

★　　★　　★

The girl in the moonlight hung from a rope affixed to the guardrail on a highway overpass. It must have been a spectacular demise. Her face was swollen and dark with trapped blood; if he saw a picture of her in life, he wouldn't recognise her. To him she was only this dead, bloated thing, her delicate green dress in ghastly contrast to what it contained. She hung utterly still, no matter the weather around her. Her body lit when the moonlight touched it, vanished when it did not. On a cloudy night she would come in and out of the world, strange bands of beauty and decay.

Like the woman in the hotel, she had a message she wanted to deliver to anyone who could hear. "I'm sorry," she said. The rope made her voice thin and high-pitched, like something from a cartoon. "I'm sorry."

"I forgive you," he told her, but it didn't matter. It was too late.

★　　★　　★

There were others. More than he could see in a single night. Some of them manifested according to certain patterns; others were irregular, stuttering like faulty lamps. Before The Day, he'd never believed in ghosts. Afterwards, he saw them everywhere. The world was teeming with them. Filthy with them. People had no idea. Frankie was the only other he'd met who saw them too. Maybe that was why he kept him at bay: it suggested a flaw in the man, a wound that Allen lacked the strength or patience to acknowledge.

Allen followed his customary, circuitous path home, marked by these stations of loneliness. An old man in his ghostly wheelchair, patrolling his alley with ceaseless repetition. A couple tangled in their crushed bicycles on the roadside, weeping as they inspected their own ruined bodies, each unaware of the other. A young woman stalking a riverbank where a homeless community once stood, still wracked by schizophrenia in her death, still raving at the ghosts even ghosts couldn't see.

Allen spent a little time with each. He listened to them if they had anything to say, and he talked to them when he was inclined to. It didn't matter that they couldn't hear him.

By the time he made it back home, the night's chill had worked its way into his muscles. The sun would be up very soon. He didn't have to plan what would come next: he was a creature of routine now. He moved without having to think. He'd eat something for breakfast and then he'd settle into the couch with a six-pack of beers parked at his feet, and he'd stay there until sleep took him.

His path was such that he came to the house in which he kept a small apartment from the rear this time, and that meant he'd have to walk past his truck. He paused at the tree line, looking out at the overgrown back yard, a field of weeds and tall grass corralled by a chain-link fence. Somewhere under that over-growth were relics of the dog that used to live there. Beside the fence, parked on a gravel path which too had succumbed to weeds, was the blue Ford pick-up. It was covered with a tarp but that wasn't enough to disguise its fallen state. All four tyres had lost their air long ago, and a few years' worth of pollen crusted whatever the tarp didn't cover. Its engine hadn't turned over in nearly a year.

The truck had sat unmoved since someone had brought it home to him a couple days after The Day. He couldn't even remember who it was. Someone who'd since disappeared from his life, anyway. In the time since, it had served as a home for all manner of beasts: raccoons, birds, mice, wasps.

Allen planned to walk around it and head straight for the front door, like he sometimes managed to do, but instead he approached the driver's door and lifted the tarp so he could peer inside.

The sky was still dark, light staining the eastern ridge. The truck's cab was empty. He could barely see anything at all.

He'd been drunk on The Day. He was drunk in all his best stories, the ones with real punch. Fighting with Natalie, sure, old news. It was a hot day, brutally hot, and the fights came easy those days. But he didn't hit her, the way some folks liked to say. He never hit her. It was something he used to be proud of, as though a lack of that particular wickedness made him a case of special merit.

But the fight. It had been one of the bad ones, and Shane was squalling like a tornado in his highchair, he just would not shut up, and Natalie had said you can both get the fuck out. Get the fuck out and give me a minute's peace, please Jesus.

And he'd said all right you fat bitch, maybe you'll see us again, maybe you won't.

And he'd yanked Shane from his highchair and installed him on the floorboard of the truck's passenger side, where he'd be safe from falling off the seat should a sudden stop be required, as it sometimes was when Allen drove under these conditions. Shane settled down then because he liked riding in the truck, and he cooed with satisfaction as Allen put it in gear and hauled all that rusted misery out onto the two-lane blacktop (cooed, because at eighteen months he still hadn't started talking, not shown the slightest interest, and even then Allen couldn't blame the kid for that – who the hell would want to talk to a set of parents like them?), gunning that gasping, dry-coughing engine the whole three miles to the bar where Allen had made such a celebrity of himself over the years.

And, you know how it is, you can't bring a kid into a bar. You're not an animal after all.

You stick around here, Shane. Daddy'll be back in ten minutes. One beer, maybe two. No more than that. And the beer tasted so good, and he was telling good stories that day. He was on his game.

Anyway.

It was a hot fucking day.

Allen opened the car door. The smell of mildew belled out at him, and when he climbed inside he had to brush spiderwebs out of his hair and off his clothing. He felt something crawl across his neck and he brushed at that too.

"Shane? Can you hear me?"

He listened, as he always listened.

A sharp wedge of grief pushed its way into his throat. His eyes watered and his lips trembled. "Please, Shane." He waited for something to manifest, anything: his son, weeping for consolation; or some gaping darkness, a hungry revenant here to pull the skin from his face, to stuff his lungs with fire, to fill his guts with the magnitude of what he'd done.

He waited. A spider descended on a thin line, passing in front of his face. He watched it anchor a strand of web to his shirt, then crawl back up, connecting it to the steering wheel. It worked slowly and methodically, as though he were just another fixture of the truck.

The well of the passenger seat was empty. That was all right. He would continue to wait. Maybe that was the problem; he'd been too impatient. Shane was small, he couldn't really walk yet. It might take him a while to get here from wherever he was coming.

"I'll wait for you, honey. Daddy's not going anywhere. He's going to stay right here."

The spider continued to work, half a dozen strands already fixing him in place. Others joined it. The truck's cab filled with heat as the day wore on. Eventually he dozed, his dreams turbulent: the sun a burning, open eye; his body leaking blood in a steady tide.

When he awoke, it was night again. Webs integrated him into the truck. The world outside was open to the cool avenues.

Something tickled the back of his neck. A spider, or a hand.

Allen would wait and see.

THE CARE AND FEEDING OF HOUSEHOLD GODS

Frank J. Oreto

Paul started the day's third load of laundry and shoved the detergent back on the shelf. He paused, struck by something familiar in the plastic jug's shape. *Easter Island.* Those mysterious stone idols in *Ripley's Believe It or Not!* he'd gaped at as a kid. The handle formed the nose. The slope of the jug provided the long cheekbones. *Needs eyes. Did the Easter Island heads have eyes?* Paul listened for the kids. No crying, only the sounds of *PAW Patrol* on TV, solving problems with the power of friendship.

Paul dug through the shit-we-always-need drawer and found a red Sharpie. He took down the jug and started drawing. Two wide triangular eyes, the red circles of the irises slightly too close together. Slashes for the cheekbones. Finally, a thin line of a mouth, the ends sinking into a judgemental frown. Back on the shelf, the jug gazed down, cold and unsympathetic.

Not Easter Island, Paul decided, *better.* "Behold, Washor, god of all laundry."

"Daddy, Sam smells funny," said Billy from the living room.

"Okay, Billy. Thanks for the update."

"Her pants are brown."

"No, they aren't, they're blue." *Aw shit.* "I'm coming, Billy." He turned to go but stopped short. Had to show Washor the proper respect. "Oh, great Washor, I beseech you, by the power of your holy phosphates: Make my whites whiter and my colours bright. And do what you can about the poop stains."

With two kids under five, Paul didn't get a lot of downtime. Lunch, snacks, park for a playdate, feed Hamilton the hamster, attempt naps, find escaped Hamilton the hamster. And of course, the constant diaper changes and ever more laundry. The day blurred.

"What's that, Daddy?" Billy gestured to Washor glaring down at them as they pulled clothes from the dryer.

"Oh, just a little arts and crafts project Daddy did. Like him?"

"He looks mean."

"Nah, but he does take laundry very seriously." Paul shook out a tiny onesie. "No poop stains. All praise to Washor." He looked down at Billy expecting a grin. The boy found poop hilarious. Instead, Billy's face scrunched in distaste as he stared at the laundry god. *Everybody's an art critic.* "Go check on Samantha, buddy. Make sure she hasn't escaped the playpen. Don't wake her if she's asleep."

"Okay." The boy tiptoed off, pleased with his stealth mission.

Paul pulled more outfits from the dryer. Damn if the whites weren't a bit whiter. He reached up to give Washor a congratulatory fist bump then thought better of it, settling for a solemn amen.

Rebecca got home around seven. Her arrival was always the worst part of Paul's day. Alone with the kids, he didn't have time to notice his shortcomings. When Rebecca walked through the door, he saw everything through her eyes. Clothes on the sofa. Crumbs on the floor. She rarely complained. Instead, she'd walk in after ten hours of work and start folding blankies.

They'd made a deal, Rebecca worked fifty hours a week at the university, and Paul quit his sous chef job and took care of the house and kids. She brought home the bacon. He cooked it up in a pan. He wasn't holding up his end, and that failure made him miserable. Rebecca gave Paul a kiss and a smile showing nothing but love and exhaustion. *It's me. I'm projecting my disappointment in myself on the woman I love.* But self-awareness made him no less miserable.

"I'm going to pour some wine," said Rebecca. She draped a dishcloth over her shoulder and took Samantha from him. "You look like you could use some too." Billy grabbed her free hand and sang, "Mommy, Mommy, Mommy."

"I'll pour the wine. You dispense hugs," said Paul.

"What's for dinner?"

"Dammit." Paul set down the wine and pulled open the oven. "Slightly burnt roast vegetables… with some eggs I haven't started yet. Hey, didn't I used to cook at a fancy restaurant?"

Ten minutes later, they sat at the table, cajoling and cleaning the kids by turn. Billy refused the singed veggies, while Sam threw everything she could reach onto the floor.

"Daddy made a mean art and craft," said Billy around a mouthful of egg and ketchup.

"Your Mom was talking, Billy."

"No, I always go on about work. Let's hear about the arts and crafts."

Paul told Rebecca about the detergent jug's transformation into the god of laundry. "It's silly. But having Washor up there – I don't know – it kind of helps."

Rebecca nodded as she tried to spoon egg into Sam's firmly closed mouth. "A lot of cultures had little gods to help them around the house. The big-league deities were always busy with wars and such."

"Yeah, but back then people believed in the things."

"People believe a prayer to St. Anthony helps them find their keys. Your arts and crafts probably works the same way. The laundry runs smoother because a tiny bit of you believes the great god Sudzy is in charge. Takes the pressure off you."

"Washor."

"What?"

"He's called Washor."

"You suck at names."

"But, I'm not crazy?"

"Oh, totally nuts," said Rebecca. "You worship a bottle of soap. Whatever works though, right?"

"Yeah. Whatever works."

The next day Paul expanded the pantheon.

"Billy boy, fetch me the Elmer's glue and a sheet of your finest construction paper." Paul raided the dry goods. Macaroni outlined the face, broken spaghetti for hair. Dried limas for eyes.

"I like this one better, Daddy."

"He does seem more laid back. I think it's the candy corn teeth. Inspired choice."

"Thanks. What's his name?"

Paul taped the new deity on the refrigerator, looking over the magnetic poetry tiles for inspiration. "Hot Pot, god of food and cooking."

As the days went on, Paul made more deities. A playdough head with a dust bunny beard became Vah-Coom, god of clean floors. An old circular saw blade, plastic googly eyes held on with caulk, became Handee, lord of small repairs. He even dug out the bride and groom cake topper from Rebecca's keepsake box, proclaiming them 'Get-It-On', gods of fun and absolutely no fertility. His southern Baptist mother wouldn't have approved, God rest her soul, but Paul thought his pantheon was kind of fun. And even though making the gods took time out of his day, their creation didn't put him any more behind than usual. In fact, things were going pretty smoothly.

Not of course because of my handicraft pantheon. No. The kids were getting older. Even a few weeks made a big difference in what Billy could do to help and what Sam didn't do to cause problems. *I could just be finding my groove.* But maybe the gods did help. Not in a miraculous way, but like Rebecca said: they took a little pressure off. Instead of ripping the kitchen apart looking for the potato peeler, Paul took a deep breath and asked Hot Pot. The pause let him calm down and find what he needed. *Power of prayer, Mom. You'd be proud if it weren't for my choice of gods.*

Something damp and multi-legged squished beneath Paul's bare foot as he stepped into the laundry closet. "Ewww, Jesus," he said, then reconsidered. "Washor." Paul peeled away the crushed silverfish, holding it up to the detergent god. "Oh, great and powerful Washor, I offer up unto you this life as a good and proper sacrifice." He thought of laying the insect corpse on the shelf but dropped it into the garbage instead.

Guilt nibbled at him. The result of a childhood full of Sunday sermons. Maybe he should throw out the long-empty detergent jug. But wouldn't destroying the jug be as superstitious as making the idol in the first place? He loaded the dirty clothes and left, eyes lowered to avoid stepping on more bugs, not so he wouldn't have to look at the laundry god's disapproving face.

The socks matched.

Paul scanned the floor for strays. Nothing. How many times had he folded a load of laundry and all the socks matched? Never? The rest of the clothes lay folded neatly on the coffee table. Onesies that had seen a hundred washings gleamed white. He set Sam in her exer-saucer and went to the laundry closet. "You're listening, aren't you?"

The detergent jug god did not answer.

"No, I'm just crazy." *But all the socks freakin' matched. Okay, so test the theory.* Cold weather had brought the first ant invasion of fall. Paul put out traps, but there were always a few left to mop up. "There we go." A tiny line of ants marched along the wall behind the kitchen sink. He wiped a damp paper towel across their path. A dozen or more stuck, tiny legs kicking. Paul held the ant-studded towel before the face of his kitchen god. "I offer up these tiny souls to you, Hot Pot."

Paul plucked ants from the paper and crushed them. When the last ant was smashed, he felt a bit lightheaded. *What am I doing? What if the sacrifices work?* He wadded up the paper towel and tossed it toward the garbage pail on the opposite wall, dead centre. "Praise Hot Pot."

Paul moved Sam's exer-saucer into the kitchen where he could see her. "Billy!"

The thud of footsteps announced the boy's arrival.

"Hey, buddy. Is Hamilton in his cage?"

Billy reddened. "I put him back."

Paul gave his son a stern look but was too excited to be upset. "Guess what I'm making for dinner tonight?"

"Eggs?"

Paul shook his head.

"Soup... or butter noodles."

"Yeah, those are the usual options, but not tonight. You know Daddy used to be a pretty fancy cook. I'm thinking I'll make pork lo mein."

Billy looked dubious.

"Don't worry. Lo mein is like Chinese spaghetti. You're going to help." Paul cast a glance at Hot Pot hanging on the fridge. *So are you.* "First we line up everything we need. Chefs call that mise en place." Paul opened the cabinet, immediately spotting oyster sauce, sesame oil and kecap-manis even though he hadn't used those ingredients in months. *Oh yeah, Hot Pot. That's how we do it.*

Dinner was ready to plate as Rebecca walked in the door. Sam sat in her highchair with a fresh bib, while Billy carefully carried in cups of water. "Can you grab the plates, sweetie?" Paul asked.

Rebecca gave him a kiss and grabbed the plates.

"The pretty ones. Pretty plates for pretty food." He piled noodles onto the good plates and in a plastic bowl for Sam. Then snipped some green onion and cilantro onto his and Rebecca's. "Let's eat."

Rebecca dragged her last forkful of pork through the glistening sauce. "This is so tender."

"Yeah. I soaked the meat in water and baking soda before marinating. The baking soda breaks the meat down just enough, so you don't have to worry about overcooking."

Rebecca smiled at him.

"What?"

"You're talking about food the way you used to. I think you're finally hitting your stride."

Paul thought about pinching ants to reddish dust between his fingers. "Maybe you're right."

★   ★   ★

Occasionally, Paul killed a fly or maybe a moth, but his offerings were mostly ants. As long as he didn't put out more traps, there seemed to be a never-ending supply of the little bastards. And be it psychology or divine intervention, the tiny sacrifices worked. Accomplishing his daily tasks went from a rugby scrum to ballet.

He found time to write out a schedule and actually stuck to it. Playtime, cleaning, lunch, naps. There was even a slot for the mailman's arrival at 2:30. Dirt clung to the broom as Paul swept. Kitchen utensils lay in the first place he looked. He folded a fitted sheet! An age of miracles indeed. Billy whined, and Sam pooped as much as always, but everything ran a bit smoother. So, praise the gods and screw the ants.

Then came the soufflé.

Paul had just put the kids down for naps when Rebecca called.

"Hey, babe. Everything okay?" he asked.

"First off, you can say no."

"What's going on, Beck?"

"I invited Frank Stivers and his husband to dinner."

"Here?"

"Yes."

"Tonight?"

"I know it's short notice. But you've been keeping the house so well, and you've made all those fancy meals."

"So, you want me to get the house presentable, take care of the kids, and make dinner for your boss and his husband." Paul glanced at the oven clock. "And all by seven?"

"I kind of mentioned those cheese soufflés you used to whip up. I told Frank they were the reason I married you. Frank's a big foodie. He and his husband have eaten dinner at Al Burgess's house twice. Al keeps giving me smug looks."

"He's the guy you're up against for the promotion, right?"

"Yeah. I know I shouldn't have invited them but..." She let the words trail.

Paul's mind raced. Did he have enough eggs? Or any gruyère at all? He looked at the dishes in the sink. Heard the whomp-whomp of laundry that would need to be dried and folded. "Okay, babe."

"You're sure?"

"Yeah. I'll make the house look perfect and cook an impromptu gourmet meal before seven."

"Oh God, I'm sorry. This is crazy."

"No, I can do it. Nobody gives my wife smug looks."

"I'm not the worst wife in the history of wifedom?"

Paul laughed. "Nowhere near. I think I have chicken thighs in the freezer. I can do a braise, maybe something Moroccan. There's a lot of French influence in Moroccan cuisine so the soufflé will work."

"I love when you talk all pompous about food, baby. Seriously. Thank you, thank you, thank you."

"You're welcome. Now, I got to go. Lots to do."

"All right. See you tonight. I'll get wine."

Panic set in. When would he clean the bathroom? Sure, he'd kept the house minimally neat and functioning, but a dinner party for Rebecca's boss? With a promotion on the line? That was a whole other level.

"All right, Hot Pot." Paul pulled open the cabinet. The soufflé dish wasn't there. "Shit." He looked up at the face of his kitchen god. Was there an emptiness where before he'd felt a connection? What the hell did that even mean? He was afraid to open the refrigerator and see what food was on hand.

"I'll check the bathroom. Maybe it's not as messy as I think." Paul ran for the steps, cursing as he stepped on scattered Legos. Upstairs, the bathroom was terrible. *I can't do this. All the ants in the world aren't enough.* A dark thought drifted into his mind and latched on with claws. *A proper sacrifice.* He crossed to the kids' room. *Just to check on them.* Billy lay sprawled asleep on his race car bed. Sam sat up in her crib and stared at her father.

Paul froze. Sometimes if he didn't react… sure enough, Sam blinked once then twice and laid back down. Paul waited until her breathing levelled. *Okay, I checked on them.* But he didn't leave. Instead, he crossed the room to the plexiglass box housing Billy's pet hamster.

Ants weren't going to cut it. *What are you thinking? Your so-called gods are just psychological crutches like Rebecca said. They have no real power.* He took a deep breath and walked out of the kids' room. In his hands he cradled Hamilton.

Paul did not know hamsters could scream.

Hamilton didn't make a sound until laid on the plastic cutting board, then he let loose a wavering howl. Paul imagined Billy coming into the kitchen. His bleary eyes filled with confusion, then fear. *What are you doing with Hamilton, Daddy?*

He grabbed a thick cotton dishtowel and pressed it over the hamster. *Take your kid's hamster back upstairs.* "No. I have to make braised Moroccan chicken and a cheese soufflé." Paul stood poised on a knife-edge of indecision. Then Hamilton gave a muscular jerk, almost rolling off the cutting board. Without thinking – not true, he was thinking, thinking about soufflés and promotions and a good and proper sacrifice – Paul brought his fist down in a sharp, hard arc. He heard the snap of small bones, but the noise was distant, nothing to do with him. He brought his fist down again and again until the thing beneath the dishtowel stopped moving. Then the hamster was gone, dishtowel and all. On the porch in an old Amazon delivery box.

Paul found himself back in the kitchen, on his knees, denying what he'd done so hard the act almost went away for a few seconds. Then he staggered to his feet and vomited. It was okay, he needed to clean the sink anyway.

He got started. Changing diapers, dusting. Eggs and gruyère right where he needed them. Paul couldn't remember ever even buying the saffron he sprinkled in the braising sauce. He cleaned the bathroom with no worries about the chicken burning. His gods owed him that much. Footsteps sounded on the porch. Paul looked at the time.

2:30, mailman!

Poor broken Hamilton lay on the porch in his cardboard coffin, looking for all the world like a package to be delivered. Paul ran downstairs, past Billy on the couch and Sam in her playpen. "Just bills?" he asked, swinging the door open.

The postman handed him some circulars and paid no attention at all to the box. "Something smells mighty good in there." He was right. Dinner was good. In fact, dinner was perfect.

Rebecca's boss, Frank, turned out to be a broad-faced gregarious man built like an NFL lineman. His husband was even larger and sported a Brian Blessed-sized beard. They laughed loudly and possessed appetites to match their size. If Paul hadn't been so busy hating himself, he would have liked them. Still, he laughed when the room called for laughter and gave heavy-handed pours of the expensive wine Rebecca picked up. Frank raved about the food, asking questions about ingredients and techniques.

Well, you start by turning the oven to 300 and sacrificing the family pet. Aloud, Paul spoke about pan-browning the thighs and how the even heat of the stove was so important. By the end of the evening, Rebecca beamed. She walked the men to the door, promising to have them over again soon.

"Oh, no, our place next time," they insisted.

She waved the men into the distance then turned to Paul. "In Al Burgess's smug face," she shouted and threw her arms around her husband. "I should have never asked, but you did it. The house looks like you rented Martha Stewart. And the food… I thought Frank was going to start singing when he tasted your soufflé. Thank you so much. I'm going to be so grateful to you tonight if the kids don't wake up." She paused. "What's wrong?"

Tears streamed down Paul's face. The dam had finally burst. Guilt and self-disgust poured out. "I killed Hamilton." The confession gave Paul no relief because of the lies that followed. He had not accidentally stepped on the hamster after Billy let Hamilton out of his cage for the hundredth time. But that was the story he told Rebecca. The story he'd repeat despite his son's tearful denials. Until, by the time they buried the box in the back yard, Billy would believe he'd been at fault after all.

I have to lie, Paul told himself. *Because sacrificing my son's hamster to a jug of detergent is not an acceptable fucking story.*

Rebecca hugged him even harder. "Billy didn't notice him missing?"

"No. He never pays Hamilton much attention. Except when he decides the thing needs to roam free." Hamilton's last muffled screech echoed like an accusation in Paul's head.

"We can tell him in the morning." Rebecca took Paul's face in her hands. "It wasn't your fault, babe. There's nothing you could have done."

But there was something he could do now. Paul extricated himself from Rebecca's embrace. On the mantle sat Vah-Coom, the cleaning god. Paul snatched the head from its perch, crumbling the dried playdough.

"What are you doing?"

"Just getting rid of some stuff. The whole household gods thing feels a little weird. I'm the one who cleaned the house. I made dinner. They don't get to share the credit. You go on to bed. I'll be up in a few minutes."

"Okay. Does the whole Hamilton tragedy mean my gratitude should be expressed some other time?"

"Yeah, I think so. But I'm expecting you to be just as grateful tomorrow night." He tried to sound upbeat and failed. That was okay. His lies explained his mood. In the kitchen, he pulled Hot Pot from the fridge.

Later, after Rebecca slept, Paul even took the wedding topper from the bedroom and returned it to the keepsake box. The rest of his pantheon went one by one into the trash after being wadded, torn or otherwise desecrated.

Only one more god to go. Paul opened the doors to the laundry closet. Washor sat on his shelf, seeming as permanent and immoveable as one of the giant stone idols it resembled. Paul threw the empty jug to the floor and brought the heel of his dress shoe down onto its centre. Pressure shot the lid across the tiles along with a last splash of blue soap. "Die, you fucker," Paul whispered. He took the crushed jug to the kitchen counter. A pair of heavy shears jutted from the knife block. Paul shoved one of the blades through Washor's sloping cheek and cut. His hands shook with fatigue as minutes later he dropped the twenty-odd pieces of plastic jug into the garbage. The bag of gods went into the big metal can on the side of the house. Paul slammed the lid onto the can with a satisfying clang.

They buried Hamilton the next day, a tearful Billy officiating. Billy told Paul he forgave him and asked for a turtle because turtles had shells and wouldn't squish so easy. Billy's mixture of abject grief and easy acceptance brought Rebecca and Paul to tears, though for different reasons.

Over the next few months, Paul tried to put his brush with madness behind him. He was okay with the clothes not being as clean, and he went back to making eggs for dinner three days a week. When Billy's fifth birthday party came, Paul only flinched a little as the boy opened the box with his new pet turtle inside. Rebecca got her promotion, and a bit more money came in. Maybe they'd buy one of those robot vacuums. Life without gods wasn't so bad.

★   ★   ★

"You okay?" Paul asked as Rebecca pushed food around her plate. He'd tried making pork lo mein again. Not as good as when Hot Pot helped, but okay. "Your stomach still bothering you?"

Rebecca had come down with a bug a few weeks before. Low-grade annoyance mostly, but she'd not been able to shake the nausea. They even got a home pregnancy test. Negative, thank God.

"I'm okay, hon. Just a lot of stress at work." Rebecca didn't look at him when she answered.

"Is there something you're not telling me?"

"Secrets are bad," said Billy with all the wisdom of his five years. "Sharing is caring."

Rebecca shot Paul a look, and he backed off. "Hey buddy, leave your mother be. She had a long day." After dinner, he asked again.

"I went to the doctor. I didn't want to worry you."

Paul suddenly felt balanced on a high, thin rope. "Okay, now I'm really worried. What did the doctor say?"

"They found a growth in my abdomen. Probably nothing. The body's a weird thing."

Paul fell off the tightrope. Images of cancer wards filled his mind.

"I'm going back tomorrow for a biopsy. Let's not worry until there's something to worry about. Please?"

"I'm coming with you."

"No, you got the kids to watch. The procedure's just a little outpatient thing. I'll go in on my lunch hour."

"Are you nuts? Take the day off."

"No. If I stay at work, I'll be distracted, not bouncing off the walls waiting for the doctor to call."

"You're sure?"

"Yeah. If the biopsy is more involved than I thought, I'll call."

"So, I'm supposed to act like everything's fine?"

"Yes. Now, let's go give those kids some ice cream."

Paul didn't remember falling asleep that night. Only opening his eyes to see his mother, kneeling at the end of the bedroom before the altar of the First Southern Baptist church. The wooden cross of Paul's youth had been replaced by a plastic detergent jug with a Sharpied-on face.

"Pray with me, son," said his mother as she turned from the altar, her voice a dry rasp. "You've fallen away from God and been punished. But everything can still turn out all right if you pray with me."

Paul shook his head. "I don't even go to church anymore."

His mother crawled onto the bed and up to where Paul lay. Her body brushed against the sheets with a sound like the rustling of dead leaves. She took his hand, her mouth moving in a whispered exhortation. "It works, Paulie. The power of prayer." Her blackened tongue brushed cracked lips. Breath puffed out, carrion foul. "All you need is a good and proper sacrifice."

Paul shoved blindly outward, his hands bursting through a body as fragile as ash. He rolled from the bed, heart pounding. Eyes searching the empty bedroom. The sight of Rebecca, asleep on her side, kept the scream in Paul's throat tamped down. He laid back beside her and waited for the sun to rise.

Morning finally came with all the requisite tasks of feeding and dressing the kids. Paul stood last in line for hugs as Rebecca headed for work.

"I'll call you after the biopsy," she said.

Paul nodded and gave her a kiss. "Thanks, it's all going to be fine." He watched the Dodge pull out of the driveway, hoping the words weren't a lie.

He played with the kids all morning. No getting distracted by clothes to wash or rooms to clean. Soaking up all the love and laughter he could. After lunch, Paul checked Sam's diaper and set her in the playpen with a few toys to toss around. "Yo, Billy," he yelled. His son ran into the room.

Paul knelt beside the boy. "Do you think you could hang out here with your sister and maybe watch *Monsters, Inc.*?"

"No," said Billy "*Monsters University.*"

"Okay, deal. Daddy's got some work to do."

Billy was already putting the Blu-ray in the machine.

While the kids amused themselves, Paul recreated his gods. Recreated was the wrong word. *You can't kill a god by wadding up a piece of construction*

paper or slicing and dicing a plastic bottle. I only destroyed their images before.
The gods remained, devising a punishment for their wayward disciple.
A punishment not on him but on the woman he loved. Paul felt his
household gods all around him. Waiting for new vessels to fill.

First Hot Pot, then Vah-Coom and Handee. Sam followed Paul with
her eyes as he placed the new-forged deities around the living room,
forming a circle gazing inward. Billy never looked up from the television.

"You know I love you, right Billy?"

Billy nodded. "I love you too, Daddy."

Paul stepped in front of the TV, squatting down, so he and Billy were
eye to eye. "I want you to know, sometimes people do bad things for
really good reasons. Does that make sense?"

Billy pursed his lips. "I guess so."

"It's okay, you watch your show." Paul stood back up. The kid was
five, of course, he didn't understand. *He never will, and neither will Rebecca,
but she'll be alive and healthy.*

Paul's phone buzzed. The text read **Heading into the biopsy.
Nervous.**

Everything's going to be all right, Paul typed. A partial
truth. He went to the laundry closet and got the new jug of detergent.
This one was red, but the colour didn't matter one bit. *Hell, I probably
don't even have to draw the eyes and mouth.* He could already feel power
coming off the thing. Paul drew the face anyway.

He held the new Washor in the crook of one arm like a child. With
his other hand, he took his twelve-inch chef's knife from its plastic blade
protector. Paul carried them both into the living room where the rest of
the pantheon waited. He set the knife and god on the couch. From her
playpen, Sam watched him with sleepy eyes. Paul gave her a wink. "Billy,
I need you to go upstairs to your room for a little while."

Billy didn't answer until Paul picked up the remote and turned off
the television.

"Dad!"

Paul crossed the room and picked Billy up, hugging him. "Upstairs to
your room."

"But it's almost over."

Paul sat his son down on the bottom step. "Room, now. And no
coming down until I call."

Billy looked over Paul's shoulder. "Your arts and crafts are back."

"Yeah, for a little while."

Billy turned and marched up the stairs.

Paul checked the time. 2:15. Sam lay on her back now, small chest rising and falling. Paul wanted to hug his daughter to him. But he didn't. Better she stayed asleep, easier. He sat for a few minutes, Washor on the couch beside him. Rebecca's biopsy was probably over. He hoped she wasn't too worried. The results would turn out fine. He would see to that.

"Power of prayer, Mom. Like you said. All I need is faith and a good and proper sacrifice." Paul picked up the knife and went to the playpen. He brushed Sam's tiny pink cheek with his fingertips. Then he straightened and walked from where his daughter still slept to the front door. The time was 2:30. Paul tightened his grip on the chef's knife. The mailman should arrive any minute.

YELLOWBACK

Gemma Files

Brendan's phone said October 31st, which meant the workday began with Alistair making the same old joke about how you couldn't tell Halloween had been cancelled on account of public health, because everybody was still wearing masks. To which Brendan could have pointed out that Halloween had been cancelled since he was five, but didn't, because it seemed mean. He even made sure to smile, mouth hidden inside his own mask's hot, wet fabric pocket; experience had taught him Zoomers actually *could* tell the difference if they were looking at your eyes, which they always were. Keep eye contact, smile at the jokes, no matter how many times he'd heard them. Alistair was a nice enough old dude, after all, and jobs doing things Brendan liked to do were hard to come by – probably always had been. But most especially now.

"Be back to take over at noon," Alistair reminded him, "and you should maybe think about ordering in, by the way. I hear it's gonna be *extra*-crazy out there tonight."

"Oh yeah? Why?"

"Check your feed, man: There's an anti-vax demo scheduled, bunch of idiots who don't wanna take their booster shots, so there's twice as many cops out as usual and they're all running facial rec checks. That same dumb-ass shit about undocumented D'Vatzers maybe sheltering in the place down by the Shoreline, in buildings that cleared out after last year's tidal creep." Alistair crammed his hat on, wound a knitted scarf the length of both Brendan's arms twice around his mask and zipped up, sighing. "Anyhoo, I got a test to take for that upgrade in the a.m., so I need at least five hours' sleep before I start studying – you get into trouble, do *not* call me first, okay? Good kid."

He waved going out the door, which sealed shut behind him, audibly. Brendan waited a full minute, then slipped his other phone out from under the desk – the disposable scrambler he'd bought this afternoon, on his way up, from a dude on the train – and texted Nazneen.

cops r pulling masks tonight, stay safe

The dots rolled over, so he knew she was reading it, ready to reply. After a moment, her words appeared, making his stomach flutter: *need to see u*

at work rn, come by the back

too hot. u need to meet me. joe chih mins.

Brendan stared down at the words, quick-blooming across the screen, fast as Nazneen's thumbs could go. That woman typed faster with gloves on, outside, than Brendan did at home.

He could tell her it was far too early to take a break, or that he couldn't risk losing his job over getting caught helping her out when there was going to be twice as much pork as usual on the menu. But as ever, he already knew he wasn't going to; her use of periods alone implied urgency.

be there in 15, he texted, and got out his keys. And the fact that this decision later proved to be the only reason he didn't get arrested this Halloween was hilarious, particularly in hindsight.

★   ★   ★

Extract from the American Medical Association's Instructional Bulletin #372, June 2022, "Fundamentals of D'Vatz's Syndrome ('Yellowback')", pp. 23–27:

Where does the disease come from?
The first cases of D'Vatz's Syndrome, or Chambers' Sarcoma (after the first two scientists who isolated the disease's DNA markers in infected patients), are thought to have occurred as early as 1985, though little attention was paid to them due to the burgeoning AIDS crisis, and their relatively remote location in clusters across the Iran/Iraq/Afghanistan area of the Middle East (from which the colloquial name "Yellowback" derives, from the Pashto *sha-zhairh*). The first recorded case in North America occurred in 2010, around the same time American military personnel began returning from the conflict in Afghanistan, though the disease did not gain public notoriety until fashion model Gianna Capparelli contracted it in 2013. Since then, the number of cases has risen exponentially. If current trends hold, a full ten per cent of all North American females may expect to contract DS.

What kind of disease is DS?
The syndrome has some features of a fungal infection, but also some features of neoplasmic cancers, scabbing and leprosy. No viral or bacterial agent has yet successfully been isolated; however, the patterns of outbreak development suggest some form of aerial or contact transmission. The disease can be detected prior to symptom onset by a DNA scan of the patient, and has so far only been observed in patients with a double-X chromosome.

How do the primary symptoms progress?
A normal period of incubation has not yet been confirmed; the longest known period between DNA marker detection and initial active manifestation was three years and seven months. The disease's progress is measured in four stages:

Rashing. The patient develops a visible, highly itchy rash over the facial area, neck, and upper chest and shoulders. This stage is often accompanied or preceded by reports of ambiguous pain or general discomfort, and lasts on average approximately three to four weeks.

Blistering. The patient develops heavy pustules and blisters over the same area, shedding most layers of the epidermis, which grows back with a distinct yellow tinge (the source of the disease's popular name). Yellowish or orangeish discolouration of the irises may occur as well. This stage lasts approximately two weeks.

Masking. A heavy yellowish-brown scab-like tissue begins to grow over the affected area, occurring first as isolated lesions and then spreading to join together. Surgical removal is impractical, as the tissue alteration includes acutely heightened nervous sensitivity and a concentration of anticoagulants, making both anaesthesia and successful healing prohibitively difficult. Ultimately, the "mask" will cover the entire affected area, often closing over eyes and nostrils; the impeded airways frequently induce sleep apnea, which is thought to contribute to the likelihood of coma (see under *Secondary symptoms*, below). Untreated, this stage generally lasts from sixteen to twenty-four weeks, though extended periods of dormancy can be achieved (see *Treatment options*, below). However, heightened stress levels, as well as social and psychological comorbidities, often cause serious health debilitation in general.

Unmasking. The infected tissue has become so genetically altered that it triggers an immune-antibody response, causing the mask to separate completely from the cranium. The process has an extremely rapid onset, usually concluding in less than ten minutes, and almost always leaves the patient's facial area completely debrided; if the infection has entered the patient's eyes, or the maxillary or facial bone, this tissue too will be shed. Prognosis beyond this stage is extremely poor. The event itself causes extreme levels of pain, often with severe accompanying blood loss; patients who cannot be quickly anaesthetised and treated show a >97% mortality rate from shock and exsanguination. Those who do survive the initial event show a >91% mortality rate within the week, rising to >99.5% within two months, overwhelmingly due to onset of sepsis in the exposed tissue.

★　　★　　★

Joe Chih Min's was a food truck, not a restaurant; you had to subscribe to a very restrictive app to find out where it was going to be within the neighbourhood, and since it never stayed anywhere more than two hours, it made for a fairly efficient place to check in with somebody who wasn't supposed to be out on the street, for fear of automatic arrest, no-bail detention and getting shipped (or shipped *back*) to Quarantine Holding.

Going by her own testimony, Nazneen had been out of QH for upwards of a year now; they'd met in the spring, when she'd taken shelter in Alistair's bookstore from a stalker – she'd eventually had to knee the guy's 'nads just to drive him off. *Six months gone and I haven't infected anybody yet,* had been almost the first thing she'd told him, *even if you did have the second X-chromosome to bond to.*

Brendan had just shrugged, trying to play it cool, before replying: *Kinda making an ass of U and… you, potentially. In terms of gender presentation, I mean.*

And here she'd paused to study him again, a bit more intently, before twitching the scab where her left eyebrow used to be, dismissively. *Don't think so, no,* she'd said, after a moment. *Sure, you're soft on the outside, but you also got a full-ass beard, not stubble with attitude. And I'm pretty good at spotting facial plugs.*

I identify as genderqueer, he'd muttered, into that same luxuriant growth. *Just to say.*

Oh, cool. I identify as someone with a fatal disease whose parts happen to match the neurology; nice to meet you.

Prickly, smart and inaccessible – Brendan's kryptonite trifecta, all wrapped up in one double-masked package. He couldn't have stopped himself from falling for her if he'd tried, which he really probably should have. And yet.

Here they were.

Today Joe's was parked around the corner up on Maitland Terrace, behind the demolition site that used to be a diploma-mill 'institute' before going tits-up sometime during second or third lockdown. The truck itself was an unmarked dark blue van, doing its business out of open back doors. Most of the customers wore hard hats and masks, a few obvious homeless wore neither; none were Nazneen. Brendan paid cash for a Korean Street Toast sandwich and ate it standing there, mask down over his beard. He was on the verge of giving up when a light tap on his shoulder made him jump.

"Sorry," Nazneen murmured, but he could hear her smirk in her voice.

"Yeah, sure," he muttered, yanking his mask back up. "This better not take long. If Alistair calls the store and I'm not there, I'm screwed."

"Yeah, I know. Problem is, this can't wait." She handed him yet another fake prescription slip. Between her parka's raised hood and her mask, her eyes glinted – luminous black, still beautifully-shaped, with only a hint of cataract on the left iris. "We need somebody to get this for us, now."

Brendan scowled down at the slip. "Promethazine – that's new. What for?"

"Do you care?" But even her usual snark sounded half-hearted; she sighed, adding, "Look, I'll come by after work, and explain. Just..." She waved back towards Yonge Street, in the direction of that Rexall's they'd used twice before. "I'll wait here, 'til Joe's gone. If it's after that—"

"Up the alley, I remember. Keep out of sight."

He saw one eye crinkle, hinting at a hidden half-smile. "That's why I picked up this," she said, slipping a classic horny red-devil mask out of her pocket. "Makes it hard to see, but it should keep the assholes off. For tonight, at least."

"Not the assholes in blue," he reminded her. "Or the King."

"Fuck the fucking King."

More for display than anything else, probably, but he got it – nothing about Toronto's very own D'Vatzer-obsessed serial killer in this week's feeds, but that could change anytime, and they both knew it. "Just put that on," he told her, turning his back.

Inside the store, he passed the clerk the slip and thumbed his phone unlocked, automatically scanning to see if the keyword search-string he'd bookmarked had been updated yet. *TENTH 'UNMASKING' HOMICIDE KEEPS POLICE GUESSING* was still the most recent link, so he clicked through, re-familiarising himself with the details: *Toronto chief of police Alexander Marcus confirms that the body found October 9th under the railway bridge at Queen Street West and Dufferin is yet another victim of the serial murderer variously dubbed 'The King', 'The Unmasker', 'The Defacer' and 'The Façadist' by multiple news-aggregator sites... No identity as yet established, due to advanced stage of D'Vatz's Syndrome, lack of ID and apparent homelessness, plus condition of the body. As with previous victims, infected facial 'mask' was removed from the scene. An artistic reconstruction of the victim's original face will be available on the Toronto Police Services website once completed, and the public is asked to assist in identification...*

One of Nazneen's bunch? He hadn't asked her; not like she'd volunteer that sort of information, anyhow. Every person she lost was like losing a part of herself, probably – that was the way people put it, at least online, just talking about the pandemic, and D'Vatz's came with a death sentence already attached... but then again, so did life, in general. It was hard enough to process, even with medication. Brendan had to think most neurotypicals did the same thing he did about it, just in different ways: i.e. distracted themselves from the ticking clock by fixating on what was in front of them, for exactly as long as that would keep them too occupied to remember. The next task, the next episode, the next game, the next whatever sort of high left the best aftertaste. The next fuck, plus the relationship mechanics surrounding it.

Brendan hadn't ever gotten close enough to Nazneen even to hug her, let alone anything else. He barely felt those sorts of things for most people, including his own parents. Yet somehow, over a remarkably brief time, she'd managed to become the single best distraction he currently had. Which meant a lot – enough so he'd do whatever it took to stay close to her, and she knew it, well enough to exploit it. He didn't resent that, though. Given her situation, it was totally understandable.

The pharmacist rapped on the counter's plexiglass sneeze-shield, startling him. "For your wife?" he asked, eyebrows hiking, as he handed Brendan the orange plastic phial. "Or family member?"

"Uh – family."

"Well, congratulations. Good news in bad times, hey?"

The hell? "Uh yeah, thanks," Brendan answered, perplexed, already trying to type "promethazine" into the search engine one-handed as he stepped back outside. Which explained why he was halfway up the block before he looked up to see police cruisers parked around the bookstore. *His* bookstore. With an ambulance in their midst, waiting. The red and blue lights circled, flashing, calm and silent.

Fuck.

Without letting himself think about it, he crossed the street, not hurrying, not looking back. He didn't allow himself to run 'til he was back on Maitland, well out of any possible sightline.

Joe's van had left and Nazneen was indeed up the alley, sitting on the kerb, alone. She leapt to her feet as he accelerated; it was almost funny to see how quick the alarm in her eyes flashed to relief, then back to alarm again, with a side-order of dismay. "Did you get the – okay, good – no, fuck, never mind. Cops, yeah? They see you?" He shook his head, panting too hard to speak. She swore again, and grabbed his arm. "Goddammit. Come on."

★   ★   ★

From Toronto Police Services Case File #3A24-2034, Homicide

    Evidence Item #17: Transcript of Voicemail Left for Det. Inez Machado, 2034/10/13 0244

    [NOTE: Distortion-filter used on call rendered some words uncertain; marked where relevant.]

Detective. I'm the one who carved those signs inside the masks, after I took them off. I know you haven't released that detail to the press. Haven't found the right [combination?] yet, though. Obviously.

I'm calling because I need you to do something. Understand, I'm not blaming you, or your colleagues – you're just doing what you have to. So am I. This isn't personal. But truth's supposed to matter. And I am *not* an unmasker, a defacer – definitely not the [King?]. [Not any more than (any/ all?) of us are (going to be)?]. If I have to be anything, call me… a seeker.

It's not about hating these people, either. I mean, I do hate them. But that's [incidental?]. I just need what [they're becoming?]. To go where they're pointing the way. See what they're teaching us to see.

It's going to happen to all of us, sooner or later. I'm only expediting the inevitable. We'll laugh together, afterwards. And I don't think I'm going to need too many more tries to [make it work?].

Keep your family safe, Inez. Until after.

★   ★   ★

Down to the Shoreline, past the Creep's most recent markers; Nazneen and Brendan, hammering hard through greasy, oily water, half Lake Ontario, half… other stuff, polluted at best, irradiated at worst. The slushy top layer sprayed higher than the rest, slopping almost to Brendan's crotch, and he couldn't help but wish he'd worn a cup.

Harbourfront had been gone for a while now, tsunami blowback from that crap in New York. Nazneen and the girls she nested with fought a constant losing battle to stay just far enough out that it wouldn't be worth even the cops' time to come after them, the places where yellow and orange zones crossed over, just skirting the red. And when things got too dangerous, they'd even boat out there, using a raft cobbled together from extra air-mattresses… but they hadn't done that for a while, according to what Nazneen had told him.

They can't be trusted, Brendan, his mother had warned him, not all that long ago – and she got all her news straight from the CBC, old-school, though in podcast form rather than radio broadcast. The "nicest" nice person he knew. But even she was convinced that since nobody knew exactly where D'Vatz's came from, let alone how it operated, this could only mean people suffering from it were… tainted, somehow, on almost a moral level. Which definitely jibed with the way everybody else seemed to treat them. Some scientists thought it was pheromonal, though that was just a theory – nothing had ever been proven, quite probably (as

290 • BEYOND THE VEIL

far as Brendan could figure, using the Darknet's nameless equivalents of NuGoogle) because no one had done any sort of experimentation aimed at confirming or denying it. They preferred to just scoop Yellowbrows up and tuck them away in QH, so no one would have to deal with them who hadn't already volunteered for the privilege.

I was training for Forensics, back when I was a med student, Naz had told him, *so I never worked with patients – all I ever saw were individual tissue samples. But I was there for nearly a year before I got diagnosed, and I'll tell you this: All those press releases about 'promising avenues of investigation'? Total bullshit. Our lab, we never found a single bacterium or virus we didn't recognise, not even a goddam prion or a toxic agent, and we'd've damn sure heard if somebody else did. I'd bet good money we're not dangerous, except maybe to ourselves.*

How so?

She'd shrugged. *Not like I can go by anything but anecdata, but given what I saw in QH, let alone in the squats? Unmasking seems to go a lot faster, around other D'Vatzers.*

But if it's dangerous to keep you guys in proximity, then why—? But the equation came together so fast he didn't even have to complete his own sentence, let alone watch Nazneen shoot him one of her patented *how dumb is you, dog?* brow-twitches. *You think QH is designed to trigger as many unmaskings as possible, as fast as possible,* he finished, at last.

Cheaper than a bullet, she agreed. *And if we're all in the same place, it's easier to just cremate us real fast and shove us in a hole, without having to deal with too much oversight.* She paused, still watching him. *Now, ask me the real question. I know you're dying to… so to speak.*

What real question?

'But Naz, if being around other Yellowbrows kills you faster, why the hell would you break out of QH just to shack up with a bunch of other scab-faces?'

Brendan hoped that wasn't supposed to be *his* voice she was mimicking. But: *I don't have to,* was all he said. *I know why; you already told me, practically that first night. Because they need you.* (*And you need them,* he could have added, easily. *Closest you'll ever get to being any kind of doctor, now. Even if it does mean you have to deal with real people.*)

Again, though, that seemed mean.

"Sure I'm not gonna scare off you guys's…" he began, hesitantly, unsure how best to proceed, without being insulting. To which Nazneen snapped back, cutting him off in mid-word-grope—

"...customers? Clientele? Those sad Yellowflesh hate-fuck fetishists we make our bribe money off of, for if and when the cops come calling?" She didn't even bother slowing down. "We try not to shit where we eat, in general. And the ones desperate enough to come to us aren't gonna be scared off by one stranger they don't recognise. So no."

"Okay, then. That's good."

"It is, isn't it? Especially for you."

One good thing about D'Vatz's, she'd told him, back when he was still too shy with her to follow up on her previous hints that foraging and sex work provided her personal enclave's economic baseline. *Nobody with full Yellowback seems able to get knocked up, at least not for long – automatic miscarriage, usually around the same time most chicks would be taking a test. It's messy, but then... so's everything else, right?*

"True enough," he muttered, following along behind.

Naz's nest was in one of the buildings still poking above the waterline on the edge of what was left of the Leslie Street spit, once the top floor of an abandoned auto repair shop. After drying off best they could with a knot of ragged towels left by the door, he and Nazneen moved further in, finding the rest of the nesters gathered in what had been the shop's office lunchroom. It surprised Brendan how well the women had adapted. The windows were all sheathed in cardboard to conceal the light, which came from arrays of heavy candles backed up by the occasional LED flashlight, back-reflected by taped-up sheets of aluminium foil. Furniture was limited to ratty cushions, worn mattresses, a few folding chairs probably donated from some church's basement, but everything had been organised as neatly as possible. Through a serving window that opened into the kitchen, he could see a couple of women sorting through piles of unlabelled cans and plastic bags full of expired bread products, plus a basket crammed with dumpster-dive fruit and veg; for not even vaguely the first time, he hoped none of them were gluten-intolerant. Large jugs of water, probably boiled over that open fire in the long-dry sink, took up half the kitchen counter. And sure, the air tasted funky from unwashed bodies in proximity plus mildew and rust, but it wasn't like Brendan hadn't smelled worse locker rooms. This was... pretty homey, for homeless people.

"Hey, Naz," wheezed one of the kitchen sorters, a heavyset woman in almost full mask, with dark-skinned hands. "Good food run haul, for once; want me to set anything aside for—?" Then she stiffened, somehow seeming to sense Brendan, even lurking behind Nazneen's shoulder. "Fuck's *he* doing here?!" she demanded.

All eyes – those still visible, at least – turned to Brendan, who swallowed. He'd met some of these women before (one at a time, on the street, as Nazneen handed the drugs he'd helped her scam off to them), but seeing all of them together in one place at once was – disquieting, even for him. All had their outside masks off but were *physically* masked up to some extent, most worse by far than Nazneen, to the point where telling age or ethnicity was difficult; nobody's face completely gone, though (*yet*, he tried not to think). Whatever trust he might've earned by complicity in Nazneen's crimes, it clearly wasn't enough to outweigh years of hard-learned paranoia. Even translated through those half-visible, rotten banana-scabbed features, their expressions hit him like a slap: wariness, suspicion, resentment. Even contempt.

Like *he* was the dangerous one. The disgusting one.

"He's *here* 'cause the fucking cops found him, Retta," said Nazneen, flatly. "So we're taking him in, 'til he can make other arrangements – he's earned that, at least. Don't you think?" She strode to the kitchen window and set a green plastic bottle on the shelf. "That's to stock us up on our vitamins again, and Retta—" another plastic orange phial, which she tossed straight to the other woman "—here's the refill on your duloxetine." She turned. "Annie, meanwhile – you here? Or…?"

"I'm here," a high, unsteady voice answered, from somewhere in the back. "Did you get it? Please tell me you got it."

"*Brendan* got it," Nazneen pointed out, "so thank him."

"Oh God, thank God. Thank you. Both." A slight figure pushed its way through the group, shrouded in a heavy woollen blanket. The girl's face was near-completely masked over, but one bright blue eye stared out of the lumpy yellow-brown mass her head had become; the third of her mouth still visible smiled, in pitiful relief. "I had to sit with my head in a bucket for two hours today. Please, God, let this work." As she reached for the phial, the blanket slipped, revealing achingly scrawny limbs, skin piss-coloured beneath a ragged green summer dress. So thin, all over, except for her face. And—

Brendan boggled. Was that one of those medical-curiosity gigantoid-size tumours people watched YouTube videos about removing? Everything under where her breasts should be bulged out, almost nauseatingly. Then he remembered: *Promethazine.* The doctor had prescribed that to his sister, two years ago.

For her morning sickness.

"Holy *shit*," he yelped. "You're pregnant!"

Annie jerked back a step, automatically, though her single eye flashed: *No, eh?* While the rest of the room silenced itself in a rush of indrawn breath. But Nazneen simply sighed.

"Okay," she said, at last. "Well, now you've *got* to stay."

Brendan stared at her. She wasn't smiling – though she rarely did, especially when she was joking. None of the others were smiling either. His stomach sank. "Or – what, exactly? You'll *kill* me?"

Now it was her turn to stare. "*No*," she snapped back. "Fuck's wrong with you, man? We just need this shit kept on the down-low, at least until Annie stabilises. So you hide out here a day or two at the most, and by the time we find you somewhere else to go, it won't even matter anymore…"

("Hopefully," Brendan heard Retta mumble, almost into her collar, from the kitchen.)

"Sorry," Brendan said to Annie. "That was rude. I just… didn't think that could happen."

Annie nodded, shrugging. "Yeah, me either – so it must've happened before I got ill, I guess. Right, Naz?"

"Only way," Nazneen said. "Unless you agree with that whole 'no one knows where it comes from, must be fuckin' *magic*' proposition the streams're so fond of."

"Ou don *ow*, dough," another woman put in, from the back, her voice so mushy she needed subtitles. "Uh ean, *un* uh us do. Weh *CAHnt*."

Nazneen cocked her head, shooting this dissenter a glare she very likely couldn't even see, given how overgrown she was – all Brendan could recognise was a single upper row of teeth, half-blocked by a lip swollen three times normal size and flared inside out. She had one hand slapped up over her tracheotomy tube, blocking it to produce what little sound she was still capable of; the girl next to her hugged her around the shoulders, shushing her, gently disengaging her fingers one by one. That last part seemed to deflate Nazneen, who sighed. "Claire, just rest, okay?" she told her. "It's a disease, but who cares, seriously? Nobody that matters."

Again, Annie nodded. "I'm due this week," she explained to Brendan. "That doesn't change. But Naz's a doctor – almost – and Heather there has her doula's licence, so… yeah. Whatever happens, happens. And soon."

This time, Nazneen nodded too, her mouth set at a slightly grimmer angle.

"*Very* soon," she agreed.

★   ★   ★

Alistair, who kept track of all sorts of heinous shit, had once shown Brendan what he thought was evidence that there was a ring of weirdos making "completion" films out there, Yellowback porno videos that ended with somebody reaching in from above to rip the girl's mask off just as the guy fucking her climaxed. Brendan told him it sounded like an urban myth to him, not quite snuff and not quite not, with some bullshit *True Detective*-style mythology mixed in; Alistair couldn't completely argue the point, not when with every fresh post to the thread, rumours of what could be glimpsed underneath the mask got weirder and weirder. "This one guy says he saw one where the girl didn't even have any face at all under there," he said, scanning further. "Just meat and bones and, like, fat…"

"… and eyes, right?"

"Nah, not according to him. No eyes, at all."

"That just means it came off too soon, that it wasn't dried out and *ready* to separate, so whoever it was pulled it off early, like a scab. So the eyes got stuck inside."

"That's fucking sick, man."

"No shit, Alistair. Can we maybe talk about something else, for a while?"

All this stuff he'd tried so hard to block out, coming back to him now in fitful dribs and drabs, between half-grasped snatches of light, painful sleep. *I heard some of them just disappear when their masks fall off, like poof, dissolve into ash, or shit; they go somewhere else, someplace men can't go… My cousin used to message me on a Cryptocom app from QH; near the end she told me she could barely sleep anymore for nightmares, and her last post said she'd started seeing shit when she was awake, that she couldn't tell which was which anymore – colours were reversing on her, and there were mountains. She said the sun was black, and it ran backwards… There was a woman in my neighbourhood who vanished, but I think she just crawled away somewhere to die, like a cat. I'm betting she's probably under somebody's porch somewhere, and come spring someone's gonna get a really shitty surprise – seems a hell of a lot more likely.*

He could have written it all off as typical web bullshit if not for comments like that one: brutal flashes of misery, convincing by sheer weight of awfulness. Plus the last post Brendan had read, before slamming Alistair's computer shut so hard it startled them both, comprising only two words above an embedded image of a brown-and-yellow, red-streaked *thing*, crumpled inside a plastic neonatal crib: *My daughter.*

God, he hoped it had already been dead.

In his half-doze, he couldn't stop imagining how it must have sounded, in that delivery room. When had the moans of pain turned to screams? His brain slapped poor Annie's clogged-up face on the unknown mother, and he flailed in his blankets like a rat in a trap: *Christ, no, out, let me OUT—*

Then he jerked upright, finding the screams were real – two voices, equally panicked. And one of them was male.

Naz and Retta were halfway down the main corridor when he burst out to join them, flinging his whole bulk at the door of what the nest called their 'service' room – the place they used for the johns too eager, poor or ashamed to provide their own. On the mattress, Claire struggled against her customer with a frenzy nobody could mistake for even the freakiest stripe of fucking; both bodies were red-splattered, air flooded with hot copper stink. Brendan and Nazneen dove onto the guy, got their arms under his and yanked him off, still yelling. As Brendan hung on, grimly, his grip blood-slippery, they wrestled the john to the head of the main stairway and threw him down – he landed at the bottom, hard, with a combination splash/shriek. Brendan felt Nazneen brace herself, probably anticipating a roaring return charge, once the guy regained his balance. But—

—then the man looked up, and it hit them both, clear as a slap. This guy wasn't angry. He'd never *been* angry.

He was *terrified.*

Oh, shit.

Leaving the john to flail his butt-naked way back across the channel between their building and the next, Nazneen and Brendan turned, as one. The screams had already stopped, and it was easy to see why: Claire lay limp, shrunken-looking skull seemingly fused with the mattress, indistinguishable from the stain spreading around it – blotched crimson, an oozing starburst. Her tube was out, hole spraying mucus. Between long, bubbling breaths, her nude teeth shone scarlet.

Nearby, a yellow-brown, bowl-shaped oval thing lay slightly folded in on itself, cracked edges trailing shreds of raw red tissue. From the back, only one tiny slit remained where a mouth might once have been.

Nazneen was shaking. "Fuck," was all she said. "*Fuck*."

"Naz," Brendan started to say, the very first time he'd ever dared use the diminutive, but she just snarled at him, shaking him off; shining trails silvered her puffy, spotted cheeks, their discoloured sections already threatening to merge. Repeating, as she did: "Ugh, ahhhh… fucking, fucking *fuck*!" Like a building collapsing, she crumpled, bending at waist and then knees until she was face down on the floor, fists smacking the dirty linoleum with dull, steady thuds.

Brendan recoiled, unsure what to do until Retta stepped up from nowhere behind him, her hand on his shoulder. "Take her away," she wheezed. "It's done – we'll deal with it. Try and keep her calm, get her to sleep."

"But—"

"Just *do* it, boy. We're gonna need her later, with Annie."

Which was true, and she wouldn't be much help if she stayed locked in the loop of her current grief, her fear, her anger. He bent, got his arms around her, and lifted; it shocked him how light she was, as if her anguish had hollowed her out. For lack of any other idea, he carried her back to his cubby and sat down with her among his blankets, holding her to him. Helplessly, he fought back his body's reaction to the hot, damp feel of her sobbing breaths on his neck.

Eventually her grip eased, her breathing quieted. He thought she'd fallen asleep when her hand fisted itself in his beard and hauled his head around. The kiss hit him like a body-slam; half her mouth was hard and crusted, the rest soft and wet and warm; the smell of her hair flooded his nostrils, rank and sweet at once. Her other hand descended to cup him, and he groaned with the pressure. His hands broke all control, seizing, pulling, sliding between layers, finding and gripping sweaty skin. Naz only yanked harder on his beard and moaned between his lips.

Conscience forced words out of him, between gasps. "Naz – this isn't – you don't—"

"Shut *up*," she snarled. And pushed him down on his back.

He took her at her word and tried to make as little noise as possible, though he couldn't suppress a choked groan at the end, seconds before her own hand and bucking hips brought her to a teeth-gritted, silently shuddering conclusion. She slumped, hair hanging down, chest heaving in the still, damp air. Then without warning, she half-slid, half-shoved herself off him and rolled herself into the blankets, facing away from him. "Don't look at me," she rasped.

But I don't want to look at anything else, he just barely managed not to say. *I'd look at you forever if you'd let me.*

Even he could tell how that would sound, though. He remembered the night they'd met, Naz crouching behind the counter as he scanned the outside to make sure she could get away clean, muttering to herself as she shrugged her coat back on and wrapped her scarf up extra-high, extra-tight: *This whole thing, it's a wet dream for garden-variety misogynists, let alone the incels, the crip-fuckers... I mean, none of them really think we're human anyways, so this is just the icing on the cake. But 'not all men', right? And you, you actually seem okay, but I bet you wouldn't've looked my way before I started growing patches, got this thing. Now I'm a freak, though, I'm* fascinating.

I just want to help, he'd told her. And: *Oh*, she'd replied, after a long, slow blink, eyelids already too stiff to narrow any more. *So you're* another *sort of fetishist.*

At last, back in the now, he made the decision to cup one spread hand over her shoulder blades and let it rest there, lightly; she didn't respond, but didn't move away, either. What light remained slowly drained from the room, leaving them in darkness.

"I shouldn't have done that," she said, at last.

"I... didn't mind."

"Oh, no shit." Her voice turned acid. He was weirdly happy to hear it. "Guess that takes care of next Valentine's – wait, no; odds are, I'll be *long* dead by then. Want me to will you my mask, after?"

That hurt, but not enough. "I *said* I'd help you," he told her. "Get you what you needed. So if you needed *that*, and now you need – I don't know, to be alone, then I get that too—" Then he stopped, as cold shot through him. "Fuck," he breathed.

She let out a hiss. "Okay, you're right, I'm sorry. I'm being a bitch."

"No, no, no. Don't move." He couldn't take his eye from the

window, that blocky silhouette atop the next building over. "Remember that guy you kicked in the nuts, outside my store? The one you thought was an undercover cop?"

"Our meet-cute? Sure. Why?"

"'Cause…" Brendan swallowed. "He's outside, over there. On the other roof."

*   *   *

The guy was gone by the time Brendan got over there, but Naz hadn't needed confirmation. When he got back, she was already in the lunchroom, telling everyone they were blown; the burst of protests in response held disappointment, anger and fright, but no real surprise. Soon enough, they were breaking down all the moveable goods and starting to inflate the raft. *We'll move out around 4:00 a.m.*, Naz told him, amidst the rush; *Annie first, then everything else. Deadest time on the street, let alone the Lake.*

It'd sounded good to him, at least 'til he woke to the sound of furious retching: Naz, doubled over, in the corner of the room. She tried to push him away, feebly, when he went to help, but gave up and fell back against him as the spasms eased, more annoyed and bewildered than afraid. Then they both realised they could hear other people puking. Brendan helped Naz down the hall, stopping to let her check every possible hidey-hole; he could feel her dismay and confusion mount as the count of the stricken rose. By the time they'd gone through everyone, nearly a third of the group lay exhausted; the whole floor stank of bile and acid. *Nobody's going nowhere*, Retta managed, finally. *Not now.*

Not everybody's sick, Nazneen muttered.

We ain't leaving anybody behind, Naz.

Fine. A day, to rest.

A blink, then. And by the time he looked up again, almost a week had passed. Too late, not that they knew it.

Not yet, anyhow.

*   *   *

Around noon, in the middle of the latest police newscast Brendan's search-strings had flagged for him – nothing about the King or their nest, thankfully, just some noise about a maybe-inside-job equipment theft from an unidentified downtown precinct – Annie's water broke. By the time night fell she was howling uncontrollably, deep in the throes of full labour. They made a heap from all the bedding for her to burrow inside, stripped from the waist down; Naz was checking her vitals and making her take sips of water as Heather tried to talk her through it, Retta intermittently levering Annie up so she could squat and bear down, panting. Brendan, meanwhile – who'd only ever seen birth as footage on YouTube – was stuck in the corner with one of the window-coverings partially peeled open, obsessively checking to see that guy hadn't reappeared, just trying to keep out of it.

Is she going to die? he'd almost asked Naz, near the start, but stopped himself by cycling through a Terminator menu of her potential replies: *Oh, definitely, just like everybody else – but wait, you meant WHEN, right?; why no, child, no one ever really dies; fuck you, asshole.* So now he just stood there scanning the black water outside, the next building's slumped outline, watermarked by wave-reflected moonlight.

Didn't help that everybody else was still sick too, but then again, you wouldn't expect it to. He could hear them like a weird under-chorus, supporting Annie's pain through rough mimicry – groaning, puking, groaning again. The promethazine had helped while it held out, but it was long gone now, not that there would've ever been enough to go around in the first place. Brendan was still amazed it had worked as well as it did...

'Cause it's not like they could all *be pregnant, now. Right? That, that's just—* (impossible)

Another thing he couldn't possibly say to Naz, another subject he was too scared to broach. Especially since in *her* case, because of his participation, it was a genuine possibility.

Don't worry about it, that's what she'd tell him, if he did. Automatic miscarriage, remember? But – when was that supposed to happen, exactly? Sooner, rather than later; he was almost sure. So why it was still going on nearly six days later, that would be the question...

"*Jesus!*" Annie screamed, behind him. "Jesus, *please, Jesus!*" Like she thought He would appear next to her, stroke her sweat-soaked head, if she only did it loud enough. Light up the whole nest with His Sacred Heart's burning. And: "Ugh," he heard Naz answer, nauseated, turning aside to grab the communal bowl and retch into it; saw Retta reach for her hand and fist it, tight.

"Take it easy, baby," she wheezed, possibly addressing them both. "S'alright, okay? You're doin' fine. Right, H?"

Heather, reassuring, almost as mushily: "Uh huh, absolutely. Just squeeze, release, squeeze, release, squeeze—"

Downstairs, the front door suddenly broke open with a violent crack, as if kicked; Brendan heard the splash of water spraying everywhere, boot-broken. Then he was up and moving, somehow, passing Naz; she bounced to her feet as well, bowl flipping, all but racing him to the top of the stairs while Annie howled yet again, wordless with pain. They were almost at the top when he heard a noise he didn't recognise, some sort of buzzing hum ratcheting up within seconds to an electronic shriek, a giant lightbulb turning on – Naz yanked him back by his hair, pulling him down to where she crouched. "Cover your *eyes!*" he thought she yelled, under the mounting whine, so he did, but not quite fast enough to block out all of that giant burst of bright white light exploding up the stairs with a deafening detonation, turning everything around them negative.

Flash-bang, sonic grenade? Combo of both? Police gear for sure, the sort designed for crowds, but even with the split-second slice of a look Brendan'd been able to grab before whatever-it-was went off, he'd seen only one guy – *that* guy, had to be. No backup. What kind of cop tried to bust a nest all by himself, without calling for surrender first—?

(*Well, the kind who steals his equipment from his own station. Obviously.*)

Retta yelled from behind him, unintelligible through his ringing ears. Naz screamed back, more terror on the visible half of her face than he'd ever seen. "Get her *out!*" he half-heard, half-read in her mouth – her voice sounded like they were underwater. "Get Annie out of here, *now!* It's *him,* goddammit! It's been him all along!"

Him? "That cop?" Brendan blurted stupidly, blinking hard to get the spots out of his vision. "You *know* the guy, or—?"

"*No,* fuck it!" Naz pulled his head close with one hand. "It's *him!* The fucking…!" Then the buzzing whine whirled up again, and they hunched down together against another *boom* of blinding light. But Brendan didn't need to hear the end. He'd understood. His guts wrenched at his spine.

The King.

Boots mounted the stairs, stomping hard – Brendan shied away, taking Naz with him, as some sort of throat-set projection mic squealed awake. The scrambled vocal it emitted was like articulate feedback jacked to 11.5, each vowel firework-popped, louder than a bomb. "HARRRRRBINGERS!" it roared, translating whisper to scream as the man rose out of the stairwell, following inexorably behind Brendan and Naz as they tore down the hall towards Annie's room. "PARRRRRIAHS! CARRRRRCOSITES! FROM THE CITIES YE SHALL BE CAST OUT, AND IN THE WASTELANDS YE SHALL FORRRRRAGE IN VAIN!"

Annie greeted them with another shriek, a fresh explosion of piss and blood jetting to soak the sheets even as Heather tried to stuff a wad of it up inside her and Retta pulled hard, dragging her onto her feet as she chanted, "*Go, go, go, GO—!*" But in the next instant they were both caught in mid-jackknife themselves, spasming with new sickness, then bam, down on the blankets with Annie, flailing helplessly. Brendan gaped, aghast, watching their own crotches darken, like the flasher's tone had thrown them both into spontaneous auto-abortion.

"We're so fucking *fucked*," Naz gasped in Brendan's ear, then broke off, grunting in agony; he didn't have to see where she was clutching to understand the same thing must be happening to her, with equal immediacy. He eased her down and turned as a black figure appeared in the door, head helmeted and faceless, inhuman and angular in its body-armour; above his shoulder, to his right, hovered a high-buzzing miniature defence drone, the thing that had hit them with the flash-bangs. One hand brought something pistol-shaped down, its aim centring – on Naz.

Brendan flung himself at the King in pure reflex: he got one hand on the weapon and forced it up, his sheer weight enough to send them both staggering back into the hall. Then the other man's training kicked in and he flipped Brendan over his knee, slamming him to the ground so hard Brendan saw stars again, all the breath and strength crushed instantly out of him. The King held his weapon on Brendan for a second before dismissively turning away. He strode into the room and stopped, helmet angled down at the helpless women; the drone followed behind, its wasplike buzz threading through the cries of pain and fear like a bonesaw, pitiless and terrifying.

He lifted his free hand to his helmet and adjusted something. The voice that came from the drone was a quarter the volume it had been, but still loud enough to scrape the skin. "NAZNEEN HIKAR, HEATHER BRRRRRAIDIE. I WANT THE CHILD."

"*Annie's* child?" Naz spat. "Screw *you*, stormtrooper."

"UNIMPORRRRRTANT. THE *CHILD.*" The pistol-thing gestured sharply at Annie, still writhing and moaning. Retta must have thought that would give her enough chance; she lunged up and charged at him, but her pain and his reflexes were too much. The weapon whipped back. A blue-white line of light struck her with a *crack* like a thunderclap: all her limbs kicked out at once, like a dead frog jolted with current in some high school bio lab, and then she fell. Before she'd even hit the ground the weapon was pointed at Naz again. "GIVE ME THE CHILD!" the man roared.

"It's not *out* yet, you idiot!"

"THEN *GET. IT. OUT.*"

Even that mightn't have broken through Naz's shock. But the next sound did: Annie's agonised moans, already diminishing, suddenly died in a hissing strangle that ended in a flat *shlupp*, like a vacuum container sealing shut. Heather wailed and scrambled forward. "Oh, fuck, Naz," she sobbed, "her mask! She's blocked up! She can't breathe! Fuck, Naz, *help me!*" She caught Annie's hands and held them down as the girl bucked and kicked, before Naz flung herself on top of her, digging in her back pocket for her Swiss Army knife. "Tracheotomy!" she gasped. "Somebody get me a straw – Brendan, Heather, hold her down, *shit*—"

"NO!" The King stepped forward; for the first time his voice betrayed something like fear. "FIRRRRRRST CHILD OF THE NEW RRRRRACE! THE ONE BORRRRRN TO BRRRRREAK THE WORRRRRLD OPEN! SAVE IT, NO MATTER HOW—"

"Asshole, you want me to cut her *open?*"

The man didn't even answer, just lunged forward, jerking his side-piece up – extendable truncheon with a kevlar edge, tooled sharp: *I will if you won't,* in other words. As he did, though, Brendan leapt up to grab the drone out of the air and smash it against the wall, feedback squeal audibly ripping through the man's helmet; he staggered, which gave Brendan enough time to hurl himself onto the man again, from behind. They went down together, truncheon skittering away across the floor; Brendan pounded the man's head against the floor until, on the fifth or sixth blow, something snapped. The whole thing came off like an ant's head, tumbled across the room, rolled up against Naz's feet; she kicked it away, sliding her knifeblade into Annie's throat. A horrid, high whistling pierced the air.

"*No, goddammit!*" bellowed the King, shoving up against Brendan's weight. "Not like this! No fucking way!" He twisted, but Brendan shoved his face against the floor with one arm; it only muffled his shouting. "You *know* how many of these fucking bitches I took apart, asshole?! How many masks I had to peel off? And they were all fucking *wrong*, goddammit! Every mask I looked through, every sign I carved, *nothing*! Nothing *worked*!

"But then I heard." His breathing steadied; his movements stilled. "I heard how they were finally getting pregnant. All of them. And I knew if I could find the one, the *first* one, the mask of the one *chosen* – then *that*... would be the one. The one that'd finally – finally – let me *see*."

"See *what*?" Brendan blurted, despite himself.

The man's head whipped around. Wild eyes glared out of a scab-like, yellow-brown mask, ringed in black stitches crusted with blood; the bottom half was torn open where his jaw's movements had cracked the desiccated tissue. Brendan screamed, jerking backwards; before he could recover the King twisted and shoved, hurling him off. Brendan hit the floor hard, wind knocked out of him for the second time in two minutes, and scrabbled back as the man clambered to his feet. Blood trickled down the stolen mask and dripped to the floor.

"The other world, shithead," the King whispered, his mouth moving behind the ragged brown tissue. "The *real* world." From his belt, he drew something very much not regular issue – long and angular, a plexiglass triangle blade, wine-dark with stains. "The one I saw, in my dreams. The lake, two suns. Black stars."

Brendan stared up at him, gasping for breath.

A whole new type of cry filled the air, shocked and hungry, angry, *betrayed*. From between Annie's legs, Heather fell back on her butt, arms full of something pink, wrinkled and squalling. Naz slowly took her hands away from Annie's throat, watching as the hollow pen sticking up from it quivered and twitched. Annie's breast rose and fell. Retta, who had just begun to roll over, lay still and frozen. In Heather's arms the baby wailed, tiny mouth gaping.

"Heather?" Naz husked.

Heather's voice was thick. "She's okay," she gulped. "She's fine. She's perfect. Oh, God, Annie, I wish you could see her…"

"She will," said the King. His smile was so wide it tore "his" mask even further. He held up the knife. "Least I can do for her. Give her one look, before I go…" He moved towards the women, past the unconscious Retta. Brendan struggled to rise and couldn't, still crumpled with pain and anoxia. Heather crabwalked backward, the baby in one arm, but Naz threw herself in front of Annie, holding her bloodied penknife out.

"Don't you fucking touch her, asshole," she rasped.

The King stared at her. Then he spun and hit Naz right in the breastbone with a flashing roundhouse kick, knocking her yards backwards; the penknife clattered into the corner. "You fucking *BITCH!*" he screamed at her. "Don't you *get* it? I was *right!* I was *right all along! I did this! My dreams were right!*" He shifted his knife to an overhand grip, lifting it above his head, and stepped towards Nazneen—

"Who said they were *your* dreams, you insect?"

The voice was strange. Clear, but muffled, as if speaking through cloth; and oddly buzzy and muted, like a bad microphone in an echo chamber. Slowly, Annie sat up, one hand holding her breathing-tube in place. The other came up to her mask, flattening itself against the rough surface…

…and slid it off. The brown-yellow oval dripped clear, viscous fluid to the floor. Silently, without fuss, Annie set it aside in the blankets.

Brendan had never really known what was supposed to make someone beautiful. What he felt for Naz was mostly about who she was, her smell and voice, her movements; he'd never even really seen her whole face or body, not truly. But Annie's unmasked face seemed to blaze, so brightly he wanted to cover his eyes. Her skin was smooth and perfect, lips full and blushed with health, and her wide eyes shone a brilliant amber-gold, irises no colour he'd ever seen on any real person before, ever. This was beyond beauty. Beyond human.

The King's knife fell to the floor with a clatter. A second later, he sank to the floor himself, falling onto his knees. His hands lifted, empty and imploring. "Yes," he hissed. "It was you, all along. Lend me your mask. Please. I want to – I need to *see*."

Annie smiled. With a flickering movement, she plucked the tracheotomy tube from her throat and flung it away; the tissue rippled in its wake, sealing up. "Why?" she asked. "You already have one of your own."

For one final second of incomprehension, the King goggled at her through his mask. And then a sharp hiss split the air; smoke curled up, with a foul, acrid stink. The King's hands flew to his face, ripping and tearing, but the mask-tissue was *moving*, sealing itself to his flesh beneath even as it crawled and spread like spilled sewage, covering him over. He screamed, and screamed again, lunging to his feet and twisting around, only the force of his shrieks keeping the tissue from sealing over his mouth. Arms windmilling, he staggered towards Heather and the baby, smoke billowing around him and the sizzle of his dissolving flesh growing ever louder.

Without warning, a massive roar drowned all other noise. The building shook. The ceiling broke apart like an invisible wrecking ball had torn through it, and the walls fell away to either side. Cold night air crashed down upon them; wind extinguished the candles in a gust. The King fell with a thud, hard enough to break his screams for a moment; beyond him, the lights of Toronto flickered and went out, drowning the city in the dark. Sirens and screams came floating over the water, until the King's voice rose over them in fresh peals of anguish.

Revulsion seized Brendan like something utterly alien, something beyond either instinct or decision – like he was staring at some rotten pulpy sluglike *thing* whose mere existence brought his gorge boiling up. He grabbed the King's stunner pistol from where he'd dropped it, rolled upright, and tackled the other man, hammering at his skull with the pistol butt; and even as they toppled over together, Naz had joined the scrum, driving the man's fallen knife into his waist beneath the armour over and over again, then above the armour through his neck, choking off his screams in bloody gurgles. Her mask split and cracked and fell away as blood spurted over it, as transfigured as Annie's had been, a thing of wild chaos and storm to Annie's eerie serenity. She dropped the knife, plunged her hands into the dying man's blood and wiped it over Brendan's mouth; it burned like liquid fire, making him ravenous and horny all at once. Without transition they were embracing, kissing, smearing the blood all over each other's faces as the body of the King crumpled and shrivelled between them, and Brendan realised it didn't seem at all strange that they were laughing.

"Good," said Annie. She had risen to her feet, taking her baby from Heather's arms; it nursed at her breast as Heather, also unmasked, clung to one of her legs in a storm of blissful weeping. "All new ages begin with sacrifice. This… was worthy." She looked up at the stars. "It is time."

Time? Brendan mouthed. He looked at Nazneen, but her grin was too wide for fear. They watched Retta crawl over and press her unmasked face to the floor at Annie's feet. Something stirred dimly in Brendan's mind at that – some hard-to-recall doubt, a faint feeling of wrongness – but it passed. He was here, with Naz; *with* her, as he'd never dared dream he could be. That was worth a bent knee, or two.

"The tide turns," said Annie. "The true face of the world revealed. All will admire it under their proper stars, at last." Her voice rose to a cry. "Unmask! *Unmask!*" She lifted one arm high, and the earth's rumble echoed up through the night. Staring up at the field of stars, Brendan's mouth fell open. The sky was *rippling*. Around every star grew a web of black cracks, like ice fracturing over black water, or dead dry skin peeling; through them leaked something like black-purple ink, or boiling tar. The screams echoing from the extinguished city took on a slow, awful resonance, maddened choir-singers reaching for impossible chords, a harmony beyond.

Brendan looked at Naz. She kissed him, then took his hand and put it to her stomach. "Unmask," she whispered.

His guts gave an awful lurch; whether joy or terror, he could not have guessed.

But I wear no mask, he thought.

BIOGRAPHIES

Angeline B. Adams and **Remco van Straten** have written about the arts, culture and folklore for a variety of publications, and their short stories have appeared in several anthologies, most recently *Air and Nothingness Press's The Wild Hunt*. Their work is steeped in a shared love for folklore and history, and draws on elements of Angeline's Northern Irish childhood and the northern Dutch coast where Remco grew up. Their first collection *The Red Man and Others* has now appeared in print.

Nathan Ballingrud is the author of *North American Lake Monsters* (basis for the series *Monsterland*) and *Wounds: Six Stories from the Border of Hell*. His first novel *Strange* will be published in 2022.

Dan Coxon is an editor and writer based in London. His fiction has appeared in *Black Static*, *Nightscript*, *The Lonely Crowd*, *Unthology*, *Not One of Us*, *Humanagerie*, *Nox Pareidolia*, and Flame Tree's *Terrifying Ghosts* anthology, among others. His anthology *This Dreaming Isle* was shortlisted for both a Shirley Jackson Award and a British Fantasy Award. His non-fiction has appeared widely from *Salon* to the *Guardian*, and a collection of his short fiction, *Only the Broken Remain*, was published by Black Shuck Books in November 2020. He is an editor at award-winning publisher Unsung Stories and works freelance at momuseditorial.co.uk

Jeremy Dyson is best known as one quarter of comedy group *The League of Gentlemen*, co-creator of the hit West End show *Ghost Stories* and co-writer/director of that show's 2017 film adaptation. He has published three collections of short stories, including the Edge Hill Award-winning *The Cranes that Build the Cranes*. In addition, he co-created the BAFTA nominated TV series *Funland*, and the Golden Rose winning all-female comedy show *Psychobitches*, as well as writing for *Tracey Ullman's Show*, *Killing Eve* and the upcoming *Good Omens 2*.

John Everson is a staunch advocate for the culinary joys of the jalapeño and an unabashed fan of 1970s European horror, giallo and *poliziotteschi* cinema. He is also the Bram Stoker Award-winning author of twelve novels, including his latest New Orleans occult thriller, *Voodoo Heart* from Flame Tree Press. His first novel, *Covenant*, was a winner of the Bram Stoker Award, and his sixth, *NightWhere*, was a finalist for the award. Over the past twenty-five years, his short stories have appeared in more than seventy-five magazines and anthologies. He has written licensed tie-in stories for *Kolchak: The Night Stalker*, *The Vampire Diaries* and Jonathan Maberry's *V-Wars* universe. *V-Wars* was turned into a ten-episode Netflix series that included Everson's characters Danika and Mila Dubov. For more on his fiction, art and music, visit johneverson.com.

Formerly a film critic, journalist, screenwriter and teacher, **Gemma Files** has been an award-winning horror author since 1999. She has published four collections of short work, three collections of speculative poetry, a Weird Western trilogy, a story-cycle and the stand-alone novel *Experimental Film*, which won the 2015 Shirley Jackson Award for Best Novel and 2016 Sunburst Award for Best Adult Novel. She has a new story collection out from Grimscribe Press, *In This Endlessness, Our End*, and another upcoming.

Stephen Gallagher is the author of fifteen novels including *Valley of Lights*, *Down River*, *Rain* and *Nightmare, With Angel*. TV work includes an award-winning *Silent Witness* and a stint on Stan Lee's *Lucky Man*; he's also written for *Doctor Who*, *Murder Rooms*, *Chillers*, and is the creator of Jerry Bruckheimer's science thriller series *Eleventh Hour*. He is a Stoker and World Fantasy Award nominee, and has received British Fantasy and International Horror Guild Awards for his short fiction.

Christopher Golden is the *New York Times* bestselling author of *Ararat*, *Snowblind*, *Red Hands* and many other novels. He is the co-creator, with Mike Mignola, of the Outerverse horror comics, including *Baltimore*, *Joe Golem: Occult Detective* and *Lady Baltimore*. As editor, his anthologies include the Shirley Jackson Award-winning *The Twisted Book of Shadows*, *The New Dead* and many others. Golden is also a screenwriter, producer, video game writer, co-host of the podcast Defenders Dialogue, and founded the Merrimack Valley Halloween Book Festival. Nominated ten times in eight different categories for the Bram Stoker Award, he has won twice, and has also been nominated for the Eisner Award, the British Fantasy Award, and multiple times for the Shirley Jackson Award. Golden was born, raised, and still lives in Massachusetts.

Lisa L. Hannett has had over seventy-five short stories appear in venues including *Clarkesworld*, *Fantasy*, *Weird Tales*, *Apex*, *The Dark* and *Year's Best* anthologies in Australia, Canada and the US. She has won four Aurealis Awards, including Best Collection for her first book *Bluegrass Symphony*, which was also nominated for a World Fantasy Award. Her new collection *Songs for Dark Seasons* is out now. You can find her online at lisahannett.com and on Instagram @LisaLHannett.

Peter Harness was born and grew up in Yorkshire, but now lives on top of a hill in Sweden. He mostly writes TV shows like *Wallander*, *McMafia*, *Jonathan Strange and Mr. Norrell* and *Doctor Who*. Occasionally he writes a film, like *Is Anybody There?* In his spare time he forges letters from obscure British TV personalities of the 1980s, and is working out how best to make a living out of that.

Matthew Holness created and starred in *Garth Marenghi's Darkplace* for Channel 4 and his short films include *A Gun For George*, *The Snipist* and *Smutch*. His stories have appeared in *Black Static*, *At Ease With the Dead* (Ash Tree Press), *Phobic*, *The New Uncanny* and *Protest* (all Comma Press). He wrote and directed the 2018 horror feature, *Possum*, and his audio adaptation of M.R. James' 'The Ash Tree' for Bafflegab Productions recently won Best Drama Special (Gold) at the 2020 New York Festival Radio Awards.

Toby Litt has published novels, short story collections and comics. His most recent novel *Patience* was shortlisted for the Republic of Consciousness Prize 2020. His story 'The Retreat' won the 2020 Short Fiction/University of Essex Prize. He runs the Creative Writing MFA at Birkbeck College, and blogs at tobylitt.com. When he is not writing, he likes sitting doing nothing.

Bracken MacLeod is the Splatterpunk, Bram Stoker, and Shirley Jackson Award-nominated author of the novels *Mountain Home*, *Come to Dust*, *Stranded* and *Closing Costs*, from Houghton Mifflin Harcourt. He's also published two collections of short fiction, *13 Views of the Suicide Woods* and *White Knight and Other Pawns*. Before devoting himself to full-time writing, he worked as a civil and criminal litigator, a university philosophy instructor and a martial arts teacher. He lives outside of Boston with his wife and son, where he is at work on his next novel.

Josh Malerman is the *New York Times* bestselling author of *Bird Box*, *Black Mad Wheel*, *Unbury Carol*, *Inspection*, *A House at the Bottom of a Lake* and *Malorie*. He's also one of two singer/songwriters for the Detroit rock band the High Strung, whose song 'The Luck You Got' can be heard as the theme song to the Showtime show *Shameless*. He lives in Michigan with the artist/musician Allison Laakko.

Mark Morris (Editor) has written and edited almost forty novels, novellas, short story collections and anthologies. His script work includes audio dramas for *Doctor Who*, *Jago & Litefoot* and the *Hammer Chillers* series. Mark's recent work includes the official movie tie-in novelisations of *The Great Wall* and (co-written with Christopher Golden) *The Predator*, the Obsidian Heart trilogy, and the anthologies *New Fears* (winner of the British Fantasy Award for Best Anthology) and *New Fears 2* as editor. He's also written award-winning audio adaptations of the classic 1971 horror movie *Blood on Satan's Claw* and the M.R. James ghost story 'A View from a Hill'.

Karter Mycroft is an author, musician and ocean scientist who lives in Los Angeles a little too far from the beach. Their short fiction has appeared in *Zooscape*, *Coppice & Brake*, *Misery Tourism* and elsewhere. They're also a member of the bands Squid Cult and Manic Carbon. You can find them on Twitter @kartermycroft or at kartermycroft.com

Frank J. Oreto is a writer of weird fiction living in Pittsburgh, Pennsylvania. His work has appeared, or is upcoming, in *Pseudopod*, *Unnerving Magazine*, *The Year's Best Hardcore Horror* and *Vastarien*. When not writing, Frank spends his time preparing elaborate meals for his wife and their always-hungering offspring. You can follow his exploits, both literary and culinary, on Twitter @FrankOreto or on Facebook at fb.me/FrankisWriting.

Lynda E. Rucker has sold dozens of short stories to various magazines and anthologies including *Best New Horror*, *The Best Horror of the Year*, *The Year's Best Dark Fantasy and Horror*, *Black Static*, *Nightmare*, *F&SF*, *Postscripts* and *Shadows and Tall Trees* among others. She has had a short play produced as part of an anthology of horror plays on London's West End, has collaborated on a horror comic, and won the Shirley Jackson Award for Best Short Story in 2015. Two collections of her short fiction have been published, *The Moon Will Look Strange* and *You'll Know When You Get There*, and she edited the anthology *Uncertainties III* for Swan River Press. A third collection is forthcoming in 2021.

Priya Sharma's work has appeared in venues such as *Tor.com*, *Interzone*, *Black Static*, *The Dark* and *Nightmare*. *All the Fabulous Beasts* (Undertow Publications) is a collection of her short stories. *Ormeshadow* (Tor) is her debut novella. She is a multiple British Fantasy Award and Shirley Jackson Award winner.

Lisa Tuttle has been writing strange, weird and fantastic fiction since the 1970s, and is a past winner of the John W. Campbell Award, the British Science Fiction Award and the International Horror Guild Award. She is the author of a dozen novels, and half-a-dozen short story collections, the first of which, *A Nest of Nightmares* (1986) was recently reprinted by Valancourt, who have just published her most recent, *The Dead Hours of Night* (2021). She lives in Scotland.

Aliya Whiteley's novels and novellas have been shortlisted for multiple awards including the Arthur C. Clarke Award and a Shirley Jackson Award. She has written over one hundred published short stories that have appeared in *Interzone*, *Beneath Ceaseless Skies*, *Black Static*, *Strange Horizons*, *The Dark*, *McSweeney's Internet Tendency* and the *Guardian*, as well as in anthologies such as Unsung Stories' *2084* and Lonely Planet's *Better than Fiction*. She also writes a regular non-fiction column for *Interzone* magazine.

FLAME TREE PRESS
FICTION WITHOUT FRONTIERS
Award-Winning Authors & Original Voices

Flame Tree Press is the trade fiction imprint of Flame Tree Publishing, focusing on excellent writing in horror and the supernatural, crime and mystery, science fiction and fantasy. Our aim is to explore beyond the boundaries of the everyday, with tales from both award-winning authors and original voices.

•

Other titles in this series:
After Sundown

Other horror and suspense titles available include:
Snowball by Gregory Bastianelli
Thirteen Days by Sunset Beach by Ramsey Campbell
Somebody's Voice by Ramsey Campbell
The Queen of the Cicadas by V. Castro
The Haunting of Henderson Close by Catherine Cavendish
In Darkness, Shadows Breathe by Catherine Cavendish
The House by the Cemetery by John Everson
Voodoo Heart by John Everson
Hellrider by JG Faherty
Sins of the Father by JG Faherty
Boy in the Box by Marc E. Fitch
One by One by D.W. Gillespie
Black Wings by Megan Hart
Stoker's Wilde by Steven Hopstaken & Melissa Prusi
Stoker's Wilde West by Steven Hopstaken & Melissa Prusi
The Playing Card Killer by Russell James
The Portal by Russell James
The Dark Game by Jonathan Janz
The Raven by Jonathan Janz
We Are Monsters by Brian Kirk
Greyfriars Reformatory by Frazer Lee
Those Who Came Before by J.H. Moncrieff
August's Eyes by Glenn Rolfe
Creature by Hunter Shea
Misfits by Hunter Shea
Screams from the Void by Anne Tibbets
Your Turn to Suffer by Tim Waggoner

•

Join our mailing list for free short stories, new release details, news about our authors and special promotions:

flametreepress.com